Catherine Robohm

Paul Watkins is the author of nine novels and the memoir *Stand Before Your God*. He attended the Dragon School, Eton, and Yale and currently lives with his family in Princeton, New Jersey, where he teaches at the Peddie School and Lawrenceville Academy.

ALSO BY PAUL WATKINS

FICTION

Night over Day over Night

Calm at Sunset, Calm at Dawn

In the Blue Light of African Dreams

The Promise of Light

Archangel

The Story of My Disappearance

The Forger

Thunder God

NONFICTION

Stand Before Your God

The Fellowship of Ghosts

The
ICE
SOLDIER

The
ICE
SOLDIER

Paul Watkins

PICADOR

HENRY HOLT AND COMPANY

NEW YORK

THE ICE SOLDIER. Copyright © 2006 by Paul Watkins. All rights reserved. Printed in the United States of America. No part of this book may be used or reproduced in any manner whatsoever without written permission except in the case of brief quotations embodied in critical articles or reviews. For information, address Picador, 175 Fifth Avenue, New York, N.Y. 10010.

www.picadorusa.com

Picador® is a U.S. registered trademark and is used by
Henry Holt and Company under license from Pan Books Limited.

For information on Picador Reading Group Guides,
as well as ordering, please contact Picador.
Phone: 646-307-5629
Fax: 212-253-9627
E-mail: readinggroupguides@picadorusa.com

Designed by Meryl Sussman Levavi

Library of Congress Cataloging-in-Publication Data
Watkins, Paul, 1964–
    The ice soldier / Paul Watkins.
        p.   cm.
    ISBN-13: 978-0-312-42650-7
    ISBN-10: 0-312-42650-X
    1. World War, 1939–1945—Veterans—Fiction. 2. World War, 1939–1945—Italy—Fiction. 3. Alps, Italian (Italy)—Fiction. 4. British—Italy—Fiction. 5. History teachers—Fiction. 6. Mountaineering—Fiction. 7. Mountaineers—Fiction. 8. Soldiers—Fiction. I. Title.

PS3573.A844I23 2006
813'.54—dc22

                                                        2005046237

First published in the United States by Henry Holt and Company

First Picador Edition: January 2007

10 9 8 7 6 5 4 3 2 1

The
ICE
SOLDIER

PART

I

ONE

"Is he dead?"

I opened my eyes.

The face of an old woman came slowly into focus.

I knew I wasn't dead.

What I didn't know was how I came to be lying on a rain-soaked London street in June of 1950.

My name is William Bromley and, until that moment, I had lived secure in the belief that the gods were looking out for me.

Firstly, through nothing more than luck, I had survived the war.

Secondly, despite the fact that jobs were far from plentiful, I had a steady post as a teacher at a small private school in London called St. Vernon's. This provided me with long holidays and time to take advantage of my membership at the Montague Club, where I had many acquaintances but very few close friends. Nor did I have any romantic attachments, which suited me just fine.

Thirdly, I had a place in the country, where I could spend my holidays. This was thanks to my father, who lived in a quiet Cotswold village named Painswick. When the school term ended, I traveled there by train and spent my days rambling through the woods, or hiking up a bald-topped hill that over-looked the distant mountains of Wales.

It does not sound like a very exciting kind of life, and indeed it wasn't. I'd had all the excitement I wanted for one lifetime in September of 1944. I felt like a man who had once been granted three wishes by a turbaned, cross-legged genie out of a lamp, and who had since spent two of those wishes just to stay alive. I kept that third wish in reserve, hoping that I'd never have to rub the magic lamp again.

Up to now, everything had been going more or less per-fectly, but one thing the gods will not stand for is the joy of perfection among us mortals. Even the tiniest whiff of such contentment and they begin to scheme, plotting the chaos that will bring this happiness to an end. It is a law of the uni-verse that anything perfect must be wrecked for its audacity in claiming to be so.

Something you can say in the gods' favor is that they aren't boring in the way they go about wrecking it. Each time, they use a different strategy. This keeps life interesting, I sup-pose, during those dull days up on Mount Olympus. Their methods even have a morbid sense of humor, although if you are, as I was, the butt of the joke, it's sometimes hard to see it at the time.

✳

IT WAS A FRIDAY afternoon. I had finished up my classes for the week. The history papers I'd collected from my students remained in an uncorrected clump inside the old Hardy fishing bag I used as a school satchel. The bag was a heavy thing, its leather and canvas stiffened from afternoons spent slung across my back when I sat in the rain on the banks of the river Cherwell, taking a break from my studies at Oxford to tempt a few pike out of the tea-brown water. And the Parker 51 pen I used for marking, with ink that advertised itself as "red" but which looked to me more like fresh blood as it flowed from the little gold nib, remained tucked inside my chest pocket. Until Sunday evening, that pen and those papers would remain untouched.

As I did every Friday afternoon during the school year, I made my way downtown to the Montague, where I planted myself in a chair close to the radiator. This was where I always sat, with my back to the wall and a good view of the entranceway.

Barber arrived soon after, bearing a tray on which lay the daily paper while two bottles of Château Figeac teetered back and forth with the motion of his shuffling feet.

Barber was the caretaker of the club and he had held his post for longer than most of the club's members had been alive. Old age meant that he was more taken care of than he was actually taking care. When you asked him for something, he would usually wander off, forget what he'd been asked for, and you would find him asleep in the library half an hour later.

Barber had the look of someone who had once been more substantial but had been worn away by the years, as a piece of glass is scuffed down by the sea. Now he was a student of his own disintegration, and often spent hours just staring at his hands, which were anchored to his wrists like two small, featherless birds.

This particular day was a cause for celebration, because Barber had remembered not only to bring me the correct paper, but even the right kind of wine. The contents of these bottles was to be shared with my best friend, Stanley Carton. Soon he would come through the door, shaking the rain from his umbrella and shivering dramatically, something he did no matter what the weather was outside, in a way that always reminded me of an old blackbird ruffling its wings. Then he would stride towards me across the red-carpeted room, eyes widening as they adjusted to the soothing darkness of the czar's green walls.

Once we had dispensed with any gossip about old schoolmates, most of whom were also members of the Montague, we would settle down to our drinks. Over the next few hours, we would polish off the wine. At the end of this we would, with great solemnity, forgive the world for all its many sins.

By Monday, all bets would be off and the world would have returned to its previous unforgiven state. But on Friday afternoons, Stanley and I made our peace with the planet, which always seemed easier to do after six glasses of Bordeaux.

Glancing at the paper, I read the grim announcement that North Korean troops had crossed the border into South Korea and seemed to be ignoring the United Nations Security Council's demands that they withdraw. Unsettling as this news appeared, I was still getting over the war I had finished with only a few years before, and had no room in my head for contemplating another. My eyes drifted to the story of a British climbing expedition soon to depart for Patagonia.

At that moment Stanley appeared. He handed his coat and

umbrella to Barber and marched towards his seat, pausing only long enough to give his trademark shiver.

Stanley had a long Roman nose, blond hair so fair as to seem white, and sleepy-looking eyes which were never quite as asleep as they seemed. He was extremely agile and moved with fluid, catlike motions. He was also incredibly stubborn, which meant that he never did much of anything unless he felt like doing it. If he had ever shown interest in sports at school, he would have been an excellent long-distance runner, but Stanley was not inclined to be ordered about in the rain by a man with a whistle and a starter pistol.

It was this combination of stubbornness and agility which had later made him into such a good mountaineer, a sport neither he nor I discovered until university. In the mountains, he had no one to obey except himself, which was as close as a man like Stanley could ever get to heaven. For a while, it had seemed as if mountaineering would become a lifelong fascination to us both. But circumstances had changed. Now those climbing days were a thing of the past and we had become, each in our own way, outcasts from the mountaineering community. What we'd once had in common as climbers, we now shared as two people who no longer climbed. We even referred to our binges at the Montague as "The Weekly Meeting of the Society of Former Mountaineers."

I had known Stanley for most of my life, not only from Oxford but from Eton and the Dragon School before that. Spend fifteen years elbow to elbow with another person and there isn't much mystery left in either of you, though it does permit you to sit together in silence, which is a thing more difficult to achieve than any art of conversation. This was one of the foundations of our friendship and the reason I so valued our time at the club.

Stanley came to a stop in front of my chair and gave a ridiculous salute. "What is your plan for the evening, Mr. Bromley, sir?"

I looked up at him. "My plan is to drink heavily and agree with everything you say."

"Excellent decision!" He slid into the opposite chair, snatching the paper from my grasp as he sank into the leather cushions. "And how are the pigeons?" he asked.

I had ongoing strife with pigeons on the windowsill of my flat. "Bloody pigeons," I said. "One of these days . . ." I made a gun with my thumb and index finger.

"And unlike most people I know who threaten to shoot things, mostly me, you actually possess a gun."

Quite illegally, I had held on to my Webley pistol from the war. It presently resided in a seldom-opened trunk under my bed, along with several other worn-out pieces of kit from my days in the service.

Stanley opened the paper with a dramatic rustle. "What's wrong with the world today?"

"Korea's gone all to hell," I replied.

Stanley glanced at the headlines. "Silly buggers," he said as his eyes wandered across the page. "And as for the mountains of Patagonia . . ." He folded the paper and skimmed it onto the windowsill. "They're just another pile of rocks as far as I'm concerned."

I knew perfectly well that he could have found Korea on the map. It was simply his way of reaching the same conclusion as I had when I read the news. He knew where Patagonia was, as well, just as he knew the whereabouts of every other mountainous region on the planet. This, too, he felt obligated to deny.

Just after I gave up climbing, it used to be that any talk of mountains would unsettle me. Lately, though, I was pleased to find that it had less and less of an effect. To prove it to myself, I rolled a smoke. With steady hands I held the fragile paper along the line of my thumb and index finger. Then I sprinkled into it just the right pinch of tobacco, swiped my tongue along the edge of the paper, and rolled the cigarette shut.

"You know," said Stanley, "I don't understand why you still use that little tin as your tobacco box."

My "little tin" was in fact a ration box given out to all Special Operations soldiers in the war. The box was painted green, although most of the paint had worn off by now, revealing the gray glimmer of bare metal underneath. Stamped into the lid of the tin were the words EMERGENCY RATION. PURPOSE OF CONTENTS: TO BE CONSUMED ONLY WHEN NO OTHER RATIONS OF ANY KIND ARE PROCURABLE. NOTICE: NOT TO BE OPENED EXCEPT BY ORDER OF AN OFFICER.

The contents, two hard bricks of gritty-tasting chocolate, had long ago been consumed. I'd kept the tin all the way through to the end of the war and saw no need to break the habit now. It was just the right size for storing tobacco and fit neatly in my coat pocket. This was the practical reason for keeping it, though not the only reason.

To me, the little box had become a mark of my survival. Its dents and scratches were more of a medal than the one I kept in its velvet-lined presentation box.

"It's all bashed up," continued Stanley, swishing the wine through his teeth, which he did every time before he swallowed, as if he were trying out some new flavor of mouthwash. "We ought to take a walk down to Asprey's and get you a decent one. You don't have to roll your own anymore, either."

As if to emphasize his point, he had by now fished out his own silver case and was tapping a prerolled cigarette vigorously on his monogrammed initials.

It was not Stanley's fault that he could not grasp the meaning of the box. I had been the one to change, not Stanley, not the club, not the mountains that we used to climb before I went away to war.

Stanley had not gone to fight, and that was why he could not understand. His father had pushed him to join the same regiment in which he and a long line of men in the Carton family had served. But the father's gentle and then not-so-gentle persuasion fell on deaf ears. Stanley announced that he would refuse to join up with his father's regiment, or any other regiment for that matter. The idea of a conscientious objector in the family so horrified his father, who ran a factory that canned meat for the army, that Stanley was hurriedly installed in the company as his father's "personal assistant." The war made Stanley's father a very wealthy man. The Bully Beef his father canned was a mash of pasty white fat and lurid red flesh. It was standard issue to the troops, no matter where they were serving. Soldiers in the jungles of Burma poured it in a greasy liquid from heat-bloated tins and men in the Arctic hacked the meat from its metal housing with the tips of bayonets.

As an employee of this vital company, Stanley had the right to wear a brass badge that read ON WAR SERVICE. By wearing the badge on his lapel, he was able to fend off the ugly stares of men in uniform, or women handing out white feathers, which signified cowardice, to any man wearing civilian clothes who looked as if he ought to be a soldier.

He was proud of this badge and kept the brass highly polished, so that it stood out against his dark jacket. As soon as the war was over, however, he threw that badge off Waterloo

Bridge, spinning it out across the water like a skipping stone. Since he had discarded this once-powerful trinket, it made sense to Stanley that I should also put away the relic of my own war days.

But it did not make sense to me. I was not yet ready. Nor was I the only one.

Under the shirt of the bowler-hatted banker who managed my meager accounts still hung the remains of his dog tags. At the school where I taught, the head groundskeeper carried a bullet that had nearly ended his life. It hung on the end of a watch chain straddling his waistcoat pockets. The head of the school's math department slept with a Luger beneath his pillow. And I wouldn't part with my emergency-ration box.

Now and then, as I traveled on the train to my father's home in Gloucestershire, I would be fixing myself a cigarette and sense that someone was watching me. I'd raise my head and come eye to eye with some old soldier, who knew exactly what the box was, and what it meant to carry one.

Having been with us in those moments when we stood on the verge of oblivion, these talismans served to remind us that we were still alive. Sometimes the only way to avoid being overwhelmed by what we had seen was to cling to those symbols of the days when we had taken life for granted, which none of us could ever do again.

I could have told Stanley all this, but I doubted he would understand. For the same reason, I'd never spoken to him in any detail about what had happened on the mountaineering expedition which had closed that chapter of my life for good.

I carried on rolling my smoke.

By now, Stanley was stretched out in his chair, feet up on a cushioned stool and joined heels making a V with his outward-pointing toes. He puffed his cheeks and noisily exhaled.

"What's the matter?" I asked.

"I'm in love," he sighed, the way a person might confess to having lost too much money at the races.

I made a vague attempt to sit up. "Sounds serious," I said.

"Oh, it is," he replied.

"Well, who's the lucky girl?" I asked. I wasn't completely sure I wanted to know. One didn't normally discuss one's romances at the club. You could talk about almost anything else, but not about love.

"Her name," said Stanley, "is Helen Paradise."

"Hell and Paradise?"

"Helen," he said slowly. "Hel-en. You've got the Paradise part right, though."

"You're kidding," I told him. "What kind of name is that?"

"French, I think. The name used to be Paradis." He pronounced it *Paradee*. "But then they came over here and changed it."

"Paradise," I said. "You're bloody joking."

"Paradise," he sighed again. "It's true."

"God."

"She's giving a lecture series at my uncle's club."

I gritted my teeth in anticipation of the tirade which usually followed the mention of Stanley's uncle.

The man's name was Henry Carton and he was president of the London Climbers' Club. Many years ago, Carton had made a name for himself as a mountaineer. He was best known for having scaled a previously unclimbed peak in the Alps and for nearly dying in the process.

It was Carton who had first drawn me and Stanley to climbing, and we were not the only ones. Few people had done as much as Carton to ensure the popularity of mountaineering, not only with those who climbed but also with those who had never, and would never, set foot in the mountains.

In Carton's day the act of climbing, particularly in the Alps, had been considered a rich man's sport. At the turn of the century, the cost of getting to the Alps, of purchasing climbing gear, of hiring porters and guides, and of securing membership in various mountaineering societies had kept it that way. The mountains were the province of the climbing elite. Above all, this elite was an English elite, and even if they were grudgingly forced to accept the French, Swiss, German, Austrian, and Italian climbers who made their way into the hills, and whose countries owned those mountains in the first place, one thing they would not tolerate was what they saw as the lower classes of their own society. Women, too, were frowned upon. Mountaineering clubs either barred them from membership or obliged them to wear full-length dresses when they were climbing.

By the 1930s, when Stanley and I started climbing, all that was changing fast. Women had discovered that they could scale mountains just as well as men, and had long ago discarded the recommended dresses for trousers instead. Travel to the Alps was no longer as costly as it had been, and mountaineering societies had dropped the requirement that only those who had been above twelve thousand feet could apply for membership.

Henry Carton had no use for the old elitism of the mountaineering establishment. "Social Climbers Climbing Socially," he called them. Climbing was for everyone, he maintained, and anyone who didn't climb had missed out on one of the greatest joys on this earth.

For a man who preached this sort of doctrine it was a

particular disappointment that his own nephew, who had once showed such promise as a mountaineer, should have given it up. Now these two men, who had once been mentor and pro-tégé, regarded each other only with disgust.

The strain between them was made worse by the fact that, after the death of Stanley's father in September of 1945, only weeks after the end of the war, Stanley had quit the family meat-canning company and was looking forward to a leisurely existence of living off his inheritance. Unfortunately for Stanley, his father had anticipated this and, being a man of solid work ethics, had placed his brother Henry in charge of the inheritance. With this came the discretionary power to distrib-ute the money to Stanley in whatever amounts Carton saw fit.

The result of this was that Stanley soon found himself employed as his uncle's assistant at the club. Here, Carton had calculated, he could not only keep an eye on his nephew but could also ensure that he earned an honest living.

"Is your uncle still making you miserable?" I asked Stanley, remembering the days when they had not hated each other quite so much.

"I should say he is," Stanley growled. "I'm not his assistant. I'm his bloody servant. He tells people I'm his Nitty Gritty Man and has me doing all the boring paperwork. Whenever I stick my head up from the accounts books, he starts making suggestions as to how I could better myself. I know that nothing would please him more than to hear I'd taken up mountaineering again. But he'd better not hold his breath, what little he's got of it. He may have talked me into climbing once, but I'm damned if he'll do it again."

Both Stanley and his uncle were equally obstinate. That was why I had no hope for any reconciliation between them.

"Why don't you just get another job?" I had asked him this question before, and he never liked answering it.

"I can't be bothered," he said.

But the truth was, and we both knew it, that his uncle did not work him very hard, and to earn as much as Carton paid him Stanley would have had to find a real job, with real hours and slim holidays. As it was, Stanley's efforts at the club were slack at best, no matter how hard Carton tried to push him. He kept irregular hours, took endless lunch breaks, and seemed to be under the impression that the Christmas holiday lasted until February. More than this, it seemed to me that the two men had grown so accustomed to being at each other's throats that they had, in a way, forgotten how to exist any differently.

"Look, you really haven't heard of her?" demanded Stanley, returning to the topic of his latest romance.

"What's her name again?" I asked.

"Helen Paradise. I told you."

I shrugged myself a little deeper into my chair. "I'd remember a name like that."

"You'd remember if you saw her, too." He held a wine bottle upside down over his glass, shaking the last drops from its dark green mouth. "I first spotted her when she came in to hear a lecture in the last series we had at the club. Well, then we happened to get talking—"

"You mean you threw yourself at her feet."

He ignored me. "—and then it turned out she was also a mountaineer and then she got invited to give the next lecture series."

"You mean you begged your uncle to let her give a talk."

"I didn't beg," he sniffed. "I just mentioned it to him as a possibility."

"How many times did you mention it?"

"As many as it took," he said exasperatedly. "Anyway, she's exactly my type."

"I don't know about your taste in women," I muttered. By this, I meant that I knew all too much about it. There had been several dismal and expensive failures. Many times I had accompanied Stanley and whatever woman had currently captured his heart to the fanciest restaurants in London: the Ash Grove, Tamesin's, and La Borsa. There were moments in those evenings when the sweat of witty banter was glistening on Stanley's forehead and I would catch the eye of these sad and beautiful women—they were always beautiful and always sad—and we would tell each other with a glance that this was not going to work. And while these glances were exchanged, Stanley would continue to ramble through his usual jokes, Adam's apple quivering in his throat like a bobber on a fishing line. It wasn't Stanley who made these women sad. They were sad before they met him and for reasons that had nothing to do with his feverish charm. Stanley and I referred to them as "Melancholy Angels," and often debated whether they were sad because they were so beautiful or whether their sadness was, in some twisted way, the very source of their loveliness.

Whatever the answer, Stanley was drawn helplessly to this sadness just as the women were drawn to his laughter and precariously punch-lined anecdotes, and his money, of which he had more than most people, despite his uncle's choke hold on the trust fund. The difference was that these women were drawn to him only in a transitory way, as a diversion from their sadness, and when they no longer found him diverting, they would leave. Stanley, on the other hand, lived in a world of perpetual hope in which true love was not a thing to be ridiculed and, if found, would last forever.

There were nights when Stan and I walked back to the club, having said good night to the woman, and I would dread the moment when he'd ask how I thought it had gone. We both knew exactly how it had gone, and Stanley would be in the process of what seemed to be one long exhaling of breath, as he slowly returned to himself. With me, he had no reason to be anything other than who he was, and if he had been this same person when he was with the ladies, they might have liked him better for it. Or perhaps the Melancholy Angels would have steered clear of him to begin with. But something clicked in him when he was trying to impress these ladies, and he became like a dancing bear, lumbering about on the stage, without reward, without dignity, without a chance.

I would never tell him it was useless. It was important to let Stanley decide that for himself. I would always say, "There are possibilities."

And so, for a while at least, he would bask in the glow of potential. It was what the French call *l'extase langoureuse*. An ecstasy of languishing.

The next day, or the day after, we would be talking about something completely different and Stanley would suddenly exclaim, "No, it's pointless."

Then I would know he had put away his dreams, at least with this particular woman. And as for the woman, we might see her again at some party, on the arm of some other languishing and grinning man. She was also languishing, but it had nothing to do with the men whose hearts she broke. What she languished for, no joke could mend, no bottle of champagne, no warmth of adoration.

"You must meet her," he said.

"I'd be happy to," I lied, because it was understood that I would lie.

"She's doing another lecture at the Climbers' Club tonight," he continued. "You could come along. I'll introduce you."

I narrowed my eyes at him. "Your uncle and I haven't spoken in years."

"All the more reason for you to come! Besides, I don't need you to meet him. I need you to meet her."

"What sort of climbing has she done, anyway?"

"Well, she's just returned from photographing a lot of the mountains down in the Alps, including that one which is named after my uncle."

Carton's Rock, as it had been named, was a jagged pinnacle of stone and ice which rose almost sheer out of a glacier called La Lingua del Dragone, the Dragon's Tongue. It lay in a section of the Italian Alps known as the Val Antigorio, north of Turin, and jutting up towards the St. Gotthard Pass. The Dragone glacier covered a large area in the mountains west of the town of Formazza. It was here that Carton had found himself, in the summer of 1905, having taken a wrong turn at the village of Crevoladossola on his way down from Switzerland to Milan.

By the time he realized his mistake, he had traveled a considerable distance north along the only road which ran through the Antigorio Valley and stopped to spend the night in Formazza before retracing his steps towards Milan.

At a guesthouse in Formazza, Carton met another Englishman, whose intention had been to travel out across the Dragone glacier. Until that time, the glacier, and in fact the whole area around it, had received very few visitors. Bigger mountains and less dangerous glaciers could be found just across the border in Switzerland.

It had never been Carton's intention to go out on the ice. Until he met the Englishman, he had not even known of the

glacier's existence. He had not intended to do any mountaineering on his trip, and had come to the Alps only on the
advice of his doctor, as a cure for the asthma he'd had since
childhood. After hearing the Englishman's description of the
wild and barren landscape of the glacier, Carton grew curious.
He would have remained merely interested if the Englishman
had not revealed that he was suffering from gout and would not
be able to make use of the guide he had hired. The Englishman
kindly offered to let the guide take Carton instead, and even
offered him the use of his mountaineering equipment.

Invigorated as much by the Englishman's stories as by the
Alpine air, Carton accepted. The next day, instead of heading
south on his original course, Carton traveled west along a dirt
road to the village of Palladino; no more than a cluster of
houses on the banks of a lake called Vannino. Palladino was
the last outpost before the mountains, and the closest starting
point for a voyage across the Dragone glacier.

At Palladino, Carton was met by the guide, who, after
hearing Carton's explanation, agreed to take him instead.

At first light the following day, the two-man team set off.

Two weeks later, Carton staggered into Palladino alone,
starving, snow-blind, with the skin sunburned off his nose and
cheeks and his fingers so badly frostbitten that he spent a week
with his hands in a bath of vinegar before he regained feeling
in them.

The story he told was that after several days of grueling
exertion over the ice of the Dragon's Tongue and up the
Dragon's Teeth, the two men reached the tallest of these jagged
peaks, shook hands, and started down again across the glacier.
They were roped together, testing the snow ahead of them
with their long ice axes. At some point on the descent, the
guide fell through a thin patch of snow, beneath which lay a

crevasse hundreds of feet deep. Carton was able to roll onto his stomach and jam his ax into the snow to provide an anchor. The ax caught fast in ice which lay beneath the snow, stopping his slide, but when the rope came taut it broke. The guide fell into the abyss, leaving Carton by himself up on the glacier. It took Carton seven days to find his way back to Palladino.

Despite an exhaustive search, the body of the guide was never found.

Having seen that glacier for myself, I knew how lucky Carton had been to survive. To call the glacier the Dragon's Tongue, and Carton's Rock the Dragon's Teeth, was no mistake.

When Carton returned to London, his hands bandaged and face still badly burned, he was front-page news in every paper in the country. Inspired by the unexpected attention, he rented out a small dance hall in Ealing and gave a lecture to a half-filled space about his experiences, which he titled "Peril in the Heights." It soon became clear that Carton knew very little about mountaineering, but this did not seem to matter. What mattered was that he had survived in spite of how little he knew. Even more important, he knew how to tell the story, hurling himself across the stage, flailing his arms in the air, retrieving from his ice-burned brain the most obscure but telling details.

The next week, he rented out the hall again. This time the place was full.

Throughout the months ahead, two, three, four times, the same people showed up to hear Carton describe the sight of the guide as he slipped away to his death. The eyes of the audience grew wide as he held up his hands and spoke of his frozen fingernails turning black and falling off, of the blood he coughed into the snow as the altitude punished his lungs.

Despite what he had endured, he always finished his talks by speaking of the view once he had arrived at the summit. He told his audience it was the most beautiful sight he had ever seen, like something out of a dream. This view, which only he had ever glimpsed and lived to tell of, since Carton's Rock remained unclimbed except by him and the unfortunate guide, became a thing of mythic beauty, beyond all earthly comparison.

In these lectures, Carton steered clear of formal moun-taineering terminology, most of which would have been mean-ingless to his audience. Instead of *verglas*, for example, he said "icy rock." Instead of *firnspiegel*, he said "icy snow." *Col* became ridge, *couloir* became *gully*, and so on.

The lecture series went so well that the following year, after spending his summer traveling through the Alps, he rented a larger dance hall. The second year's lecture series, given twice a week, on Monday and Wednesday nights, was augmented with paintings of the Alps which Carton hung on easels on the stage. Wearing a tweed mountaineering suit and carrying an ice ax, he walked among these paintings as if he were the "Wild Huntsman" of German mythology.

The hall was always full.

I myself had been to see him, when he came to give a lec-ture in Oxford. I'd only gone because Stanley had nagged me and Stanley, who had never been to one of Carton's talks, had gone only because his uncle had promised him a free dinner at the Randolph Hotel afterwards.

If I had to name the single thing which first drew me to mountaineering, it would be the darkly resonant voice of Henry Carton. Even Stanley, who had almost turned into an art form his ability to remain unimpressed by everything he saw or heard or did, became swept up in the momentum of his uncle's words.

Carton spoke with such urgency that it seemed as if his very life depended on our seeing what he was trying to describe. He talked in epic phrases. Even the way he paused to catch his breath had something grand about it. Sometimes he clawed at the air, grasping for images like a man catching leaves as they fluttered to the ground before him. Other times, his head thrashed from side to side, as if the colors which vibrated in his head would burn through the bone casing of his skull if he did not set them free with words.

For Carton, the Alps were the ultimate proving ground. Up there, all that one could be and all that one was would become clear. Carton was the only man I had ever heard use the word *honor* who wasn't trying to sell me something. In the Alps, Carton told us, no climber could be sheltered by his wealth, or by his social connections, or his clever turns of phrase. In the mountains, you learned who you were, for better and for worse.

"There are those who climb," he said, "and those who dream of climbing. For some, the dream is all they need, and perhaps they are the lucky ones. But not all of us can be content with dreams alone. We are drawn up to the stony rafters of the world, like migrating animals who travel thousands of miles without knowing why they do this, only knowing that they must. Those who have been to these places know that they are not only worlds of rock and snow and ice. They are worlds of bleak but unforgettable beauty. To those who climb, the mountains are part of a dream, which we all have when we are young. It is the dream of wanting more than anything to know who you really are. The poet Friedrich von Schiller once wrote, 'Hold Fast to the Dreams of Your Youth.' This we must all do, or else we risk forgetting what it means to be alive."

Carton finished his lectures so exhausted that it was hard to imagine how he would ever be able to speak of the mountains again. But he did. Night after night, his energy never subsiding.

It wasn't long before he bought the dance hall outright and rebuilt it as his own club. Few of its members were actual climbers. The Climbers' Club had no membership criteria other than that people had to be interested in mountains or, failing that, at least interested in Carton.

Carton also gave private lectures, in which he guaranteed to reveal information "too horrific" for his regular audiences. For this, he charged extraordinary amounts of money and never revealed the names of those people who received the private lectures. He also swore these private audiences to secrecy, forbidding them to disclose the "terrifying facts" kept hidden from the regular audiences. Because no one knew who these private audiences were, the rumors surrounding their identities soon included most of the famous people in Britain, including the royal family. And because swearing a group of people to secrecy was a virtual invitation to gossip, more rumors emerged concerning the "facts."

This was, of course, exactly what Carton had hoped for.

One story was that Carton had discovered the remains of an actual dragon frozen in the ice and had shown his high-paying audience one of its teeth. Another story was that Carton had been guided back to safety by the ghost of a mountaineer who had died on the Dragon's Tongue over a century before. Carton never admitted to any of these, but he never denied them, either, so the rumors flourished.

Carton was a force of nature, so much larger than life that he became, in the eyes of his audiences, as mystical a presence as the mountains he described.

His only critic was a man named Joseph Pringle. Pringle was a small, slope-shouldered man with big ears and impossibly small eyes. He rarely smiled, and his fashion sense had come to a halt some fifty years before. His clothes were almost exclusively black, and instead of a tie, or any modern concept of a tie, he wore a large floppy neck scarf knotted into a bow. The neck scarf shambled off down his front and across the lapels of his heavy woolen coat, which buttoned all the way up to the throat but on which only the top button was fastened.

Pringle had spent many years climbing, particularly in the Alps, and had several first ascents to his name. Like Carton, Pringle had originally been sent to the Alps by a Harley Street doctor, although in Pringle's case in the hopes of curing chronic eczema. Pringle's eczema remained unchanged, but he fell in love with the Alps and soon became what was known as a "peak bagger," obsessed with being the first to climb as many mountains as he could. One story often told about Pringle was that while vacationing in Turin, he read about a man who was attempting a small but unclimbed peak in the Cottian Alps near Monte Viso. Unable to rein in his competitiveness, Pringle decided he would get there first and steal the prize of first ascent. He raced up to the mountains, half-killed himself climbing the peak, and when he returned, ready to gloat about his victory, learned that this unnamed man attempting the climb was, in fact, himself.

But Pringle was old now and his days of climbing were over. He had instead become a curator of sorts. Throughout his life, the man had gathered thousands of pages of information about the Alps. He subscribed to every mountaineering journal and read every book on the subject of climbing. Few of these escaped his criticism. There was almost always some error which required a letter from him to the editor demanding a correction. For example, if a climber spoke of having been able to see Monte Rosa from the summit of the Breithorn on a certain day, Pringle would consult the weather bulletins, all of which he had saved, and if the bulletin had indicated cloud, he would be sure to send a scathing letter discrediting the climber's claim.

Pringle's appearance at a lecture on the subject of Alpinism would send a shudder of dismay through any unfortunate speaker walking out onstage. During the lecture, Pringle would take notes on a miniature chalkboard which he carried with him. The tapping and scratching of the chalk on the board was enough to ruin anybody's concentration. At the end, when the floor was opened for questions, Pringle's stubby arm would be the first to rise.

He was so nitpicky in his fact-checking, and so blunt in his delivery of the truth, that Pringle had managed to make enemies of almost everyone in the climbing community. Most people were too terrified to speak ill of him. He had made a business of ruining reputations, and it was with particular energy that he set about ruining Carton's.

For Pringle, the disregarding of a fact was a personal insult. Facts were for him the most beautiful of all things, as hard and precious as diamonds. But for Carton, that diamond fact was a thing to be held up to the light, to be twisted and turned and examined for its angle of greatest interest. And if he believed that the fact might be of better use to him if it was held up in just such a way, or turned even slightly, to achieve that particular wide-eyed look of wonder—part horror, part fascination, part incredulity—he would make it so. Each summer he returned from the Alps with new and hair-raising stories for his audiences.

He also accumulated a collection of artifacts which had

been expelled from glaciers. Anything which fell down a crevasse would, sooner or later, be tombed in ice and carried
through to the glacier's end. The movement of these glaciers
had been studied enough that when something, or someone,
disappeared down a crevasse, it could often be predicted to
within a year or two when that thing or person would reappear.

Carton established contacts among the Society of Alpine
Guides and quietly bought up the relics of mountaineering
disasters. These included ice axes, clearly marked to men whose
lives had ended decades before and whose bodies had never
been found. He purchased the bones of Alpine cave bears,
which had been extinct for thousands of years. There were
shreds of clothing, spewed out in slow motion by the ice; their
tattered edges seemed to prove the violent ends of those who
had once worn them.

And then there was Archie.

One year, thirteen members of the Climbers' Club were
invited to a Saturday lunch in the club's dining room. There
was some uneasiness as to why Carton would have chosen
thirteen people, when the superstition attached to the number
still meant that hotels did not have a thirteenth room, that
hunting parties never comprised thirteen people, and that you
did not invite thirteen people to a luncheon.

The guests arrived to find fourteen places laid for dinner.

Who was the fourteenth guest? they asked.

Carton would not say.

Just as the meal was about to begin, Carton rang a small
brass bell and the waiters wheeled in something that caused
two people, both of them men, to faint.

It was a skeleton sitting in a chair. The bones had been
wired together and then strapped to the chair, but not before
it had been dressed in a gray suit with a red tie bearing a white

skull-and-crossbones design. The skeleton had been wired in such a way that its arms were folded across its chest. This, combined with the grinning teeth, served to give Archie a cheerful and irreverent expression, much like Carton himself.

Carton never disclosed exactly where the skeleton had come from, saying only that he'd picked it up in the Alps and that it had been found near a glacier.

The skeleton bore no signs of identity and the clothes had been added later, so it was impossible to say who the person had been, although one guest, who was a doctor, did confirm that the skeleton belonged to a man.

Once again, rumors circulated. The most persistent of these was that the body had been stolen from the old morgue in the hospice of the Great St. Bernard Pass. There, the bodies of those who had become lost in the mountains were gathered to await identification. Because of the dry air and the fact that many of these bodies were never claimed, some had become mummified. Even though Carton had never seen the place, he described it in vivid detail to his audiences, based on stories he had himself been told.

Pringle wrote Carton a letter that began, "You Brute!" and listed the names of forty vanished mountaineers whose skeleton Archie might be. Carton had the letter framed and hung it in the men's bathroom at the club.

Soon after, Archie was moved to the head of the table and the Saturday lunches developed into a regular event. At these lunches, Archie would be toasted by the guests, who always numbered thirteen. Carton drank to Archie from a battered pewter mug engraved with the initials E.B. This had emerged from a glacier near Trélatête and almost certainly belonged to the infamous guide Emil Boileau. Although it had never been proven, Boileau was said to have murdered several of the climbers who had hired him in the early 1800s. He would lead them high into the mountains, to places from which they would never be able to return without his help. Then he would demand money, which, if not paid out immediately, would result in the deaths and disappearance of the climbers. Boileau drank heavily, even when climbing. According to legend, he would throw the bodies of the climbers he had killed down bottomless crevasses and toast them with a tankard full of brandy. His own end came when he found himself unable to kill a particularly beautiful young woman. He became so deranged that he threw himself down the crevasse instead, tankard and all. The tankard, bruised by its journey through the shifting glacier ice, emerged almost a century after Boileau's death, and was immediately acquired by Carton. How much truth there was in the story of Emil Boileau didn't matter to Carton. What mattered was the legend.

Thousands flocked to Carton's lectures, hoping for a glimpse of Archie, who was sometimes sitting behind Carton on the stage, sometimes appeared after the intermission, and sometimes could be found in the front row of the audience.

Membership in the Climbers' Club tripled.

Archie became, in the words of Carton, "the most popular man in London. And the thinnest." People posed for pictures beside him. Carton took to swinging his arm around Archie in the middle of the meal, squinting out at the dinner guests and remarking, "Well, Archie, what do you think of the view?"

The greater Carton's popularity became, the more he added to his shows. He brought in blond, blue-eyed "Alpine maidens" in traditional costume. The fact that these women never spoke but only smiled led to some speculation as to whether the maidens were actually from the Alps, although no one truly cared. Nor did they care when the Saint Bernard dogs

Carton brought in turned out to be boxers, or even when the stuffed and tattered bird which he claimed was the last of the dreaded baby-snatching lammergeier vultures in the Alps turned out to be of a more common variety.

It was all about the show, and if the show was sometimes short on fact, Carton made up for it with the energy he put into his presentations. He reenacted not only his own ascent of the Dragon's Teeth but also many other mountaineering epics, in particular those which involved some loss of life. These included the notorious Hamel expedition to Mont Blanc, which ended in the deaths of three men who were caught in an avalanche. He also gave his own interpretation of Whymper's 1865 ascent of the Matterhorn and the subsequent deaths of four of its members. He would stand on his toes, grasping at imaginary rock holds, hauling up make-believe companions at the end of invisible ropes, pausing only to wipe genuine sweat from his forehead.

Carton's next venture, a plan to lead an expedition back to the Dragon's Teeth, was cut short by a bout of pneumonia that ruined his already asthma-scarred lungs. After that, he had trouble even climbing the stairs of his club. Although the lecturing continued, his mountaineering days were over. The strain began to show on Carton's face and in his voice. Carton's talks were filled with awkward silences as he fought for breath.

By the time he hired Stanley, the Climbers' Club had begun its slow decline.

Nowadays Carton usually invited other mountaineers, like Hell and Paradise, to do the speaking for him.

Stanley was still going on about her. "She gave me a look, and I looked right back!" He pointed a finger at his eyes, as if the force of her glance had left a gash across his pupils. "And I tell you something happened. Now she is all I can think about.

We've been out to lunch several times. We've had picnics in Hyde Park. She's fascinating. Everything she says is just brilliant, and the photographs are pretty amazing, too. Some of them are on display at the club. You've just got to come and meet her."

I glanced out the window, hoping for some inspiration that would provide me with an excuse not to go. But there was only the brick facade of the bank on the opposite side of the road, and the space between sieved by gently falling rain. There was a grayness in the air, which made the moisture seem less like rain than a failing of my sight.

"Don't try and get out of it," said Stanley, reading my mind. "I want to know what you think of her."

I heard a clock chime quietly in another room. After waiting out the count, I turned to him. "No, Stanley," I said, "you don't."

His eyebrows arched. "I don't?"

"No," I told him, doing my best to put aside the comfortable beehive hum of the wine inside my head, "you don't want to know what I think of her. You want me to tell you what she thinks of you."

Stanley breathed out sharply through his nose. "I suppose you could say that." Then he held open his hands and smiled as if to say, "So we are agreed."

"I didn't say I'd come along. Besides, does this woman know you don't climb anymore?"

He brushed my words aside. "Once she's got to know me a bit, the old charm will kick in and she won't care if I do or not."

It occurred to me that the only person on whom Stanley's old charm had worked was himself, and the only thing which had been charmed was his belief that he actually had any. With women, anyway. I might have told him this, seeing as he had just spoiled our weekly booze-up, but it was at this moment that my entire world began, very slowly, to fall apart. It began when I heard the whispered name of a man I hadn't seen in years.

"*It's Wally Sugden!*" hissed a voice.

"*Just about to leave for Patagonia!*" said another.

"*Sugden's at the Montague!*"

"*I thought he'd given up his membership.*"

"*Who cares? Let's give it back to him.*"

The whole club filled with these admiring whispers, which echoed through the bar and through the sitting room, up the stairs, and into the guest rooms where no one ever stayed.

At the mention of Sugden's name, the breath caught in my throat and I felt sick. The memory of him was tied, as if by tiny threads, to all the other memories I had been trying so hard to forget. Now I sat with teeth clenched, trying to remain in control, and praying that those other nightmares did not come tumbling one after the other from every darkened corner of my brain.

A member of the close-knit group of mountaineers at Oxford, which had included Stanley and me, Sugden was the only one who had continued to climb. Since the war, he had gone on expeditions to the Himalayas, the Rockies, the Jotunheimen mountains of Norway, and now was on his way to Patagonia. He had become a national hero; many believed he was Britain's best shot since George Mallory and Sandy Irvine for reaching the summit of Everest.

He had parlayed this hero status into a wildly successful car dealership.

The *Evening Tribune* often carried ads which featured a picture of Sugden in his climbing gear, complete with goggles, boots, and a coil of rope across his shoulders, standing along-side the latest model auto. Beneath this picture were the words "Trust in the Man. Trust in the Machine."

Now the sight of Wally Sugden, who once hung around the Montague but had not been seen here in years, astonished everyone. Everyone except Stanley, anyway.

Despite the fact that he and Stanley had gone to the same school, once climbed together, and were members of the same club, each represented the polar opposite of the other.

Sugden was a square-faced, broad-shouldered man with slightly squinting eyes that told you he meant business and a perpetual smirk, which made you feel as if you had to choose your words carefully when speaking. He had been extremely popular at school. At Eton, he was captain of every team he played on, and he played on almost every team. He also possessed the kind of unshakable confidence that assured him of success. Sugden had been senior prefect in my house at Eton, where he'd developed the annoying habit of wandering into my room, whether I was there or not, and eating all the food in my cupboard. I often found him sitting with his feet up on my desk, shaking the last crumbs from a packet of chocolate-covered biscuits down his throat.

I more or less put up with this because Sugden seemed to have no idea he was doing anything objectionable and it would have been considerably more work trying to explain this to him than to go out and get a new packet of biscuits.

Stanley, by contrast, was captain of nothing. He had the intelligence to be top of every class but, as if on principal, never was. He was also athletic, but stubbornly refused to be a "team player" in soccer, rowing, or rugby, sports which occupied the majority of our school year. As a result, he was relegated to the lowest teams and regarded with suspicion by people like Wally Sugden

I recalled Stanley leaning against a goalpost on a soccer pitch reserved for teams made up entirely of people who either couldn't or, like Stanley, wouldn't play. This field was kept out of the public view, behind a thick bramble hedge down by the river. The masters who refereed the matches were kindred spirits to these players. They began the games late, finished them early, and allowed the halftime break to last forever. Sometimes the ball would get kicked into the hedge, at which point both teams would become embroiled in a philosophical discussion about who should go in and get it.

There were times I envied their lack of ambition, while out on fields with names like Agar's Plough and Dutchman's, people like Sugden and me engaged in ruthless competition, as if our very lives depended on the outcome.

There were several of Stanley's former teammates at the Montague. Most of them were too intelligent for their own good, and the majority, unlike Sugden, had failed to make their way in society. It was most likely because of this that Sugden had stopped coming to the Montague. He considered himself to be in a different league.

But now Sugden stood with his arms outstretched and a huge grin on his face, waiting until he had attracted adequate attention before saying whatever he had come to say. From the glazed look in his eyes, it was clear he had been drinking heavily.

Long after the others in the room had stopped what they were doing, in anticipation of Sugden's announcement, Stanley continued to chat, refusing to play the man's game and despising the others for their shameless adulation of a man like Sugden.

At last Sugden spoke. "I," he boomed, "have returned!"

The room burst into applause.

"And I just wanted to stop by and see the old crew before I head off to Patagonia."

More applause. Some people even cheered.

"And I also wanted to tell you that I have, prior to my departure, fortified myself at that Greek restaurant across the road by eating an entire plate of testicles!"

These words produced the most profound silence that I had ever heard descend upon the club. Even late at night, when the place was almost empty, and the last of the dozing members were snoozing in their chairs, you could hear more in the snuffling breaths and ticking of clocks than you heard after Sugden made his comment about the testicles.

Even Stanley fell silent. Then, with a defeated sigh, he turned to face the man, who still stood with his arms open, welcoming the astonishment of the masses. "Whose?" asked Stanley in a frosty voice.

Sugden lowered his arms. "Oh, it's you," he said, unable to hide his irritation.

Stanley gave him a cheeky little wave.

"I should have known I'd find you skulking about in here," said Sugden.

"So are you going to tell us who these testicles belonged to or not?" demanded Stanley.

"A sheep, I suppose. How should I know?" Sugden already seemed to be regretting his appearance at the club.

"They were unlikely to have belonged to a sheep," remarked Stanley.

"A goat perhaps," said Sugden. "It doesn't matter."

"It matters to the goat," replied Stanley. "Were they fried?

Or baked? Or pickled? Or did you just gnaw them off some unsuspecting member of the animal kingdom?"

Sugden forced a smile back onto his face. He turned away from Stanley and continued with his story, addressing the others in the room. "They were on the menu. The chef had them written down as 'A Feast of the Gods.' I asked what was in this feast of his, but he tried to fob me off on something made with cucumbers."

"If they were in fact cucumbers," said Stanley.

Sugden ignored this. "So I said to him, Look here, Themistocles, you've got this thing on the menu and I want to try it, so bring me out this Godly Feast and I'll have a go at it. Well, after much babbling in the kitchen they bring me out a plate of these testicles. Fried and all sliced up."

There was a collective wincing in the room.

"But did you know what they were?" asked Stanley, the frost in his voice giving way to genuine disbelief.

"Not at first, but then the waiter told me."

"I'd have shot him," said Stanley.

"More than once, sir," added Barber in a shaky voice.

"When he told me," explained Sugden, twisting one hand in the air, "well I just thought, You've gone this far, you might as well finish the job. So I ate the lot. And I tell you, they were marvelous. They give you strength, apparently. They'll even cure you if you're ill. What do you think of that?" he called across to Stanley, convinced he now had the upper hand.

"I have never yet exclaimed 'Heavens to Betsy,'" replied Stanley, "but I feel the time is fast approaching."

At that moment Sugden caught sight of me. The angle of my chair had almost kept me hidden. His already squinting eyes narrowed even further.

Now the sickness I had felt before grew so strong that I could barely breathe. The reason he had such an effect on me was simple.

Sugden and I were the only survivors of one of the worst mountaineering disasters to take place during the war. As leader of that group, I had been cleared of wrongdoing by a board of inquiry. The board was by headed by none other than Henry Carton, who even saw to it that I was awarded a medal. But as far as Wally Sugden was concerned, the blame for what went wrong still lay upon me. No board of inquiry or medal on my chest could change Sugden's mind, and the fact that I no longer climbed only strengthened his conviction.

In truth, Sugden was right. I did blame myself for what happened. It didn't matter if the army had acquitted me, because I could not acquit myself. I had been over it a thousand times in my head and even if I could not imagine making different decisions than the ones I'd made, I had still made them and those men, who had been some of my closest friends, had still died. Even the thought of it was more than I could bear, so I had imprisoned all those memories deep in the dungeons of my brain. That was why I no longer climbed. I knew that the feel of the ropes, the sound of hidden streams beneath the rocks, the scrabble of boots over wet stone, and the pain in my fingers from gripping tiny ledges would bring those memories back into the light. Then I would become their prisoner, and not the other way around.

I had tried to convince myself that I'd put the whole business behind me, and that those images had perished in their walled-in prison cells. But the sight of Wally Sugden, and the dread it woke inside, told me the pictures were still alive, still dangerous, scrabbling at the walls as they attempted to escape.

Sugden had finally had enough of Stanley's jibes. "I was

wondering," he said in a voice everyone could hear, "whether you and your friend might like to come along."

"Come along where?" asked Stanley.

"Why, to Patagonia of course!"

The blood drained out of Stanley's face. He tried without success to assume an air of nonchalance. "We don't climb anymore," he said casually. "We are the—"

"'The Society of Former Mountaineers,'" said Sugden. "Yes, I know what you call yourselves. But why bother with such a long name when one word would do to sum it up?"

Everyone knew what that one word was meant to be. Sugden was calling us cowards.

This time Stanley had no answer for him.

Sugden turned away and smiled and faced the room. "I'll see you when I get back!" he shouted triumphantly.

Another burst of applause. Now the room became very lively.

In the midst of this, I stepped out to get some air. The once-happy thrumming of the red wine had now become an annoyance. I wanted it to go away. I muttered something to myself about the world getting itself all back-to-front, and the reason for my going into the Montague being to escape from the very confusion that I was now leaving the club to avoid.

I stood there on the sidewalk, as men and women stepped past me on their way home from work. Raincoats swished about their knees and umbrellas tilted down over their faces. The sound of their shuffling feet merged with the rumble of passing cars.

I looked down the avenue, mesmerized by the silver lights of oncoming vehicles and the red dots of taillights from cars speeding in the opposite direction. In the murky dusk, the glow of those lights linked together until they became like two necklaces, one of pearls and one of rubies, laid side by side across the grayness of the city.

The sight of it unsettled me, but I could not understand why. Everywhere around me, colors began to throb. Solid objects rippled, transforming themselves into nightmarish creatures. I realized I was sweating. The evening breeze cooled the moisture on my face, but instead of soothing me, it felt as if my skin were being eaten away. My vision tunneled, then snapped back to normal and slowly began tunneling again. Everything began to fall apart, as if the entire planet had suddenly come loose from its path across the universe. The comfortable world I thought I knew was sliding away into darkness. I felt myself carried along with it, like a passenger on the deck of a sinking ship.

The next thing I knew, I was lying in the street.

The old woman was staring down at me. Pale, inquisitive faces clustered behind her.

Beyond them, raindrops fell from the twilight sky.

"Is he dead?" the woman asked.

"No," I replied. "He is not."

TWO

T HE NEXT MORNING, having decided to spend the weekend
  at my father's place in the country, I strolled along the
platform at Paddington Station towards a west-bound train.
The place echoed with the sound of voices and machines.
People weaved among spider-webbed shadows cast down from
the glass roof high above. My eyes fastened onto moments
plucked out of the chaos:

An old man in a worn green mackintosh, having set down
two suitcases, takes off his cap, retrieves a handkerchief, and
wipes the sweat from his forehead.

A newspaper vendor announcing that the government of
South Korea is evacuating the city of Seoul, and mispronounc-
ing the word as *See-owl*.

A young man with short red hair and a scar on his cheek
hugs a woman maybe fifteen years older than himself. She
kisses him on the mouth. Two old ladies are standing nearby,

both wearing hats with silk flowers on the brims. One of the old ladies looks away but the other stares at the couple kissing.

A man my age is sitting at a table in the tea shop. He is reading a book and stirring his tea at the same time.

These pictures and sounds all vanished in a blur as I hopped aboard the 9:05 express train bound for Swindon. There, I would change to a smaller train that would take me as far as Stroud, in Gloucestershire. From Stroud, I would find a taxi to Painswick, where my father lived and where I was born. Or perhaps I would walk, as I did when I came home from the war. I would never forget the sound of my hobnailed boots on the road that morning as the sun rose, nor the sweet and heavy scent of elder flowers growing in the mist-clogged hedges, and the pink foxgloves which speckled my trench coat with dew as I brushed by.

I was always glad to get out of the city on the morning train, and treated myself to breakfast in the dining car. I carefully sipped my tea and spread marmalade on racks of toast while the countryside of Berkshire rattled past. I looked out at the luminous yellow fields of rapeseed and saw the barges inching their way like giant river rats along the soupy green water of the canals.

At the Stroud station, I paused to roll a cigarette beside a wall which, during the war, had been decorated with a recruiting poster that read, "Have You Done Your Bit?" in bold red letters. The picture was of an officer, of course, who appeared to be returning on leave, or perhaps at the end of his service. He wore a soft-peaked cap and a heavy overcoat, and had a pipe jutting from his mouth. At his feet lay a half-open pack, bulging with various war souvenirs—a German helmet, a Luger, and a pair of binoculars. But it was his smile that I remembered most clearly. It was a peaceful, sleepy grin, like that of a cat on a windowsill on a sunny afternoon. It was the smile of not being in danger anymore. The smile of going home. That poster went up in the first year of the war and remained up until it was so faded and torn that the soldier had almost disappeared. But each time I passed by, I remembered his smile and hoped that it would be on my face someday soon.

It was late in the afternoon before I reached Stroud, so I opted for a taxi to take me on to Painswick. My father's place stood smack in the middle of the village, opposite a greengrocer's shop, which put on a seasonal firework display of bright green leeks, baskets of cherries, tomatoes, or the shimmering feathers of pheasants, gunned in the woods up near the village of Slad.

My father had lived here all his life. Before retiring, he had taught for twenty-five years at the local school. During that time he had been a heavy smoker but the day he quit teaching, he threw away his cigarettes and never touched the stuff again. All that remained of those years of tobacco and chalk dust was a clock on the mantelpiece, given as a token of thanks by the school board, and a yellow stain on the ceiling above his reading chair, from all the years of rising fumes.

Until I went away to school at the age of seven, this village was my home. After that, even though I returned for every holiday and could have found my way around the place blindfolded, it never felt like home again.

I fished the key out of the flowerpot beside the front door and let myself in. The back door was open, and I could see right through the darkness of the house to the garden, where my father sat on a three-legged wooden stool. His eyes were closed, chin lifted towards the afternoon sun, which made his face look as if it had been hammered from a sheet of burnished copper.

"Hello, Dad!" I shouted as I walked across the brick-red floor, trying not to chip the tiles with the iron-shod heels of my boots.

He turned his head sleepily towards the sound of my voice. "Is that you, William?"

My father seemed to be getting thinner these days, both his body and his hair. Elaborate attempts to comb it into seeming as if he had plenty left only made his scalp more obvious. He wore heavy clothes, no matter what the weather: flannel shirts and tweed waistcoats with horn buttons and a stiff oilcloth jacket when he went striding up and down the lanes.

I saw myself in the color of his eyes, in the shape of his lips, and in the way he stood when he was thinking, hands in pockets, staring at the ground, heels touching, one foot pointing forward and the other almost to the side.

"Is it the holidays already?" he asked.

"Not yet," I said, dumping my pack and stepping out into the garden. Sunlight glared off the yellow Cotswold stone. I sat on the edge of the garden wall and stretched and yawned. "I'm just down for the weekend. Taking a break from the city."

"You wouldn't catch me going up to London. Dirty, smelly place." My father had a loathing of the city. To him, it existed as a kind of twilight realm, dislodged from the rhythms of the natural world; a place where people went who had died but did not yet know they were dead.

"I fainted the other day," I said, changing the subject.

"Did you?" His hands rested on his legs, fingers dangling down over his knees.

"I don't know what happened." I shook my head.

"Cup of tea?" he asked.

"Yes, all right."

He stood and slapped the dust of gardening off his large

hands. "I've been sorting out the beans," he said, nodding at the trellis he had made on which the plants were climbing. "They've got to have everything just right or they won't grow, and every year they want it a different way and I've got to figure out what that is."

"Yes," I said vaguely.

As he headed into the kitchen, my father rested a hand on my shoulder. "Welcome back." Then came the noisy splash of him filling the kettle. I watched him scooping the tea from the tea tin, using a broad spoon made of brass. He leveled off the spoonful with a slow sweep of his index finger. Then he lit the gas on the stove and rested the kettle on the whispering ring of blue flame. Taking two mugs off the shelf, he turned them right side up and brought them to rest upon the bare wood kitchen table, which had not seen a tablecloth since the day my mother died.

We never talked about my mother.

My father woke up one morning thirty years ago and she was lying dead beside him, having suffered a stroke in the night. She was buried in the Painswick churchyard, with its finely sculpted trees which reminded me of poodles with silly haircuts.

My mother left behind the ghosts of her habits: the precise way blankets were folded, canned goods stored alphabetically, clothes hung out to dry, and different china patterns used for different days of the week. Slowly, my father had exorcised these ghosts, replacing her habits with the simpler efficiency of his own.

These days, my father and I got along well enough, but we got along as strangers do. When he sent me away to the Dragon and Eton, it had the effect of alienating him from his colleagues at the local school. My father understood that this was likely to happen, and when it did, he bore it well, believing his sacrifice to be worthwhile. What he had not understood, since he had not gone to these places, was that by sending me away to live among people so different than himself he acquired a son even more estranged from him than he was from his resentful colleagues.

The water in the kettle sighed as it drew near to boiling.

My father stood in the doorway to the garden, hands in the pockets of his heavy corduroy trousers, whose lines and rich brown color were like the furrows of a freshly ploughed field. He rolled his neck, cracking the joints of his spine beneath the weathered skin. "You ought to stay longer," he told me. "For good, I mean. There's jobs for you here, and I don't just mean in teaching."

Although my father made a valiant attempt to hide the fact, he was clearly disappointed that I had become a teacher. Somehow, my having chosen the same profession as his own seemed to undermine all the sacrifices he had made on my behalf. He refused to believe that I actually liked teaching, since he had grown to loathe his work years before he'd actually retired. But he'd stuck with the job, because he could do it and didn't have to think about it much.

It was not like that for me. I enjoyed the pace of life at school, and the way my duties bounced from the classroom to the sports field to St. Vernon's Officer Cadet Corps. The "Corps" amounted to fifty spotty-faced boys who, if they had been born ten years earlier, would have been made into second lieutenants, posted off to various regiments, sent to the front, and, with few exceptions, would have ended up as names on war memorials.

As an officer in the Corps, most of my duties involved having lunch with visiting officers who were scouting out

talent for their own regiments. They would be given excep-
tionally strong gin and tonics, followed by roast beef—it was
always roast beef—and very good wine in the headmaster's
private dining room. Then, after port and the best Cuban
cigars, they would inspect a march-past of the cadets, say a few
rousing words, and fall asleep in chauffeur-driven cars on the
way back to their barracks.

Once a term, the cadets would be trucked out to Salisbury
Plain, where we would conduct map-reading exercises and
stage various mock attacks on Imber village, whose inhabitants
had been forcibly evicted by the army years before. Its buildings had been torn down and rebuilt in concrete, in order to
be fought over by generations of soldiers in training. Of the
original town, only the church remained, its cemetery overgrown and its stained-glass windows dusted green with pollen
in the springtime.

While the cadets were busy shooting one another with
blank ammunition, I would sit in my rickety canvas-and-wood
campaign chair outside a leaky tent. There, along with the
other two officers on staff, I would make sure everything was
going more or less according to plan. The other officers, both
veterans of the war, were also teachers. Higgins taught math.
He had a permanently reddened face and squinting eyes from
his days with the Long Range Desert Group in Libya.
Houseman, head of the English department, had spent several
years chasing U-boats around the Mediterranean. There were
times, particularly at night, when the rolling, treeless hills of
Salisbury Plain would remind him of the ocean. We would sit
and smoke, while Higgins would call out the eerie war cry of the
Touareg tribesmen he had met in the Sand Sea of Calanscio.

We were all slightly mad. We might have been mad before
the war, but we were definitely that way now.

The only difference between us was the way we dealt with this madness. Unlike me, Higgins and Houseman made no attempt to put the past behind them. They lived like men home on leave, with no thought of preparing for the future because, in their minds, there really was no future.

If word had come through that the war had resumed and that they were being recalled to the front, they would have been ready to go in half an hour.

Until then, they carried on as they had done before, suspicious of anything civilian and still speaking in the jargon of the war, with its words plucked from Urdu, Swahili, and now-outdated military terminology. For example, any foray beyond the gates of the school was referred to as a "decko" or a "shufti." For Higgins and Houseman, these shuftis were usually to buy "zbib," their name for alcohol, or tea, called "char," or cigarettes, known to them as "buttys." Occasionally, after class on a Friday afternoon, Houseman would make a decko out to see a woman, never referred to as anything other than a "bint." Hard as he tried to keep these bint shuftis secret, the nervousness always showed on his "clock," or face, and his usual nonchalant demeanor, standard for any British officer, was replaced by an expression Higgins called "windy." In general, however, Higgins and Houseman spent their time contentedly within the grounds of the school, where, after Friday afternoon parade, they changed back from their uniforms into the "mufti" of regular clothes. Then they reconvened in the orderly room to drink a grueling mixture of brandy and champagne called a French 75, after the French artillery pieces which nearly finished off the Germans at Verdun, and which definitely finished off Higgins and Houseman until the start of classes on Monday morning.

I envied them sometimes. For them, the past was not a

thing to be overcome but instead to be endlessly reinhabited.
The past was a known quantity. For Higgins and Houseman,
it was the safest place to be.

For me, however, the past was like a maze from which I
had yet to escape.

Whatever our approach to the madness this had caused in
us, St. Vernon's provided a niche in the world where it was all
right to be crazy. In fact, it was even expected of us by the students. There was nothing more boring to them than a quiet,
conservative teacher, mild-manneredly trotting out his lessons
day after day. The teachers they would remember were the
ones who ranted and waved their arms about and drew unintelligible scrawls on the blackboard to illustrate their equally
unintelligible trains of thought. But these men loved the sub-
jects they taught, with the madness of those who cannot understand why everyone else is not enchanted with algebra or the
anatomy of locusts or the last hemlock-drugged words of
Socrates. We knew those were the ones they would remember,
because we remembered them ourselves.

My father, I suspected, was one of those quiet men.

"But I like being a teacher," I said.

"Of course." He shrugged off my words. "But a man with
a medal can do as he pleases."

At the mention of this topic, which he always brought up
with a lightness in his voice as if it had never occurred to him
before, I sighed and fumbled in my pocket for my tobacco tin.
My thumb passed over the rubbed-down letters—EMERGENCY
RATION—as I took out the box to roll myself a smoke. That
medal was one of his favorite topics of discussion. Having
brought me up on a steady diet of lectures stressing all I could
do for my country, he now regaled me with stories of what
my country should now be doing for me. Tucked away in his

garden with his temperamental runner beans, this all made sense to him.

The medal was the Military Cross, which I was awarded in 1945 after an assault on a German stronghold during that same mountaineering disaster which had marked the end of my climbing career. I gave my father the medal to look after and he kept it on the mantelpiece, displayed in its velvet-lined box. The cross itself was shiny silver and flared out at the ends. Crowns were emblazoned at each end and the cypher of King George, GV, was in the center and 9.9.44 engraved on the back. The ribbon for the cross was white with a purple stripe running down the middle.

A combination of bad eyesight, flat feet, and weak spine had kept my father out of serving in the Great War. Of his many friends in the village, most of whom had either volunteered or been conscripted, many had not returned. Half of them, I had heard, had died in a single attack on Polygon Wood in the third battle of Ypres. They had been reduced, in less time than anyone would have thought possible, to a handful of anecdotes and moss-filled names on the war memorial. It seemed to me that my father had fixed upon this medal as a justification not only of my participation in the Second World War but also for his lack of participation in the first one.

My unwillingness to discuss with him the circumstances under which I was awarded the medal only increased the gulf between us.

"Summer's almost here." I changed the subject, leaning forward to grasp the mug of tea that he held out to me as he emerged from the kitchen. After the death of my mother, he had dispensed with the niceties of china. Now he drank out of brown enameled mugs and ate off blue-and-white-speckled enameled plates.

He sank down with a sigh onto his chair and nodded at the rosebuds, each one clasped in its green skin as if by hands drawn together in prayer. "I love the roses," he said.

My father had been growing roses for as long as I could recall, and he had always tended them with a gentleness reserved for them alone.

Sometimes, when I came home on holiday, I would wait until my father had gone to sleep and I would go out and pee all over those precious roses, because he seemed to love those flowers more than he loved me.

"This is the time of year I used to dread when I was teaching," he said.

"Dread?" I wrapped my hands around my mug of tea and felt the heat radiate through my palms. "But why? It's gorgeous here."

"I know. That's the trouble. Once the warm weather arrives, the young women start dressing in their"—he flapped his hand, scattering biscuit crumbs—"their pretty clothes. And then the young men stop paying attention to anything except the young women. And how can you keep their attention when all the smells of summer are blowing in through the open windows? How can I even keep my own attention going?" He punctuated all this with slurps of tea and nibbles at his biscuit. "Taking a walk before dinner?" he asked.

"Yes." I set down my tea mug on the garden wall and stood.

"I thought you might."

I decided to walk up the hill and watch the sun go down. Hundreds of times I had trudged this path, which wound its way along the edge of town, past a golf course and up to a round-topped mound of earth where, before the days of telephones and telegraphs, signals could be sent by flashing lights between here and the eastern mountains of Wales, which were called the Brecon Beacons.

My father used to make this walk almost every day, in the company of a bull mastiff he'd named Trouble. He had bought the dog a few years after the death of my mother, and quickly became a doting servant to the beast. Even if he didn't feel like walking, he had to take the dog out and run it around or it would have torn the house to pieces. The sight of my father being pulled up the road by the huge animal, with its apricot-colored fur and fierce black face, and the sound of my father trying to control his pet with shouts of "Trouble! Trouble!" provided the town with one of its more enduring comedies.

When, after ten years of tyrannical rule, Trouble made his last trip to the vet's, my father stopped his daily walks. Now he rarely strayed beyond the street on which he lived.

By the time I had reached the top of the hill, I was soaked with sweat that pasted my shirt to my back. I stood beside the waist-high concrete block that marked the summit and looked out over the valleys beyond. It was dusk. The evening air was heavy with the smell of approaching rain. Mist was rising from the hollows, and the Severn River glinted in the distance. The time-blunted mountains of Wales stood ranked against the horizon, each one a different shade of smoky blue or violet.

Before I went away to school, my father used to bring me up here on Sunday evenings, with no regard for the weather. Sometimes we'd arrive at the top and see nothing but rain and fog. But other times, those distant hills would blaze under the banners of sunset. At that time, I gave no thought to climbing them. From where I stood, such a thing appeared impossible. Their vastness frightened me and yet it drew me to them. Later, I would learn that the mountains of southern Wales were barely ripples in the ground compared to the stone giants of the Alps. But back then, the way they reached into the sky seemed beyond all measuring. It was not until twelve years later, in my second year of university, that I first climbed one of those Welsh hills.

Inspired by Carton's lecture, both Stanley and I had signed up for a mountaineering trip to the Brecon Beacons sponsored by my Oxford college outing club.

For three days, we tramped above the tree line, through bogs where sheep skulls bleached among the reeds and over crags of lichen-painted rock. We slept wrapped in horse blankets with our boots for pillows while the night wind strummed the guy lines of our canvas tent. I didn't realize how the experience had changed me until I got back to Oxford. In the week that followed, I was restless. Oxford seemed more crowded than ever and I, who had never been out of step with the frenzied pace of academic life, suddenly felt as if I had become a stranger there. Agitation hovered over me like the beating of huge wings. It caught me by surprise to realize it was my time in the mountains which had done this to me. The clarity of thought which came from climbing, from being in a world not clogged by the gridwork of roads and playing fields and days, whose hours were not marked by the tolling clock of Tom Tower, was something I no longer wished to live without.

For Stanley, the dangerous straightforwardness of what it meant to walk where no path showed the way gave him a sense of purpose he had never experienced before. Without the hindrance of rules designed to make him into the kind of team player he would never be, he obeyed instead the life-or-death laws of the mountains.

For Stanley, as it was for me, the world had finally begun to make sense.

From then on, we went on as many mountaineering trips

as we could: to the Derbyshire Peak District, to the Highlands of Scotland and the Lake District. It was not long before we were determined to explore the higher elevations of the world. In those days, for a mountaineer of limited means, all roads pointed to the Alps. In the summer of 1936, as soon as the semester ended, we grouped together with four other students: Armstrong, Whistler, Forbes, and Sugden, each of whom had done some previous climbing on their own. All of us headed for Chamonix. Nobody had much in the way of savings. We traveled as cheaply as we could, sleeping on our rucksacks in the baggage car as the train made its slow and jolting way down through France.

At Chamonix, we camped in the shadow of Mont Blanc, mesmerized by the Mer de Glace glacier and the red granite spires of the Chamonix Aiguilles. With my five companions, I climbed the Aiguille du Plan, the Aiguille du Gouter, and Mont Maudit. By the time we returned to England in late August, we had all been changed forever. From then on, when we were not climbing, we were thinking about climbing.

During the school year, I was a student of history, Latin, and French. But every day I spent beyond the classroom I taught myself the languages of rock and cloud and ice.

We did everything we could to earn enough money to take part in expeditions.

Armstrong tutored Latin at a boys' school. He had the face of a bloodhound: a jowly frown and patient, friendly eyes. His movements were slow and methodical, as if he had all the time in the world to spend with fidgety students almost half his age. His pupils must have known from the moment they caught sight of Armstrong, outfitted as he always was in heavy tweeds and corduroy, that they could never break him down the way they might have done with other teachers.

Whistler worked in the Ashmolean Library. His sole task was to locate books which had been placed in the wrong locations, retrieving volumes which had been lost sometimes for more than a century. Whistler was perfectly suited for this work, due to his almost unbearable fastidiousness. When we were climbing and the contents of our rucksacks generally became tangled masses of dirty clothes, biscuit crumbs, and carabiners, only Whistler's remained as it had when we had started out: each piece of equipment in its place, each type of clothing stored in its own specially labeled canvas bag. For Whistler, spending his afternoons among lost books was an almost holy task. He would emerge into the squid-ink black of an Oxford winter night and join us at the Bull's Cellar for a drink, dust in his spiky red hair and his freckled face wearing an expression of triumph normally reserved for the carved stone faces of kings in Westminster Cathedral.

Sugden, meanwhile, fixed punts for a Cherwell River boathouse. It was a job which, by his own reckoning, any fool could do. This was not true, of course, and we all knew it, but it was typical of Sugden to make light of his achievements, if only to hear us contradict him, which we were of course obliged to do. Repairing the punts required the exact planing of curved hull strips, the removal and refitting of nails without causing damage to the wood, as well as waxing and polishing. All of these tasks Sugden attacked with such ferocity that he was left to himself by the boathouse owners, who trusted his work and feared his temper in almost equal measure.

Forbes resorted to mending nets at the cricket practice fields, where he gained a reputation for climbing the large nets like a spider, a sailor's twining needle in one hand and a jackknife clamped between his teeth. Of all my climbing friends, I knew Forbes the least. But none of us knew him, really. He was a tall man, broad-shouldered and always faintly smiling, as if the laughter of some recently shared joke was just fading from his lips. But even this smile seemed like a kind of camouflage to keep the world at bay. His hair, once a mop of curly blond, was thinning prematurely and so he usually wore a hat with a long brim, which only added to his anonymity. Without ever being unfriendly, he seemed to need us less than the rest of us needed one another. Even Sugden and Stanley, locked in a rivalry which was driven more by instinct than by anything they could explain, had formed a bond of mutual animosity. Forbes had no bonds, at least none we could name. In this way, he was perhaps better suited for climbing than we were. There is a kind of loneliness up in the mountains which can be cherished only in small doses by those who do not wish to be driven mad by it. Forbes carried that loneliness in him long before he ever set eyes on the jagged spires of the Alps. What drew him to the mountains was some strange familiarity, something he seemed to know about them which would always be a mystery to us.

Stanley, for his part, didn't have to work, but was obliged to beg his father for an increase in his monthly stipend.

And me, I sold a pint of blood a month for six months in order to buy a new tent. I became like one of those people who live only to hunt, and for whom the year is divided not into weeks and months but into the seasons for hunting various animals. For me, as for the others, there was a time for climbing mountains, a time to earn money for getting to the mountains, a time for refurbishing my gear, a time for testing ropes, a time for getting in shape, and a time for reading about mountaineering. Everything else seemed somehow irrelevant.

Only those who do not climb mountains ask why people climb them. For those who climb, the answer is both obvious

THE ICE SOLDIER | 55

and almost impossible to explain. Perhaps the simplest answer is that life is infinitely simplified when you are climbing. The everyday concerns of livelihood, of social standing, of overdue bills and futureless romances all fall away before the vast and overwhelming absolute of the mountain. Aside from an ice ax, a few carabiner loops, and a length of rope, there is nothing to rely on but yourself and those with whom you climb. On the precipice not only of the world but of your own existence, you look back with a mixture of pity and contempt at those who fuss away their time on the wheel of the working day.

"But it doesn't accomplish anything," my father would say. "Not for the common good, I mean. What you stand to lose is completely out of proportion to what you have to gain." And he was right. I didn't know how long I could just keep mountaineering and have everything else exist as a means to do more mountaineering. But my knowing he was right didn't change how I felt about it. Obsession, since this was what it had become, did not require the cumbersome baggage of reason.

For the first two summers, the six of us made our way back to Chamonix. We climbed the Grandes Jorasses, Mont Blanc, the Petit Dru, and the Grands Charmoz.

We formed what seemed to me a perfect team, each with his own talent which benefited the group as a whole.

Whistler could fix anything, especially the fiddly stoves and camera equipment we brought with us.

Forbes was our cook, piously minding the soup kettle and the rationing of food.

Armstrong spoke the languages of the Alps, not only French and German but Italian as well. And when these failed, he spoke in Latin. Without him, on our first trip down, we would probably have misunderstood the directions offered to us by a variety of train conductors, and would have ended up on the other side of Europe.

Sugden was our most aggressive climber. The few times we were forced by weather or an impassable route to turn back, he took it as a personal insult. There was no doubt in my mind that if it had not been for the moderating effect of the rest of the group, Sugden would have killed himself simply in refusing to accept defeat. He was absolutely without fear, and so intolerant of fear in others that there were times when, if it had not been for Stanley, we might have pressed ahead with climbs which we should more sensibly have abandoned.

The only one of us who regularly stood up to Sugden was Stanley. Whereas the rest of us did our best to avoid argument, Stanley seemed to revel in it. What annoyed Sugden most about these confrontations on the mountainsides was that Stanley was quite simply a better mountain climber than anyone else in the group. With his natural agility, it was taken for granted that Stanley would be in the lead when we came up against stretches of any serious technical difficulty. So when the route ahead began to look unclimbable and Stanley started making noises about turning back, the rest of us knew that this time the mountain had beaten us.

Sugden, who hated giving in to anything, hated even more that Stanley's judgment in these matters carried more weight than his own.

Once we climbed above the tree line, it was always left to me to make the final choice. This role had evolved without any debate or argument. The very lack of argument was perhaps the thing that decided it. Neither Whistler, Forbes, nor Armstrong had any wish to lead. They shared among themselves a certain quietness of character which did not jibe with taking charge.

Stanley didn't care for leading either, except when it came to the actual climbing. He disliked giving orders almost as much as he disliked taking them from anyone else.

Sugden would gladly have led us, but most probably to unmarked graves on some unclimbable peak, simply because the concept of turning back was so repugnant to him. So he could not lead, because the rest of us would not have followed him. Sugden knew he was wrong for the job, although his pride would never have allowed him to admit it. Nevertheless, he seemed constantly on the alert for any opportunity to exert control over the rest of us.

So it fell to me to make decisions when decisions had to be made. Up on the mountainside, someone had to choose what route we took, when we stopped to rest, where we camped, and, ultimately, when neither Sugden and Stanley could agree, if reaching the summit was worth the risk involved.

Among the three who could have taken charge, it was no great boast to say I was the only choice. Despite the fact that this role came to me more or less by default, much as the teaching did later on, I found to my surprise that I was suited for it. It was one of the more helpful realizations of my life to learn that, just because something had come along unexpectedly, that did not mean it was any less important than the plans I'd worked out in advance. In preparing for our mountaineering trips, I discovered that I had a seemingly inexhaustible energy for sorting out the little details which drove people like Stanley to distraction. And, unlike Forbes and the other non-leaders of our group, I did not mind the burden of decision making. Finally, when difficult choices had to be made, I found I could think clearly and calmly, while Sugden spat and swore and raged at the mountains which beat us, as if they had done it on purpose.

As we descended from the glacier fields, I would cajole Sugden and Stanley to set their differences aside, since even on successful climbs they managed to find things to argue about. Knowing them both as well as I did, and resorting to silly games I invented, such as asking each person to name three things he could not live without, I was usually successful. By the time we returned to civilization, Stanley and Sugden would be as close to friends again as they had been before we'd left.

I played my part with such sincerity that the others took to calling me "Auntie," a title I pretended to despise. And if I was sometimes not entirely successful in my diplomacy, fatigue usually stepped in to finish the task.

Coated with the white dust of dried sweat and the gray dust of the scree slopes, we pitched our tents at campsites like the Boule d'Or, where we were regulars and where Madame Thibodeaux would hold a place for us each year. We were also known at the nearby Piton café, where we drank ice-cold "demis" of Stella Artois and lingered over bowls of white-bean cassoulet. At the end of our third summer, the owner of the Piton, Monsieur Rancourt, took our picture in front of the café, framed it, and hung it above the bar, along with the pictures of other climbing teams who had made Chamonix a second home.

As time went by, we spent less time in Chamonix, and grew tired of the incessant booming of mini-cannons, which the hotels would fire off when their guests had summitted Mont Blanc. These guests, when they reached the top, would signal with bright scarves or flashing mirrors to people waiting on the hotel balconies, bottles of Bouvier at the ready. The town had become a magnet for the kind of tourist known to local Chamoinards as "Pioux-Pioux": people attracted to the trendiness of mountaineering rather than the climbing itself. One could see them gathered outside the Hotel Tremblay, late in the summer mornings, by which time any serious climbers would long since have set out. The Pioux-Pioux wore the latest mountaineering fashions and were content to let their guides lug their gear. Even with the loads they had to carry, which sometimes included birds in cages and dogs in miniature copies of the tweedy hiking clothes worn by their owners, these guides were to be pitied more for the humiliation they endured than for the physical exertion of their jobs. Most of the Pioux-Pioux halted at the first patch of ice, drained the contents of their whiskey flasks, and retreated to town.

In the summers that followed, we did our best to follow in the footsteps of mountaineers like Mummery, Stephen, Whymper, and Tyndall, whose well-thumbed memoirs we carried with us everywhere. This brought us to places like Grindelwald, Murren, Kleine Scheidegg, and Zermatt, where we camped above the town in a small forest called the Erikawald. There, in August, dozens of camps would spring up and the woods would echo with the sounds of every language in Europe. We were students, most of us, and in a shingle-roofed shrine to the Virgin Mary, erected at a crossroads in the wood, abandoned textbooks from the universities of Freiburg, Oslo, Warsaw, Paris, and Verona lay stacked. They were used either for reading material on rainy days or for starting fires, depending on the quality of the book.

It was here that we heard stories of more distant mountain ranges. The Rockies, Patagonia, the Himalayas. Our nights were filled with plans for future expeditions.

Back at Oxford, with finances a continuing problem, I made a wise switch from selling blood to writing about our expeditions in the *View*, the *Climber's Gazette*, and other Alpine journals. The publications didn't pay much, but with the articles we began to establish ourselves as a mountaineering team worthy of following in the footsteps of earlier climbers, as well as their guides; men like Emil Boss, Melchior Anderegg, and Jean-Baptiste Aymond, whose names were almost too sacred to be spoken aloud.

We became known as the Lucky Six, after the old dice roller's expression. This was because of the way we seemed, to others, to be gambling with our lives. But it was also because of the way that our luck was holding out, since we had never suffered any mishap. This luck we did not take for granted. In the summer of 1938, climbers were dying at a rate of two a week on the slopes around Chamonix.

Our good fortune came to an end when war broke out in September of 1939. By January of the following year, I and the rest of the Lucky Six had been called up.

We went our separate ways.

Whistler and Sugden went into the navy, Forbes joined the merchant marine, and Armstrong became a sniper in the army. Stanley, engaged in his "vital war service," went into his father's Bully Beef factory. Having authored several articles on mountaineering, I was appointed as a climbing instructor for the Royal Marines at the Achnacarry barracks in Scotland. Achnacarry was used mostly for the training of commandos, and later for American Rangers. There, I lived a spartan but relatively safe existence until August of 1944, when I was asked by the commanding officer at Achnacarry to assemble a handful of men skilled in mountaineering for an unspecified task in Europe.

The commanding officer's name was Sholto Lindsay. He had cavernously dark eyes, spiky gray hair, and usually wore a kilt, both on and off duty. Lindsay owned the land on which the

Achnacarry base had been built. In exchange for the use of the land, the army had put him in charge of running the base, a task he performed with humorless efficiency.

On the day he asked me to assemble the team, Lindsay and I were out on the training ground beside a twenty-foot-tall wooden fence, off which soldiers were jumping into a pit of mud. The point of this exercise was that they should emerge from their fall with their rifles ready to shoot. We lost at least one man a week during training on this fence, from broken legs, dislocated hips, and damaged spines. Several had refused to jump at all. When this happened, their lockers were cleaned out and their mattresses rolled up and tied to the squeaky black frames of their beds. They were sent away and their names were not mentioned again. They were not pitied or envied. They simply vanished, as if they had never existed.

We stood beside the mud pit, and as each soldier landed, a wall of cold slime sprayed across our uniforms.

"You can take a week to sort out a list," said Lindsay. Oblivious to the dirt that spackled his face and clothes, he puffed on a small-bowled pipe, speaking to me with the pipe stem gripped between his teeth.

"I don't need a week, sir," I replied. "I can give can you the names right now."

He cocked an eyebrow at me. The pipe jerked upwards as he clenched his teeth. "Can you indeed?" he replied.

I gave him the names of the Lucky Six.

"Right, then," said Lindsay. "You'd better start tracking them down."

The only one who refused the offer was Stanley. "I can't," he said when I called him on the telephone. "I'm sorry. I just can't. I refuse to get involved in this madness."

"What madness?" I asked. "This mission?"

"No, William. The war. That madness."

Stanley's refusal to join us came as no shock to me, although I knew there was more to it than he was telling me just then. I could not bring myself to be angry at him, but that did not stop the others when they heard about it, especially Sugden. For the rest of us, the chance to climb again and the importance that was being attached to this task, whatever it was, gave us all a sense of purpose which we had not felt since we were last together as a group.

For myself, I wondered if my father might at last find some meaning in the path I had chosen to follow.

It took two months, but by the end of that time the five of us were assembled at Achnacarry.

In the weeks ahead, we went on daily marches, for distances ranging between ten and twenty miles, carrying fully loaded Bergen rucksacks. These were very similar to the ones we had used on our own before the war. The only difference was that in addition to our regular gear, each pack was weighted down with two parcels. Each parcel contained four bricks wrapped in canvas. As part of the training, we were also given instruction in low-level parachute jumps. We started out by jumping off towers wearing parachute harnesses attached to ropes, but we quickly moved on to actual jumps from the side door of a Dakota transport plane flying only three hundred feet above the ground. For this, we wore the heavy rimless helmets of the Royal Parachute Regiment and Dennison jump smocks, with their green-and-brown camouflage pattern which seemed to have been applied by a monkey with a paintbrush. Once I got used to the idea of hurling myself into space, the jumps weren't actually that difficult, since the chutes were the static-line type and opened of their own accord as soon as we leaped from the plane.

There was such a thing as a reserve chute, normally attached to the chest. But our Polish parachute instructor, a man named Zimanski, informed us a little too cheerfully that we were jumping so near to the ground that these reserve chutes would not have time to deploy if the main chute failed. In other words, if our main chutes did not open, we would not only be dead but would literally break every bone in our bodies.

"Even those little ones in your ears," said the instructor, pinching the air between his thumb and index finger to show us how small the bones were.

Zimanski wore a black beret, as opposed to the red berets of the Royal Parachute Regiment. He had been part of what was known as the Free Polish Brigade, made up of those who had managed to escape from the German occupation of their country. Zimanski had been a member of a brigade under the command of General Sosabowski and had been involved with Operation Market Garden, the battle for the Arnhem bridge-head. The men of Sosabowski's brigade were pretty much slaughtered as they crossed the Rhine, and I'd heard that only a few made it back. Zimanski never talked about this, at least not in English. When he got drunk, however, which he did every night without exception on a homemade alcohol called *spiritus*, he would burst into our barracks when we were sleep-ing, turn on the lights, and yell at us in Polish. At times like this, it was impossible to imagine that he was even related to the quiet, broadly smiling man who taught us in the daytime. Invariably, Zimanski would be hauled out of our barracks by the military police. He never put up a fight. As soon as he saw the red caps of the MPs, he would sit down on the floor and wait to be dragged off. The next day, he would be back to his old self and seemed to have no memory of his tirades from the night before.

We were also put through a course in the use of various weapons, including the Sten submachine gun, the Webley revolver, and the Sykes-Fairbairn fighting knife. We also practiced throwing Mills bomb grenades and learned to hold our genitals when they went off only a few feet away on the other side of the practice trench, or risk being neutered from a vacuum created by the blast.

With little else to discuss, we speculated endlessly about what we would be asked to do and where we would be sent.

The training ended with a climbing exercise on a rock face overlooking Loch Amon. The tannic acid in the ground had stained the lake water almost black. A local legend held that in 1900, a boy had tried to swim across it on a dare. He had traveled halfway across when a huge creature rose up from below and dragged him down.

I was glad to turn my back on the loch as we began our climb. Despite the added weight we had been asked to carry, the ascent was easily accomplished and by the end of the day we had marched back into camp through the pouring rain. We were peeling off our wet and dirty clothes and listening to the showers groan and creak as warm water finally began to pour through them, when Sholto Lindsay came in, kilt swinging about his knobbly knees.

"Report to my office in fifteen minutes," he said, then turned on his heel and walked out again.

All thoughts of rest evaporated. We knew this was the moment when we would be told where we were going.

There was no time to shower. We piled into any dry clothes we could find and shambled into Lindsay's office, having dashed across the empty parade ground under the steadily falling rain.

In Lindsay's office, I was astonished to see, sitting comfortably at Lindsay's desk, none other than Henry Carton. He was not wearing a military uniform. Instead, he had on a Norfolk jacket made of impossibly thick wool and a turtleneck sweater which bunched around his throat. His cheeks were rosy and the bristles of his mustache looked as stiff as pencil leads. Carton was leaning back in Lindsay's chair as if he owned the place.

"Gentlemen," said Lindsay, closing the door, "you know who this is."

Of course we did.

"Due to Mr. Carton's expertise in the specific nature of your task," continued Lindsay, "he has very kindly volunteered to help us out."

Carton had been smiling at us, but now the smile flickered and died. "Where is my nephew?" he asked. "Where is Stanley?"

"He didn't sign up with us, I'm afraid," said Lindsay.

Carton stood suddenly, sending his chair scudding back against the wall. "Why didn't you tell me?" he spluttered.

Lindsay cleared his throat. His face turned red. "I wasn't at liberty to give out any specific names over the telephone."

"But when you mentioned the group, I assumed they'd all be here." Carton looked stunned. His eyes fanned across us. "I thought he'd finally come to his senses, instead of wasting away in that bloody sausage factory!"

"It's all right, sir," said Sugden quietly. "We feel the same way."

The rest of us glared at Sugden, because he had no right to speak for all of us.

Carton glanced around the room, as if he did not know

where Sugden's voice had come from. "It's bad enough that he dodged his military service, but now he's gone and let you down as well!"

This time, nobody replied.

In the quiet of the room, we heard the wheezing of his ruined lungs.

"Where's the phone?" demanded Carton.

"There's one in the orderly room," said Lindsay.

Carton stamped out of Lindsay's office and across the parade ground to the leaky, tar-paper-roofed hut which served as our orderly room.

For a while, we all just stood there in silence.

Then Lindsay spoke. "I wouldn't want to be that chap Stanley right about now."

We mumbled in agreement.

A minute later, Carton reappeared from the orderly room and walked back to Lindsay's office. His face was red, his hands clenched into fists. He swung into the room and slammed the door, then returned to his place behind the desk. He was out of breath from even that short walk. "It's no good!" he said. "The little beggar won't listen to reason."

Carton fumbled behind him for the chair and sat down heavily. He reached to the sides, spreading his arms like wings, and gripped the edges of the desk, as if it were the only thing anchoring him to the world. He blinked. There were tears of rage in his eyes.

Lindsay pulled down the blinds and flipped on the light. Rain tapped at the corrugated iron roof. The remains of a coal fire smoldered in the grate. Lindsay sat himself down by the fire in a chair whose stuffing was bursting out of a dozen broken seams. He propped his feet, which were encased in boots so mirror-polished that they looked as if they were made of glass, upon an empty ammunition box. Then he folded his arms and nodded at Carton to begin.

Carton tried to compose himself. He tilted his head first to one side and then to the other, cracking the bones in his neck. For a moment, Carton stared at the green paper of the blotter on Lindsay's desk and pursed his lips, as if he did not know how to begin. Then he breathed in sharply and raised his head, looking at each of us in turn. "You're going to Italy," he said. "How does that sound?"

"A damned sight better than the North Atlantic," replied Forbes. His old half smile was gone. Instead, after two years of serving on a convoy ship, he bore the permanent expression of someone who has just seen a bad traffic accident.

"I'm afraid it's not going to be any sort of sunny holiday," said Carton. "You're going into the Italian Alps. Actually, you're going to climb *my* mountain. That's why they've brought me in here, since I'm the only one who's ever done the climb who's still alive to talk about it."

We glanced at one another, smiling nervously. It was not a nervousness brought on by any lack of confidence. Looking back, I could not recall why we were so sure of ourselves. When you are trained to believe you are the best, and failure is never discussed, the idea of not succeeding becomes unthinkable.

There was a rustling behind us and we turned to see that Lindsay had pulled down a detailed map of the Alps on a rolling oilcloth screen. At first, I saw the map as just an over-whelming tangle of brown gradient lines, blue veins of rivers, and blank areas of white. The outer reaches of these white areas formed crooked fingers, marking the borders of the Lingua del Dragone glacier. Etched with blue contour lines like the swirls on a human finger, the map made the glaciers seem clean and unimposing. But I knew it was really a desert of dirty ice, trenched with thousands of crevasses, exposed to the wind, their surfaces melting by day and freezing by night. Out there in the middle of the white sea, like a tiny island, was Carton's piece of rock. The summit ran along a north-south ridge, which I knew would be mined with cornices. These were waves of snow blown into overhangs, like the crests of breaking waves. Sometimes it was hard to tell what was solid ground and what was a cornice. If you fell through one, you might find nothing below you for thousands of feet. I could see from the contour lines that it rose up sheer on the eastern and northern sides. Anyone climbing it would have to approach from the south. The nearest height mark showed 3,374 meters, which was the summit of the Blinnenhorn, more than a thousand meters lower than the Matterhorn, and over six hundred meters lower than the Eiger; but as with the Eiger, height was not the challenge here. Even from the map, the loneliness and desolation of the rock was clear to see.

Then Whistler voiced the question that was on all of our minds. "Why are we going there?" he asked.

"You're to set up a radio transmitter," said Lindsay. "It's what's known as a 'splasher.' Planes use it to home in on. We've been losing a lot of planes over the Alps recently. The Allies have got aircraft flying out of bases in the Po Valley to the south. They're heading north to hit targets like Ulm, Augsburg, and Colmar. This means they have to fly right over the mountains to reach their targets. On the outward missions, they're flying at altitude and in formation, but when they're on the way back, most of these planes are on their own and sometimes flying quite low. The navigators have been getting lost because they can't see the ground on account of the usual cloud cover and also because even when they can see the ground, the landscape changes with every snowfall. And there aren't any beacons for them to use, so they end up either going down too low in order to try to get a visual bearing, in which case they crash into the mountains, or they run out of fuel, in which case . . ."

"They also crash into the mountains," said Carton, finishing Lindsay's thought. "Each of you is to carry the components for assembling this beacon, which you should be able to manage in addition to your regular climbing gear. Once the beacon has been turned on, aircrews will be able to pick up its signal and, because of its precise frequency, will be able to tell where they are, even if they can't see the ground. Major Lindsay has told me that the whole thing can be bolted together in under an hour and that once you have installed the batteries, the machine will function for up to three months, by which time, with any luck, the war will be over."

"That is correct," said Lindsay. "The beacon itself will be contained within a steel case. All you've got to do is assemble the beacon, open the case, pull a metal strip off the top of the battery so that the machine can begin drawing from it, install the beacon in the case, and turn the bloody thing on. Those bricks you have been carrying correspond to the weight you'll each have to manage with the various components."

Carton explained the plan as best he could. He began by telling us that the mountain had been chosen because of its remoteness, and because there were no German troops in the area. We were to be parachuted in to an alpine meadow, beside a wood known as the Pineta di San Rafaele, above the village of Palladino. This was the only place they felt confident about our being able to parachute into safely. From there we would follow a dirt road until we reached the edge of the Lingua del

Dragone glacier. Carton produced a hand-drawn map to show the road and its surroundings.

"What's that?" I asked, pointing to a neatly drawn square at the point where the road petered out into a dotted line around the edge of the glacier.

"It's an old customs house," said Carton. "Around the turn of the century, a road was built from Palladino up towards the Albrun Pass. The Italians call this the Bocchetta d'Arbola. The plan was to link up with a road being built by the Swiss from the village of Binn on the other side. In the end, they didn't use the Palladino road because of avalanches. They diverted it to the town of Goglio, farther south."

"Here!" said Lindsay, jabbing at the map and evidently pleased with himself to have found the spot.

"The customs house above Palladino was built but never used, but the old road still exists and you'll be following it to the border at Albrun. All of these roads are unpaved. The whole setup is fairly primitive, and the crossing itself hasn't been used in years."

Carton went on to say that from the dropping point above Palladino, we had about a six-kilometer trek to the customs house, and from there another five kilometers across the glacier. "But that's as the crow flies," he added. "In reality, boys, the journey will be much more demanding. It's just the nature of travel over glaciers."

Once we had climbed the mountain and set up the beacon, we would return to the road and proceed into neutral Switzerland. At the border, which had been closed since the beginning of the war, we would be met by members of the British Special Operations Executive, the SOE, and transported back to England.

"There's no report of enemy activity in the area, so you shouldn't run into anyone," said Lindsay. "You should have the mountains to yourselves."

We smiled and shifted nervously.

"When do we leave?" asked Sugden.

"Day after tomorrow," answered Lindsay. "We are losing a couple of planes every week in those mountains, so there's no time to waste. Bromley has been appointed head of the team. You will answer to him as of now."

Sugden breathed in suddenly. "Is that really wise, sir?"

Oh, God, I thought. Sugden's up to his old tricks again. And Stanley isn't even here to shut him up.

But it seemed as if Carton had as little patience for Sugden as his nephew. "I beg your pardon?" he asked, eyebrows raised with indignation.

Sugden stepped forward. "What I mean, sir, is that Bromley hasn't had combat experience."

"With any luck," said Lindsay, "there isn't going to be any combat."

"But that's just it, sir," replied Sugden, turning to face Lindsay. "I'd rather rely on experience than luck."

"Who led you before?" demanded Carton.

It was Forbes who answered. "Auntie did, sir."

"Auntie?" boomed Carton. "Who the hell is Auntie?"

"I am, sir," I said quietly.

Carton's eyes narrowed. "Then it's Auntie who will lead you now."

Lindsay stood and cleared his throat again, to show that the meeting was over. "Gentlemen, you can have the next twenty-four hours off. After that, you'll be going nonstop until you reach Switzerland."

Following the briefing, Carton asked me to stay behind. When everyone else had left the room, he told me to shut the door. "Why do they call you Auntie?" he asked.

While I explained, he folded his arms and rocked back in his chair, a tight-lipped smile on his face.

When I had finished, he nodded approvingly and sat forward in his chair. "Well, Auntie, I've got a present for you." Then, from a faded canvas kit bag, he brought out a wooden stick with a gray lump on the end of it about the size of a clenched fist. He set it down on the desk. "I was going to give this to Stanley, but I think you'd better have it instead."

"What is it, sir?"

"It's a trench club," he replied. "I carried it during the Great War. In the trenches, a rifle was not always the best weapon to have. It was too long and awkward in such a confined space, especially if you had another sixteen inches of Enfield bayonet on the end. A revolver was all right, except it might get jammed with mud on the way over." Carton picked up the club and slapped the lead ball into his palm. "We called this a priest, and what we did with it we called the blessing. Like this." He wrapped the leather cord around his wrist and grasped the club about halfway up. Then he stood back from me, holding the club down at his side. With a flick of his wrist, he brought the club up to connect with the imaginary man's jaw. With another flick, he brought the club around and swung it into the side of the man's head. The whole movement did look vaguely like the blessing of a priest. "We were reduced to fighting the way our ancestors fought, even back before the first of Caesar's barges scudded up the river Thames. Go on. Pick it up."

The club was surprisingly heavy until I realized that a hole had been drilled down the middle and a lead pipe fitted inside.

With the addition of the lead ball at the end, even just rocking the stick back and forth in my hand allowed me to feel the force it would carry if swung hard. "Thank you, sir," I told him, "but surely I won't need it." I had so many questions for him, about everything to do with mountaineering. I wanted to tell him that he was the one who had gotten me started in climbing, then to sit down and have a conversation that lasted for hours, but I never got the chance.

"I need to make something absolutely clear to you," he said. "Once you get there, you've got to push on no matter what. SOE says there are no hostiles in those mountains, but we don't know that for certain. You can't turn back, even if it doesn't look safe. Do you see? The beacon is what's important. More important than your friends. More important than you. God forbid you'll ever have to make that choice, but if you do, you'll know what decision to take."

I held up the priest. "I wondered why you gave me this."

"You're not a mountaineer anymore," he told me. "You're an ice soldier, and the rules are different now."

It had grown dark, and I made my way back to the barracks with the priest under my coat. I was determined to sleep for as long as I could before I left, but knew that any rest would be unlikely. The days of training and uncertainty about where we would be sent had left me with the kind of fatigue that could not be cured by a good night's sleep, or even two or three. During the past weeks, parts of my mind had begun to shut down, robbing me of things such as my sense of taste and my sense of humor and shortening the fuse of my temper. The result of this was a general feeling that the boundaries of my world were closing in around me. But within this claustrophobic bubble, other senses came to life in a way they'd never done before. My sense of hearing had improved. The colors of this dreary world of mud and treeless hills and dirty khaki wool seemed to vibrate in the corner of my vision. In the canvas webbing of my belt and water bottle, each crossed thread came sharply, almost painfully into focus. My oiled mountain boots seemed to glow under the film of mud and ditch water which permanently coated them, as if the leather were alive.

I spent that night staring at the curved sheet-metal ribs of the Quonset hut's roof, which made me feel like Jonah trapped inside the belly of the whale.

Early the next morning, rather than go mad sitting around Achnacarry, the five of us loaded our packs and hiked back through the hills to the edge of Loch Amon. It took most of the day to get there, but by late afternoon we had made camp by the lake. After cooking up cans of beans in our mess tins, we lay out on our rain sheets, watching the wintry sun go down beside the inky water of the loch.

In the moment that the sun dipped below the horizon, the air filled with a strange and pinkish light. It sifted through the atmosphere, until everything was tinted with the softness of its shimmering. I had seen light similar to this in Switzerland, where it was known as alpenglow. But this was no ordinary alpenglow. We stared around us in amazement, at the dull gray rocks which now were smoldering like molten glass, at our faces, in which the ghostly white of our skin had been replaced by the burnishing of a vanished sun. It was as if a supernatural spark had ignited the dust from which the universe had been born. Even the blackness of the lake began to pulse with this fiery shimmer. Suffused into this poppy red was a strange paleness, which seemed to be a second kind of light existing in the same dimension as the first. It was a diamond light. A white light. Crystalline and clean. All around us, this miracle sky blazed and glittered. Gradually it faded, as the embers of the fire simmered out. The flickering whiteness also died away.

And then it was night. Stars blinked out of the blue. Still too stunned to speak of what had happened, we lit a fire with gnarly scraps of wood scrounged from the mostly treeless hills. The dew settled heavily, like glassy beads upon our woolen clothes. Fog slithered out of the reeds beside the lake and we huddled for warmth, wrapped in our rain sheets, while the mist took human shape and wandered among us.

The morning after, we woke up in a world of grounded clouds and Sunday morning calm. The only sound came from the trickling of water from the streams which fed the lake.

Only then did we talk of the strange glow and its meaning.

Edward Whymper had undergone a similar experience on his way down from the summit of the Matterhorn in 1865. With the team members roped together for safety, one man slipped and would have dragged the others to their deaths if, as had happened to Carton, the rope had not snapped. Four of the men fell four thousand feet onto the Matterhorn glacier below, leaving Whymper and the two Swiss guides, a father-and-son team named Taugwalder, precariously balanced on the mountain. Immediately following the accident, three huge crosses appeared in the sky. Even though this could be scientifically explained as a solar fogbow, the men saw it as a sign of hope that they would survive.

For us, too, the fire of the alpenglow could mean only one thing. We had been lucky so far. Even with one of us missing, we felt sure that our luck would hold.

❋

Now, BEHIND THE MOUNTAINS of Wales, just where the sun had gone down, the sky was banded red and white—a distant, fragile echo of that same mysterious thing I'd witnessed years ago.

Suddenly, I wished I had not come up here on this walk. I should have stayed home with my father. Better yet, I should have never left the city. A terrible anxiety swarmed around me.

I wanted to leave but could not move. It was as if my legs had sunk into the ground.

That same light was burning through clouds, but now it had transformed into something nightmarish and cruel. The air began to smolder in my lungs. I could not breathe. My clothes were catching fire. My skin fell away in blazing shreds.

I opened my mouth to scream and flames poured out.

The world began to tilt, mountains slamming into mountains, cascading over like a vast lineup of granite dominoes. The gory streaks of sunset slid vertically into the sky.

❄

I WOKE UP WITH dew on my face.

My first thought was that someone had covered me with a ratty old blanket. Through hundreds of tiny pinprick holes in the cloth, I could see daylight. Then I realized it was night, and I was looking at the stars.

I sat up and peered around, gently massaging a bruise where my head had hit the ground.

A fox was standing by my feet. He stared at me for a moment, then vanished without a sound.

I made my way home in the dark, barely needing my sight as the way was so well known to me.

My father had already eaten, but the pot of lamb stew he had prepared was still warm on the stove.

We sat by the fire while I ate, washing down the stew with

a mug of murky greenish-brown cider bought from a farmer down the road.

My father had taken off his shoes and socks, rolled his trousers up to his knees, and propped his heels up on wooden stool to warm his toes by the fire. The rest of him was hidden behind a copy of the weekend paper. "Look," he said, folding the paper and handing it across. "Didn't you go to school with that chap?"

I found myself looking at a photo of Wally Sugden. He was standing with the other members of the Patagonia expedition, just as they were boarding a BOAC plane bound for South America. Their clothing was emblazoned with the names of their sponsors. Tucker's Jam. Benzo Motor Oil. Falconer Athletic Clothing. The team members were all giving the thumbs-up and doing their best to imitate Sugden's trademark smirk. "Yes," I said. "We were at school together."

"He's that car-dealer chap!" My father's face lit up. "Trust in the Man!" he announced in a deep voice. "Trust in the Machine!"

"That's him." I chewed my lip for a moment before continuing. "Actually, I'm going to a mountaineering club next week."

The paper rustled as he lowered it. "Are you starting all that up again?" He did not look happy.

I shook my head as I swallowed a piece of potato, noticing that my father's toes wiggled when he spoke.

"Then why on earth are you going?" he asked.

"It's a favor for Stanley. He's got his sights set on another girl, and she happens to be a member of the London Climbers' Club."

"That's the one run by his uncle, isn't it? He's the one who got you your medal."

"That's him, Dad. Yes."

My father rose to his feet and walked towards the kitchen, where the dregs of some overbrewed tea still lingered in his chipped Brown Betty pot. Before he left the room, he paused. "Have you given any thought to joining one of the clubs in the city?"

"I'm already in a club."

"Yes, but I mean . . ." He paused while he hunted for the right words. "Well, the Montague . . ."

"I like it at the Montague. Why should I change?"

He gestured at the Military Cross in its box on the mantelpiece. "After all you went through to get that thing, and the schools I paid for you to go to, I don't understand why you didn't take the opportunity to advance yourself, William." The way he spoke, his words sounded rehearsed, as if he had been waiting a long time for the right moment to say what he was saying now. "God knows I would have."

I had been shoveling the last of the food into my mouth, pretending not to listen. But now I let my spoon clatter into the empty bowl and glanced up at him. "Would you, Dad?"

"In a heartbeat!" he replied and headed off into the kitchen. When he came back, he settled once again into his chair, polishing an apple against his trouser leg. It was a local kind called a pippin, its grass-green skin streaked with orangey red. When he bit into the apple, the sharp crunching sound made me wince. It was as if he had taken a bite out of my head, teeth cracking through the bone of my skull.

"Are you all right?" he asked, chomping on his mouthful.

"I think so," I replied, momentarily pressing my hands to my face. "I think I must be tired."

"Well, you've had a long day." Then the sound came again; that tearing, cracking sound.

I flinched, teeth gritted.

"What's the matter?" he asked.

"Can you not eat that apple just now?"

"Why ever not? Is there something wrong with it?" He inspected the apple, as if to find half a worm dangling from the part he had bitten.

"Just . . . please." I had no idea why I'd suddenly become so sensitive to this noise, but I knew for certain that I could no longer tolerate it.

"You need to get some rest, William." My father leaned forward and tossed the apple into the fireplace.

We both watched sparks fly up from the place where it landed among the glowing coals. And then there was no sound except the hiss of its juices turning to steam.

✻

THAT NIGHT, LYING IN BED, I thought back to the old recruiting poster at the Stroud station—the confident and blissful smile on the face of that officer heading home from the war after he had Done His Bit. In a silly way that man, that drawing of a man, had become my hero during the war. I wanted to wear that same contented smile and to be sure, as he was sure, that all he had endured would trouble him no longer when he at last reached home again.

The difference was that the drawing of the man never did reach home. He lived in that exquisite in-between place, when the hope of returning to all that was familiar and secure was close enough to grasp but had not yet been grasped. What that man never had to learn was that the image of home which he had clung to when he was away could not be found. The smells and sounds were the same. The colors of the flowers in the hedgerows which he passed by, having walked because there were no taxis, were all as he remembered them. Everything was there, except the most important part. This was the part that had convinced him to go on living when it seemed as if everything around him was dead. That part was missing.

I wish I could have seen a picture of that man after he reached home and was lying back in his bed, so unused to its softness that he would end up sleeping on the floor, wrapped in his greatcoat, as I did. I wish I could have seen the look on that man's face as he lay there, having realized that the reason the all-important part of home could not be found was that it had never existed at all. Instead, he found a place where people forced him back into a past he was trying to forget. They reminded him of squandered opportunities, not understanding that the one great opportunity, to be alive, was something he could no longer take for granted as they did.

I waited until I could hear my father snoring in his bed; then I went out and pissed on his roses.

THREE

WHEN I CAME DOWN for breakfast the next morning, my father was at the stove, frying up eggs and humming "Guide Me, O Thou Great Redeemer." He wore his best white shirt and suit trousers. His braces hung down the backs of his legs and his suit jacket hung on a chair beside his spit-shined shoes. When he heard me come into the room, he looked at me over his shoulder and smiled. "Coming to chapel?"

"How many times have you asked me that and when have I ever said anything but no?"

He chuckled. "Just wearing you down, I suppose. I'm like one of those missionaries, you see. The ones they send off to live among the cannibals. I just keep making a nuisance of myself until eventually you'll give in just to shut me up."

"Or I could roast you and eat you." I yawned, helping myself to a mug of tea.

"I expect you would find me a bit chewy. I'm a little past my prime." He took some tomatoes out from the broiler and tinned beans from a pot on the stove, loaded them onto the plates of sausages and eggs. He set one in front of me and the other in front of himself.

I reached behind me to the cutlery drawer, feeling sleep-cramped muscles stretching in my back. I fished out some knives and forks and handed one set to my father.

As we tucked into our breakfasts, the strange events of yesterday seemed far behind me.

The church bells started ringing, long hollow notes which echoed out across the rooftops of the town.

Although he had eaten only a few mouthfuls, my father set down his knife and fork. "Right, I'm off," he said. He dabbed a handkerchief against his mouth and stood up from the table. "You can have the rest of mine, if you want. You stay here and read the paper, while I go and pray for your sins," he added as he pulled on his jacket.

"That's good of you," I replied.

He swiped an apple from the bowl on the windowsill, tossed it in the air, and caught it in his palm with a satisfying slap. "That business last night," he said. "Better now?"

I nodded. "I don't know what it was."

My father stepped out into the street and pulled the door behind him. His route to the church took him right past the kitchen window, down the path on which cows were herded to the market. When I was a child, I used to press my face to the diamond-shaped glass panes, each one held in place by dull strips of lead, and watch the cows bring their wet black noses up to the window as they passed. Now I saw my father striding by, the uneven view through the panes making his body seem improperly assembled. The kitchen window was open and I could hear the sound of his footsteps. I was leaning forward to tap on the glass and give him another smile before he headed off to sit among the somber pews of the church when he lifted the apple to his mouth and took a bite.

I froze, and in that moment I was no longer reaching out towards the window, no longer in the kitchen of my father's house on a quiet Sunday morning.

❋

As if glimpsed from the crust of a meteor falling to earth, I saw the craggy vastness of the Alps with its elephant skin of glaciers, bared teeth of rock, and blinding sheets of snow. Now, coming closer, I could make out the Dragone mountains. Below them, tucked in a luminously green valley, lay the town of Palladino, its jumbled shingle rooftops patched with yellow moss. Beside the town, a shimmering lake reflected the blue sky. From there, I focused to a narrow stripe of trail which climbed up to the treeless hills. There, high on that trail, five figures were moving slowly forward, bent low with the weight of their packs.

One of those figures was me.

Tumbling now into the shell of my body, I saw through my own sweat-stung eyes and felt the burden of my pack and heard the shuffle of our boots across the stony ground.

We were moving single-file up the customs house road. On one side of the narrow dirt track was a steep drop down towards the Palladino Valley. On other other side, beyond a wide stretch of boulder-strewn ground, was a lake formed by runoff water from the Langua del Dragone glacier. On the far side of the lake, the glacier itself reared up out of the water, scabbed with dirt and glowing blue inside. Somewhere out there, hidden from view by the rise of the glacier, was Carton's Rock.

It had taken us most of the day to climb the steep road from the meadow where we had landed by parachute just before dawn. As soon as we hit the ground, we gathered up our chutes, located the drop canisters, and sorted out our gear. Within twenty minutes, we were on the move.

It was late afternoon before we cleared the last switchback of the mountain path and emerged onto level ground. Here, the boulder fields of glacial moraine extended to the glacier itself. The path continued along the edge of a lake in which great chunks of ice drifted with the dignity of swans across the silty green water.

We stopped to catch our breath. It had been a hard walk carrying so much gear, but the higher we climbed, the safer we felt. Even though none of us had been to this part of the Alps before, the shape of the terrain and what it demanded of us was so familiar that I began to feel as if we had somehow leapfrogged time itself, returning to those days before the war when the most complicated thing in our lives, and the only thing that truly mattered, was being up on the high ground, doing exactly what we were doing now.

As the shadows of the afternoon began to stretch towards evening, the wind picked up, as it always seemed to at the end of the day in the mountains. Turning our backs on the glacier, we sat down against a wall of rock. There, sheltered from the chilling breeze, we brewed up tea on a paraffin stove. The straps of our rucksacks were dark with sweat and the treads of our boots clogged with grit from the path. Some of the Greenland wax rainproofing had rubbed off my anorak and onto my hands, making them smell of beeswax. I took off my wool cap and let the sweat cool in my hair.

Each of us was lost in thought as we stared out across the vast expanse of snowy mountaintops. The valleys which separated these peaks from one another were hidden from view. They seemed not to exist at all. It looked as if the world had shrugged, closing in upon itself like an accordion, swallowing the greener world below and leaving only the jagged tips.

I allowed myself a moment of congratulation for having brought us together again. I felt genuinely sorry for Stanley, that he had somehow gotten himself so tangled up in his stubbornness and in that silly feuding with his uncle that he had missed out on this great adventure.

Until now, we had climbed for what it brought to us personally. Even in our little group, which mattered to me more than any other bond of friendship, there was a necessary solitude. No matter that we would soon be roped together, depending on one another's movements for our very survival, there were moments when it was just you and the mountain. And then, sometimes, the stabbing of your cramponed boots and the swinging of your ice ax became so focused that it was no longer just you and the mountain. It was just you. As if you and the mountain were the same thing. As if you were climbing some part of yourself. How little sense that made to people who had not felt it, and yet how real it was. How undeniable. But now that selfishness, if this was what it could be called, had been set aside. Knowing that lives would be saved by this mission, the purpose of our being here was richer than at any other time up in the mountains.

As the deep breaths of our exertion slowly returned to normal, we sipped our tea and nibbled on dry army biscuits.

Soon the sun would dip behind the mountains. Then the light would fade quickly. I planned for us to get as far as the abandoned customs house, spend the night there, and then head out across the ice at dawn on the following day. Since we were still too low to have a view of Carton's Rock, I would not feel secure about our route until I had our objective in sight.

It was time to move again. Our cooling sweat had begun to chill us. We packed away the stove, flicked the last drops of cold tea out of our tin mugs, and shouldered our rucksacks.

About five minutes later, just as I was wondering when we would come in sight of the customs house, I heard the first gunshot.

At first, I did not believe it was a gun. In that fraction of a second before I realized we had come under fire, I thought it was ice cracking somewhere out on the glacier.

I turned to see that Whistler had fallen. Part of me was trying to believe that he had simply slipped, but then I noticed that he was lying facedown, not moving, his pack spilled open and his neatly labeled bags of clothing and food about his shoulders. Only then did I understand what had happened.

We tumbled into the ditches, Sugden and Forbes on the side closest to the slope and Armstrong and I on the side nearest the lake.

"It came from out there." Armstrong gestured towards the dusty ground between us and the lake. Somewhere, behind one of those boulders, hid the man who had shot Whistler.

We both looked back to where Whistler lay on the road. He still had not moved.

On the other side of the road, I saw Sugden's face appear and then disappear as he ducked out of sight.

Beside me, Armstrong checked his gun. It was a modified Enfield which he had used in his duties as a sniper in the hedgerows of Normandy. The wooden stock had been cut down to reduce its weight, and the telescopic sight was wrapped with a strip of burlap for camouflage.

Carefully I raised my head until I could see over the edge of the ditch. Then I lifted my binoculars and scanned the lichen-crusted boulders, looking from rock to rock, searching for movement. Tufts of white cotton grass swayed in the breeze. Miniature tornadoes of dust spun along the water's edge.

"No luck?" whispered Armstrong.

I lowered the binoculars and wiped the sweat out of my eyes. "Nothing yet."

"Where the hell did he come from?" asked Armstrong. "They told us there wouldn't be anybody up here." Armstrong crouched beside me, rifle laid across his thighs. The paint-splash camouflage pattern on his Dennison smock made him seem like a shadow in this world of earth and stone.

I returned to scanning the ground beyond. In the instant I raised the binoculars above the rim of the ditch, I saw movement. A helmeted figure carrying a rifle swept past like a ghost among the rocks. He was there for only an instant. Then he was gone behind a large stone which stood about knee-high and whose top was as smooth and flat as a table. "He's on the move," I whispered. My mouth had gone bone dry.

Then came the faint grating sound of Armstrong chambering a bullet in his rifle.

"Take a look," I whispered.

Armstrong set aside his gun and peered through the binoculars.

"Do you see the big flat rock?" I asked.

"Got it," he replied.

"He's behind that."

Armstrong handed me back the binoculars, then took up his rifle and adjusted the range on his sights. "Tell me when he shows his face."

I went back to staring through the sweat-smeared lenses. My teeth were gritted so tightly that I thought they would crack. Every muscle in my body was clenched. My eyes ached from staring.

Then I saw him again. The sniper had crawled around to the side of the rock. His sharply angled helmet was covered with dried mud. If he stayed still, I could barely make him out.

"I've got him now," I whispered to Armstrong. "He's on the right-hand side of the rock."

Slowly Armstrong raised his gun and eased the barrel forward between two stones which lay across the top of the ditch.

I slid down until my head was at the level of his boots, watching as he dug his toes into the ground to brace himself. I could hear his breathing.

Armstrong wiped the sweat of his palm on his jump smock. His breathing changed. It became deeper and heavier, almost like that of a man asleep. But his eyes were open, cheek resting against the oiled red-brown wood of the gun stock.

I drank all the water in my canteen, even the gritty dregs which always lurked at the bottom, before refilling it in the milky-silted runoff in the ditch. Then I pressed my hands against my face and rubbed the dirt from my eyebrows. I felt exhausted and we had not yet even set out across the glacier. I thought about Whistler. I wondered if he was still alive and was just lying motionless until the shooting stopped. I had an image of him down in the Bull's Cellar in Oxford, when he had just come off a day of working at the Ashmolean. Armstrong had reached across and mussed up Whistler's hair and the dust of the library had wafted into the air, scenting the pub with the smell of antique books.

Then a sharp, crunching crack scattered the gentle picture from my head.

✻

AND IT WAS IN this moment that I returned to my father's kitchen, fingers still outstretched to tap upon the glass. But my father was gone. The sound of his biting into the apple, which had somehow brought to life that memory, still echoed in my head. I had no idea how long I had been standing there. The clarity of that memory had been so sharp that for a moment I could not be sure which was real.

For a while, I just sat at the table, while the sounds and smells of the house slowly filtered back into my brain, until I knew for certain where I was. Then I went upstairs and shaved and dressed, and packed my overnight bag, ready for the trip back to London. All the while, I was wondering why that day of Armstrong's death should have returned to me after all this time of lying dormant in the catacombs of my brain.

When my father returned from church, he found me on the doorstep, sitting on my duffel bag beside the remains of the iron rail fence which had once stood in front of the house. The railings had all been cut down during the First World War, to make use of the iron. Now only nubs of the metal remained.

"I've sent for a cab," I told him.

"So soon?" he asked. He looked sad but not surprised.

"I have to, I'm afraid." I smiled weakly. "Too much work to do back in the city."

"Damn the city," he murmured. "Damn what it does to people."

The cab arrived and I shook my father's hand good-bye.

I went to let go but he kept his grip on my palm.

"Something's not right with you, boy," he said.

"Something's not right," I agreed.

The cabdriver got out of his cab and stretched. Then he put his hands in his pockets, tilted his head back, and stared up at the sky.

"It's to do with that medal, isn't it?" asked my father.

"I don't know," I told him. "Perhaps."

"I wish you'd never won it!" he blurted out.

This caught me by surprise, given how much he liked to talk about it and the fact that he kept it on display.

"All this time," he went on, "I've been trying to pretend that whatever it cost you—"

"Cost me?"

"Yes!" he blurted out. "Cost! Not in money perhaps, but in other things. I'm not such an old fool as I don't know that a good number of the people who won the M.C. died winning it. It cost you all right. And I expect you'll be paying for it, one way or another, for the rest of your life. That's why I make so much of it. So as we can both pretend that what you did was worth it. I know you don't like it when I bring up the subject, but how else can you know I am proud of you?" By the time he had finished, there were tears in his eyes.

I hugged him then, which I had not done in years. I smelled the coal-tar soap he used, and the faint lemony scent of his hair oil. "Dad," I said, "I'm so sorry."

"Whatever for?" he asked.

"I peed on your roses."

He stood back, but kept his hands resting on my shoulders. "I know that," he said. "You've been peeing on them for years."

"You knew?"

He shrugged. "They don't seem to mind."

As the cab drove away past the cemetery, people were still emerging from the darkness of the church. The vicar stood off to one side, hands clasping a Bible to his chest, smiling at the old ladies who clustered around him, flowers pinned to their hats.

The last I saw of my father, he was standing at his front door, one hand raised to wave good-bye.

I knew he must be thinking about going back into that empty house, putting on the kettle for a cup of tea, and trying to get used to the silence once again.

FOUR

"THERE SHE IS," whispered Stanley. He had been standing in the doorway of the Climbers' Club, greeting people as they filed in to hear the lecture. But as soon as he saw me, he pulled me to one side and pointed out Miss Paradise.

The air seethed with cigar smoke and the beehive hum of talk from the thirty-odd people in the room. This smoke tinted the light a dusty blue, like the bloom on an unripe plum. The main room had high ceilings and a wide and darkly wooded staircase which rose to a landing. The landing was taken up mostly by a huge blue-and-white Chinese vase, which contained a number of short-handled and viciously pointed Zulu assegai spears. The staircase then turned right, climbing out of sight among the heads of trophy animals. Their big glass eyes looked down haughtily on the people in the room and the flared nostrils of their hard black noses made them seem like they were breathing in the smoke. It was as if, in their years of hanging on the walls, they had acquired the habit of tobacco.

"I can't see her," I told Stanley.

"The one in the woolen britches," he hissed, jabbing his finger towards the far end of the room. "How can you miss her? She's the only woman wearing trousers."

I still couldn't see her. My eyes had gone out of focus at the well-dressed muddle of people that had confronted me as I'd stepped through the huge double doors.

I had found, as time went by, that I did less and less well with busy places. Seeing this company of tuxedoed men and long-gowned women, my first reaction had been to turn around and walk back out into the dark. But Stanley was still tugging at my arm and pointing, and Carton, standing at the top of the landing with one hand in his pocket and the other clutching a cigar, had already fixed his nephew with a disapproving stare.

Unlike the more formally attired guests, Carton wore his trademark heavy suit made of brown-and-green-flecked keeper's tweed. A few people filed past him on their way upstairs. Carton stood between them like a rock in a slow-running river, glaring at Stanley.

Now Carton's gaze traveled from Stanley to me. His eyes narrowed slightly. He seemed to know my face, but not well enough to put a name to it.

We had not spoken since that day at Achnacarry.

Carton looked considerably grayer than when I'd seen him last. He now resembled a fierce old dog.

I'd hoped he might not recognize me after all this time.

But Carton had not forgotten. With a sudden, stabbing movement, he jammed the cigar in his mouth and began to make his way down the stairs. For a while, he disappeared among the little crowd of people, as he was not a tall man. Soon he reappeared, elbowing aside anyone foolish enough to remain in his way. He waved at me. His wave was not like the waves of other men, that open hand which shows no weapons in its grasp. Instead, Carton held his fingers outstretched and horizontal, as if he were casting a spell. Then he was standing in front of me, wheezing slightly. Jutting from his outside chest pocket was a line of fresh cigars, like bullets in a hunting vest. "Bromley! Is that you?" he asked, completely ignoring Stanley. He spoke as if he had gone blind. I half-expected him to stretch out his hand and begin patting his fingers against my face.

"Hello, sir."

"Bromley! I heard some rubbish about how you'd given up climbing!" He barked all this out in one staccato tirade, and it was only because he paused to draw a breath that I could respond at all.

"Sir," I said, "it is true." The last person I wanted to talk to about this was Henry Carton. I wished I'd never come here. I should never have let Stanley talk me into it.

Carton's mouth shut, teeth clacking together. It seemed only with difficulty that he forced his jaw open again. "What is true?" he asked.

"What you heard, sir. I don't climb anymore."

"Nonsense!" he barked and plugged the cigar back into his mouth. Then he turned to his nephew. "Aren't you supposed to be greeting the guests?" he asked, lips curled around the damp stub of tobacco leaves.

"I am greeting them," chirped Stanley. "Mr. Bromley here is a guest."

"But what about all the others? And what about the guest lecturer? Has she shown up yet?"

"She has indeed," said Stanley. "I was just on my way to"—he paused, choosing his words like a man choosing food from a menu—"to make sure she has everything she needs."

"You stay away from Miss Paradise," snapped Carton. "The last thing she needs is you traipsing around after her."

But Stanley was no longer listening. His eyes were fixed on the far side of the room.

I followed his gaze, and then at last I saw her.

Helen Paradise was of medium height, with broad shoulders and a suntanned face which made her blue eyes seem to glow. Her brown hair was streaked with blond and gathered at the back. She looked as if she had done her best to hide all femininity under heavy woolen britches and a short jacket, both of which were khaki overlaid with a green windowpane plaid. They were proper mountaineering clothes but looked slightly ridiculous among the formally attired people who made up the rest of the room. She gripped the stem of her champagne glass as a person might do if preparing to use it as a weapon.

Miss Paradise was so different from the willowy and doomed-by-beauty ladies who had previously caught Stanley's attention that I began to wonder if he really had gone and fallen in love. Properly this time. As yet, however, I could not grasp what Stanley saw in her.

The doors of the lecture room had been opened. People were making their way inside. I noticed that not all of the chairs would be filled. At the far end of the room I could see a podium, on which a glass of water rested, covered by a white handkerchief. On either side of the podium were large pictures of mountains. I recognized one of them as the rounded peak of Mont Blanc, and the other as the crooked witch's hat of the Matterhorn.

"Well, you'd better start showing people into the hall," Carton told Stanley, his voice heavy with exasperation. "The talk's just about to start. And you stand at the back. I don't want you nabbing seats from any of our paying guests."

"I'm looking forward to the lecture, Uncle," said Stanley, mocking him with the formality in his voice.

"And let's not pretend," replied Carton, "that your enjoyment has a damned thing to do with mountaineering."

Despite the harshness of Carton's words, it seemed to me that there was no real anger in them. There was something else, too, about the way he dealt with Stanley. It was something which defied the words he spoke and showed itself more in the language of his body. This was a kind of distant melancholy, mixed with a gentle pride in the willfulness of his nephew. The source of these emotions, whether they brought to life in Carton some memory of his dead brother or even of himself, lay so deep beneath Carton's barricade of gruffness that I wondered if even he knew where they came from.

"Right, then!" said Carton, terminating the conversation with Stanley as if he were hanging up a telephone. Then he turned to me. "Bromley, you come find me in a little bit. I want to talk to you about something." He screwed the cigar back into his mouth and, without another word to Stanley, did an about-face and ploughed back into the crowd.

"Who the hell does he think he is?" muttered Stanley.

"He knows exactly who he is," I said. "That's why people either love him or they hate him."

"Well anyway," said Stanley. "What's your opinion?"

I looked at him questioningly.

"Of her!" He jerked his head in the direction of Miss Paradise.

I thought of all the times I had played along, not wanting

to hurt his feelings. But now I found myself thinking of something I had never considered before. It was not the feelings of Stanley, nor my own, but the feelings of Helen Paradise. "I am your friend, Stanley," I began.

"Of course you are!" he snorted.

"And I would never do anything to hurt you," I continued.

"I know that! What are you babbling about?"

"And so you will believe me when I tell you that you haven't got a hope in hell with that woman." It gave me a shock even to say it, and I saw the same jolt pass from me to Stanley as the words made their mark.

"You can't say that," he stammered. "You haven't even met her."

"I don't need to. Let's go over to the Montague and have a bite to eat." I turned to leave, feeling as if I'd already stayed too long. Running into Carton again had rattled me more than I'd expected.

"Oh, can't you just hang on until the end of the talk?" pleaded Stanley. "It's only an hour. That's all I'm asking."

I was just about to tell him no when Carton's booming voice summoned me up the stairs.

He had returned to his perch on the landing, at the place where the staircase changed direction. He seemed to like the confines of the space and paced back and forth like a captain on the bridge of his ship.

"You'd better do as he says, Auntie." Stanley flashed me a smile. "He is my uncle, after all."

Knowing there was no escape, I made my way wearily towards him, conscious of the old man's eyes boring into the top of my head as I plodded up each red-carpeted stair.

Before I reached the landing, he was already heading for the top of the stairs. "Come on!" he commanded. He led me down a green-walled corridor, which was lined with water-color prints of the Alps, to a door which he unlocked using a large brass key.

"You're not going to hear the lecture, sir?" I asked, in a hopeless gesture to fend off the other lecture I knew was coming my way.

"Don't need to hear the talk," he replied, struggling to catch his breath. "Talk's not for me. Talk's for them downstairs." Then he flung the door open and marched inside.

The apartment was smaller than I had imagined. The robin's egg–blue walls seemed to soak up the light. A tiny bedroom looked out over the street, and a crow-footed bath filled up the bathroom, which was floored with black and white tiles the size of sugar cubes. The sitting room had a small couch in front of a fireplace, and various pieces of rock took the place of clocks and Staffordshire china dogs on the mantelpiece. The rocks, obviously souvenirs from his climbs, were each about the size of a grapefruit and all roughly the same shape. What set them apart were the colors. One rock was pink like boiled salmon. Another was arsenic green. Another black like coal but smooth, as if it had been tumbled in a river. One rock was white, but lined with tiny threads of gold. At the far end, I recognized the coarse red granite of Mont Blanc. Behind the rocks lay his ax-headed climbing stick. Its polished wood seemed to breathe in the dim light.

His small bookshelf was lined with mountaineering classics dating back to the 1700s, including Cox's *Travels in Switzerland*, Barde's 1785 edition of *Nouvelle Description des Alpes*, and Pinkerton's *Voyages and Travels*.

With his back to us, in a chair in front of the empty fireplace, sat a man in a heavy tweed coat and matching trousers.

He even had on a matching hat, and it was not until I came a little closer than I realized it was Archie.

I stood in front of the well-dressed skeleton, looking at the hollow eye sockets and the folded arms, whose hands were wrapped in gray doeskin gloves.

"Had to get gloves on him," said Carton. "Some of the guests complained that the sight of the fingers made them lose their appetites. The face never bothered them, though. Don't know why."

"You honestly don't know whose skeleton this is?" I asked.

Carton shrugged, to show that not only did he have no idea but not knowing didn't bother him. "He is whoever they want him to be. Sherlock Holmes. Jack the Ripper. Hannibal. I've heard them all. The only rumor that ever actually offended me was when I heard someone say it was the skeleton of my guide. It bothered me so much that I had to hire someone to prove that it wasn't."

"But how did you do that?"

"Got some scientist to calculate when his body would be coming out of the glacier, and that's not for another twenty years." Carton took off his jacket and hung it on a peg made from an antler bone. "Make yourself comfortable for a few minutes. I've got to sign some documents for the club's board of trustees." He nodded to a small room, no bigger than a closet, where a desk was piled with ledgers and pieces of paper stabbed onto long nails, and torn-open envelopes littered the floor. "The bastards are drowning me in bureaucracy. I won't be long. And then I want to talk to you."

While Carton sorted out his papers, I wandered into his study. On its wall above a little fireplace hung his old climbing ax. It was of a type known as the Kennedy style; its tempered-steel head double-screwed at the top and triple-screwed into the wooden shaft at the sides. The metal of the ice-ax head glowed with a bluish patina. Stamped into the iron was the manufacturer's logo: Herder/St. Gall, the best maker in the world. The spike at the other end had been blunted by use. The wood itself was dark from sweat and beeswax polish. I brought my face close to it and smelled the distant honeyed fragrance.

On the other walls were photographs of Carton on various mountaineering expeditions. In most of them, he wore a round-topped hat and moleskin breeches and leaned on a tall hiking staff. Across his chest, he carried a coil of rope. It was strange to see him looking so much younger, as I had not been able in my imagination to peel away the time which had splintered his face with gray stubble and creased the skin around his eyes like the tributaries of the Nile.

One picture in particular caught my attention. In this, Carton stood beside a fountain, in the center of which a statue of a horse reared up on two legs. The skin on his nose and cheeks was darkened and scabbed, his brow hidden beneath a shallow-crowned felt hat. His hands were wrapped in bandages. His eyes looked haunted, and his overall expression was one of disbelief. He stood there like a man about to be shot by a firing squad.

It was some time before Carton reappeared. He came into the study, walked over to the picture I'd been looking at earlier, and tapped his finger against the glass like someone tapping a barometer to check the pressure. It was as if he expected the figure in the picture to move and get on with whatever it had been doing before it posed for the photograph. "That was after I came down off the Dragon's Tongue," he told me.

"Judging from that picture, I'd say you were lucky to have made it out alive."

"I *was* lucky," he said softly, but then he breathed in suddenly, a rasping hollow gasp, and announced in a much louder voice, "And so were you! You could have been the best mountaineer in Britain by now."

"I'm quite happy with the way I am, sir."

"Oh, save that for your friends who don't climb mountains!" he spluttered. "You aren't happy! How could you be? No more than I am now that I can't climb mountains anymore. But the difference between us is that my body is the thing that let me down. My bloody useless lungs! What's wrong with you," he said, laying one stubby finger gently against my forehead, "is inside there."

I stepped back, leaving his finger touching only the air, as if it were pressed against an invisible wall that separated us. "You know perfectly well why I stopped climbing," I said.

"What's gone from me is gone for good," said Carton. "But what you've lost can still be found again." His voice was filled with frustration, as if his words, not just his lungs, were failing him.

I had no answer for him. His words were like a razor swiped across my face.

We returned to the top of the stairs.

By now, the lecture had ended. The doors of the lecture room swung open and the audience members once again swarmed around the food table, which had been restocked with sandwiches and urns of tea.

"I must attend to my guests," said Carton. "I love them all, but sometimes I despise them, too."

"Why is that?"

He glanced at me. "Because they are content among the borrowed revelations of their sheltered lives."

"If it wasn't for that," I said, "they'd have no use for you."

He smiled then. "And that is why I love them, too."

We made our way down.

Carton paused on the landing and we looked out over the sea of heads. Plumes of cigarette smoke rose like charmed snakes to the rafters, carrying with them the jumbled happy voices of the crowd.

Carton squared his shoulders. He seemed to be bracing for the ordeal of small talk that lay ahead. He slapped me on the back and strode down into the main room, a Cheshire cat smile bolted to his face.

Catching sight of Stanley among a cluster of men who had gathered around Miss Paradise, I made my way towards him.

"You spoke so well," Stanley was saying. "I am certain you will be remembered among the ranks of mountaineers like Meta Brevoort, Mary Mummery, and Lily Bristow."

The other men stared at Stanley.

By the time Stanley finished comparing Miss Paradise's career with those of half a dozen other female mountaineers, two of the four men had already departed. The remaining pair looked back and forth from Stanley to Miss Paradise as if following a tennis match.

"You do know a great deal!" said Miss Paradise. From the way she looked at him, it was clear they were already friends. The windburned creases which I'd noticed on her face before she'd begun her lecture had disappeared. A softness had entered her eyes. It was as if a mask had been removed and, amazingly, Stanley was the one who had removed it.

Now only one man remained, the other having drained

his glass, stared into the bottom as if he had no idea where his beverage had gone, then wandered off in search of more.

"I wanted you to meet a friend of mine," said Stanley, turning towards me and neatly blocking out the last man, who took his cue and vanished.

Helen Paradise stared at me for a moment, her lips pressed together and her forehead lined with concentration. "You're William Bromley," she said. "The climber!"

"That's right," I replied.

"I thought . . ." she began.

"Thought what?"

She blinked, as if I had breathed dust into her eyes. "Well, I thought you had died in the war."

"No." I tried to smile. "Still here." I was confused as to why Stanley had not mentioned me before, especially since the topic of mountaineering must have come up between them.

"Still causing trouble!" exclaimed Stanley, determined to keep the mood upbeat.

"It's just that I heard a lot about you and your climbing before the war and then nothing afterwards." She sipped at her champagne. "I just assumed."

"No, well, I . . ." I began, but had no idea what to say next. What she'd just said had derailed me completely. I stared down at my shoes. "I've just not really been around much. I mean . . ." I glanced up.

She was no longer listening.

Instead, she and Stanley were staring at each other, lost in some happy, wordless conversation of their own.

Seeing that my reason-for-leaving excuse was not required, I made my way across the crowded room.

But then a voice called after me. It was Miss Paradise. "You're coming back?"

Stanley's eyes fixed upon mine, telling me I'd better stick around.

"Of course!" I smiled. "I've just got to sort something out. I'll be back in a minute." I strode away, as if I knew where I was going. In truth, I had no idea. Two minutes later, having wandered down some passageway near the kitchens, I ended up in the men's bathroom, where I found myself a quiet stall and sat down to have a smoke. I'd go back out in a minute. After making a silent promise to myself that this was the last time I'd let Stanley talk me into anything, I rolled myself a cigarette. I had just fished out the box of matches when the door swung open and I heard the voice of Henry Carton.

"I told you to leave her alone!"

Then I heard Stanley. "It's none of your business."

My lips pressed down on the cigarette. I breathed in the heavy, sweet smell of unlit tobacco.

"It doesn't look right." Every time Carton spoke, he sounded like a train announcer. "You're a host here at the club. You're supposed to be looking after the guests. After *all* of them. Not just traipsing around after one of them and ignoring the rest."

"Uncle Henry, what does it matter how it looks? I love her."

Carton clicked his tongue, then launched into something else. "Why the hell aren't there any new magazines out on the tables?"

"The subscriptions have expired, Uncle Henry."

"Well, renew them, for God's sake, why don't you?"

There was silence, but even in that quiet, I could hear the air being drawn into Stanley's lungs.

Then Stanley exploded. "Because one month from now, the club won't even exist! Didn't you see the empty seats in the lecture room tonight? Why don't you just face it, Uncle? The board of trustees has got it in for us. Every week they make you sign away a little more of the place."

I had never heard Stanley mention any of this before. I knew that the club was not the same grand place it had once been, but I'd had no idea they were in such trouble. I sat very still, the cigarette balanced between my lips, box of matches resting in the palm of my right hand, and one blue-tipped match pinched between the thumb and index finger of my left hand, ready to strike.

"What the hell am I going to do?" asked Carton, punctuating his words with the splash of peeing in the urinal. "Without this place, I'm nothing." There was a rustle as Carton did up the buttons on his fly. "Come on then," he said. "Let's go and get this over with." His heels clacked out over the tiles. The door opened and a sound of chatter rose and fell as the door closed again.

I imagined Stanley following him, eyes cast down and loping like a scolded dog. Believing they had gone, I touched the head of the match to the box, ready to strike. But then I heard a sigh.

Stanley was still in the room. "You've got it the wrong way round, you old fool," he mumbled. "It's without you that the place is nothing."

Those were the first compassionate words I'd heard him say about his uncle in a very long time.

The door thumped shut a second time, and then I knew I was alone. But in the quiet of that room, his words lingered like the fluttering of tiny wings.

After smoking half the cigarette, I stood and flicked the butt into the toilet, where it fizzed and floated, turning circles.

I didn't have it in me to go back into the room and make conversation. Stanley was doing fine on his own and Carton did not need me to tell him good-bye. Out in the hallway, I turned right and exited the building through a side door, which deposited me in an alleyway. A streetlamp threw a harsh glare down the alley, which was slick and black, as if the bricks and cobblestones had all been sprayed with oil.

As soon as I stepped into the alley, I saw a figure kneeling on the cobblestones. It was a man. He wasn't exactly kneeling. He was resting on one knee, right arm steadying himself against the ground. His head hung down. A trickle of saliva stretched from his mouth, as silver as the strand of a spider's web.

Then I heard a voice, which I recognized immediately as Carton's.

"Get up, damn you!" he said. "Get up or get it over with!"

Even though I couldn't see Carton, I had no doubt it was Stanley he'd been cursing and that Stanley was the one down there on the cobblestones. Carton was standing over him, hidden in the dark. My face went hot with anger. All that talk he had given me about his bloody lungs and how weak he was now and he still had the strength to knock his own flesh and blood to the ground. I stepped towards them, ready to help Stanley to his feet. And if I didn't have my temper back by then, I decided, I might just knock Carton about a bit and give him some of his own bloody medicine.

I looked into the shadows, trying to spot Carton, but he wasn't there. Then I realized that the man on the ground *was* Carton. Stanley was nowhere in sight. Carton had been swearing at himself.

The anger evaporated. Now all I felt was confused. "Sir?" I said, and touched Carton on the shoulder. "Do you need some help?"

Slowly, the old man raised his head and looked me in the eye. "Damn it," he said. "Damn everything."

"Are you all right?" I asked.

He nodded, turned his head, and spat. "Help me up," he said, his voice gone faint and hoarse.

I helped him to his feet, noticing as I lifted him by the arm that he had laid down a handkerchief on which to rest his knee.

The cigars which he kept in his breast pocket had fallen to the ground. I gathered them up and handed them over.

Carefully, he put them back where they belonged and tapped them into place with his finger.

Then I picked up his handkerchief and gave it to him.

He touched the cloth against his mouth before putting it away in his trouser pocket.

"Do you need a doctor, sir?" I asked.

Carton shook his head and at the same time gave a great rumbling cough, which ended with a rattle from his throat. "Nothing to be done. The show's over."

We were both looking down the alleyway towards the street, where the silhouettes of departing guests flitted beneath the lamplight.

"Heading home, were you?" he asked hoarsely.

"Well, I've got to teach tomorrow, and there are some papers I haven't marked yet."

He grunted. "I suppose I must have sounded a bit daft, cursing myself like that."

"No, sir. Not really." I felt sorry for him. For the first time I understood how hard his life had become.

"I can't help it," he said. "I get so frustrated that I can't do things anymore. I want to go back to climbing mountains. I want to undo all that mess I got you into back in the war."

"You didn't get me into it, sir."

"But I didn't get you out of it, did I? And perhaps I should have. I ought to have known."

"Nobody could have known, sir."

"Sometimes I think Stanley knew." The words came out very slowly, almost as if he had forgotten how to talk. "Instinctively, I mean. He's got good instincts, that boy." In the streetlamp's silver light, cut through with blind man's black as jagged as a shard of glass, I could make out a sad smile upon Carton's face. "That new woman of his, for example. At his age, I'd have fallen in love with her myself."

"Yes, sir," I said, but the truth was, I could not imagine him being in love with anyone, or anyone being in love with him, either. He seemed too much larger than life for that, even broken down as he was now.

"It would be easier for me," continued Carton, "if Stanley was simply a dead loss. Then I could content myself with giving him the occasional pat on the back and a box of cheap cigars at Christmas. But he's not a dead loss. He's capable." He nodded in agreement with himself. "He can do anything he sets his mind to. It's his father, my own brother, who spoiled him. Let him do anything he wanted and, what's worse, got him out of doing anything he didn't want to do. Since my brother's death, I've tried to mend things, but I think perhaps it is too late. I tried to get him interested in mountaineering again, but he seems to have made up his mind about that."

"No one would climb with him," I said. "Not after Sugden spread the word about his refusing to come with us. Stanley could have gone off on his own, but he was too proud for that. So he just walked away."

Carton looked up and down the alleyway, as if to see his nephew disappearing. Then, slowly, he turned back to me.

"And now that you've walked away as well, Bromley, what is it that gets you out of bed in the morning? What keeps you sane?"

Instinctively, I reached into the right pocket of my jacket, pulled out the old ration tin, and felt the rubbed metal in my hand. "I don't know if I am keeping sane, sir. To be honest, I'm not sure I am keeping going. My thoughts never used to go back there. To that place."

We both knew what I was talking about.

"But lately," I said, "things have been reminding me."

The way the light struck his face now, Carton's eyes had disappeared. What remained was only the darkness of empty sockets. He looked like the skeleton who, I realized, had in all likelihood become his closest companion apart from Stanley.

Carton let go of my shoulder.

I felt the warmth where his hand had been. Now I shuddered in the cold.

"Don't let the demons drag you down," he said.

"What do you mean?" I asked.

Carton didn't answer my question. Instead, he gently set his hand against the side of my face.

Against my cheek, I felt that his fingertips were callused, the way all mountaineers had callused hands. It was as if, in some secret way, he had tricked the world and never quit his climbing.

"Do they still call you Auntie?" he asked.

"Sometimes, sir. Those who are left."

"Of course," he said. Then, almost in a whisper, he added, "You'll be fine. You wait and see."

Before I could ask what he was talking about, Carton turned away into the dark. A rectangle of light appeared in the wall as he opened the door, and disappeared again as he closed it behind him.

Alone in the alley and hidden by the night, I felt an unfamiliar lightness in my heart. Part of me could not help believing that Carton's words would come true, even if I did not know how, simply because it was Carton who had spoken them.

For the first time in as long as I could recall, the simple act of drawing breath into my lungs became a pleasure. It was as if, for a moment, I had been set loose from the confines of my body, free to drift above the rooftops of the city and out among the hilltops of the clouds.

FIVE

I WAS SITTING IN the faculty lounge at St. Vernon's, slumped with a lukewarm cup of tea on a tired leather couch. Miss Kidder, the headmaster's assistant, was delivering mail to the faculty pigeonholes. I studied the way her dress rode up her calves as she stood on her toes to reach the higher boxes. The dress was off-white with little red flowers printed on the cloth. Her short black hair was stark against the pale skin of her neck.

"Would you like some help?" asked Higgins, who sat in a mirror image of myself on the couch against the opposite wall.

We'd just had our lunch and, with half an hour still to go before the next class, Higgins and I were trying not to fall asleep. Houseman, on the other hand, had wangled his class schedule so that he had the next period off. He lay dozing on a wooden bench behind the table in the corner, a copy of Caesar's *De Bello Gallico* over his face.

Higgins and I did not bother to lower our voices, because

Houseman could sleep through anything. One night, we'd gone into his room, which was on the ground floor of the faculty housing block. The two of us had carried his bed, with Houseman in it, out into the middle of the playing fields. And that was where he'd woken up in the morning.

"Would you like some help?" repeated Higgins, making no effort to get up.

Miss Kidder turned and glanced at him. "No, thank you," she said, and flashed him a humorless smile.

When she left, Higgins would have something to say about that smile.

It was understood that not only Higgins but Houseman and I, too, were in love with Darcey Kidder. Each of us had settled on a different tactic to win her heart. Higgins chose the route of polite conversation, which never worked because he ended up talking to himself. Houseman played hard to get, which so far had proved completely effective, although not in the way he was hoping.

As far as I was concerned, she was so beautiful that I could barely bring myself to look her in the eye. From the first time I'd seen her, she'd had, in the delicate contours of her face and the electric blue of her eyes, a beauty that seemed so familiar that I felt sure I must have met her before, even though I knew I hadn't.

We had all agreed that we didn't stand a hope in hell with Darcey Kidder. Sooner or later, someone with better prospects than three underpaid teachers would come along, and that would be the last we'd see of her.

Secretly, I refused to give up hope. Instead, I prayed for a chance to be alone with her, away from the magnifying glass under which any rumor of love among the faculty was placed. But those chances were hard to come by, and the risks of being made into a fool were great on either side. The time will come, I told myself. An opportunity will present itself. The hard part was learning to be patient.

I heard footsteps in the hall.

A moment later Stanley appeared in the doorway.

"What are you doing here?" I asked.

Stanley had never stopped by St. Vernon's before. The fact that it was a school seemed enough to make him steer clear of the place. He looked a little flustered. "Where did you disappear to last night?" he asked me. "Helen and I searched all over the place."

Rather than go into it just then, I introduced him to Higgins, who nodded hello over the rim of his chipped and brown-stained tea mug.

Darcey Kidder took the opportunity to duck out. The clip-clop of her feet faded away down the corridor.

"That there is Houseman," I said, pointing to *De Bello Gallico*.

Houseman's eyes flickered open, a flash of mahogany brown, then closed again.

"Looks like he's laid out for a wake," said Stanley.

"Ah," sighed Higgins. *"Quid dicam de ossibus? Nihil nisi bonum."*

Stanley fixed him with a look he reserved exclusively for people who quoted Latin or poetry or anything in any foreign language.

Higgins was not paying attention. Instead, he leered at the pigeonholes, as if Miss Kidder were still standing there, returning the desire in his stare.

Stanley and I walked out into the school courtyard.

A line of boys emerged from a classroom and shuffled by, clutching their armfuls of books. One by one they greeted me.

Stanley watched the little troop go past, a combination of pity and disgust whittled into the creases around his eyes. When they had gone, he turned to me and asked, "How on earth do you remember all their names?"

"It's not that hard," I said.

"School," said Stanley, and shuddered. "Well, I'm not calling you Mr. Bromley, except when I am drunk or about to get that way."

"And I will not assign you any homework."

He winced. "Homework! God. I'd forgotten about that."

I was about to say that he had been forgetting about it for as long as I had known him, but he had obviously come here on another matter, so I let the moment pass.

We walked out of the courtyard and onto the playing fields, where the groundskeeper was busy repainting the lines of the cricket pitch with a one-wheeled machine that looked like a cross between a plough and a baby's pram.

At the far end of the fields, ranks of chestnut trees lined the horizon like green clouds.

The peaceful scene drew a sigh from my lungs.

But Stanley did not sigh. For him, the world of academic institutions was racked with painful recollections.

I was used to this uneasiness in people who came here from the outside. I'd felt it myself when I'd first arrived at St. Vernon's. I had never given any thought to teaching before and had only taken the job to buy myself some time before moving on to somewhere else. The longer I'd waited for the answer about what that somewhere else might be, the more I'd realized that the war, and the changes it had brought to my life, had removed not only a plan for the future but even the future itself.

I woke up each morning surprised to find that I was still

alive. This phenomenon had thrown me into a permanent state of amazement. The smallest things, like the blue flame balanced in the old spoon in which I melted black polish for shining my boots on Sunday afternoons, or the smell of toasted granary bread, or the sound of a distant train clattering along the tracks in the middle of the night, would bring to life in me a bewilderment that lasted for days. Such apparently trivial details, I had to remind myself, had long since been taken for granted by most people around me, or else had never been noticed at all.

The result was that while they ploughed ahead with their lives, I was content to drift, without the ambition, lust for money, or the need for recognition which so underpinned these other lives that anyone not caught up in the same pursuit must, these people assumed, be either mad or lazy or hiding even greater ambitions than their own.

There was a faint squeaking sound behind us, and a moment later Darcey Kidder rode past on her bicycle. She was heading alongside the playing fields to the little house she rented on the other side of the road which bordered the school grounds.

Higgins could see her house from the living room of his flat above the school library. The ceiling of this flat was sharply angled, since it was, in effect, the attic of the building. This meant that Higgins spent most of his time moving around it hunched over like Quasimodo. Despite the ridiculous level of discomfort, he kept the room because it meant that he was, by his own calculation, only fifteen seconds in a flat-out run from his classroom. This meant he could roll out of bed at 7:50 for an eight o'clock class and still get there on time.

Higgins held weekly blackjack tournaments in this flat for anyone who cared to join. Usually, it was just him and

Houseman. Only rarely did I give up my Saturday evenings to join in, since I saw enough of them during the week.

Even while we played cards, Higgins kept a huge pair of binoculars on the table. They were made by Busch-Rathenow near Berlin, and the right lens was fitted with a ranging grid. He had gotten them off a German artillery officer at a place called Sidi Rezegh in North Africa. The artillery position had been overrun and most of the crew had surrendered, but the officer had pulled out a broom-handled Mauser and, aiming wildly, shot the cap off Higgins's head. "It was a new cap, as well! I'd just had it sent down from Hobson's!" he'd told me. There was no need to ask whether the German's binoculars had outlasted him.

Now and then, Higgins would lift the binoculars and peer through his living room window at Darcey Kidder's house across the playing fields.

He never saw anything except a light behind closed curtains, but when her lights went out, he would announce with a sigh, "She's gone to bed."

Then each of us would silently imagine what it might be like to lie beside her, to hear her breathing, and to see, in the soft glow of the streetlamp through the curtains, the pulse of her heart beneath the milky skin of her neck.

"*Tamam,*" Houseman would say quietly. This meant—in Arabic, I think—that everything was as it should be.

Stanley watched Miss Kidder floating past, his eyes fixed hungrily upon her.

"One at a time, Stanley," I said.

"Right," he said.

"I'm glad you're here, Stan," I told him.

"Yes?"

"I'm actually a bit worried about your uncle."

"Are you?" he laughed. "Well, you're always fussing over people. But I wouldn't trouble yourself about him."

I told Stanley about finding Carton in the alleyway.

Stanley shrugged it off. "He's always coughing. He can't help it. I think he spends a fair amount of time spluttering away out there in the alley. That's where he goes to be alone."

"It's just that he seemed . . ." And then I did not know how to go on.

Stanley waited patiently for me to find the words.

"Fragile," I said, eventually.

Again, he laughed at me. "I've heard him called a lot of things, but never fragile. Good Lord, William, he's as tough as old boots! He's practically indestructible. He gets in his dark moods from time to time, but he's not fragile. There's nothing wrong with him that hasn't been wrong for as long as anyone can remember. That's just who he is. Trust me."

I had no choice but to do just that. I hadn't seen Carton in years, and Stanley saw him all the time. Who was I to guess at the old man's mental state? I felt a little foolish even for bringing it up. "So how are you and Miss Paradise?" I asked, glad to change the subject and guessing that this was what Stanley had come to discuss.

But instead of launching into his usual tirade, he merely shrugged, jangled the change in his pockets, and jabbed at the ground with the toe of his shoe.

"Oh," I said sarcastically, "so now, after years of telling me everything whether I wanted to hear it or not, you have decided to tell me nothing."

"This time is different. I told you it was." He was watching the groundskeeper rather than making eye contact with me.

"She's not like those Melancholy Angels," I admitted. "But what do you see in her? That's what I don't understand."

The groundskeeper turned and began to make his way slowly back along the length of the cricket pitch, white paint striping the close-cropped grass. With each footstep, the brass watch chain hanging from his waistcoat pocket swung and glinted.

Stanley began to pace along the white line of the cricket-pitch boundary, as if walking a tightrope. "All the other women have shared two things in common. They all knew exactly what they did not like, which amounted to just about everything. The other thing they had in common was that they had absolutely no idea what they did like. They could have any-thing, of course. If their rich parents didn't pay the bill, they could easily find someone gullible like me who would. But they didn't know what they wanted. Mostly they waited for other people to tell them what they should want, and then they wanted that for a while before moving on to something else."

I tried to recall the faces of the women who had passed in and out of Stanley's life. They flickered before me like a shuf-fled deck of cards.

"But Helen knows exactly what she wants. How can I not fall in love with that? How can this time not be different?"

Everything he said made sense. I understood perfectly why Stanley could become attached to someone like Miss Paradise. But in the end, it would make no difference. This time seemed as doomed as all the rest. More doomed, even, if that was pos-sible. I could see it all happening in slow motion. The uncor-rectable imbalance of emotions. The inevitable disaster, despite the promise that this time would be different. With Stanley, every time would be different. But the difference this time would be that his heart might get properly broken.

"And she likes me," said Stanley. "It's not the same old dog-and-pony show where I spend all my time trying to keep

THE ICE SOLDIER | 119

them amused because I know they'll leave the minute they get bored. That was why I wanted you to stay last night. So you could see that we really do get along together."

I turned on him. "But why?" I demanded. "I see why you like her. But . . ." I couldn't even say it.

Stanley had to finish the sentence for me. "Why does she like me? Is that what you can't figure out?"

I stared at the ground. "I'm sorry," I muttered.

"Why don't you ask her yourself?"

"Oh, right," I muttered.

"No, I mean it. She said she wanted to meet you."

"Why didn't you mention me to her before? She said she thought I had died in the war."

Stanley stopped on his tightrope, turned, and began to walk the other way. The soles of his shoes were powdered white from the dried paint. "I don't know," he huffed. "I asked her about her and she asked me about me. I don't know any of her pals, either. But now that we are getting along so well, she wants to know what kind of friends I keep. And what's wrong with that?"

"Nothing. Sorry."

"That's the way it goes with relationships. You ought to have one someday, and then you'd know."

"All right!" I held up my hands in a gesture of surrender.

"Anyway, you're all set for lunch on Saturday at the Climbers' Club. She's giving her last lecture. You're to meet her afterwards in the dining room."

The school bell rang.

"I have to go," I said.

Stanley slapped me gently on the arm. "You'll be there, right?"

I nodded.

"Try not to exhaust yourself saying nice things about me," said Stanley. "If the subject comes up, I mean."

"Don't worry. I'll tell her you're magnificent."

"Do you promise?" he asked suddenly.

"Of course I promise. Don't be ridiculous."

We set off across the courtyard in different directions, Stanley towards the street and me towards the classrooms, where students shambled in, carrying their bundles of books.

"Remember your promise!" called Stanley, as he disappeared through the school gates and out into the constant rolling thunder of the city.

❋

WALKING DOWN THE PORTOBELLO ROAD, I felt the particular energy of London on a Saturday afternoon. Sunday, it would be different, and during the week it would be different once again. But Saturdays had something special and I loved them the best.

Almost every Saturday morning during the term, I caught a No. 10 bus from just outside my flat, which would bring me to the top of the Portobello road. From there, I'd stroll down the hill to Ladbroke Grove. I could have gone straight to Ladbroke Grove on the No. 17 bus, but I liked to wander with the Portobello crowds past antique stalls, the vendors lost in their obsessions of leather suitcases, binoculars, fountain pens, and walking sticks. Beyond them, where the road leveled out, I passed by fruit sellers with cigarettes wagging from their lips who called out in almost indecipherable Cockney, praising the ripeness of tomatoes, the newness of potatoes, the freshness of leeks.

When I reached Ladbroke Grove, I would roam among the old bookstalls, returning home after dark with bread and cheese and a wicker-wrapped bottle of Italian wine to keep me company. Then I would spend the night reading whatever dusty volumes I had bought that day, drinking the wine from the bottle, and eating lumps of cheese off the end of an Opinel knife.

During the school year, St. Vernon's did not allow us much free time, so I guarded my Saturday afternoons carefully. But today was different. Miss Paradise was waiting.

The dining room of the Climbers' Club was small, with walls the color of custard. There were no windows, which made the place feel stuffy. This was offset somewhat by several paintings of mountain landscapes. One showed the Bellevue Spa at Kleine Scheidegg, hunched in the shadow of the Eiger. Another had a view of the Matterhorn from the chapel at Platten, and there was a photograph of the shrine to Our Lady of the Snows at Lac Noir, its sepia print glowing in dusty brown light.

All of the tables were filled. A hum of talk mixed with the clink of spoons in soup bowls.

At the long table, which ran the length of the left side of the room, sat Carton with his twelve guests.

I had forgotten about Carton's Saturday lunches, and quietly cursed myself for not remembering.

Beside Carton sat Archie in his gray suit with his red skull-and-crossbones tie.

Carton saw me standing in the doorway. He grinned and raised his battered tankard in salute, then drank from it and grinned at me again.

It sent a shudder down my back. His bared teeth looked the same as Archie's, and I thought back to that night in the alley, when Carton's eyes had vanished in the shadows. Despite Carton's grim bravado, that strange fragility I'd glimpsed in him before was still there now. It seemed to hover around him, like the smoke of his cigars. But I didn't know what it meant, or if it was just my imagination. There was nothing I could say about it anyway, not without feeling like a fool, as I had done when I'd mentioned it to Stanley.

I scanned the room until I saw a woman sitting by herself at a table near the kitchen door. It took a second glance before I realized this was Miss Paradise. She was not wearing her heavy mountaineering clothes this time. Instead, she had on a navy blue dress with a white collar and white fringe on the ends of the short sleeves. Her face was almost hidden by a small white cloche hat, which had a flower tucked into the brim.

She was studying the menu card, but looked up and smiled when I walked into the room. It was a lovely smile, so open and honest and unlike Carton's skull-smirk from the other side of the room that the first thought through my head was, Oh dear, I am going to fall in love with this woman.

"I was afraid you wouldn't show up," she said.

"Why?" I asked as I took my seat opposite her.

"Because then I'd be summoned over to Carton's table to hobnob with his guests and have my picture taken with his skeleton. Which smells, by the way."

I didn't want to get started on Carton. "That is a very pretty dress," I said.

"A bit of a change from that frumpy climbing gear, isn't it? The mountaineering kit was Carton's idea." She handed me the printed menu card. "I think he wanted to give the impression that I was just in off the glaciers. I told him I'd rather not, but as I suspect you know by now, he's not very easily swayed. I just keep telling myself that each lecture I give, no matter what gear I'm sporting, earns me enough to spend another week up in the mountains."

I liked her already, and I began to wonder if I could get through this lunch without liking her too much. The next hour passed quickly, as we exchanged stories of the lengths to which we'd gone to earn money for our various expeditions. I told her about selling my blood and she gave details of a disastrous month as a pastry chef in Edinburgh, which ended with her being not only fired but banished from the whole of Scotland by the hotel manager.

We talked about the cafés of Chamonix, the endless train ride down to Switzerland, and other things we had in common, each of us recalling the most minute details of this other life we had both lived but shared only as memories. I barely noticed the metallic-tasting vichyssoise and the lamb with a bitingly acidic mint sauce that passed under my nose during the course of the meal.

She spoke about the heavy photographic equipment, the way the cameras would seize up in the cold, and trying to reload film canisters with frozen fingers.

"But the results were worth it," I said, remembering the photos I had seen in the lecture room when we'd first met.

She smiled. "Now they seem worth it, but I'm not sure you could have convinced me of that at the time." She reached down under the table and retrieved a leather folder from where it lay at her feet. "Look at this one," she said, and laid before me an eight-by-ten-inch photo.

I recognized it immediately. It was Carton's Rock, taken from the edge of the glacier. The rock looked like the gnarled end of a chisel, streaked with snow, the precipice as black as ink and the snow like porcelain. I knew she must have walked up the same gravel road I had traveled with Sugden, Forbes, Whistler, and Armstrong.

It was a brilliant photograph. She had captured perfectly

the fierce loneliness of the place, which spoke as much of the fear of mountains as the lure of those remote places. I glanced across at her, wondering if she knew I had been at that same spot where she'd taken the picture, and what had happened there.

"It's Carton's Rock," she said. "I'm giving it to Mr. Carton as a present. He hasn't seen it yet."

I realized that she did not know. Not yet anyway. But it was bound to come out sooner or later, and I was already dreading the moment when it did. I handed back the photo. "He's going to love that," I said.

"Too bad I didn't get any closer," she said. "I hear that the view from the top is one of the great wonders of the world." Helen went on to explain how she had used a red filter to highlight the contrast between the black and the white. "That's a trick I learned from studying Ansel Adams," she explained. She was just starting to tell me who Ansel Adams was when I asked her something that had been on my mind since I'd first set eyes on her.

"How did you ever get started in mountaineering?"

"Well." She rested her elbows on the table and folded her hands together. She looked around the room and back to me again, as if she had been searching for the right place to begin. "I started climbing because I was told that I shouldn't." Then she raised one finger, correcting herself. "No. Actually I was told that I *couldn't*. When I was eighteen, I went on holiday with my family to Switzerland, where my two brothers and my father planned to climb the Schilthorn. When I asked if I could come along, my father said absolutely not. I was expected to stay in Grindelwald and keep my mother company. My father went on to say that no woman should attempt a climb like that and, even if they could, it would be unladylike. So the next year, I went back and climbed it by myself. After that"—she let her hands fall open—"I didn't care what people thought about a woman climbing as long as I could keep at it."

It was only then that I began to see how much she and Stanley had in common. Both had been pressured to conform to the wishes of their families, and each had responded by doing the opposite. It seemed a great and unfair irony to me that the same stubbornness which drove her towards mountaineering had helped to push Stanley away from it, by refusing to become his uncle's protégé.

By the time we'd finished our meal, the lunchroom had emptied out, and the waiter was staring at us desperately through the porthole window of the kitchen door.

Taking pity on him, we had our coffee in the main room, beneath the jutting heads of the trophy animals, who seemed, despite the blank stare of their glassy eyes, to be listening to every word we said.

"Stanley thinks the world of you." She dropped a little jewel of brown rock sugar into her coffee cup.

"We've known each other forever," I said.

"He's quite charming," she said, raising the cup to her lips.

I felt a twisting in my chest. I wished we were not talking about Stanley. Just then, I wished that Stanley did not exist. I stared at her straight nose and her softly rounded cheekbones and the way her eyes closed a little when she smiled, and I wondered suddenly if I would ever again be content to wander home alone on a Saturday night, with my bottle of wine and a crumbly-paged book for a companion.

"He knows a great deal about what's going on in the mountaineering world these days," she continued.

"Yes. I think he follows things pretty closely in the various publications." I was staring at the pattern of the red, black, and green Berber carpet on the floor, chewing the inside of my cheek.

"But there's the practical side, too," she added. "The trip you and he have planned, for example."

I looked up from the carpet and stared at her. It was as if she had leaned across the little coffee table, whose surface was strewn with old club bulletins, and slapped me in the face. "The trip," I said. I did not say it as a question. I just pronounced the words.

"Yes. The one to the Himalayas. It sounds fascinating."

"The Himalayas," I said, remembering the way Stanley had made me promise to say nice things about him. He must have known this would come up. That was why he had not mentioned me to her earlier. I wondered what other lies he had told.

"I've always wanted to go there," she said dreamily.

In that moment, a blinding madness took hold of me. I had not been lonely before, but now I was terribly lonely. I wanted, with a few well-chosen words, to ruin this business with Stanley and Helen, so I could have my own chance of happiness with her. It did not matter that Stanley and I had been friends most of our lives. Nor did it matter that he had trusted me to speak well of him to this woman whom he loved. Nor did I care that this would mean the end of our friendship. I did not even care if things might not amount to anything between me and Helen Paradise. All I wanted was a chance.

She was looking right at me, smiling with what I felt sure was some kind of expectation. I wondered, Can she know what I am thinking? How can she not know? But does she want the same thing? Does she understand the risk?

"I . . . ," I said.

"Yes?" she asked. Those bright blue eyes. The half smile on her lips.

The words that I wanted to say to her hung trembling in the air around me, shuddering with the nervous energy of hummingbirds. But I could not speak them, because I was not sure what she was thinking.

I glanced down at my plate and sighed.

When I looked up again, her face had changed. The hard-staring focus had drifted from her gaze. She was still smiling, but now it was a different kind of smile.

Then I was certain she had known my thoughts. And too late I understood the meaning of that stare.

Now all that remained for us was to pretend that nothing had happened.

The madness slowly faded, like sand trickling away through a sieve.

I began to see clearly again. Whatever possibilities had existed between me and Helen Paradise would have been ruined if I'd buried Stanley now. Maybe not at first. But I would not be able to forgive myself and gradually that would eat away at whatever happiness I'd gained by my betrayal. The two things could not have balanced out.

I thought about the gamble Stanley had taken by lying. For a person like Stanley, the ridicule of a lie being discovered would normally have outweighed any benefits of telling it. This time, in his desperation, he had risked everything. Stanley had done what I'd been too afraid to do. He really did love her.

Then I felt as sorry for Stanley as I did for Miss Paradise, because I was beginning to think that perhaps she loved him, too. "You're fond of Stanley, aren't you?" I asked.

She was about to speak, but at that moment the waiter appeared and informed us quietly that the club was closing for the day.

We collected our coats and walked out into the street.

It occurred to me that if I hurried, I might still reach the bookstalls down in Ladbroke Grove before they shut. I could almost feel the texture of the old books' spines as I traced my fingertips across their backs.

Helen shook my hand. "I'm sure we'll see more of each other," she said.

As I jumped aboard the bus, a fine rain had begun to fall. Through the blurred glass, I watched the bright lights of shop windows flickering past. I wished I could have told her that everything would be all right. That she and Stan really were meant for each other. But it wouldn't have helped. Neither my silence nor my words would keep the lie in check. Sooner or later it would come out. It was inevitable. What happened after that was in the hands of the gods, who were, even now, dismantling the flimsy scaffold of my own life.

❉

I DIDN'T HEAR FROM STANLEY during the week that followed. The next Friday, I begged off going to the Montague for our usual Forgiving of the World. It seemed only a matter of time before things fell apart between Stanley and Miss Paradise, and I did not want to be there when it happened.

On Saturday, instead of spending the evening reading in my room, I stayed up all night with Higgins and Houseman, drinking whiskey out of pewter tumblers and eating stale biscuits from a slightly rusty tin. When the biscuits were gone, Higgins produced a box of cigars the size of bulrushes. For the rest of the evening we puffed on these and played blackjack with Swan Vesta matches for bets. Sometime after midnight, Higgins and Houseman got into an argument about whether the much publicized Schuman Plan for pooling the coal and steel resources of western Europe was a good idea. When they began cursing each other in Swahili, I took the opportunity to stagger home to my flat.

On Sunday morning, despite being slightly the worse for wear, I resolved to find Stanley and discover what had happened. If nothing else, I wanted to reassure him that I'd done nothing to hasten the breakup I felt sure had already come.

Knowing that Stanley wouldn't roll out of bed before eleven o'clock, and still with several hours to go before then, I strolled down to the newsagents and bought my usual three papers. The newsagent was asleep with his head on the counter, so I left the money on the register.

Following my normal Sunday ritual, I stopped at Mrs. Reave's Tea Shop. It was the only place open on a Sunday morning. As usual at this hour, I was her only customer.

"Tea and two slices, Mr. Bromley," said Mrs. Reave, removing a heavy tea mug from the shelf and setting it down beside a steaming pot of tea. She was not asking me what I would have. She was telling me, and her voice had the finality of a judge passing sentence.

Mrs. Reave was small and bony. Her face was pinched, with a thin slit of a mouth lipsticked bloody red. She kept her hair tied in a bun so severe that it pulled her face into the likeness of someone walking into a hurricane wind. She had few good words to say about anyone or anything, but she did make a good cup of tea. Her world revolved around the making and pouring of hundreds of cupfuls a day, and the endless manufacturing of toast, served always in sets of two slices. On these slices, she swiped huge gobs of half-melted butter and delivered

them to a clientele which covered many ranks of London society. Tramps with clothing so dirty it looked like gunmetal sat
beside silver-buttoned policemen, who in turn sat beside more
or less gainfully employed people like me. Here, there was no
room for more than passing comments, as Mrs. Reave did not
like people who dawdled. To show she meant business, there
were no decorations in the tea shop. The walls were bare
except for a large chalkboard, on which the menu had been
written. In addition to tea and toast, it offered beans (spelled
"beens"), sausages, broiled tomatoes (spelled "tomartoes"), and
the dauntingly vague special of "fish."

Holding a mug of tea and a plate of toast, Mrs. Reave slid
towards me on the worn-down soles of her shaggy slippers. It
looked as if she had trampled two small rabbits to death and
was now using them to polish the floor. "Hear what happened
to those chaps up in the mountains, then?" she asked, clunking
the mug down in front of me.

"No, I haven't," I replied. "What mountains?"

She nodded at my newspapers. "It's all in there."

I snatched up one of the papers. There, splashed across
the front page, alongside news that Seoul had fallen to the
Communists and the American air force was bombing North
Korean troops, was an announcement that Sugden's team had
returned early from Patagonia, having lost two men in an
avalanche.

According to the report, on the morning of June 20,
two members of the expedition, named Bertram Culshaw and
Arthur Dalvey, left their camp at the base of El Cajon, making
for their second camp halfway up the mountain. From there,
they planned to proceed to a third camp, and from there to
reach the summit on the following day. By the time they
reached the second camp, it was June 22. On the following

day, the two men were spotted from the base camp, heading up towards camp three. Later that day, a blizzard set in, and nothing more was heard from the two men. Three days later, the base-camp team, which included Sugden, began a search-and-rescue mission and arrived at camp three after an all-day climb. They found the tent belonging to Dalvey and Culshaw and continued on towards the summit, but with the blizzard still blowing, and no sign of the men, the rescue team was forced to turn back and make its way down to a lower camp. A second search was launched when the blizzard cleared two days later, in the hopes that Dalvey and Culshaw might have reached one of the lower camps, but there was still no trace of the men. The team was forced to accept the fact that no one could have survived out in the open at that altitude. There was some speculation as to whether the two men might have reached the summit, but the papers said that it was "beyond doubt" that they had perished.

The King had sent a message to the families of Dalvey and Culshaw, which the papers also printed. "They will ever be remembered," it said, "as fine examples of mountaineers, ready to risk their lives for their companions and to face dangers on behalf of science and discovery."

"Well," said Mrs. Reave as she slid the toast expertly across the table, "if you ask me, they shouldn't have been up there in the first place. What were they after, anyway? There's nothing there but snow, at least as far as I can gather."

"You're absolutely right, Mrs. Reave," I said, hoping she would leave me in peace to read the other papers.

"Right about what?" Her brittle hands fastened on her hips.

I sighed. "About whatever point you are trying to make."

She eyed me suspiciously, tilting her head to the side and back again in a gesture that reminded me of a parrot. "It's just daft is all," she said. "You'd be the first to agree, wouldn't you, Mr. Bromley? You're a nice sensible chap. Got yourself a steady job teaching those toff kids. Don't go running around taking unnecessary risks. Isn't that right, Mr. Bromley? We all took enough risks in the war. Even those of us who stayed at home. The war made life cheap. Now we got to make it precious once again."

"Well said, Mrs. Reave," I told her. And this time I meant it.

"Don't you think," she continued, "that those two blokes would rather be sitting here beside you having a nice cup of my tea instead of being frozen solid on some mountain in Parsimonia?"

"I think it's *Patagonia*, Mrs. Reave."

"Doesn't much matter where it is if they're dead, does it?" With that, she retreated behind her barricade of cups and saucers and began furiously sweeping the floor with a worn-out broom. A moment later, she stopped and looked out at the street. "Quiet today," she muttered, as much to herself as to me. "Even for a Sunday."

After saying good-bye to Mrs. Reave, I headed out into the street. There, I stopped and looked around. A sadness filled the damp and dreary street. I could feel it, in the same way I could sense the approach of rain. It was as if the great life of the city itself, made up of all the millions of lives within its boundaries, had sighed at the deaths of those two men. And suddenly London looked a little more run-down, the bricks a little dirtier, the rooftops of the houses bowed like the backs of tired horses.

Just then, I noticed a man sitting on my doorstep. It took me a second to recognize that the man was Stanley. He sat hunched over, staring at the pavement, the end of a cigarette smoldering between his fingers. I realized he must have come to tell me about his breakup with Helen. "It's over then," I called to him as I crossed the street.

Stanley glanced up, bleary-eyed. His hair stuck up in tufts. He looked like an owl knocked out of its nest. "If that's the way you want to put it," he replied, flicking his cigarette into the gutter.

"She told me everything," I said, as my thoughts returned to normal. "I don't blame you, Stan. I might have done the same thing in your shoes."

"What are you talking about?" he asked.

"About you and Helen," I said uncertainly.

Stanley shook his head. "It's my uncle."

"Carton? What about him?"

"William, he is dead."

A picture appeared in my head of Carton kneeling in the alleyway, the handkerchief placed carefully beneath his knee. "What happened?" I stammered.

"I got a call from our family doctor. Apparently my uncle called him and told him to come by, but when the doctor got there, it was already too late."

"I'm awfully sorry, Stan" was all I managed to say. "His lungs must have given out."

Stan glared at me through bloodshot eyes. "I feel like a murderer," he said.

"That's ridiculous!" I spluttered.

He shook his head slowly. "You told me something was wrong with him. I should have listened to you. Instead of that, I just passed it off as business as usual."

"You were right, though, Stan," I explained. "He was like that all the time. Coughing and spluttering. You said so yourself. I didn't know what I was talking about." I would have said anything to make him feel better.

Stanley pulled his coat around him as if there were a cold wind blowing. "Poor old Uncle Henry," he muttered.

"Look," I said. "I'll cook us up something to eat. Afterwards we can go down to your uncle's club to see if there's anything we can do to help. That's better than sitting around doing nothing."

He nodded and rose wearily to his feet.

✳

I FRIED EGGS AND BACON and spread marmalade on toast, all of which Stanley ate in thankless, brooding silence. When at last he shoved his plate away, I sat down at the opposite end of the table. "Better?" I asked.

"Much better, thank you." He reached across to the pot of marmalade, fetched his teaspoon from the saucer, and began to eat the marmalade by itself. "So she told you everything, did she?" he asked without looking up.

"Well, the stuff about our upcoming trip to the Himalayas, anyway."

He managed a weak smile.

"You know," I said, "I don't think you needed to tell her all that."

He wagged the teaspoon at me. "Of course I bloody did!" Now that the topic had changed to Helen Paradise, Stanley recovered some of his energy. "I had a pretty good idea what she'd think of me if I told her I'd quit climbing."

"How the hell are you going to get out of it?"

"With your help of course!" He got up from the table and began to pace the room, still waving the spoon. "All you have to do is back me up when I tell her the plan fell through on account of my uncle's death. If we both say it, then she'll have to believe us."

"You shouldn't ask me to do a thing like that."

He clicked his tongue. "If you thought you might be falling in love with somebody, wouldn't you resort to anything to keep them in your life?"

I shrugged uncomfortably, because I did not know.

"Oh, but why am I asking you?" he snapped. "You've kept the world at arm's length for so long that you probably have no idea what I'm talking about." With that, he flopped onto my couch, placed a cushion over his face, and fell asleep so quickly that he didn't even hear me tell him to bugger off.

Stanley slept all morning and halfway through the afternoon, while I tried reading the papers. Mostly, however, I thought of what he had said about me keeping the world at arm's length and wondered if it was going to be like this forever.

Late in the afternoon, I was just getting ready to wake Stanley, so that we could go over to the Climbers' Club before it closed, when the bell rang downstairs.

I went down, opened the door, and found a tall, elderly man waiting in the street. His white hair was combed straight back on his head and he wore a suit made of heavy reddish-brown wool. The toe caps of his black shoes were spit-polished and he was carrying a small brown briefcase, on which the brass latch was also polished. "I'm Dr. Webb," he said.

"I didn't call for a doctor," I told him.

"I'm actually looking for Stanley." Dr. Webb cleared his throat. "I was told he might be here."

"Oh. Yes, he is." I stepped aside. "I beg your pardon."

"You're William Bromley, aren't you?" he asked.

"That's right, sir."

"Sorry to barge in on you like this. I expect you know what it's about."

"I think so, sir."

"How is Stanley taking the news?" asked Dr. Webb. "Doing all right, is he?"

"More or less, but he's asleep at the moment."

Dr. Webb stopped. "Do you suppose I should come back later?" he said without turning around.

"I think it would depend on what you have to tell him."

He thought about this for a moment. The fingers of his left hand drummed on the banister. "I'll wake him," he said quietly.

Stanley was already awake when we walked in. He sat upright on the couch, rubbing the sleep from his eyes. "What time is it?" he asked.

"There's someone here to see you," I told him.

Through bleary eyes, he blinked at the man. "Dr. Webb!" he exclaimed, and rose to his feet.

The two of them shook hands.

"Dr. Webb is the Carton family physician," Stanley told me, "although given that I am the only one left, I hope he has found other means of drawing income."

Dr. Webb gave a short, flustered laugh. "I'm here because I've got some news that I think you should hear. I didn't want to say it over the phone. I felt I ought to tell you personally."

"That doesn't sound good," muttered Stanley.

"Do you want me to leave the room?" I asked.

"No," said Dr. Webb. "That won't be necessary. What I have to tell you is that Henry Carton committed suicide."

Stanley blinked at him, too shocked to speak.

"That can't be right," I said. "His lungs were giving out. He was dying anyway. You must be mistaken."

"It's true, I'm afraid," said Webb.

"But what happened?" asked Stanley. "I mean exactly."

Dr. Webb winced. "Surely there's no need to go into the details . . ."

"I want to know what happened," demanded Stanley. "I want to know exactly and I want to know now."

Dr. Webb sighed and then nodded. "Carton had called in to say he was having more trouble than usual with his breathing. I went straight over, but by the time I arrived, it was too late. He'd hung himself. One end of the rope was tied around the horns of that wildebeest on the stairs. His neck was not broken, but his windpipe was crushed. As I told you on the phone, I found him myself, so there can be no doubt about it being suicide."

Now I was the one who felt like a murderer. Or at least someone who had not prevented one. I had seen he was about to break. That thing I'd called fragility. It had not been my imagination after all.

Webb glanced down at his shoes and up again. "I'm sorry to be the bearer of such bad news."

We stood there in silence. I heard the clock ticking in my bedroom.

Webb looked at his watch. "Stanley, you had best come with me now. There are many things that need to be arranged."

Obediently, Stanley went to fetch his coat.

I saw them to the door and then went back upstairs.

That night, as I was lying in bed and trying to fall asleep, an image appeared to me of Carton. It was as if I were looking down at him through the dark glass eyes of the animal. I saw him alone in his club, sitting on a chair he had fetched from the dining room and neatly fashioning the noose. He tied the thirteen-banded knot, swung it over the horns, and pulled it tight. I saw the expression of calm determination on his face, the way his mustache twitched. With a grunt, he climbed up onto the chair and fitted the noose around his neck. He stood there for a while, looking out over the shadows of his club. Then, with a savage jerk, he kicked the chair out from under himself. His back thumped against the wall. The horns creaked as they took the weight. The blood vessels burst in the old man's face. His eyes rolled round to white and his lips turned blue. The last of his cigar-smoky breath trailed out into the dust-speck constellations drifting through the room.

❄

THE END OF THE TERM was only one week off. The seniors had already begun their mental graduation from the school, which took place long before their bodies were permitted to depart. Although I couldn't blame them, I sometimes felt as if I ought to be conducting séances, in which I'd have a better chance of making contact with them than in the teaching of my class.

I finished my last lesson for the afternoon and shuffled over to the department room for a "brew-up" with Higgins and Houseman before the weekly faculty meeting.

I arrived to find them in their usual positions—Higgins sprawled on the couch reading the sporting news, and Houseman lying on his bench, *De Bello Gallico* shielding his eyes.

But I saw, beneath the visor of that tattered book, that his eyes were open, his head leaned slightly to one side. Following his gaze, I turned to see Darcey Kidder standing at the pigeon-holes, delivering the weekly paychecks.

A second glance at Higgins revealed that he was only pretending to read the paper. In reality, his eyes were fixed on Darcey Kidder.

"Oh hello!" I said cheerfully.

This earned me one annoyed grunt each from Higgins and Houseman.

Darcey Kidder glanced at me. "Hello, Mr. Bromley," she said, and immediately turned back to her task.

For a while, the only sound was of the paycheck envelopes sliding into the wooden slots and clicking against the back wall.

"Would you like some tea?" I asked Miss Kidder, as I poured myself a cup.

Higgins glared at me. Offering Miss Kidder tea, and being refused, was his department.

Houseman's eyes glinted from under his book.

"No thank you," replied Miss Kidder. "I've just had a cup. Besides, I don't think they give you the same stuff as they give us in the headmaster's office." She wrinkled her nose, to show that our tea was decidedly inferior.

Higgins laughed uproariously, as if this was the funniest thing he'd ever heard.

Houseman pretended to remain asleep.

Miss Kidder stood back from the pigeonholes, having delivered the last of the paychecks. "Enjoy your weekend, gentlemen," she said. Then she strode out of the room, but as she did so, something slipped from her pocket. It was a small blue fountain pen with a golden arrow for a clip.

It hadn't even hit the floor before Higgins was lunging to catch it. Houseman also sprang into action. His book spiraled into the air.

The two men, both of them with arms extended, collided head to head, with a sound like two coconuts knocking together. They fell back, groaning, but Houseman struggled to regain his balance. By now, the pen had landed on the tattered carpet. Houseman's fingers were just about to close around it when the book, which had been silently pirouetting up in the rafters of the room, fell and smacked him on the head. With a sigh, Houseman subsided onto his back. The two men lay there, stunned and blinking at the ceiling.

This allowed me to step forward, pick up the pen, and stride out into the hall on the trail of Miss Kidder.

She was heading down the center of the corridor, the heels of her shoes clicking against the polished wooden floor. Her dress swished in rhythm with her stride. The notices pinned to corkboards on the walls fluttered slightly as she passed.

"Miss Kidder," I said. Then I changed my mind and shouted, "Darcey!"

She stopped. She turned. Her face was nearly hidden in the gloomy shadows of the hallway. "Yes?"

"You dropped your pen." I held it up so she could see.

"Oh!" She checked her pocket. "So I have." She retraced her steps to me and held out her hand. "Thank you, Mr. Bromley," she said.

"You're welcome, Miss Kidder." I set the pen in her hand and watched her fingers close around it.

She stood there, not moving, looking me right in the eye.

I opened my mouth to ask her out for a drink, for tea, for any excuse to spend some time with her.

But before I could get the words out of my mouth, she thanked me again and turned away.

"You're welcome," I replied, and watched her go.

I wanted to call out to her, but something seemed to paralyze me and I only stood there in silence. It's just nerves, I told myself. Nothing to worry about. Next time will be different.

Back in the common room, Higgins and Houseman were still on the floor, rubbing their heads.

"You gave it back to her!" blurted Higgins. "Bloody oozlebart!"

"Whatever that means," I said. "Of course I gave the pen back to her."

"What did you go and do that for?" mumbled Houseman.

"What else was I supposed to do with it?" I asked.

"Keep it!" they chorused.

"And take it home," continued Higgins, "and guard it with your life."

Houseman rose shakily to his feet. "You just don't get it," he told me.

"But I got the pen, didn't I?" I replied.

They scowled at me, but then their anger faded into curiosity.

"Did you ask her out?" inquired Higgins.

"Timing wasn't right," I said dismissively.

This answer seemed to satisfy them.

"She's a lovely bint," said Higgins dreamily.

"Smells nice," added Houseman.

"*Sarkam?*" asked Higgins, which was his way of asking the time in God knows what borrowed language.

I looked at my watch. "Damn," I said. "We've only got ten minutes until the faculty meeting."

One thing the headmaster would not tolerate was lateness to faculty meetings. It was one of his favorite pastimes to point out to anyone shambling into his chambers after the four o'clock bell had rung that we had no right to expect punctuality from our students if we could not be punctual ourselves. The year before, he had even fired a faculty member for consistently showing up late to these meetings. What was more, he insisted that we show up in what was called "standard change." This meant smart jacket and tie, not the tired old stuff in which we taught our classes.

I kept a set of standard change clothing in the storage closet in my classroom, in order that I wouldn't have to go home to dress again and then come all the way back to school.

I raced across the courtyard, threadbare tie flapping around my neck.

Five minutes later, I emerged from the storage closet, spiffed out in my standard change, to find Dr. Webb standing in the classroom.

He was so out of place that for a moment I couldn't recall who he was. "Hello again," I said, once I had remembered.

"Sorry to keep dropping in on you like this." Webb peered around the classroom, taking in the various maps on the walls and names scrawled on the blackboard.

"Peloponnesian War, is it?" he asked.

"That's right," I said hurriedly. "Athens, Sparta. Lots of blood and treachery. The students seem to like it." I glanced not very subtly at my watch. "You've caught me at a bit of a bad time. I've actually got to go, I'm afraid."

"Ah, of course. Then I suppose I should get right to it." He reached into the chest pocket of his jacket and pulled out an envelope. "I have a message for you," he said.

"From whom?" I started walking for the door.

"From Henry Carton." He held out the letter. "The late Henry Carton, I should say. Perhaps you would like to read it."

I stopped in my tracks. "Is this some sort of joke?"

"I assure you it is not." By now the letter was quivering slightly in his grasp. "I found this letter on his body. It contains a request. Several requests, actually, one of which concerns you."

I heard the sound of running in the courtyard and saw a couple of junior teachers dashing past, doing up their ties as they went. I turned back to Webb. "Why didn't you tell me when you came by yesterday?"

"Because I needed to speak to you in private."

"Look, Dr. Webb, can this wait a bit? I've got to be at a meeting in about three minutes."

"No," he said. "It really can't wait."

I sighed. "All right," I said. "What are these requests?"

"Carton asked that his body be embalmed."

"Embalmed? What? Like an Egyptian mummy?" I laughed. "Well, I can't help you with that! My knowledge of history doesn't go back further than the Greeks."

"No." Webb smiled faintly. "That is what he asked of me. It's what he asked of you that I am here about."

By now I should have been arriving at the headmaster's chambers, leaving me just enough time to take my seat between Higgins and Houseman before the headmaster breezed in and shut the door behind him. "Look, I've got to go. Otherwise . . ."

"Otherwise what?"

"Otherwise I'm done for! The headmaster—"

Webb cut me off. "What I have to explain to you is that Henry Carton wants his body to be placed in a sealed metal coffin and transported to the Alps"—and here he paused—"by you."

I narrowed my eyes. "But there must be funeral directors who can transport bodies overseas. I'm sure it happens all the time."

"It's a little more complicated than just transporting him, Mr. Bromley. He would like his body taken to the top of Carton's Rock."

Just then, I heard the school bell ring. Now the headmaster would leave his study, walk down the green-carpeted corridor to the side door of his chambers, which was his own private entrance. He would complete this little journey by the time the clock struck four. Then the main doors would be closed. Attendance would be taken. The meeting would begin.

As the last bell died away, I felt my heart sink. "Oh, God," I muttered. "The headmaster is going to ring my neck."

"I'm sure that your headmaster, like Carton himself, has complete confidence in your abilities. The only sticking point for Carton was whether Stanley would be up to the task."

I stared at Webb. "You mean he wants Stanley to do this as well?"

Webb nodded.

"Well, you can stop right there!" I shouted and did not care that I was shouting. "Stanley wouldn't sign up for a job like this. Not in a million years."

Webb looked confused. "Actually, he's already agreed to do it."

I felt the breath catch in my throat. At first I couldn't believe it. But then I understood. "He's trying to impress that woman is all! He won't do it! He'll find some excuse. He's good at that."

"In the event that this falls through," continued Webb, "Henry Carton will be cremated and his ashes scattered in the Thames off Waterloo Bridge."

I thought about the ashes, the million flecks of gray sinking into that greasy brown tide, joining with all the nameless Celts and Romans and Vikings and Normans whose bones lay crumbling in its mud, and the now-tarnished brass of Stanley's ON WAR SERVICE badge, which he had thrown from that same

bridge into the water years ago. To insist upon such an anonymous and undignified finale was, for Carton, as much of a
statement as being dragged to the top of a mountain. He had
made this an all-or-nothing proposition.

"You would be setting off as soon as your teaching duties
are completed for the term," continued Webb. "That's in about
two weeks, isn't it?"

"One week actually. Exams begin tomorrow."

"According to the letter," Webb continued, "you would
need to get up the mountain before the first snow falls, which
I'm told might happen as early as September. Carton has provided a small budget, as much as he could afford, so you will be
able to hire a few guides. If all goes well, you could be back by
the end of the summer." Now he paced across the classroom
and came to a stop in front of the window which looked out
onto the courtyard. "In the event that you are successful,
Stanley is to be placed in charge of his own inheritance.
Otherwise, the bank is to dispense it in the same amounts as he
is currently receiving, which I gather Stanley does not consider adequate."

"And me?" I asked.

He glanced back. "Nothing," he said. "Not a penny."

"Why should I do this?" I demanded. "Give me one good
reason."

"I can't," he replied. "I am only delivering the message.
Perhaps Mr. Carton thought you knew the answer for yourself."

We stepped outside the classroom and I walked Dr. Webb
to the school gates, where a car was waiting for him.

Webb got into the car, then rolled down the window and
handed me his card. "I need to have your answer by the end of
tomorrow. I can't hold things off any longer than that. You can

telephone me at my office." Then his car sped off, joining the streams of traffic heading in and out of the city.

When he was out of sight, I took the old tin from my pocket, ready to roll myself a smoke. But a sudden gust of wind tipped it out of my grasp. The tin landed with a clatter on the road. Crumbs of tobacco and the rolling papers spilled out. Quickly, I bent down to pick them up, but the breeze got to them first and swept them away.

Without thinking, I ran out into the road, chasing the little bits of paper. It was only when a car narrowly missed me that I stumbled over to the narrow concrete verge which separated the lanes of cars. A second later, a car ran over the tin and flattened it.

The fragile cigarette papers flitted about in the air.

Oblivious to the oncoming traffic, I stared at the drifting white shapes.

I was remembering something, but at first I could not tell what it was. This was no nightmare, as the sound of the apple had been. The emotions of this other memory had begun to reach me before the memory itself. They were strong but muddled, a kind of exhilaration bordering on fear, but not fear itself. There was hope. There was determination.

And then at last I began to see. Those cigarette papers were transforming into the substance of the memory. As the picture came slowly into focus, everything around me started to disappear. It was as if the place in which I stood had begun to dissolve. The particles that held the solid world together were flying apart and behind where they had been this memory was still alive, still happening, as if it were not in fact a memory at all. Rather, it seemed as if everything that had happened to me since then held no more substance than a dream.

I felt myself drawn forward through the tattered veil of this peaceful London evening.

Then all about me was the rush of air. The canopy of a parachute mushroomed above my head. I drifted downward through the night sky, the sound of the plane already fading. In its place I felt more than heard the great familiar stillness of the mountains.

SIX

I T WAS STILL DARK when we leaped from the Dakota. I heard the rustle and thump of our parachutes deploying, then looked down to see our cloudlike shadows drifting over the Palladino Valley. A few seconds later, we landed in the dew-soaked grass of a meadow beside the San Michele woods.

By the time we had stashed the chutes, unloaded the drop canisters, strapped on our gear, and found the road, the sun was rising on a clear, cold day.

Now that we had begun our climb we were in full view of anyone who looked up to the hills. Despite this, there was no sense of danger. Palladino looked so peaceful down below, wisps of smoke rising from its crooked chimney pots.

For the first quarter of a mile, as the road climbed steeply, the path was more or less intact. Beyond that, just after the first bend, the going became much harder. Portions of the road had collapsed, leaving gaps in the path over which we had to jump or else move with the slow precision of tortoises, to avoid setting loose any more of the earth. In other places, the ground from above had slumped down, so instead of jumping over gaps, we now had to climb across the loose earth and stones of these small avalanches.

Our progress was slow. The weight of our packs and the added burden of the beacon parts soon had us all soaked in sweat. It was a beautiful day, however, and we found it almost impossible to believe that away to the south, whole armies were clashing together. The first reminder we had of the war was a series of contrails in the sky, great chalky cat scratches, at the tips of which we could just make out the planes themselves. From where we stood, the planes were a luminous white. They looked like chips of ice up in the blue. Separate streams of condensation from the engines on each wing merged to form one trail behind every plane. There seemed to be hundreds of these trails, but it was impossible to count since some planes were flying directly above others, so that when the planes were directly above us, the lines blurred together into one huge path across the vault of the sky. Only after they had passed could we hear the rumble of their engines.

We watched and listened for a while, trying to imagine the men up in those planes, swathed in sheepskin, the pilots trying to stay in formation, the gunners watching the frost build up on the barrels of their .50-calibers, the navigators squinting down upon the brightness of sun off snow and seeing the world below as we had seen it on the map at Achnacarry—a smooth, clean maze of ice and stone, the height of mountains measured only by the shadows they cast across the surrounding glaciers.

Turning back to the crumbling path, I thought how for the next few days we would measure this world not with maps and the blink of an eye but in sweat and the shuffling of our boots.

The road jackknifed twice more before it leveled out, by which time we were well above the tree line. Here, the ground was covered with stunted grass and lichen. Snow clung to the hollows. Icicles dripped from the lips of stones. Some of these were huge and had been propped at precarious angles by the glaciers which had left them behind.

Our original schedule, as devised by Carton, had allowed us two hours to reach this place. But either because he had misjudged it or because the breaks in the road and the weight of the gear had slowed us down so much, we did not get to the level ground until midafternoon and still had several kilometers to go before we reached the customs house.

The schedule didn't seem to matter much, however. We were on our own now, and appeared to have the entire range to ourselves. Scrabbling up the mountainside on that beautiful autumn day, there were times when I almost managed to forget that we were carrying weapons, and that we had been ordered to kill anyone we came across between here and the Swiss border.

Shortly afterwards, we stopped to rest and brew up tea.

Then, shouldering our packs, we continued along the gravel road. It was bordered on both sides by ditches, along which a shallow but steady stream of water splashed over the stony ground.

My body swung once more into the rhythm of the march. My vision narrowed in on the heels of Whistler walking before me and the tidily rolled ends of his canvas pack straps.

It was only a moment later that I heard the strange, dry,

popping crack which I at first failed to understand was the sound of a gun.

Whistler tripped, or so it seemed to me. He fell down hard on his face and the heavy Bergen pack slipped over his head.

I stumbled to avoid tripping over him. Once I had regained my balance, I reached down to help him up, still wondering what that sound could have been and thinking that it must have been the ice cracking out in the glacier.

Then I saw Sugden and Forbes scrabbling down into the ditch on the other side of the road. Armstrong jumped for cover, landing with a splash in the ditch nearest to me. Then he turned and shouted to me. His face was white.

I looked from Armstrong to Whistler, and then out towards the glacier and the lake. My gaze swept over the boulder-strewn ground. Only now did I fully grasp that we had come under fire

"Come on!" shouted Armstrong.

I stumbled towards him.

His hand reached out to me, fingernails dirty with gun oil.

I dropped into the ditch beside him.

Hurriedly I took out my binoculars. With Armstrong ready to shoot, I scanned the ground between us and the lake, from where the shot appeared to have come.

After finally locating the sniper, I ducked down and indicated the spot to Armstrong. Slowly, the way people sometimes move in dreams, he raised his rifle and took aim.

I crouched beside him, breathing hard. My head rested against the side of the ditch. The binoculars were still clutched in my hand.

Then I heard a sound right by my face, like someone biting into an unripe apple. Armstrong's face became a blur. His legs gave way and he fell in a heap at the bottom of the trench.

Armstrong lay on his back with his legs twisted under him. His hands were thrown out to the sides and his fingers curled gently over his open palms. His head looked lopsided, squashed like a stepped-on loaf of bread. It seemed to be pressed into the wall of the ditch, but then I realized that the left side of his face was missing. A bullet had gone through his right ear and come out somewhere around his left cheekbone. His mouth was open and his shattered teeth were stained red.

Immediately after came another gunshot, which made me flinch and close my eyes. When I opened them again, I saw Sugden running across the road. He tumbled in beside me, breathing hard. The rim of his helmet, its surface roughened by sand sprinkled over the paint when it was wet, cut a sharp line across his brow. "I got the sniper when he came out from behind the rock," he said. As his eyes met mine, a look of horror spread across his face. Immediately, he began tearing at his pocket, trying to pull out one of the field-dressing bandages we all carried.

"It's no good," I told Sugden. "Armstrong's dead."

"This isn't for him," replied Sugden, his breathing shallow and fast. "It's for you."

"But I'm not hurt," I told him. Then I touched a hand to my face and saw blood on my fingers. "It's not mine," I said, pointing a red-smeared finger at Armstrong.

Sugden paused, the half-unraveled bandage clutched in his hands. Almond-colored eyes glowed in his sunburned face. "Oh, Christ," he whispered.

Now Forbes left cover and made his way across the road. He stopped in the middle, grabbed Whistler by his pack straps, and dragged him to the edge of the ditch before jumping down beside us.

We could see for certain that Whistler was dead. His eyes remained open. The bullet had gone in through the right side of his chest. It must have hit him in the heart and killed him instantly.

Armstrong's blood tinted the water sluicing past my feet.

I glanced at Sugden and Forbes. Each of their faces bore the same pale mask, which blurred their features into the same hollowed-out expression of fear.

"There couldn't just be one man up here by himself," said Forbes, his voice trembling. "He must be part of a patrol."

"Then why was only one man shooting at us?" asked Sugden.

We squinted at one another in the bright light, sweat dried powdery and white in the corners of our eyes.

"He might have been a sentry," I said hopefully.

"Guarding what?" demanded Sugden, but before anyone had time to answer, he had figured out the answer for himself. "They're in the customs house," he said.

But if this was true, then how many were there? We did not even know if the customs house existed anymore.

Forbes took off his glasses and rubbed his reddened eyes. "What are we going to do?" he whispered, more to himself than to us.

"We must turn back," answered Sugden. His breathing was shallow and fast.

I stared at him. It was the first time I had ever heard him speak of turning back from anything.

"There's no point going back," I told them both. "Switzerland is that way." I pointed up the road in the direction we had been going.

"Then let's just forget about the beacon and move on into

Switzerland," Sugden protested. "We can't do the job. Not now. Not with two men gone." He scratched at the side of his face, leaving red lines through the dirt that pasted his skin.

Then I remembered what Carton had told me back at Achnacarry—that the beacon was the most important thing. More important than me. More important than my friends. I had not believed for an instant that it would ever come to this, but now I knew what choice I had to make. "We will still make the climb," I told them.

The two men stared at me in silence, as if they could not believe what I'd just said.

I met their gaze and held it. "The rules are different now," I whispered.

Sugden turned away and spat. "What do you say, Forbes?" he asked.

"Sugden," I said as firmly as I could, "it's my decision."

He turned on me. "I don't care about your decision! I want to know what Forbes thinks." Bringing his dirty face close to Forbes, he whispered, "What's it going to be?"

Forbes blinked Sugden's breath out of his eyes. He cleared his throat. "I don't want to be here any more than you do," he said.

I gritted my teeth. With two of them against me, there would be no hope of completing the task.

"Then it's settled!" Sugden hissed. "We head back down the valley. We'll hide out until things quiet down, then make it through to Allied lines."

"No," said Forbes.

"What do you mean?" Sugden's face was twisted with disbelief.

Forbes aimed one black-rimmed fingernail at Sugden. "If we pack it in now, Armstrong and Whistler will have died for

THE ICE SOLDIER | 155

nothing. No matter how badly I want to get out of this, I say we push on and get the job done."

Sugden's eyes darted from Forbes to me and back again. His hands curled into fists, the knuckles turning white as he squeezed the blood out of them. "Fine," he spat. "Then let's get on with it. Don't say I didn't warn you."

We prepared to move out. Pushing into some backwater of our minds the wretchedness of going through the pockets and the packs of our two dead friends, we shared among ourselves the pieces of the beacon they had been carrying. After we had redistributed the equipment, we took the food from the dead men's packs, then filled our pockets with additional ammunition. Lastly, we took their dog tags.

"We'd better go and get that other man out of sight," I said. I could see him lying out there in the open, beside the rock where he had taken cover.

With Sugden and Forbes standing by, I ran to where he lay.

The soldier was on his back. Sugden's bullet had hit him in the throat, exposing his torn windpipe and the milk-white tendons of his neck. The features of his face were sharp, his lips thin and pale. The way that death had pinched his skin, I could not tell how old he was.

He wore a greenish-gray tunic made of shabby wool, held together with gray pebbled buttons and a black leather belt. On the belt were two sets of leather ammunition pouches. One of them was open, and bullets had spilled out over the ground. Also on the belt was a green canvas bag on which he had clipped a wool-covered canteen. His helmet lay upturned beside him. The fact that he wasn't carrying a pack confirmed that he must have been using the customs house for a base.

I took his paybook from the top right pocket of his tunic and was getting ready to go through his other pockets when

Sugden called for me to hurry. I grabbed hold of the man's heavy mountain boots and dragged him behind the rock, where he would not be seen from the road.

There was no time to bury Whistler and Armstrong, so we dragged their bodies behind the flat rock and laid them beside the German who had killed them. Then we spread a ground sheet over the three men and pinned it down with stones.

When Sugden, Forbes, and I moved out, we walked in the ditch, stumbling over uneven ground and splashing through the shallow stream.

Water seeped into my boots. The weight of the extra equipment hung across my shoulders, and the muscles of my thighs strained to handle the burden of my pack. The way sloped gently upwards until we reached the crest of the rise. From here, nestled under a great overhang of rock, we at last spotted the customs house about five hundred yards away. It was a wooden log-cabin type of structure, built up against the rock itself. Flat stones of various colors, some green, some brown, some smoky blue, overlapped unevenly to form its roof. On the opposite side of the road stood a small guard-house and the supports for a wooden boom for raising and lowering across the road. Now only the supports remained in place. The boom itself lay in the water at the edge of the lake, just beside the guardhouse. In place of the boom, the road was blocked by barbed wire. It had been strung onto several X-shaped frames which were staggered across the road.

We crawled forward, so as not to silhouette ourselves against the skyline. I took out the binoculars again and looked for signs of life. Sunlight reflected off the barbed wire, showing that it had recently been placed there. The area outside the front door was protected by a chest-high crescent of sandbags.

I could also see that, just to the side of the customs house, there was some kind of stairway leading belowground.

I saw no people, however, nor any sign of vehicles or radio antennas. For a moment, I allowed myself to feel some relief that the place might have been occupied only by a couple of men. And perhaps, at the sound of the gunfire, these men had fled.

A short distance beyond the customs house, the lake curved around towards the glacier. That was the route we'd have to take to get out on the ice and begin our march towards Carton's Rock. We could not circle down below the customs house, as the mountain face formed a sheer drop to the valley floor. The site for the building had been well chosen. Anyone who wanted to travel this way had to get by under the shadow of that rock, right past the front door of the house.

The approach was entirely out in the open. There was no way we could sneak by in daylight. If anyone saw us, we would be gunned down before we'd gone more than a few hundred yards.

We decided to wait and then try to slip past in the dark. With no sign of a radio antenna, we assumed that whomever was there had no radio contact with any units standing by down in the valley. We would have to get by them, but they would have to get by us as well. They would have to cross the same open ground.

We removed our packs and took cover in the ditch. The sun was going down. In the distance we could hear the wind out on the glacier. It blew across the ice and ruffled the surface of the lake, then raked against our faces with a bone-hollowing chill.

As sunset bronzed the air, we heard the noises of engines and saw one, then two, then three planes flying overhead in loose formation. They must have been part of the squadrons we had seen earlier in the day, now returning from their mission. They were much lower than before, and I could see the white-star insignia and distinctive turned-up noses of B-24 Liberators.

I realized how little chance these planes would have stood if they had been flying through clouds on their return journey. Luck alone would bring them through these jagged hills. But soon, perhaps, they would have more than luck, and it seemed amazing to me that this small beacon might save the lives of so many men. Thinking about this allowed me to balance out what had happened to Whistler and Armstrong. The knowledge of their deaths was sinking in, past the fact of it, past the grief of it, to the cold acceptance of their bodies left behind.

Sugden, Forbes, and I took turns keeping an eye on the customs house as well as on the road behind us, in case someone approached from that direction. The third person tried to get some rest. When it was my turn, I lay with my scarf across my eyes. Sun winked through the crossed threads of the wool, which smelled of sweat and old tobacco smoke. For a while I drifted back and forth across the veil of consciousness.

As soon as the sun disappeared behind the customs house, the air became very cold. We waited through the long twilight, until a fingernail of moon rose above the glacier. Stars riddled the darkness in the east, but in the west, the sky was clouding over.

We smeared our faces and hands with mud, not only to camouflage ourselves but also to distinguish between friend and enemy once we got to the customs house. There, if we ran into anyone, it would be too dark and confusing to differentiate between German and British uniforms. Anyone with a pale face would be killed.

We moved slowly down towards the customs house, carrying all our gear. The plan was to stop a hundred yards from the barbed wire, then creep forward and see if we could shift the entanglements by hand.

The three of us spread out about ten paces apart, navigating the uneven terrain while keeping an eye on the customs house, which by now was completely hidden in shadow.

I had become convinced that the place was empty. There were no lights, no smell of smoke or food. Slithering across the crumbling earth, I was soon sweating again under the weight of my pack. The stones over which I crawled were as sharp as coral. I could feel their edges gouging my knees and the blood cooling as it trickled from these wounds. In places, the dry earth gave way to patches of damp ground, in which water black as tar welled up from the moss and leeched into my clothes. If I tried to raise myself, my arms only sank deeper into the wet earth. Whenever I stopped to catch my breath, I could hear the faint sound of the others crawling beside me. By now, the clouds had blown in from the west, and a soft rain began to fall.

We reached the bottom of the rise and were now level with the customs house. The building remained dark and silent. The wire bunched like a haze at the horizon of my little world. Wind off the glacier whistled around the roof of the guard shack. I could feel my heartbeat thumping in my neck.

We were only a hundred yards from the wire.

As agreed, we undid the straps of our rucksacks and left them lying on the ground with the rope, the climbing axes, and the equipment belts we had been issued. Sweat which had pooled against my back under the rucksack quickly chilled now that the pack was off. As soon as we had secured the customs house, we would go back for our gear, then carry on

around the edge of the lake to the departure point for our glacier crossing.

I made sure that my rifle and Webley revolver were loaded
and stuffed two Mills grenades into my pockets. From my
pack I removed the trench club I had been given by Carton.
The cold ball of lead at the end of the club seemed to glow. I
looked across at the others.

Sugden's eyes shone in his mud-crusted face. He was
watching me.

I wondered if he was waiting for me to change my mind
and give the order to fall back.

But then he started crawling forward.

I began to move as well, keeping the rifle across my back
and the Webley in my hand.

The rain was falling harder now. The black air hissed as if
snakes were slithering above our heads.

We were fifty yards from the wire when I heard a cracking
sound.

I knew immediately that it was a flare. I even saw the yellow sparks as they left the flare gun's barrel, just behind the
wire. It was as if the flash had exploded in my chest. A trail of
burning white sliced the darkness above us.

❋

THE BLARING HORN of a truck on the road outside St. Vernon's
jarred me to my senses once again. I struggled back to the
curb.

My cigarette papers lay ground into the road by the wheels
of passing cars. The rest had blown away.

Twilight blurred the traffic racing by. Now and then, one
of the automobiles ran over the flattened remains of my emergency ration tin, which clacked against the macadam.

Until that moment, I had not known what I should do.

But now I understood.

The answer lay in the passing of these cars, the two lanes of them heading relentlessly in opposite directions. They were like the streams of time itself, one flowing into the past, the other into the future. I was stuck between them, endlessly spinning around. I had to do something to get out of it, or I would be trapped there forever.

That something was to honor Henry Carton's last request.

What I needed was the courage to go through with it.

Suddenly I knew I had just made the third and final wish, which I'd been keeping all this time and hoping that I'd never have to use.

SEVEN

I WALKED BACK TO MY FLAT and trudged up the stairs, hand gliding along the old sweat-polished banister. I fumbled in the deep pocket of my mackintosh for my keys, wondering aloud what I would have for dinner. Then I unlocked the door and, swinging it wide open with a jab of my toe, was startled to see a man standing in my living room. He was glancing out the window and had his back to me.

"Jesus Christ!" I blurted and staggered against the door frame. I was trying to decide which piece of furniture to hit him with when the man turned around and I realized it was Sugden.

The way he stood there smirking, he looked exactly like his picture in the newspaper advertisement.

"Bloody hell, Sugs!" I shouted. "You just about gave me a heart attack!"

"Sorry, Auntie!" He grinned unapologetically. His face

was red, the tip of his nose and his ears flaky white with sun-burned skin.

"What are you doing here?" I asked, trying not to sound nervous. I was not afraid of Sugden. Not of the man himself. What I feared were the memories his presence kindled in my mind.

"Making some tea." He nodded at the stove. My kettle muttered as the water warmed inside it.

I hung my umbrella on the coat stand, then shrugged off my coat and laid it over a chair. "Look, Sugs," I said. "No offense, but you can't just walk in here anytime you feel like it. This isn't the bloody dorm."

"I haven't had a decent cup of tea since I returned from Patagonia," he said, staring out the window.

"I read about what happened," I told him. "I'm sorry you had a rough time."

"Where do you keep the tea?" he asked, as if my words of condolence had not even reached his ears.

"Left cupboard in the kitchen," I said, resigning myself to the fact that Sugden had not changed since school, and that he probably had no idea he was doing anything unusual by crashing into my flat. I sat down at my kitchen table and halfheartedly swept away some bread crumbs from the bare wood surface. "What is it you want? Besides a cup of tea, I mean."

"It was a bloody mess in Patagonia," he said, stepping past me into the kitchen, where he began opening and closing the cupboards. "Men dead. Sponsors all cheesed off."

"But it was an accident. At least that's what I read."

"It was indeed an accident. Couldn't have been avoided." He found the tea tin and shook it to see if there was anything inside. "The whole thing was running like clockwork. Until it went wrong, anyway."

"People will understand," I said reassuringly.

He made a sarcastic sound with his lips. The water had boiled now. He turned off the gas and poured some of the water in the teapot. Then he cradled the pot in his hands, tipped out the water, and spooned in some tea leaves. "People won't understand. Doesn't matter why things go wrong. Only that they do." He poured hot water onto the black crumbs of the tea leaves and breathed in the steam, closing his eyes. Then he threw a dish towel over the pot to keep it warm while it brewed.

"Patagonia must have been beautiful," I said, hoping to steer the topic towards something more pleasant.

"Oh, it was." He turned again to face me, arms folded across his chest. "Speaking of beautiful places, I heard someone was making travel plans for you recently."

I shook my head, not understanding.

"Oh, come along!" He snapped his fingers in the way that our old teachers used to do when we could not answer questions fast enough. "Carton. The Alps. The coffin!"

"But how did you know?" I stammered. "I only just found out myself."

He was smiling now, pleased to have the edge on me. He came out of the kitchen, sat himself down at the other end of the table, and pattered his fingertips on the wood, as if giving a drum roll before making his next pronouncement. "It just so happens that Dr. Webb is my doctor as well as Carton's. He was giving me a checkup yesterday, to make sure I was still in one piece after coming back from South America, and he mentioned this business with the coffin."

"It's an extraordinary request," I said.

He nodded. "It certainly is. And damned awkward for you as well, I imagine."

"How so?" I asked.

He shrugged. "Well, evidently Carton had never heard of your Society of Former Mountaineers." He said these last words with a mocking plum-in-the-mouth pomposity. "So look," he continued, "the reason I'm here is because I think we can both do each other a favor."

"We can?"

"Yes, I'll explain"—he jerked his chin towards the kitchen—"while you pour the tea."

Too unnerved to protest, I obediently got up and poured the tea.

"I need to get things back on track after this business in Patagonia," he began, "and since you're not going to do it, I thought it would be a perfect thing for me. The publicity would be great. The sponsors will soon be lining up again. I have to keep my eye on that sort of thing, you see. Mountaineering is an industry, just like selling cars."

"Sugs," I said. "I'm sorry to tell you this, but I'm actually thinking of doing it." I set the chipped red mug of tea in front of him.

He was staring at me. "What?" he asked.

I told him again.

"No," he shook his head. "No, that won't do at all."

I sat down at the other end of the table, ready to explain why I needed to do this. But I didn't get the chance.

Sugden's face grew suddenly dark, as if a shadow had passed through his blood. "Henry Carton was a great man," he said.

"I know," I replied, "but what's that got to do with it?"

"There are two blemishes on the name of Henry Carton," he said, "and two only. The first"—he bent back one finger until it looked as if it was going to break—"is his wretched nephew, whom I once made the mistake of calling my friend."

My jaw clenched. "You don't have to talk about Stanley like that."

"The second," he continued, "is that God-awful mess you got us into in the war."

"For the love of God, Sugden!" I said, rising slowly to my feet. "Do you still blame me for the fact that we didn't turn back after Armstrong and Whistler got killed? Have you actually thought about what would have happened to us if we had tried to make our way out through the Palladino Valley? The nearest Allied troops were hundreds of miles to the south, with the entire Fifteenth German Army Corps between us and them. It's almost as if you think I killed those men myself. Well, Carton didn't think so, and why should you?" By now I was almost shouting.

Sugden's eyes were filled with hate. "I don't think you killed them. What you did was to bring us all together in the first place. So that we went there. So that those men died."

"But I had no way of knowing what would happen—"

He raised his doubled fist and smashed it down on the table. Tea jumped from his mug and splashed onto the bare wood. "It doesn't matter if you knew!" he howled. Then immediately his voice sank back almost to a whisper. "It's the same thing as with the sponsors for my expeditions. What matters is what happened. Not how or why or what excuses you are able to make up. We can sit here talking about it until hell freezes over, but the fact remains that if it wasn't for you, those men might still be alive. You were put in charge, whether you wanted to be or not. It all comes down to you. That's all there is to it."

I felt as if I were choking. "The board of inquiry..." I started to say.

Sugden breathed out noisily. "The board of inquiry was headed by Carton, and he put his own reputation on the line to make sure you were cleared. And why? Because he let himself be swayed by that coward you call a friend." He could not even say Stanley's name.

I managed to gasp in a breath. "You don't know any of that for a fact."

"You're right." He smiled coldly. "I don't. The only fact I know for sure is that you have no right to be alive when our old comrades are dead." He looked at me for a long time before he spoke again. "But I guess that's just something you've learned to live with, isn't it?"

My hands were shaking.

He fetched his coat and stood in the doorway. "You listen to me, Bromley. This is what you're going to do. You're going to tell Dr. Webb you've decided not to go. He'll know to pass the offer on to me. I've already explained it to him. I'll get the word out to the press. I'll even put in a good word about you and your friend. That way, you won't have to walk away from this with your tail between your legs. Then I'll get some good people together and make sure the job is done properly. This isn't some offer I'm making, Bromley. This is how it's going to be." He shook the anger from his face, like a dog shaking water from its back. "Thank you for the tea, Auntie." After flashing his Trust-in-the-Machine smile, he walked down the stairs and out of the flat, leaving the door open.

I heard the striking of a match and then the click of his iron-heeled shoes as he walked away. A moment later, a faint wisp of tobacco smoke reached the place where I was sitting.

Sugden's voice still echoed in my head. It was as if a dozen people were speaking at the same time. They were all saying the same thing: that I had no right to be alive when my old friends were dead. The voices grew louder, each one shouting to be heard above the others and all of them saying the same thing.

Suddenly I understood, with total clarity, that there was only one way to make them stop and if I did not stop them they would howl at me for the rest of my life.

I walked through the kitchen and into my bedroom. There, I hauled out a small metal trunk from under the bed. I opened it, and dug around under the pile of my old service clothing, Sam Browne belt, jerkin, balaclava, and God knows what other rubbish until my hand closed around the smooth leather slab of a holster. I opened it, drew out the Webley, surprised at the weight because I had forgotten how heavy it was. I got back on my feet and started walking towards the kitchen. As I walked, I pressed the release button and brought the barrel down to check that the cylinder was fully loaded, which it was.

I had no time to think this over. If I started thinking, I would only come unraveled and not be able to go through with it. I would sit down at the table and I would finish the business. The way to do it, I thought, is with the barrel in my mouth, gun upside down with the butt pointing towards the ceiling. That way, I did not have to pull the trigger with my thumb and risk messing things up.

Entering the living room, I almost walked right past Stanley, who was standing in the doorway.

"The door was open downstairs," he said. "Where are you going with that gun?"

I stopped and stared at him. I was shaking all over and sweat was running down my face.

"Are you going to shoot those pigeons finally?" he asked. "You know, I didn't want to say anything about it before, because I thought you were only kidding, but I think it's illegal to shoot them."

I had no idea what he was talking about, or what he was doing here. "Pigeons?" I asked. My throat had become so dry that I could barely speak. Each breath felt like hot ashes drawn into my windpipe.

Stanley tugged at his ear. "Well, I heard it was illegal, anyway. Not that it should stop you necessarily, but someone's bound to hear the noise."

I looked at the gun in my hand. Then, hurriedly, I set it down on the table.

"You heard about my uncle's last request?" he asked.

I nodded.

"It's excellent!" He picked up Sugden's tea and took a sip.

"It is?" I mumbled.

"Of course! Didn't you hear? If the trip falls through, he's going to be cremated and I still get my inheritance because I agreed to go. All I had to do was *agree*. And since you're not going, I don't have to go either." He looked at me and frowned. "Are you all right? You're sweating."

I wiped a hand across my face. "Sugden was here," I said.

Stanley's eyebrows rose. "What?"

I sat down and told him what Sugden had said about taking over the expedition.

"Bastard!" shouted Stanley. "He ought to just leave you alone!"

The gun was still lying on the table.

Stanley was staring at it. "Wait a minute," he said slowly.

I looked at him.

His eyes were narrowed into slits. He gestured towards the revolver. "You weren't thinking of . . ." He couldn't finish his sentence.

"Of course not," I said.

But he saw right through me. "My God, you were!" He lunged forward, took up the gun, and waved it at me. "Don't you bloody dare do something stupid like that!"

"Careful," I said. "It's loaded."

"I know it's loaded!" he shouted, still brandishing the gun. "That's the problem!" Then he began trying to wrench the gun apart so he could remove the bullets.

"No," I said, as he twisted the gun first one way and then another. "It doesn't go like that. Give it to me and I'll show you."

"I'm not giving this to you," he grunted.

"Look, you're going to hurt someone."

He glared at me. "And you aren't? To hell with you!"

I held out my hand. "Just give me the gun, Stan."

He was breathing hard, his eyes wild. Suddenly he set the barrel of the gun against his temple.

I stood up, chair skidding back across the floor. "Put . . . that . . . down . . . right . . . now!" I shouted, punching each word from my lungs.

"See how it feels?" he asked, still not lowering the gun. "How dare you even think of checking out and leaving me to clean up the mess. You bloody coward! First my uncle and now you! You're both bloody cowards."

I breathed in slowly. "I think all three of us are cowards, Stan, in one way or another. Now you've made your point so put the bloody gun down before . . ." I fumbled for the words.

"Yes?" asked Stanley. He was smiling, and it would have been a less demented-looking smile if he hadn't kept the gun against his head.

". . . before I tell Miss Paradise about our nonexistent Himalayan expedition!"

He blinked. "You wouldn't."

"Try me," I said.

Looking a little dazed, he at last set the gun down on the table.

I retrieved my chair and sat down. Then I reached across, took hold of the gun, opened the barrel forward, and tipped the bullets out on the table. I scooped the bullets into my hand and put them in my pocket. When that was done, I set the gun in front of me.

"What the hell happened to you up in those mountains," asked Stanley, "that simply being reminded of it should . . . ?"

"You know what happened," I said. "The mission was a failure. Some of our friends died."

"But what *happened*? You've never told me."

I wanted to tell him, but I couldn't. There had been a moment, years before at one of our binges in the Montague, when he'd asked me if I wanted to talk to him about the deaths of Forbes and Armstrong and Whistler, and the failure of the mission in general. But I had guessed from the halting way in which he'd asked the question that he was asking only because he felt he ought to.

I never did discuss it with him. Since he hadn't been there himself, I simply didn't think he'd understand. Until this moment, the subject had never resurfaced. But now I realized that even if I wanted to talk about it, I could not find the words.

Instead, I just sat there.

"It must have been terrible," he said quietly.

At the sound of his voice, tears spilled down my face.

"I didn't mean to call you a coward."

"It's all right." I knuckled the tears from my eyes. "I called you one as well."

"But I am one," said Stanley. "Otherwise I would be going on this crazy expedition my uncle planned out for us."

I cleared my throat. "You aren't a coward," I told him, "because you are going on it. And so am I."

He looked at me for a long time. It was the way you would look at a stranger. "What?" he asked eventually.

"You heard me," I said.

"Would you mind telling me why?" His forehead was creased with confusion.

"Because your uncle loved you, even if he pretended that he didn't. And you loved him too, no matter how much you might try to deny it. And if you honestly do love Helen Paradise, you'll do it for her. And I hate to say this, but you're bloody well going to do it for me as well."

He looked at me with his chin stuck out defiantly. "You bastard," he said. "You rotten bastard."

"You can call me whatever you like, but you'll do this for your uncle, and for Helen and for me because we're the only people on earth who haven't given up on you!"

At first, Stanley made no reply. He got up and, with an expressionless face, walked across the room and lowered himself into a chair by the window. It was the one where I marked student papers on Sunday evenings, and I never sat in it at any other time. The tired old cushions sighed as Stanley settled into them. Then he smiled at some private joke playing out inside his head.

"What's so funny?" I asked.

He wafted his hand dismissively in the air. "All those years," he muttered.

"All what years?"

"The years my uncle spent trying to get me to take up mountaineering again. And just when I thought he was finally through pestering me, he comes back from the grave and wins his little battle after all!"

"So you'll come?"

He shrugged carelessly, as if none of this mattered to him. But his eyes gave him away. His gaze roamed around the room, and he appeared to be looking for an escape route. "Doesn't seem as if I have much choice, does it?"

"Think of it," I told him, "as one last piece of Nitty Gritty."

He coughed out a sarcastic laugh. "I always was the Nitty Gritty Man," he said. Then suddenly he breathed in, slapped his knees, and stood up. "Right," he announced loudly. "Let's go!"

"Well, I'm glad to hear you say that," I told him, rising to my feet. "But we can't just leave. There's a lot of preparation to be done first."

He laughed. "Not to the Alps, silly! To meet Helen for dinner. We're going to that Greek place Sugden talked about."

"The one where they serve testicles?"

"Exactly." He threw me my coat.

"What better meal," I said, "to celebrate the official disbanding of the Society of Former Mountaineers?"

We were halfway out the door when something occurred to me. "I'll have to meet you there," I told him. "I've got something I have to do first."

"Don't be too late." Then he shook a finger in my face. "And I haven't said I'll go. Not yet. I'm still thinking about it."

I smiled and pushed him gently out the door.

When Stanley had left, I put the Webley in the pocket of my coat. Then I went out to the street and caught a bus to Waterloo Bridge.

It was evening.

I walked out to the middle of the bridge.

People walked past on their way home from work. None of them saw as I drew the gun from my pocket and let it slip from my hand into the dark and swirling water.

I thought of the Webley sliding down into the blackness, and the silent blossoming of silt as it landed in the mud. I thought of the battle-axes of the Vikings and the swords of Roman legionnaires, who had survived their wars in this country but found that they could not endure the peace that followed. So they had thrown away their weapons, rather than turn the blades upon themselves. And somewhere down there, too, was Stanley's polished badge, which had been, in its way, no less of a burden than those tools of war which lay around it in their tombs of mud.

✻

FOR SOME REASON, the Feast of the Gods had been removed from the menu at the Greek restaurant.

"A shortage of testicles," suggested Stanley.

I was relieved to make do with a meal of stuffed peppers and avgolemono sauce.

We did not speak of making the trip.

All through the meal, I kept my eye on Stanley, trying to read his thoughts in case my attempt to persuade him had not worked after all.

But his expression gave nothing away.

After the plates had been cleared, we sat back with little glasses of ouzo.

Stanley drank his quickly, wincing at the fire it ignited in his belly. Then he announced that he was going to find the manager and sort out whether or not Sugden really had eaten those testicles.

"You're obsessed," I told him.

He winked at me and wandered off.

"I think it's marvelous," said Helen, "what you and Stanley are doing for his uncle."

"What's that?" I asked cautiously.

She sat back. Her hand slid away. "Going to the Alps, silly!"

"Oh," I said. "So we *are* going."

She looked confused. "Well, Stanley seems to think you are. He told me all about it before you got here."

I nodded. "He hadn't been exactly clear about it when we talked."

"Well, anyway," said Helen, sipping at the ouzo, "I think it's very grand."

"Why don't you come with us?" I asked. It seemed like a good idea.

She smiled and shook her head. "I'd love to, but I can't."

"Why on earth not?"

She turned the little ouzo glass around in circles. "Because I never was a member of the Society of Former Mountaineers."

"But that was just a thing we called ourselves! It didn't exist."

"It did exist," she said, "and in many ways it was more important than that other club you both belong to."

I saw what she was saying.

"And you've got to undo what it was," she continued, "each of you for your own reasons. It's a pity, really."

"It is?"

"Yes. That you won't be going to the Himalayas."

I gritted my teeth and nodded.

She started to laugh.

"What is it?" I asked nervously, knowing this must be at my expense.

Now she laughed even harder. "I knew you weren't actually going."

"You did?" My voice rose almost to a squeak. "But how?"

"Carton told me. He said I ought not to judge Stanley too harshly."

"Well, I wish you had let me in on the joke a little earlier."

"I wanted to see how you'd get out of it." She pressed her lips together, trying not to laugh again.

"Getting out of it was Stanley's job," I told her, "seeing as he got us into it."

"I suppose I should be angry," said Helen, "but I'm not."

"Because you know, as I do, that Stanley said the stuff about the Himalayas because he wanted you to like him. And I happen to know that he likes you very much. In fact, he's completely mad about you. You're why he's going to the Alps."

"Me and the inheritance."

"No," I said. "He wants his inheritance all right, but not enough to climb this mountain. The reason he's going is you."

She turned her head to one side and rested her chin in the palm of her hand. "I suppose I was afraid of that."

"Why be afraid of it?" I asked, thinking that she looked more beautiful than ever.

For a moment, she seemed lost in thought. Then she turned to face me again, and her eyes burned into my head. "What if he gets hurt? Or you?"

"I have my own reasons, for going."

"Well, I hope they are good reasons," said Helen, "and I hope you've got a lot of luck stored away someplace, because you're both going to need it."

✳

THAT NIGHT, I put in a call to Webb. I told him it was settled. We would go.

It was quiet for a long time on the other end.

I thought we had been disconnected. "Are you still there?" I asked. "Dr. Webb?"

"This comes as a surprise." Webb's voice returned, his heavy breaths reaching me through the static like the rumble of breaking waves. "I had been led to believe you'd be turning down the offer. And Stanley, too, for that matter."

"On the contrary," I told him. "Stanley and I will be leaving as soon as we can. I'll need to draw funds. A few hundred pounds to start with. We'll need to get some gear together and book passage to the Alps."

"Of course. Whatever you need. I'll have three hundred sent over tomorrow." He held his hand partway over the receiver and coughed. "The funeral reception is the day after tomorrow at the Climbers' Club. I assume you will be there."

"Of course."

"Do you really think it can be done?" asked Webb. "The climb, I mean."

"I don't know," I replied.

"The press will have to be told. There's no way to keep this quiet. Very soon, I expect, the whole world will be watching what you do."

"I think that Carton would have wanted it that way."

"I'd heard that you would never climb again." Webb's voice merged with the static so that the static itself seemed to be speaking. "What made you change your mind?"

"Something Carton told me long ago. I just didn't understand it until now."

"What was it?" he asked. "What did he tell you?"

"He said I should hold fast to the dreams of my youth."

He repeated the words I had just said. And then he added, "I understand."

"You do?" Somehow I doubted it. He didn't seem the type to understand.

"Words like that," said Webb. "They carry the weight of the world as lightly as a feather."

Then I knew that I'd been wrong. He understood after all.

By sunset the following day, just as Webb had predicted, Stanley and I and the news of Carton's last request were on the front page of every paper in the country.

❄

THE COFFIN LAY ON a long table in the middle of the Climbers' Club. Its sides were bare metal which had been polished in a series of swirls. The top had been welded shut, with brass handles bolted to its sides. The coffin was beautiful in its simplicity, and stood out against the darkly complex Persian rugs, the sleek fur of the trophy heads, and the otherworldly shaping of their horns.

It also clashed with the somberly dressed crowd which had gathered to pay tribute to Carton before he began his final journey to the mountains.

A chamber orchestra set up behind a barricade of shifted furniture played Albinoni's "Adagio" and Pachelbel's "Canon."

So many people had showed up that it became necessary to usher them in a dozen at a time. They filed past the coffin, laid flowers on it, touched it, ran their fingers along its sides, kissed it. Some people cried. Most just stared, with the same glazed and strangely hungry look that Carton had drawn from them in his lectures.

I thought of what he had said about the show being over.

But it wasn't. Even in death, he had managed not to disappoint his thousands of admirers.

Outside, through the open doors of the club, hundreds of people milled about in the street. The press was there, photographing anyone who seemed particularly overwhelmed as they emerged from the building.

Helen and I were sitting on the stairs, at that place where the big Chinese vase bristled with Zulu spears. There was nowhere else for us to sit, so we looked through the banister railing at the tweed caps and cloche hats of the people who filed through the room.

I was glad Helen was there. I felt comfortable around her. She was one of the few people I knew who understood first-hand the mountains that stood behind the legend of Henry Carton. It was what set her apart from the crowd down below, and bonded her to Stanley and to me.

With as much dignity as possible, Stanley led the mourners past the coffin and made sure, with polite taps on shoulders or kind words whispered in ears, that no one dawdled longer than was necessary.

Over the past few days, he had taken on the role of spokesman for our expedition. Each day, there were meetings with journalists, and I saw a little of his uncle's showmanship in the way Stanley avoided the topic of his inheritance and the rancor which had existed between them for so long. In fact, Stanley had nothing bad to say about his uncle, which was a first in my experience.

The interviews were held at the Montague, up on the second floor, where there was a space too grandly named the Banquet Room. On the walls hung colored drawings of people foxhunting. The pictures were supposed to show the progression of the hunt: the Scent, the View-Hallo, the Chase, and so on. Stanley installed himself at one end of the table and received a seeming endless series of journalists. Barber ran an irregular shuttle service of tea from the kitchen to the private dining room. The journalists scribbled furiously in their notepads, while Stanley paced the room, bounced his fist off the table, or seesawed on the back legs of his chair. He never seemed to tire.

In between classes, I usually managed to attend a couple of interviews each day. When asked, I chipped in the odd bit of Alpine geography or explained the difference between a piton and a crampon, but otherwise I minded my own business. I couldn't stand it for long in that little room, eyes drawn repeatedly and annoyingly to those red-jacketed foxhunting men, forever frozen in midair over a fallen tree or toasting one another with wine their lips would never touch. I always found reasons to be moving on.

Several times, I ended up having lunch with Helen down in the main dining room. She was concerned, as I was, about the technical aspects of the journey. There was the ice field of the Dragon's Tongue to be crossed beforehand. There, the danger of avalanche or of crevasses hidden below thin crusts of snow was enough to deter most mountaineers from ever reaching Carton's Rock. Once the climb began, even with no extraordinary gear to carry, all indications were that it would be a difficult ascent. But with the coffin as well, and what appeared in Helen's photographs to be several unavoidable vertical rock walls, we were not sure it could be done.

In the wake of the recent disaster in Patagonia, talk of climbing was everywhere. Not for the first time, the dangers of mountaineering, and the point of mountaineering at all, was brought into question. Editorials railed against what they saw as a needless loss of life while one engaged in a pursuit which had no purpose except to tempt fate.

Despite this, the Carton Expedition, as it was now being called, was finding in the public eye some measure of redemption for the corpses left in Patagonia. We were not climbing a mountain as much as we were honoring the dead. For that, risks were worth taking.

In the space of one week, Stanley evolved from the service-dodging bon vivant of the Montague Club, the co-president of the now defunct Society of Former Mountaineers, and the unemployed and unemployable slack-chinned wasteful spender of his father's hard-earned money to an almost saintly figure of personal sacrifice, familial love, and, the press was quick to point out, the love of Helen Paradise as well. Stanley had turned into an actual hero, a fact which he seemed both anxious to prove and just as eager to deny. These denials only made him more popular, as he had known they would.

I, on the other hand, had been cast as something of a silent partner. I was the former mountaineer, invalided out of the sport by the war, returning to the Alps to help out an old friend. Without complaint, I settled into this supporting role, rather than insist upon the facts. The alternate reality had been so quickly manufactured by the press that it seemed almost easier to be swept along by its half-truths than to remember the real reasons for my going.

The image they had created for Stanley was almost as heroic as that of his uncle. The two of them were, in a way, closer than they had ever been before. Henry Carton had become, in death, the father figure that he'd always wished he'd been for Stanley. And Stanley became the thing he had so stubbornly refused to be, which was, if such a thing were possible now, his uncle's pride and joy.

The only interruption to the smooth running of that afternoon occurred at the arrival of a little man whose antique-looking clothes and large black hat gave him a dwarfish, supernatural look. I could see nothing of his eyes, but his lips were bloodlessly thin and his nose was long and rounded at the end. Ignoring the orderly line which filed past the coffin, the man stood in the middle of the room and began waving a walking stick above his head.

"Henry Carton is a fraud and a scoundrel!" shouted the little man.

A gasp went up from the line of waiting people.

"Do you mind?" asked Stanley, his voice hoarse with sudden anger.

"You've all been cheated!" yelled the man. "The whole thing is a swindle!"

"What is?" demanded Stanley.

With a flick of his wrist, the man brought his walking stick level with Stanley's chest and kept it there as if aiming the barrel of a gun. "Your uncle thinks he has fooled the whole world. But he hasn't fooled me!"

"Who the hell are you?" asked Stanley.

"My name is Joseph Pringle!"

There was a sound almost like growling from the people in the line.

Pringle heard this, and he turned on them. "You can all just pack it in! You don't know anything. If you did, you wouldn't be here kowtowing to this man. And you!" He swung his stick to where I sat with Helen on the stairs. "You ought to have the sense to leave this fool where he is lying now, instead of risking your life for the sake of this blackguard's reputation!"

I had never heard anyone use the word *blackguard* seriously before.

The whole room stood in shock.

The press crowded into the doorway.

Pringle looked around, snorting in his breaths like a bull before it charges. "I tell you all now," he shouted, "that this journey will never take place!" Then he let out a shrill birdlike cry and, with one sweep of his cane, cleared the flowers from the top of the coffin.

This was too much for the crowd. They descended upon him. One man grabbed Pringle's walking stick, broke it over his knee, and sent the two ends clattering away into the corner of the room. They took his hat and stamped on it. They tore the buttons off his coat.

Pringle screamed and thrashed about, his pale scalp visible beneath a layer of thin gray hair, which made his skull look as fragile as an egg.

If it had not been for Stanley, they probably would have trampled him to death. Instead, Stanley pushed his way through the scrum, took Pringle by the scruff of the neck, and heaved him out among the pressmen.

Flash cubes popped and crackled. Bursts of magnesium light flickered in from outside.

Pringle cursed them all and tried to snatch their cameras.

But the pressmen only fell back out of reach and took more pictures.

At last, Pringle gave up the fight and ran away down the street, still cursing, still promising that our journey would never take place.

The viewing continued for a few more hours. The orchestra packed up at noon. By four, the journalists had gone. At five, Helen went home. At six, Stanley at last called it quits. This still left many people who had not glimpsed the coffin, so Stanley offered to open the place again tomorrow.

With the doors finally closed, Stanley sank into a chair and pressed his hands against his face.

The air was filled with the sickly smell of the flowers which had been left around the coffin. Stanley had replaced some of those that had been knocked off by Pringle, but the floor was still scattered with carnations, lilies, and roses.

Stanley let his head fall back with a groan. "What a day," he murmured.

I sat down opposite him and grunted in agreement.

"How are we ever going to move that coffin up the side of a mountain?" he asked.

"A lot of brute strength, I imagine."

"It's going to take more than that," said Stanley, raising his head. "Just look at the thing. It's made for being lowered into the ground, not sliding up a hill."

With only a few weeks before our departure, there were still so many details to sort out that I hadn't given the matter much thought. Even getting to Italy was proving more tricky than I had expected. Owing to difficulties with the airlines over transporting Carton's body in a welded-shut coffin, we had arranged to travel there by train, just as we had done in the old days.

"You did a good job today," I told Stanley.

"I think Uncle Henry would have been pleased with the turnout," he replied. "Especially old Pringle showing up. I thought he would have gone by now."

"Gone where?" I asked.

"The Alps," replied Stanley. "He spends his summers there, you know. Not far from where we're going, actually. My uncle used to say he could sense it when Pringle had left London for the season." Stanley screwed up his face and did his best impersonation of Carton's creaky voice: "I feel it, Stanley! I feel it like a freshening of the air!"

"How does Pringle propose to stop us?"

"Bury us under an avalanche of documents, I expect."

"He must have really hated old Carton."

Stanley smiled, as if about to let me in on a secret he had known for a long time. "Crossing swords with Carton was all Pringle had to live for, really. In a funny way, I think Pringle will miss him more than anybody else. Archenemies are hard to come by, and with Carton gone, Pringle's got no one left to persecute. Everyone else is either too well behaved or too afraid to stand up to him. But Carton wasn't bothered in the least." Stanley sat forward, smiling as a memory broke open in his head. "My uncle used to do a skit in his lectures where he would pretend to be Pringle. He wouldn't name him, of course, but would dress himself up like Pringle, ridiculous tie and so on, and everyone knew whom he was mimicking. He would come out onstage right at the beginning of the lecture and start saying all these awful things about Carton. About himself! Sometimes the audience, especially if they were first-timers and hadn't seen Carton in the flesh, wouldn't actually know who this man was. They'd be shocked, of course. Sometimes they would boo him. Carton would carry on listing all the rotten things Pringle had said about him, about how everything Carton said was lies, but then he would pretend that he had an itch, right in the middle of his back. Pringle was always scratching himself because of his eczema. So as part of his act, my uncle would try to scratch his back, but of course he couldn't. So he would start dancing around the stage, all the while trying to carry on with his Carton bashing. He would get so desperately itchy that he would start rubbing his back up

and down against the corner of the chalkboard he used for
illustrating his lectures. He'd look like an old bear scratching
himself on a tree trunk. Of course, by now the audience would
be howling with laughter. Eventually, Carton would reveal
who he was. Then you could hear the applause halfway down
the street."

"Did Pringle ever catch wind of this?" I asked.

"Oh, of course. Pringle makes it his job to find out about
everything, especially if it has something to do with him. He
tried suing Carton for slander, but Carton always got away
with it. The thing is that before Carton started spoofing him,
Pringle barely had a name worth slandering. It was Carton
who made him famous. The audience at his lectures wouldn't
have had any idea who Pringle was, much less the things he
said about Carton, if Carton himself hadn't told them all about
it." Stanley got up and walked over to the coffin. He rapped on
the side with his knuckles, as if expecting Carton to tap out a
reply from inside the metal box. "I'm going to miss him more
than I ever thought I would."

"What will happen to the club now?" I asked.

He glanced back at me. "Do you mean what *should* happen
or what *will* happen?"

"It's like that, is it?"

"I'm afraid so." Stanley began gathering up the dropped
flowers, clicking his tongue at the stains they had made on the
carpet. "He was going to lose the club. It had really stopped
being his club, anyway. Over the years, the board of trustees
took more and more control over the place. It didn't seem that
way, of course. Not to people coming in from the street. And as
long as my uncle was making money, the board didn't much
care what he did. But after his voice gave out, and he couldn't do

the lectures like he used to, it wasn't long before the vultures began to circle."

I remembered what Carton had said, how if it hadn't been for the club, he wouldn't have known what to do with himself.

"So the club will be gone," said Stanley, "but I think people will remember him well. Speaking of which, I almost forgot. Dr Webb stopped by before you got here. He left us something from my uncle." Out of his pocket, he pulled what looked like a large brown leather wallet. He tossed it to me and I caught it.

Turning the wallet in my hand, I saw that it was stitched shut all the way around. "What's in it?" I asked as I reached for my Opinel knife.

"Don't open it up," said Stanley. "It's got some poems inside."

"Poems?"

He nodded. "Dr. Webb said they had been put together by my uncle and are to be opened only when we get to the top of the mountain, and then they are to be read out over the coffin."

I weighed the leather envelope in my hand. "I've heard of people doing that," I said, "sorting out their own funerals in advance. Choosing the music and so on."

"And just like Uncle Henry to be one of them," said Stanley.

I went to hand him back the envelope.

Stanley shook his head. "You'd better look after that."

"Why me?"

"Which of the two of us would you trust not to lose the bloody thing?"

"I'll keep it safe," I said.

Both of us were too tired to go home. The thought of sleeping on a couch here at the club began to look like a good idea.

I was just heading up the stairs to see if I could rustle up some blankets and pillows when there was a loud knocking at the door, following by the crash of broken glass.

Someone shouted, "Blast!," followed by a muffled stream of blasphemy.

I stood on the landing while Stanley went to the door. "I'm terribly sorry . . ." he began to say, but then he exclaimed, "Oh, it's you!"

Wally Sugden staggered into the room, holding the broken neck of a champagne bottle. The rest of it lay in shards on the doorstep. Sugden looked at the piece in his hand and then threw it out into the dark. "That's right," said Sugden. "It's me." He was completely drunk. He could barely speak, let alone stand.

"I'm afraid we're closed," said Stanley.

"Who's 'we'?" demanded Sugden, but then he caught sight of me on the stairs. "Of course. I should have known."

"What do you want?" I asked.

"I've come to tell you that it's not too late! You know damned well how this is going to play out, so you might as well stop wasting my time. I warn you, if you don't play the game straight I'm going to expose the both of you publicly."

"Expose us?" asked Stanley. "Expose us for what? We've got nothing to hide."

Sugden snorted. "You don't understand. The papers will print any bloody thing I tell them to, and whether you have something to hide or not makes no difference to me or them. I'll just make something up, and the longer you two dither about trying to make up your minds, the worse it's going to be for you."

I felt the muscles clench along my jaw. Anger flashed behind my eyes. Without thinking, I reached over to the Chinese vase, took hold of one of the Zulu spears, and threw it at Sugden. The wide blade of the spear flickered through the air and thumped into the wall beside him.

He squawked and covered his head with his hands.

Stanley was staring at me.

"What the bloody hell was that?" shouted Sugden.

By then I was down the stairs, across the room, and face to face with him. I prized the spear out of the woodwork. "It's an answer," I spat. "That's what it was. You can say whatever the hell you want, Sugden, but it won't change anything. And instead of you thinking you can make things worse for us, why don't you start thinking about how we can make them worse for you?"

"I'd like to see you try," he said, slapping the dirt off his sleeves.

I came a little closer to him. "Would you, Sugden? Would you? Then tell me again about your trust in the man." I set the spear point at the hollow of his throat. "Tell me about your trust in the machine!" I shouted.

Sugden fumbled for the door and staggered back out into the street. "You're mad," he said. "You're both mad." He stalked away, turning now and then to hurl abuse at us, but he kept walking.

When he had gone, I walked back inside and shut the door.

Stanley was standing exactly where I had left him. "Were you aiming to hit him?" he asked.

190 | PAUL WATKINS

I went up to the landing and replaced the spear in the vase.
"I don't know," I said, which was the truth. What I did know
was that from this moment on, the power Sugden had once
wielded over me was gone. The nightmares were still there
inside my head, slicing the blackness of my dreams like the fins
of circling sharks, but from now on Sugden could no longer
summon them as he had done before.

❄

DESPITE THE FOCUS OF the press on me and Stanley, at St.
Vernon's Higgins and Houseman made a point of being entirely
unimpressed. In their eyes, there was something almost undignified about getting one's picture in the paper. To them, I
was just William Bromley, history teacher, sometime blackjack
player, man who pedaled around the school grounds on an
ancient rod-brake Raleigh, senior officer of the St. Vernon's
Officer Cadet Corps, man in love with Darcey Kidder.

But even the usually inscrutable Miss Kidder could not
help mentioning the change. On her next sweep through the
faculty lounge to deliver the paychecks, she said nothing at all
to Higgins or Houseman, which was usual. But just as she was
leaving the room, she turned in the doorway and fixed me with
a look. "Mr. Bromley," she said.

I glanced up from the pile of papers I was correcting.
"Miss Kidder," I replied.

Higgins and Houseman had been shaken from their tea-
drinking stupor and now were watching us intently.

"I hear you're to be leaving us," she told me, blue eyes
glowing through the strands of black hair falling across
her face.

"Yes," I replied.

"Off on some great adventure." Her lips were crooked with a smile.

"I'll be coming back, though."

"Well, good luck. I think it's very fine. We should all have great adventures," she said, casting a frosty glance at Higgins and Houseman. And then she was gone.

"I've had adventures!" spluttered Higgins. "I've been lost in the Sand Sea of Calanscio! Twice!"

"And I," Houseman chipped in, "have sunk three U-boats! What more does she want?"

We pondered this and found no answer.

The next day, just as I was packing up the notes from my last class, I heard a knock on my classroom door.

"Oh, hell," I said under my breath.

This was the time of day when a particularly needy student named Tirell would sometimes show up asking for help. I didn't grudge him asking, but I did grudge him for showing up at this time of day, when it was all I could do to stagger over to the faculty room for a cup of tea before heading home and correcting papers until ten o'clock at night. I had had office hours earlier in the day, and there were usually a few customers, complaining about assignments or pleading for extensions on the extensions I had already given them. But it was only Tirell who waited until the end of the day. He was a perfectly adequate student, but from the day he'd arrived at St. Vernon's, he had been obsessed with his grades. Tirell knew I would be tired and therefore more likely to give in and award him points he didn't deserve. I dreaded these meetings and Tirell's slippery, insincere politeness as he tried to wheedle out a few more points and bump up his grade point average. This was probably the only part of teaching I truly hated, because I was afraid I might one day tell the boy exactly what I thought of him, which would probably cost me my job.

After the knock at the door, I stayed very still, hoping that Tirell might think I had already left. Just as I was beginning to think the coast was clear, the knocking started again. I groaned loudly and shouted, "Come in!" And then I pretended to be very busy writing something in my notebook.

"Sorry to disturb you," said a voice, but it was not the whiny point-grubbing voice of Tirell. It was the voice of Darcey Kidder.

My head snapped up so sharply that I felt something crick in my neck. "Oh, it's you!" I said.

She smiled. "Can I come in?"

I stood up. "Of course."

"It's just that I can't find the daily attendance sheet, and I thought perhaps I might have left it in here."

The daily attendance sheet was carried from classroom to classroom by a senior prefect, who would be given a list of names of anyone who was absent that day. The list would then be brought to Miss Kidder, who would cross off the names of those boys who were playing away games that day, or who were sick or who had some other excuse. The list of those names remaining would be handed to the headmaster who, in my view, took a perverse pleasure in calling out the boys' names in all-school assembly and summoning them to his chambers during lunch break. "Didn't the prefect hand it in?" I asked, glancing around the room and hoping to see the clipboard with its jaundice-yellow attendance sheet attached.

"He did, but then I had to double-check something and I brought it over here. I must have left it in one of the classrooms." She clicked her tongue and sighed. "Oh, well," she said cheerfully. "Never mind."

"Are you kidding?" I asked. "The headmaster will do his nut if he doesn't get that list. I must help you find it."

"So you're off to Switzerland," she said, still smiling.

I looked at her cautiously. "It's Italy actually, but I will be passing through Switzerland. Now think," I said. "Where do you think you could have left it?"

"I'm sure I'll find it," she said casually, and sat down on one of the desks and folded her arms. "I've always thought this was one of the nicer classrooms. You do keep it up well. I think that makes a big difference to the students."

I felt a drop of sweat run down the trench of my spine. "Yes, well, I try to keep it nice," I said quietly. I glanced around at the dog-eared posters on the wall, one of which showed caricatures of Adolf Hitler and Hermann Göring sitting in the luggage rack of a train carriage, listening in on a conversation taking place between two old ladies just beneath them. The top of the poster read, "Loose Talk Costs Lives!" Another poster showed the Mediterranean during the Greek classical period. On the other wall was a huge pull-down map of the world, showing the British colonies in pink. The map was out of date and still showed that we ruled India. I had requested a new one from Higgins, who was department chair, and had been met with roars of laughter. When I'd asked what the joke was, Higgins had informed me that if he paid for a new wall map out of department funds, there would be no budget for tea, biscuits, toast, or Houseman's subscription to the *Sporting News*.

"And if you want to deprive him of that," added Higgins, "you'd better have something better in mind than a new map showing the deteriorating state of our Empire!"

"I hope to become a teacher myself," she said, tracing one pale finger down the edge of the desk.

Nervously, I wiped a chalk-dusty hand across my face. "Darcey," I said, "I'd love to talk about teaching with you, but you must focus on that list. The headmaster—"

"Will it be dangerous where you're going?"

"No," I said dismissively.

"People say you might not come back."

"People? What people?"

She shrugged. "Higgins. Houseman. They say it's a terrible risk you're taking."

"Well, they should mind their own business," I snapped.

She slid off the desk and walked over to me. Then she reached out and straightened the lapel of my jacket. "You will be careful, won't you, William?"

I squinted at her. "We need to find your list, Darcey. We can talk about mountains later."

"I'm sure I'll find it," she said, the cheerful tone gone from her voice. "It doesn't matter all that much."

"All right," I said, shaking my head.

"I'd better go." She headed for the door.

By the time I mumbled a good-bye, she was already gone.

I lowered my head and sighed, arms folded, staring at my shoes. For a long time, I stayed that way, blinking with dried-out eyes and drawing in shallow breaths from the stale air in the room. I knew exactly what would be going on in Darcey's head. She would be thinking that I was just another public-school boy who had stumbled into manhood without the slightest clue about the opposite gender.

But the truth about most ex-public-school boys, those at least who had any interest in women and who had not cloistered themselves entirely within the separate world of places like the Montague, was that they almost always knew more about these things than they pretended to.

I knew perfectly well that she had not come to find her list. I had known it from the moment she'd asked about my leaving for the Alps. That list she'd said she was looking for was, in all likelihood, already on the headmaster's desk. It had only been an excuse. So that we could talk. So that something could begin between us, away from the owl-eyed glances of Higgins and Houseman and everyone else in the fishbowl of the school. And when she had asked if it was dangerous where I was going, we both knew that the answer was yes. Caring enough to ask said everything. And when she had straightened my lapel, the gesture had held more in it than any kiss I'd ever given or received.

But I had shut the door on it, and played up the naïveté that was the refuge of people like me.

Even though I had known what was going on the whole time, I still didn't understand why I'd behaved the way I had, because for something to begin between me and Darcey Kidder was what I wanted more than almost anything, and had been since the moment I'd set eyes on her. It was not simply nerves, as I had told myself before. This was something more serious. It was as if some shadow of myself had stepped in front of me, and a voice which was mine but which I had not willed to speak had driven her off. What was it, I wondered, that caused me to turn away from the very thing I had been praying for?

PART

II

EIGHT

B Y THE TIME THE TERM ENDED, all enthusiasm for academics had, as usual, been beaten to a slow, lingering death.

At the graduation ceremony, the headmaster gave his usual brave speech about prosperity and duty to one's country. The fact that there was very little prosperity going around, a conflict in Korea, and fears of a third world war meant that the only duty on people's minds was staying alive rather than donating another generation to the slaughter.

After the speech, the faculty and parents clapped mindlessly and forever as the graduating students went up one by one to shake the headmaster's hand and receive certificates.

When that was done, I could at last devote all my energy to the upcoming journey. The public having said their last good-bye to Henry Carton, my task was to make sure they wouldn't be saying any last good-byes to Stanley and me as well.

We needed up-to-date climbing gear, but more than anything we needed to get back in shape. This meant familiarizing ourselves again with the finer points of abseiling, belaying, traversing, and rope tying and also the less fine points of simply being strong enough to drag ourselves and a coffin up the side of a mountain.

Our first attempt at training was, through no fault of our own, a complete bust. On a rock-climbing trip to the Derbyshire Peak District, we were so hounded by journalists and spectators that we never even reached the rock face we had intended to climb.

No matter where we were, the press had us under virtual siege. Sometimes it was outside our flats, sometimes outside the Montague and, in case we were not to be found in either of those places, a camera-toting scout was usually posted outside Carton's club. It was known that we stored our climbing gear there, along with Carton's coffin, while it awaited transport to the train station and from there over to the Continent.

Our deaths or our survival on this journey had become the latest topic of fascination. Evidence of this was that bookmakers had begun taking bets on our chances for success. The odds were placed at eight to one against our putting the coffin on the top of Carton's Rock, and ten to one that we would make it back at all.

Our second attempt to get some mountain training done, this time in North Wales, was even less successful, despite the fact that we managed to dodge the press on our way out of the city. We arrived by bus in Dolgellau only to discover that every single piece of mountaineering equipment we had brought with us had either been accidentally off-loaded at some point earlier in the day or, more likely, stolen.

We returned to London and found a letter waiting for us. It was from Sholto Lindsay, my old boss from Achnacarry. He had read about our troubles in the paper and offered us the use of the Achnacarry grounds, which included the rock face above Loch Amon where I had trained for my first mission to Palladino. Lindsay said he would not be there to greet us, as he had recently discovered the joys of doing absolutely nothing every summer at a villa in Portugal. But he said that we would be left alone there, and we were welcome to stay as long as we liked.

Having each purchased a new set of mountaineering gear, Stanley and I reached Achnacarry one week later in Stanley's burgundy-colored Morris Minor. The road to the camp was overgrown with thistles. Bracken, heavy with dew, leaned into the road, swishing against the side of the car as we passed.

I wasn't sure what to expect from Achnacarry. I didn't know if the camp had been put back into service, or perhaps turned into some sort of Boy Scout training area, or just left to rot. What we found was that the camp had ceased to exist. Beyond the gate, all that remained of the base was a twenty-foot-high pile of charred wood. The structures had evidently been burned and then bulldozed into a heap.

Stanley and I drove onto what had once been the parade ground but was now only a vacant lot, its asphalt cracked and pushed apart by the relentless weeds. We got out of the car and stretched and looked around. Then we walked over to the pile of wood. A fine rain was falling, that same old Scottish drizzle whose damp air no clothing could keep out. Even though the buildings must have been burned years ago, I could still detect the bitter reek of smoke. Then we turned and looked out at what had once been a bustling little village of Quonset huts and tar-paper-roofed shacks. It took me a few moments to remember what buildings had been where, but slowly they reappeared in my mind's eye, like the ghosts of houses, shimmering back to life in the fog.

"So this is where you spent the war?" asked Stanley.

"Most of it," I replied.

"Doesn't look like much now."

"No," I agreed, my voice barely above a whisper.

"Amazing how quickly the land takes things back," he said.

I nodded in agreement. I was thinking about all the people who had passed through here, and where they all were now. Half of them were probably dead and tucked away beneath white headstones in the military cemeteries of half a dozen countries. As for the rest, working in cubbyhole offices or ploughing fields or mending shoes or pulling in fishnets or whatever they did now, I wondered if they ever thought back to this place. Perhaps some of them, like me, had returned here and found only this funeral pyre.

We left the car and packed up as much of our gear as we could carry. Then, under a leaden sky, we hiked along the old assault course trails to Loch Amon. There we made camp and began our training.

For the first few days, we hauled our loaded packs up and down the hillsides, slowly reaccustoming ourselves to the weight and the strain on our backs. Then we began climbing exercises, and spent the next week tackling the Amon rock face from as many different angles as we could find. The early-summer days were long, and often, having set out at dawn, we did not return to our camp before dark. We lived off tins of soup and canned vegetables and managed, thanks to Stanley having brought along a collapsible fly rod in an aluminum tube, to pull a few trout from the lake.

We were constantly exhausted, although less and less as the days went by. It was amazing to me how quickly the old instincts returned. The only breaks we took were when we ran out of food and made the hike back to the car, whose trunk was filled with rations.

Each time we returned to the old base, I was afraid that the car might not be there. That someone might have stolen it. We were far from anywhere. The nearest village was at least six miles back, and Lindsay's manor house, which I had never seen, was nowhere in sight and would have been locked up anyway. The thought of being marooned here filled me with a quiet sense of dread.

But it was more than that. Although I was too tired most of the time to ponder anything except the physical exertion, in those moments when my mind caught up with my body, I found myself thinking about the fact that I had brought Stanley here to Achnacarry. I hadn't planned it that way, of course, but nevertheless, the sight of him here left me with the feeling that I was somehow, unwittingly, dragging him into the same death trap into which I had led the other members of the Lucky Six.

If we had done things Stanley's way, we would be back in London now and lounging at the Montague. I was the one who had persuaded him. He did not seem to grudge me this, and showed no signs of changing his mind, but I felt responsible for the fact that we were here at all.

One night in our second week, as we sat huddled under a tarpaulin watching a few pieces of rancid bacon sizzle in a frying pan, I joked that he must be regretting that I'd ever talked him into this. "I can't help thinking that I ought now to be talking you out of going, just as hard as I tried to talk you into it."

"Why?" he asked.

"If I hadn't brought the others together for that mission . . ." And then I just had to stop.

"They might all still be alive," said Stanley.

I nodded.

"And if you don't talk me out of this, I might end up dead myself. Is that it?"

"Yes," I said, staring at the raindrops that splashed off the toes of my boots.

Stanley swept the wet and matted hair from his forehead. "If you had chosen another group of climbers to go on that mission, and if those men had died, just as Armstrong, Forbes, and Whistler did, you would feel even worse than you do now."

"I can't see how."

"Yes, you would, because you would say to yourself that if you had brought along the best climbers you knew, then the odds would have been better that you might have succeeded. And if the planners of that absurd mission had figured out that you were trying to save the skins of your friends, instead of bringing together the best team that you could, then they would have refused to exonerate you from any wrongdoing. Because you would have done wrong. But you didn't do anything wrong. You did exactly what they asked you to do, and it got botched up through no fault of your own, just as most things in a war get botched up one way or another. I didn't have to fight in the war to know that is a fact. I am the one," said Stanley, "who must answer to the ghosts of those men. Not you."

It startled me to hear him say this. "I don't see it that way at all!"

"If I had come along," he continued, "then you would at least have had the best possible team. Who knows how it might have gone if I'd been there? I don't mean to say that I could have saved things. But the chemistry of our old group would have been there. And who knows what that chemistry would have counted for? It might have changed your luck completely."

"It wouldn't have stopped any bullets," I said.

"You're absolutely right," he told me, "and on one level the most noble thing I could hope for is that I might have stopped one of those bullets that took Armstrong's life, or Whistler's or Forbes's. But I'm not talking about that level. If one thing changes, then everything might change. Do you see? If one passenger more or one less had boarded the *Titanic*, then perhaps it might not have hit the iceberg and sank. If I had been on the mission, then perhaps the message might not have gotten through to the Germans about where you would be and then you never would have been shot at, and no one would have been hurt and you would have all come home as heroes. Then, instead of it being some unmentionably bad cock-up, people would speak of it the way they'll speak of the first person who sets foot on the summit of Mount Everest. Do you see?" Creases showed around his eyes, and his chapped lips drew across his teeth.

I suddenly knew what he would look like as an old man. At that moment, all the twisted logic he'd employed to convict himself in the courthouse of his brain glimmered through the mask of nonchalance he had once used to face the world.

I, who thought I knew him best, had never guessed how hard he'd been on himself all these years. But that mask had been so foolproof that I'd never thought to look behind it.

"That is why I have to go, William. Not to put things right, but to put them behind me in the only way I can. Otherwise I don't stand a chance with Helen. The past will just keep getting in the way until it ruins everything."

206 | Paul Watkins

That was when I told him about Darcey. I had never mentioned her before. Until that moment, as often happens, all talk of relationships had been a one-way street between us. But now I told him everything, even about that day when she had come to my classroom. "I don't know why I did it," I said. "I'm beginning to think I never will."

Stanley turned out to be a better listener than I'd thought. "When was the last time you had any close friends?" he asked.

"Well, you're a friend," I said.

"I've been your friend all along," he continued, "so I don't count."

"I was friends with Armstrong and Whistler . . ." I was getting ready to list off all the other members of the Lucky Six when Stanley interrupted.

"Exactly! And since then?"

I fell silent. There was Higgins and Houseman, but we were no more than fellow suitors of the same beautiful woman. I began to understand what he was telling me. After what had happened on the mission, I could not stand to take the risk of making friends and losing them again.

For both of us, much more than our survival was at stake. Even if our reasons for going were different, the urgency behind them was the same.

❄

AFTER THREE WEEKS AT Loch Amon, our food ran out and we decided we were ready. As we bounced away on the barracks road, the gates of Achnacarry wobbled in and out of view in the Morris Minor's side mirrors, then disappeared for good.

On the drive south, Stanley and I discussed the fact that although we had refamiliarized ourselves with climbing techniques and were more or less back in shape, we had not practiced moving the coffin. Since most of that dragging would take place on the Dragone glacier, and since there were no glaciers close at hand on which we could train, we had decided to leave that part of the preparation for when we actually arrived in the Alps. It was dangerous to do this. We knew that. But we had not been given enough time to prepare everything, and some elements of this expedition were simply going to have to wait.

We took turns driving, and when it was not my turn, I lolled in the passenger seat, slipping in and out of consciousness. In this state, the image of the coffin kept appearing to me, twisting first one way and then another as I examined all its angles.

We reached London late in the evening, and Stanley dropped me off at my flat.

Although I wanted nothing more in the world than to sleep for a couple of days, I knew there wasn't time. I went back to thinking about the coffin, and how on earth we were going to move it. Sitting at my kitchen table, I began drawing sketches in a notebook.

By dawn, I had filled the notebook and was down at the tea shop, drumming my fingers on the table.

"What are you all jumpy about?" asked Mrs. Reave as she set a mug of tea in front of me.

"I have invented something," I told her.

"I invented something once, a long time ago," she said, swiping a gob of butter across a slice of toast. "It was a bag."

"I think those have already been invented, Mrs. Reave."

She clicked her tongue at my sarcasm. "It was a bag for tea. A tea bag! No more fuss with all the strainers and tea leaves making life so complicated."

"Especially for someone like you."

"Well, that's my point, love, isn't it? But when I shopped it around a bit nobody wanted it. They said that people like the business of the strainer and the tea leaves in the pot. People like the whole production of it. That's what they said. And I told them, you make four hundred cups of tea a day and see how you like that production. I'd just as soon have a cup of tea and have it quick and easy."

"Who wouldn't?"

"Yeah, well, everyone except for you and me, apparently. Until, of course, they went and stole the idea and now a world without tea bags, well, that would just be totally uncivilized."

"Mrs. Reave, you were ahead of your time."

"I was a bit. I couldn't help it." She set the butter-soggy toast in front of me. "Here, are you really going to bury some chap on the top of a mountain?"

"I am, Mrs. Reave."

She walked away behind her counter, as if she needed some distance between us for what she was about to say. "I thought you was sensible."

"Sorry to disappoint you."

"I just don't want to read about you in the paper like I read about those other chaps."

By the end of that week, not only had Mrs. Reave read about me in the paper, but she had also read about my invention.

Realizing that the coffin would have to be dragged instead of carried, and also that it would not slide smoothly across the ground, I hired a metalsmith in Hampstead to install four sets of aluminum runners along the underside. Holding bars suitable for attaching ropes were also fixed to the front, sides, and back, so that it could be lifted or dragged in any direction. I also arranged for a compartment to be built on top of the coffin. Situated at the back, the compartment consisted of three sheets of aluminum. One sheet was fixed to each side and another across the back. The compartment had no roof, but the sheets were perforated with holes to allow for ropes which could tie down the cargo. This also allowed wind to blow through the compartment.

While I waited for the modifications to be completed, I kept myself busy with the final preparations, coiling ropes, checking the spring mechanisms on carabiners, searching for faults in the cloth of our tents, and pawing through the first-aid kit to memorize its contents.

One week later, I received a call from the metalsmith saying that the work was done. "It looks like a rocket," he said.

He was quite right about that, and it wasn't long before the papers began to refer to the coffin as "Carton's Rocket." Editorials appeared, debating whether inspiration for the design had come from Sir William Congreve's 1805 pattern rocket or the one designed by William Hale in 1846 or Werner von Braun's V-2. It was not surprising that by the time Stanley and I set out upon our journey we had become known, for better or worse, as the Rocket Men.

NINE

AFTER AN OVERNIGHT CROSSING of the Channel, we arrived in Calais before dawn. By that afternoon, we were in Paris, with barely any time to spare before catching a connecting train to Geneva.

It had been twelve years since I'd last set foot in the Gare du Nord, but the place seemed much the same, echoing with the voices of announcers and the chugging stamp of train engines. The damp, smoky smell of the trains mixed with the aromas of coffee and strong, cigarlike French tobacco, climbing in a fog towards the glass-paned roof.

Stanley and I made our way across the platform, carrying our mountaineering rucksacks, coils of rope across our chests and ax-head climbing sticks in hand.

Stanley sported a heavy moleskin cap which he had bought at Lillywhites. The gray-green cap flopped down over his ears, and its brim seemed to be balanced on the bridge of his nose, making him look like a gangster.

My own cap was made of close-fitting sheepskin with flaps that tied at the top and could be pulled down over my ears. The cap gave me a vaguely Russian look, which provided Stanley with a seemingly endless supply of names to call me, such as Willipov, Bromski, and the Montague Czar.

It was amazing to me that he could find humor in my cap while failing to see the absurdity of the climbing jacket he had insisted on bringing along. It was of his own design and had been put together by a very expensive Jermyn Street tailor. The fabric was heavy woolen twill and fitted with a dozen pockets: on his hips, on his back, on his chest, on his arms, and even a little one on his wrist. When I asked him what this was for, he said he couldn't remember. Then he added that whatever it was for, it had been a very good idea and as soon as he recalled its purpose, he would put it to use. As for the rest of the pockets, when he experimented by filling them with chocolate bars, goggles, penknives, spare carabiners, and so on, he found that he could barely move.

Despite all of Stanley's pockets, the leather envelope containing Carton's poems remained safely tucked away in one of mine.

Behind us, wheeled by two porters, came the coffin, now officially known as the Rocket. This procession drew a variety of stares, from astonishment to curiosity to scorn, none of which was unfamiliar to us after the past few weeks in London.

Twenty minutes after arriving at the Gare du Nord, we were on the move again. We had booked first-class tickets for the entire journey. Stanley had insisted on our traveling in style, saying that if we were on our way to give his uncle a final resting place, we bloody well deserved a decent temporary resting place on our way there. With logic like that, it was not a point worth arguing.

"I'm going back to check on the gear," I said as soon as the train started rolling.

"Please yourself," replied Stanley. He was doing his best to read a French newspaper. "You ought to just relax a bit and enjoy the ride."

"I will," I said, "but not right now."

"And for God's sake stop patting your chest."

I had developed the habit of placing my right hand over the left side of my chest, to make sure that the leather envelope was still where it should be. "Well, you can look after the poems if you want."

"I think not," he mumbled from behind the paper.

I made my way back through the carriages, passing through first, then second, and finally third class. The farther I went, the louder things became, but also the more cheerful. In first class, waiters were passing from compartment to compartment, somberly announcing the meal that would be served in the dining car. In second class, sandwiches were being sold, along with half bottles of wine, from a counter at one end of the front carriage. In third class, the passengers had brought their own food in canvas-and-leather satchels. Blue-and-white-checked napkins were tucked into shirt necks, bone-handled knives carved slices off enormous salamis, baguettes were torn to pieces, and wine was drunk from old French army–issue two-spouted canteens.

Beyond the various classes was the conductor's wagon, divided between an office and his sleeping quarters. Past that came the freight wagon. It was here that Carton's coffin had been stored, among gray sacks of mail marked PARIS VILLE, bicycles, and all our mountaineering gear.

The door had been left open a few feet, as was normal, to keep the place aired out. After I had checked on the coffin, and everything else belonging to us, I sat down on the mail sacks and watched the French countryside clattering by. The wagon filled with the dusty smell of approaching rain.

On the Rocket, I noticed how worn the runners had already become after several days of being dragged across the playing fields of St. Vernon's while we tested the maneuverability of my invention. These experiments had made me hopeful that the Rocket would perform well on the ice and hard-packed snow of the glacier.

From this uncomfortable seat, I glanced around at other pieces of our equipment, such as the long, orange-painted willow sticks, known as "wands," for marking our path, the ropes, candle lamps for use inside the tent, and new gray leather-trimmed canvas packs I'd ordered from Bergans of Norway, which had arrived only one day before our departure. The sleeping bags, stove, water bottles, and ice axes had all been carefully selected and packed away.

Besides the standard mountaineering gear, there was a crate of apples, which had been sent by my father from an orchard down the road from where he lived. Stanley and I knew we'd never be able to eat them all, but we thought we might as well bring them along.

It was the type of gesture I would expect from my father. These pippins, green and rosy-cheeked, were the distillation of the rain and sun which fell upon the village where he lived. In his life of runner beans and roses, nothing was more precious. He knew that I would understand this, and knew perhaps as well that only I would understand it.

Another piece of equipment I had brought along in order to serve our special needs was a winch. It was, in fact, the winch that the groundskeepers at St. Vernon's had used to haul the line painter up onto a flatbed, which would then be towed back to the work shed by the school's ancient Massey Ferguson tractor. In a previous life, the winch had been used for hauling a boat out of the water and onto a trailer. One handle on either side allowed the steel cable to be wound in, while a set of blunt metal teeth prevented the cable from being let out again. A switch could be thrown which would disengage the teeth and allow the cable to pay out, but while the teeth were engaged, the people winding in the cable could rest without letting the line slip. The only trick would be to find a suitable place for anchoring the winch while it was in use. I didn't know if the winch could be used where we were going, but I knew it had to be better than hauling in ropes with our bare hands, trying to pull the coffin up the face of Carton's Rock.

I had thought of the winch too late to be able to shop around for a new one, so I'd gone to the groundskeeper's hut and pleaded my case.

The five of them, the head groundskeeper and his crew, spent their time in a large shed at the far end of the playing fields. There, as I had seen through the cracked and dusty windows, they had fashioned for themselves a comfortable cave decorated with old pieces of furniture scavenged from the well-appointed classrooms of the school. There were hammocks hanging from the walls, in which they took their frequent naps, and piles of old magazines which doubled as tables. They spoke a language of rough Cockney, filled with rhyming words which stood for other words so that they seemed to be speaking in crossword-puzzle clues, decipherable only by members of their own gruff tribe. Nothing went to waste in this kingdom. Even the dregs of their tea leaves were ploughed into the compost of their vegetable garden. There, raspberries grew beside cabbages, which grew beside the deep green shoots of leeks, which grew in turn beside the jagged leaves of mint. Guarding these plants were the carcasses of rabbits, pigeons, and even mice, caught in traps and now strung up on stakes and left to rot as a warning to others of their kind.

I admired them from a distance, because it was only at a distance that they let themselves be known.

Now they sat in frowning silence while I did a clumsy impersonation of Carton reenacting his climbs. I winched the imaginary coffin up the side of a cliff, wheeling my arms as if I were pedaling a bicycle with my hands, all the while describing how necessary the winch would be to our endeavor.

When I finished, I stood panting before the men, feeling the silence swell in the room.

The groundskeepers continued to stare at me, seemingly unaware that I had nothing left to say. Just as I was about to thank them for their time and leave, they exchanged a few cryptic glances among themselves. Then one of them sat forward. His name was Mr. Dooley. To judge from the repair work on his clothing, it would have been safe to say that he had never thrown anything away in his life. His once-blue overalls were a quilt of different fabrics, sporting everything from corduroy to leather to what appeared to be pieces of Persian carpet. These patches were the badges of his rank among the groundskeepers, and all of them seemed to have known in advance that Dooley would speak for them. "Are you going to bring it back?" he asked, his Irish accent clipping the words.

"I don't know," I replied. "I might not be able to."

Dooley sat back and clicked his teeth around his well-chewed pipe stem.

"If I don't return it to you," I said, "I'll buy you a new one."

New glances were exchanged.

"Perhaps they don't make it anymore," said Dooley.

"Then you can choose whichever one you want."

More rapid eye movement.

"Any one at all?" asked Dooley.

I nodded. "I'll make you that promise in writing."

For the first time, the focus of Dooley's eyes changed. He removed the pipe from his mouth.

I felt as if I must have said the wrong thing.

"There's nothing that needs to be in writing," he said.

"As you wish," I replied.

Dooley turned to the man next to him.

This man's name was Hector Partridge. He was tall and sinewy. His skin looked kippered by tobacco smoke. One of his front teeth was made of silver, and he sucked at it as if the silver nourished him somehow.

"Hector," said Dooley. "Give the man his winch."

As I carried the winch away with me, I looked at the school grounds and the tidy gray rooftops of the school buildings and I wondered suddenly whether I would return to St. Vernon's when this journey was over.

Now, greased and with new cable fitted, the winch lay on the floor of the baggage car, neatly stored inside a wooden box which had once held a case of our favorite Château Figeac. To offset its weight and the bulk of the coffin, I had arranged, through the Italian Society of Mountain Guides, for six porters and two guides to meet us at Palladino. From there, they would accompany us to the summit of Carton's Rock.

Once my mental inventory of our gear was complete, I fetched an apple from the crate, polished it on my chest, and took a bite. The taste reminded me of the days when I had ridden to and from the Alps in baggage cars like this. Using our rucksacks for pillows, we had eaten apples and chewed Horlicks tablets instead of buying food on the train, which we could not afford. We'd slouched on the jostling floor, feet all pointed towards the center, where sometimes a candle lamp would be left burning at night. I remembered the shine on the hobnails of our climbing boots and the smell of their water-proofing.

When the weather was warm, we would slide back one of the doors and watch trees file past in a blur, our view obscured from time to time by wreaths of steam from the engine up ahead. Of all the views I had glimpsed through the doors of those wagons, one stood out more clearly than the rest. It was only a fragment, and I didn't know why it came back to me more clearly than the others. I didn't even remember when it had occurred, except that it was night and autumn was coming on, so we must have been heading north, back to England. The fields were deep in autumn mist, frozen blue in the light of a full moon. The candle in our lamp had burned out, and now the only light from inside the wagon came from the burning ends of cigarettes. Long lines of poplar trees stretched out like telegraph lines into the darkly merging sky and earth.

Now those same poplar trees, their emerald-and-white leaves flickering in the heat, cast their shadows on the sunset fields of barley. The barley stalks changed color in the breeze, from scarab-beetle green to the green of palest jade. Heat haze rose from the fields, blurring the world into a lazily sketched landscape.

From the crate sent by my father, I fished out some of the

apples which were no longer any good and threw them out the open door. The green balls arced out into the sunlight, curving beautifully as the motion of the train left them behind.

Here and there the shadows of old shell craters seemed to ride like waves across a field, and the moss-patched ruins of concrete bunkers tilted into the earth like ships sinking in that green ocean. Time was filling in the wounds, season by season, under the brittle confetti of leaves.

I stayed there until the landscape had vanished in the purple shadows of twilight. Then I went back and joined Stanley, by which time it was so dark outside that it seemed as if the windows had been painted black.

The train thundered on into the night, and at last sleep overtook me.

❄

THE NEXT MORNING, after changing trains in Geneva, we passed through Lausanne and went on towards the Grand St. Bernard Pass.

At the sight of the Bernese and then the Pennine Alps, I felt a shudder in my chest. It was the trembling of energy stacked up inside me, ready for the long days ahead.

Passing through the Val d'Entremont, the train clattered along beside the river Drance, so close to the overhanging slopes that even if we craned our necks we could not see the tops. On the other side of the river, the sharply sloping fields were sown with wildflowers—campion, monkshood, and goldenrod. Waterfalls and tiny streams which tumbled from the rocks above merged into fast-running, gray-silted rivers. These rivers roared beneath the railway bridges, spraying the windows and bending the sun into rainbows. As the ravines emerged from shadow, I found myself returning to the old habit of plotting an imaginary path along each stony slope to reach the glacier fields that lay beyond.

Turning to look back inside the carriage, I could see others who had come to climb. Their eyes were focused on the world above, refusing to be overwhelmed by the vastness of the mountains. Instead, each crag and pinnacle of rock became a mental exercise in how it could be scaled.

Others stared with rounder eyes at the quaintness of the pastures, at the overwhelming cleanliness of the houses. From time to time, their eyes passed over the barrenness of the scree slopes and the overhanging cliffs, then quickly returned to the lower ground, where flowers smudged the hedgerows with more cheerful colors than the monochrome world of rock and ice above.

Stanley sat very still, hands balanced carefully in front of his face, fingertips touching, lost in thought.

I knew what was going on inside his brain. Until now, the mountains had remained a distant prospect, more of a concept than a reality. At last the truth was sinking in. We were both wondering if, each now at the age of forty, we might have grown too old for what lay ahead. In the past, it had always been a question of willpower and skill. But that was before Stanley's knees began to ache in damp weather and before the vision in my right eye became flecked with gray if I didn't get enough sleep.

Stanley gazed at the mountains rising up on either side of the train as if they were the jaws of a vast creature which had reared up out of the earth. "Bastard," he whispered.

I knew without having to ask that he was not cursing me. He was cursing his uncle.

Stanley turned to me suddenly. "These guides we'll be hiring," he said, giving voice to a conversation which had apparently been going on inside his head for some time already.

"Six porters and two guides," I said. "They're meeting us in Palladino."

He nodded and went back to staring out the window.

❊

WE CROSSED THE BORDER into Italy and changed trains at Aosta. From there, we had to go all the way south to Turin before catching another train north to the town of Domodossola, at the entrance to the Antigorio Valley.

There were no trains into the valley, so we spent the night in Domodossola and hired a cab early the next morning to take us the rest of the way.

With all of our gear crammed inside, and the coffin tied up on the roof, the cab took us about thirty kilometers up the valley. We reached Formazza late in the early afternoon. From there, we continued on to Palladino, which already lay in the shadows of the mountains above. At the southern edge of town, Lake Vannino glimmered in the half-light.

The cab, its once-black paint now coated with a shimmering layer of khaki dust, came to a stop in the village square, beside a fountain where a small statue of a rearing bronze horse spouted water from its mouth.

I recognized it from the photo back in Carton's apartment. This was where he had stood after coming down off the glacier.

My eyes were drawn beyond Palladino's clustered rooftops, no two of which appeared to stand at the same height, to the flower-strewn green of the fields above the town. From where I stood, I could make out the little wood, the Pineta di San Rafaele, and the meadow where I'd parachuted in. Above it, etched like a lightning bolt into the rocky hillside, was the old customs house road. Beyond the ridge where the road leveled out, I could see only the eggshell whites of clouds.

The San Rafaele woods looked dark and cold. I was glad to know we would be spending our first few nights here in a hotel, while we bought provisions, acquired the most up-to-date maps, and squared away things with our guides.

But the San Rafaele woods were exactly where Stanley and I ended up, six hours later, having been rejected from the only lodging place in town.

Stanley and I sat exhausted outside our tent. Beside us, the Rocket's polished sides reflected the shadows of the trees. On the breeze, we could hear music coming from a café in Palladino. Then the wind changed direction and the music disappeared, leaving us with only the whisper of wind in the tops of the pines.

Both Stanley and I were still in shock at what had happened. We had not made reservations, partly because there had been so little time and also because it was so early in the summer that I was sure there would be places to stay. Arriving in this sleepy little village, I was still confident that I had made the right choice.

But when the manager of the Caffè Falterona told us there were no vacancies, despite the fact that he had two empty rooms above the bar, I felt I deserved an explanation.

The café owner seemed ill at ease. He pulled at his gray mustache and kept clearing his throat. "It is the coffin," he said. "There is a law against it."

"Against a coffin?" I asked, looking around the dimly lit space, at its walls patched with pictures of soccer teams torn out of magazines, and rickety-legged tables bearing heavy metal ashtrays.

"This is an old law," said the man. "There is nothing I can do."

"But the coffin is sealed," I told him. "It can be kept in a storage room if you prefer."

"Sir." He held up one hand. "It is not possible. Perhaps you should speak to the police. There is a mortuary in Domodossola. You might be welcome there."

"But that's down at the other end of the valley!" I protested.

"It took us all day just to get here!" added Stanley.

The manager shrugged and turned away.

After this, Stanley and I stood outside, hands in pockets, trying to figure out what to do next.

The sounds of children's voices echoed from the narrow alleyway behind us. Above our heads, a woman was hanging up laundry on a line attached to the opposite building by a pulley. The woman's mouth bristled with wooden laundry legs. Expertly, she pulled the pegs from between her teeth, pinning socks and shirts to the line. As she completed each task, she gave the laundry line a tug, which caused the pulley at the other end to squeak. The shirts, with arms dangling, edged out jerkily across the alley, like a row of clumsy puppets.

Meanwhile the cabdriver drummed his fingers on the steering wheel and steadily made his way through a pack of cigarettes. He no longer wore a look of cheerful efficiency. Instead, he had begun eyeing us suspiciously, no doubt wondering if we lacked the funds to pay him.

"Well?" asked Stanley.

I was looking up at the dark expanse of the San Rafaele woods, already sunk in the half-light of the evening.

Stanley followed my gaze. "Oh, no," he said. "You can't be serious."

"It won't be that bad," I told him. "Remember those days

when we camped in the Erikawald above Zermatt? Once we get settled, it'll be cozy."

Stanley gazed forlornly at a board posted outside the café, on which was scrawled a dinner menu of pasta carbonara, potatoes with rosemary and olive oil, and tiramisu. Then he turned and glared at me. "And what will we be having for dinner?" he demanded in a loud voice.

What we had for dinner was a mug of tea, the water heated over my smoky old camp stove, some bruised apples, and a bar of chocolate each, since the grocery store in town was already closed.

We persuaded the cabdriver to transport us up towards the San Rafaele woods. At the point where the paved road turned to dirt, the cabdriver jammed on the brakes and got out. At first, we thought he'd gotten stuck, but then he opened the door and stood waiting for us to join him on the muddy track, and indicated that he would go no farther.

His face showed undisguised relief when Stanley hauled out a fist-sized wad of Italian bills, which we had procured at a bank back in London. After that, his sunken shoulders straightened and he insisted on helping us unload the Rocket from his roof. "After all," he said, "it is only a coffin. We will all be in one soon enough." He shook our hands and wished us good luck, but even as he did this, he glanced over our shoulders at the gloom of crowding trees and could not hide a shudder.

The cab backed away down the muddy lane, since there was no place for it to turn around.

For a long time, Stanley and I listened to the whine of its engine in reverse. Then, having at last found a place to turn, the cabbie clanked through the gears, heading away down the valley.

"What that man said about the coffin . . . ," said Stanley.

"Yes?"

"Was he trying to make us feel better or worse?"

I did not know, and so did not reply.

We looked at the Rocket. Tiny beads of rain were gathering on its smooth and angled sides.

Stanley gave it a kick. "He knew this would happen," he said. Then he glared at me. "He *knew*!"

With our packs shouldered, we each took hold of a brass carrying handle and began to drag the coffin up towards the woods.

"I'll be glad when we get those guides sorted out," said Stanley.

"We'll see them tomorrow," I said. "I have an address in the village where we are supposed to meet them. As soon as we have bought provisions and divided up the gear, we'll head out."

A rickety wooden gate separated the lane from the entrance to the woods. The gate was closed with a chain and padlock, but there was a turnstile over which we were able, with some difficulty, to haul the Rocket. Once we were through, we moved in under the canopy of trees down a path even more muddy than the lane.

The wood was empty and damp. Clusters of greasy-looking mushrooms patched the pine-needled ground. I thought about the coarse nobility of our encampments in the Erikawald, which had made life down in the town of Zermatt seem so soft and decadent by comparison. When we'd come into town, we'd look dismissively at the tourists at the outdoor cafés, sweating in their loden coats, moleskin trousers, and hobnailed hiking boots. Few of them would climb above the tree line, fewer still across the glaciers, and none of them looked as if they would survive an actual trek in the mountains. But now I was older than some of those I'd sneered at, and the anticipated comfort of a hotel room in Palladino filled me alternately with longing and with guilt.

By the time Stanley and I pitched our tent at the edge of the wood, we were covered in sweat and had no prospects of a bath. But once the tent was up, the bedrolls laid out, and the water boiling for tea, I saw the first grudging smile on Stanley's face as he sat on the coffin, one leg crossed over the other, carefully munching the last of our English chocolate.

A sound of sheep bells reached us from pastures down in the valley.

I was just finishing up my tea when I noticed a solitary figure walking up the lane towards us.

Stanley saw him, too. "It's probably just some old codger out for an evening stroll," he said hopefully.

"Unless he's come to turf us out of the wood," I said.

"If he has come to move us along," declared Stanley, "he can bloody well save his breath because I'm not going."

Grimly we watched the old man. Now and then, we heard the metal tip of his cane click against a stone. There seemed to be something almost cruel in his leisurely pace. The man reached the turnstile and carefully climbed over it. Then he began to make his way down the main trail that ran through the woods.

I dreaded the thought of packing up the tent and trudging out to find another campsite, but as the old man turned off the main trail and began making his way towards us across the pine-needled ground, I resigned myself to the possibility.

Stanley and I both stood as the old man arrived at our camp.

"Good evening," said Stanley.

"Good evening, gentlemen," he replied, his face hidden under the brim of his hat.

We were surprised that he spoke perfect English.

"We are here," began Stanley, "in order to transport—"

"I know why you are here," he said, "and also who you are." He raised his stick and pointed it at the coffin. "And who is in there, too. I expected you to know me as well." I looked at Stanley and he looked at me.

"Actually, sir," I told him, "we have no idea."

Clearly irritated by our ignorance, the man took off his hat, revealing shaggy hair which had been tamped down by his hat into a strange gray helmet.

We recognized him instantly.

"Pringle!" said Stanley, the word having escaped his mouth only a fraction of a second before it left my own.

"That's right," he said, replacing the hat, then tilting his head back so he could fix us with his piggy and suspicious eyes.

Now I remembered what Stanley had said about Pringle spending his summers in the Alps. I wondered how on earth he had found us.

He jabbed the steel spike of his walking stick towards the rooftops of Palladino. "I hear you've had some trouble with accommodations."

"We've done all right," I said.

"Ah, but not as all right as you had hoped, judging from your time at the café this afternoon, which I must admit I watched with some hilarity from a bench across the street." The lips stretched tight across his teeth.

"How kind of you," said Stanley.

Pringle's hand clenched around his walking stick. "There's no kindness about it, as you well know, but the reason I'm here now is to offer you some good advice."

Wind sifted through the trees. It had begun to rain. The air beyond the woods turned smoky gray. Raindrops which had filtered through the branches tapped against the fabric of our tent.

"I'm here to reason with you," said Pringle, "and to make you see that you have been sent on a fool's errand. It is a needless risk of life. And for what? For him!" Once more, the walking stick, like a magician's wand, was aimed at Carton's coffin. "That man, who tried to ruin my life, is now doing his best to ruin yours. It's just one more stunt in a lifetime of stunts, and I have had to sit back and watch him misinform the public, humiliate me with his cruel impersonations, and generally bring disgrace to the science of mountaineering." He stepped towards us, which forced him to tilt his head back even farther in order to look us in the eye. "But this time, if we can all just agree on the facts, then logic can prevail over the madness in which we now find ourselves."

It was strange to hear this man speak of Stanley and me and himself as if we were all united in some common struggle against Carton.

"As soon as I heard he had died," continued Pringle, "and that he wished his body to be brought to that mountain he has claimed as his own, I knew you would be passing through Palladino. So I made sure I got here first and took the liberty of informing the café owner of a regulation that I found in the bylaws of the town, to the effect that no person who is deceased may be brought inside a public place of lodging. It's all there in black and white in the mayor's office, which also happens to be the grocery store. You can go and see it for yourselves if you don't believe me. The important thing is, the mayor believes me. And that is why you are here, instead of down in Palladino."

"I'm having a bit of trouble seeing where logic fits into all this," said Stanley.

"Yes," I added, "unless it involves tying you up and rolling you back into town like an old pudding."

Pringle gasped and shuffled backwards. The walking stick was raised yet again. "You had better reconsider your language, since you might not have noticed that my stick has a sharp pointy bit at the end!"

"It's not all that pointy," said Stanley.

"It's sort of a medium pointy," I added.

"It's pointy enough!" Pringle shouted.

"Not for what you have in mind," I told him.

"Quiet!" he shouted. "It's all a joke to you, isn't it? But people die up there in the mountains, and you might join them before long if you don't listen to me."

"Mr. Pringle," I said. "We make jokes not in spite of the fact that people die but because they die, and because, as you have pointed out, we might soon be among them. We make jokes to remind ourselves that we are still alive."

Slowly, he lowered the stick. "The fact remains that you should abandon this journey at once, before you are forced to endure any further humiliation. You owe him nothing! Even to have brought him this far is more than he deserves!"

The rain fell harder now and the last particles of daylight were effervescing into darkness.

"Well?" asked Pringle. "Will you give me an answer?"

All he got in return was our silence and the sound of the rain, through which he would soon be walking back to Palladino.

Pringle stalked away towards the trail. After only a few paces, he turned and raised his voice to us again. "This work you do," he said, "is the work of the devil!" His teeth were so clenched with rage that he could barely speak.

Briefly, we saw his dark shape disappearing down the lane before his black clothes merged with the darkness. Below, the cheerful lights of Palladino flickered like the embers of a fire.

Stanley returned to his tree-stump seat and picked up his cold mug of tea. "That does it. I'm going to finish this job if it's the last bloody thing I do." He spoke the way his uncle talked, tearing his words from the air.

"I think that's the point Pringle was trying to make," I replied.

Stanley ignored me. "If he thinks he can put us off just by making sure we don't get a bed to sleep in, he's got another thing coming."

Unfortunately for Stanley and me, we were the ones who had another thing coming.

TEN

THE FOLLOWING MORNING, in preparation for a trip into town to meet up with our guides, we made the first of many modifications to our coffin-hauling technique.

Although it probably would have been safe to leave the coffin at our camp in the San Rafaele woods, we did not dare to after the visit from Mr. Pringle.

By fastening lengths of rope around our shoulders and through the carrying loops, we were able not only to drag the coffin forward but also to stop it from sliding too quickly downhill. For the sake of the already scarred runners, I hoped we wouldn't have to drag the coffin around too much before we set out across the ice.

Now and then, as we moved along, we would hear a thump from inside the coffin, as Carton's body slumped from one side to the other. The idea of him embalmed beneath the plates of zinc seemed too abstract to be horrifying or sad. The coffin wasn't particularly heavy, which got me to thinking about the whole process of embalming. I seemed to recall something about Egyptian mummies having their insides removed, and their brains pulled out through their noses with the use of hooks. I wished I had asked Webb about it, but such questions had seemed too morbid at the time.

When we reached the streets of Palladino, the scraping of our runners soon attracted the attention of people whose houses overlooked a street called the Via Capozza. As soon as they discovered what was making all the noise, they crowded into their doorways. Unfriendly-looking women in headscarves and faded dresses held back their wide-eyed and whimpering children.

Our destination that morning was the Cooperativo di Palladino,which I gathered was some kind of communal storage space for goods moving in and out of the town. The *cooperativo* was a small tarred-wood building with green-shuttered windows. As with most of the buildings in town, the roof was made from irregularly shaped flat stones, on which grew luminous patches of emerald or sulphur-colored lichen. Beyond the Via Capozza, a few narrow, muddy side streets trailed down towards the river or wandered up towards the San Rafaele woods. Aside from a modern sign for Pirelli beer in the window of the café and concrete-pillared telegraph poles lining the road out of town, the place seemed lost in an earlier time. Even the rusty-fendered car parked next to the fountain seemed more out of place than the donkey-pulled cart tied up to a tree on the opposite side of the street.

We came to a halt outside the *cooperativo*, where Stanley made himself comfortable on a bench, feet up on the coffin, morning sunlight warm against his face.

Leaving Stanley with the Rocket, I went to sort out our

guides. As I walked inside the building, I felt that the worst of our troubles would soon be behind us. Much work lay ahead, but from now on we would have the help of experienced climbers. With their strength added to our own, the placing of the coffin on Carton's Rock seemed less of a dream and more of a certainty. Before the war, Stanley and I and the others had usually gone without guides. They were too expensive for us, and their presence took away some of the challenge. But this time, we needed all the help we could get.

The building was larger inside than it appeared from out on the street. Boxes lined the pine walls, reaching all the way up to the ceiling. Some were cases of wine, others of beer, others of canned foods like tomatoes and beans. There were also sacks of flour, large wicker-wrapped glass jars of olive oil, and wheels of Reggiano cheese. In between the various stacks was a walkway which led down to a booth, rather like a large ticket booth, behind which sat a man in a heavy woolen sweater, with a wild beard and dark curly hair almost down to his shoulders. Behind him was another storage area, containing racks of hunting rifles, shotguns, and brown metal cans of ammunition with military markings done in yellow paint.

Apart from the shaggy-haired man, I was the only one in the building.

His coal-black eyes fixed on me as I strode purposefully towards him.

"Good morning!" I said as I came to a stop in front of the grille.

"*Giorno*," he replied, still not taking his eyes off me.

I handed him the letter I had received from the Society of Mountain Guides in London, confirming the eight men we had engaged to help us in Palladino.

He looked at it and slowly lifted one arm off the desk. He let his hand fall open, with one finger pointing at me. "Do you know of the guide Giacomo Santorelli?" he asked.

I shook my head. "I can't say that I do, I'm afraid."

The man nodded, as if expecting this reply. "Then you can meet him now."

Despite the gloomy reception, I was glad that things were progressing and that I was at last able to meet one of our guides.

He opened the door to the booth.

I held out my hand. "William Bromley," I said.

He did not shake my hand but only nodded. "I am Salvatore."

I didn't know if this was his last name or his first, but it was clearly the only name he was going to give me.

Salvatore led me past the rifles to a back door, which opened out onto a narrow gravel road. On the other side of the road was a cemetery, and beyond that, across a flower-speckled field where a few sheep wandered among the dandelions, the lake's gentle waves flashed in the sunlight.

Salvatore opened a creaky wooden gate into the cemetery. The old wood was weathered gray and was patched, like the roof tiles, with scabs of lichen.

"Is he down at the lake?" I asked, thinking we were taking a shortcut.

"This way," he said.

We walked along a path among the crumbling gravestones. The inscriptions had worn off most of them. In front of each headstone, the ground had sunk down after the coffin below had collapsed. On the more recent graves, pictures of the dead had been printed onto small ovals of porcelain and attached to the stone. Stone angels with their eyes downcast stood among the graves, their once-fine features blurred like the faces of melting snowmen.

Salvatore stopped and turned. "Here," he said.

I looked at him. "What?" I asked.

He gestured to the grave by our feet.

There, barely legible in the inscription on the upright slates, I read the name Giacomo Santorelli. Above the name, a face was trapped within a dish of porcelain. Its expressionless eyes stared unblinking from the stone.

"I don't understand," I said.

"He was the guide for your Henry Carton."

The old story unraveled in my head, how the guide had fallen down a crevasse and the only reason Carton had survived was because the rope broke. "I thought that man was lost," I said.

"The grave is empty," he replied.

I saw now that the ground before the stone was not sunk down, indicating that no coffin lay beneath.

"If you come back here in twenty years," said Salvatore, "his body should appear from the glacier. That is what the scientists have told us, anyway."

"I know Mr. Carton spoke very highly of his guide," I said, not knowing what else to tell him, since it seemed a bit late for offering condolences.

"Everyone spoke well of him," answered Salvatore. "He was the best mountaineer in this region."

"I'm trying to understand," I said, as patiently as I could. "Does this somehow affect my hiring of other guides?"

Salvatore folded his arms and looked out across the lake, squinting in the glare of sun off rippled water. "No guide will go with you," he said, so quietly it was almost to himself.

"Why not?" I asked. "Did you not receive a letter from the Society of Mountain Guides?"

He nodded. "We received a letter. Yes."

"They told us everything had been arranged, and that guides were being brought in from several towns in the area."

"It was arranged, but it is not arranged anymore. The Society of Mountain Guides did not say anything in their letter about the coffin you have been dragging through our streets, or about Henry Carton being inside it. This we have learned from another Englishman who came here only a few days ago. His name—"

"Pringle," I said angrily. "Yes, I know who he is, but I would be happy to explain everything to the guides when they arrive."

Again he shook his head. "They are not arriving."

"Then they are already here?"

"They are not here and they will not be here," said Salvatore. "No guides will go with you on this journey."

"Do you think it is too dangerous with the coffin?" I was ready to explain my modifications to the Rocket.

But Salvatore only smiled contemptuously. "It is very dangerous to travel in this manner, but the danger is not what offends us."

"I didn't realize you were offended," I said, trying to remain calm. "I played no part in the death of your guide."

Salvatore turned to face me now, still squinting, as if the paleness of my northern face was hard for him to bear. "But Carton did. Henry Carton has offended us!"

"Many guides have died," I told him, "and many climbers, too."

He breathed out harshly. "It is not the fact that the guide was killed. It is the manner of his death."

"The fall?"

"The rope! It was hawser-laid rope. Do you know what that is?"

"I know what it is," I said.

"Good. Then you know that a rope like this will hold the weight of five men, maybe more. A guide checks his ropes before every journey into the mountains. When a rope is frayed or stretched, it is replaced immediately. This is the same kind Santorelli used to tie himself to Carton."

"Perhaps the rope became frayed on their journey."

He let his head fall back slightly and stared at me down the length of his blunt nose. "If this is true, then why did Carton say nothing about it? In fact, when he was asked by the police, he said it had not been frayed at all, and if the rope had been stretched, they would not have used it. And what is more, Carton did not return with the rope to offer us as proof."

"So what are you saying?"

"Only that the story Carton told us is incorrect."

"A lie, you mean."

He shrugged. "You can give it whatever name you want."

A breeze blew in off the lake, making the dandelions nod out in the luminous green grass.

"So how do you think Santorelli died?" I asked.

"I do not know. I only know that it is not the way that Carton said."

"Look," I said. "I have no more of an answer than you do, but I did not cause the death of this man and neither did my friend outside."

"But you travel in the name of Mr. Carton. That is the thing the guides will not accept."

"And what did Pringle tell you about it?" I asked, my temper flaring up. "That we were on the devil's business?"

"It is not what Mr. Pringle told us that matters. What matters is what we told him."

"Which was what?" I demanded.

"To go away. We told him to leave us alone. We do not need the advice of another crazy Englishman!" Now Salvatore began to walk back through the cemetery, talking to me over his shoulder as he went. "We are mountain guides! If a baker puts the wrong name on a birthday cake, he can make another cake. But if a guide makes a mistake, he may lose his life and the lives of his charges. Our work is very serious. We do not listen to little men like your Mr. Pringle. He thinks he knows everything about the mountains. He is like a thousand other people who go into the hills and come back to tell us what they have learned about climbing or about themselves or about the world."

"What is the harm in that?"

He turned and glared at me. "No harm at all, most of the time. The harmful ones are those who believe that they have found one thing, one truth above all others, that this is the only way it can be seen from now on, that everyone else is wrong and the rest should be humiliated for seeing it differently. These people are the dangerous ones. Mr. Pringle thinks that because he knows the height of all these mountains, and a catalogue of names and dates, he is as important as the mountains themselves. And Mr. Carton, he believed that because he was the first to climb a piece of rock in whose shadow we have lived for ten thousand years, that he was somehow in possession of that rock. Of course these two men ended up hating each other, not because they are so different but because they are so much the same. If you English were not so busy despising each other, you might find the time to understand what it means to live in the mountains, not just to visit them."

He may have said more, but I did not hear him. I was struck by an image, not of Pringle or of Carton or even of the mountains they worshipped. It was an image of Santorelli, frozen in the glacier. I saw his body suspended in the pale blue ice. His fingers were outstretched, legs halted in the motion of a swimmer, as if the glacier had enfolded him suddenly, as in the tumble of a breaking wave. But now he lay cradled in a world removed from the ticking of clocks, from the etching of years onto his skin, from the bitterness and squabbling of those who lived on with the burden of his death.

After what Salvatore had said, I knew that there could be no changing of his mind. From the way he talked, I knew he was speaking with the voices of everyone in this little town. Before Carton's coffin had ever scratched and bumped its way along the Via Capozza, they had decided what to do, and it had been left to this man to put their feelings into words.

Just as we were leaving the cemetery, I noticed three graves in a corner of the churchyard. They were newer than the graves around them, and each one carried the same inscription: QUI GIACE UN SOLDATO INGLESE, MORTO NELLA GUERRA 39–45.

I knew immediately who they must be. My eyes blurred.

Salvatore saw where I was looking. "In the summer of 1944," he said, "some Germans came through here on their way into the mountains. One week later, there was shooting. Then more Germans came. When they returned, it was said that there were several dead hidden in a truck whose canvas flap was pulled down. So nobody here saw them, or knew how many there were. But the Germans gave us three English bodies to bury, and this is where we put them. We could not find any names on the bodies, so we had to write that they were *sconosciuti*."

"Their names were Charles Whistler, David Armstrong, and Winston Forbes," I said. Tears spilled down over my cheeks, carrying the salt of old sweat to my lips, where I pushed them away with the tips of my fingers.

"They were your friends?" he asked.

"Yes," I replied. "They were."

Salvatore did not seem surprised, as if somehow the story of Carton and his guides, and of the fighting in the mountains and the bodies of the *soldati inglesi* and then our arrival here the day before had all been woven into the history of this town before the events even took place.

"Thank you for making a space for them in your church-yard," I said.

We walked to the side door of the *cooperativo*. It was cold in the shadow of the building.

"I wish that it was not this way between us," said Salvatore.

I felt as if he meant it, despite everything else he had said. I stood for one thing and he stood for another. And those two things had separated us as finally as the line between the living and the dead.

Walking around the front of the building, I found Stanley basking in the sun, heels up on the Rocket and moleskin hat pulled down over his face. He opened one eye. "All set?" he asked.

"They won't help us," I told him.

Now both eyes flicked open and he drew his heels down from the coffin. "Why on earth not?"

I explained what Salvatore had said.

"Jesus," muttered Stanley.

"I don't think he is going to help us, either." I took Stanley down to look at the graves.

There was nothing for me to say. To stand before the remains of someone who, if things had played out differently, could at that moment just as easily be looking down on your own grave is not a thing which can be bracketed with words, or set right with prayers, or even wept into making sense.

❄

IT WAS LATE AFTERNOON by the time Stanley and I arrived back at our campsite in the San Rafaele woods. We were tired from dragging the coffin. The muscles of my lower back and thighs complained in the angry, thumping rhythms of my heart.

I lit the old Primus stove and put some water on to boil for tea, of which we had very little left. Fading light showed in coppery strands through the trees. Church bells tolled the hour down in town. I heard the clop of a donkey's hooves along the Via Capozza.

It was a while before either of us spoke. In silence, we were both reaching the same conclusion. Either we would have to give up, and give up now, or we would have to carry the coffin ourselves, along with our food and the tent. It was, according to my map, eight kilometers across the glacier before we reached the gully up which we would need to travel to reach the base of the Dragon's Teeth. From there, no map would tell us how far up we had to climb, as none of them were detailed enough. We would not know until we had gone that far whether the coffin could be dragged or lifted to the summit. And I had no way of knowing if, once we were on the summit, there would even be room for a coffin, let alone enough stones lying about to construct the cairn that Carton had requested. With most of the mountains I had climbed, there was barely enough room for two people to stand on the summit.

I was afraid to speak because I was worried that Stanley would try to talk us out of it, and for the first time since I had given my word to Dr. Webb, I knew I *could* be talked out of it. I tried to think about what it would mean to have failed at this. I could imagine myself sitting at my father's house, in front of the fire with one of his tin cups of tea, and hearing him say I had done the right thing and my trying to believe it was true.

So thickly did these thoughts swirl around me that I did not feel the cool sweat on my back or the tom-tom drumming of pain in my body. I did not hear the cold wind blowing through the treetops, or even Stanley's voice, calling to me as if from somewhere down in the valley and not from right beside me. His voice grew closer and closer until at last I heard what he was saying.

"I've been trying to imagine the look on Helen's face when we show up at Victoria Station still lugging the Rocket."

"I'm sure she'd understand," I said.

"I can think of half a dozen jokes to make about it."

"I expect there are jokes to be made," I said, bracing myself for the onslaught.

But Stanley's face remained serious. "I think about Sugden and Pringle," he said, "and those people down there in Palladino who would like to see us fail before we've even started. They will be the ones to make the jokes if we give up now. And then those jokes will be the story of our lives."

I listened to him, hearing the old stubbornness in his voice and remembering all the times when he had exasperated me with his bullheaded words. But now I needed to hear them. Just as when I'd jumped from that Dakota, six years and a lifetime ago, there was no way home for me except through those mountains.

❄

THE NEXT DAY, dragging the coffin behind us like the beasts of burden we had become, Stanley and I returned to the Via Capozza. We had agreed that there was no time to lose. The longer we stayed up in the San Rafaele woods, the more likely it was that the locals would find some reason to have us arrested.

We stopped outside the grocery shop, which was the only provisioner in town. Splintery boxes of tomatoes, beans, and apples were set out under a tattered yellow awning.

Stanley took up his post as coffin guard, while I went inside, my pockets stuffed with lire to buy up whatever I could.

The shop smelled of spices, soap, and cheese.

An old woman sat beside a counter, on which oval loaves of bread were stacked. Beside the loaves were bowls of olives, green and black and another tiny kind which were a vivid bluish yellow. The woman was knitting a white baby sock. As soon as she saw me, she set the knitting down beside the bread, got up, and went out the back through a curtain made of beads. The beads rattled as they fell back into place.

A moment later, a man appeared. He was small and round-faced and wearing a shirt the same faded yellow as the awning outside. His eyes were a flat blue-gray and humorless. *"Prego,"* he said, and took his place behind the counter.

"I've come to buy some food," I said.

Almost imperceptibly, he moved his head from side to side. *"Non posso,"* he whispered, as if he were afraid to raise his voice.

"Is there a law against selling food to us?" I asked.

He shook his head.

"You are the mayor of this town?" I asked.

He nodded slowly.

"And you will not help us?" I demanded. "Not in any way at all?"

"*Mi dispiace,*" he said, and looked down at his shoes.

There was no point arguing. I turned to leave and was startled when I found myself face to face with Salvatore.

He was wearing the same thread-pulled sweater as the day before and leather breeches polished black at the knees. This, combined with his unruly hair and shaggy beard, gave him the look of a bear masquerading unsuccessfully as a man. He was holding out a can whose yellow label said SALUBRIO; it appeared to contain a stew of chickpeas and smoked ham. "Try this," he said. "After three or four days, you will get used to it."

I took the can from him, unable to disguise my confusion as to why he would be helping me now. "The gentleman says I cannot buy food here."

"You can buy here." Salvatore looked past me and spoke to the mayor in words I could not understand.

"I don't want to cause any trouble," I said.

"There is no trouble," replied Salvatore.

I faced the shopkeeper again.

He was holding the half-knitted baby sock, pinched between the fingertips of both hands. He nodded, to show that things had changed.

Salvatore said he could not stay. He wished us luck and was gone.

I loaded up the storage compartment of the Rocket with cans of beans, tinned fruit, olive oil, couscous, and cans of "Salubrio." Having run out of prerolled English cigarettes, I bought a packet of Italian pipe tobacco, cheerfully emblazoned with an Italian soldier in full *alpini* mountain-trooper gear. The fact that he was still wearing a Fascist insignia on his uniform either had gone unnoticed by the manufacturers or else the tobacco had been in the shop for a very long time. We bought no wine or bread, because they took up too much space. The salesman helped me carry everything out. When that was done, I paid him.

He folded the money away into his pocket.

"Who is Salvatore?" I asked him. I wanted to know why his words carried so much weight in this town.

"Salvatore Santorelli," replied the mayor. "He is the son of the guide who led Mr. Carton to his mountain."

Then I understood. It was Salvatore, and he alone, who could change the minds of those in Palladino. He had suffered most, and it was he who had to show forgiveness first.

Few gestures had meant more to me than the sight of that great bear standing before me, holding out that can of stew, as if he had punched through the two-dimensional image of who he had believed us to be before we arrived. But now that he had seen us, what had once seemed to be nothing more than madness, or Englishness, or even the work of the devil, had taken on more human faces, even if they were dirty faces like Stanley's and mine.

✳

BY THE NEXT MORNING, Stanley and I had been forced to make a few rules about sleeping in the same tent.

The first rule was that we no longer slept head to head. After inhaling each other's bean-soup breath all night, we decided that one person would sleep towards the front of the tent, the other towards the back.

The next rule was that although it was a good idea to remain in our bedrolls, heads peeking outside the tent, while we cooked oatmeal for breakfast, it was not a good idea for both of us to try to blow out the paraffin burner at the same time. When we did this, burning paraffin splashed in our faces and scorched off my week-old beard as well as the best part of Stanley's eyebrows. This left him looking permanently astonished, an expression he preferred to call "alert."

All through the day, we packed and repacked the storage area of the Rocket, which turned out to be more difficult than we had expected because even a slight imbalance caused the coffin to tip over when moving across rough ground. By now, not only the metal runners but the sides of the Rocket, too, had received their share of bumps from gateposts and the occasional capsize, which sent the body tumbling inside. But the seams of the coffin were holding, the carrying handles and the rope rings still secure.

I could feel the gradual strengthening of my legs and back as we hauled the coffin back and forth across the field. I was growing used to the feel of the rope around my waist and the strain against my stomach as I pulled.

The end of the day saw us slumped on either side of the stone-ringed fireplace we had built. The wood we had gathered was damp and smoked as it burned. We added fresh pine branches now and then to keep the thing going. The green needles spat and burst into flames. A stew of beans, crumbled biscuits, and pieces of cured ham bubbled and plopped in our mess tin. We leaned forward over the fire, no longer concerned about the smoke which stained our clothes and seeped into every pore in our bodies. I was just reaching forward to lift the mess tin off the flames, since the stew was starting to burn, when Stanley asked, "What's that?"

"What's what?" I replied, rummaging in my canvas sack for the plates.

"That sound?"

I looked among the dark shadows of the wood. I did hear something. It was a faint rattling, almost as if someone was chipping at a piece of stone, but I couldn't tell where it was coming from.

"There," said Stanley.

I turned and saw a wagon coming up the path which led to town. It was a horse wagon but was being pulled by two men. A third man was walking behind it. Something was on the wagon, but it had been covered by a tarpaulin.

"More visitors," sighed Stanley.

"Well, I don't see Pringle," I replied, "so that's a good start."

The wagon reached the gate which separated the muddy lane from the beginning of the field.

"Now they're stuck," I said, reflexively reaching my right hand to the small of my back, which hurt constantly from the effort of lifting the Rocket over the wooden barricade.

But they weren't stuck. The man who had been walking behind the cart stepped forward, produced a key, and undid the padlock. The two men who had been pulling the cart resumed their journey across the field and on towards the woods where we were camped.

By now, Stanley and I had forgotten about our stew and were standing with our hands in our pockets, watching the course of the wagon.

I felt sure they would continue on the road which led around the outside of the woods, although what good that might do them I had no idea, since it only led to another gate going back into town on the other side of the forest. In their silence and their stubborn solemnity, they reminded me of pilgrims bound on some journey meaningless to all but those who made it.

The men did not continue on around the wood. They headed straight towards us.

"What the hell is going on?" muttered Stanley.

When the men came to within a few feet of our campsite, they set down the long arms of the wagon and straightened their backs. They were dressed in heavy, collarless work shirts, canvas trousers, and heavy boots. They nodded in greeting, but did not smile.

It occurred to me that in spite of the shopkeeper's generosity and the kindness of Salvatore, enough people in Palladino still harbored resentment against us that they had decided to run us out of town and had brought along the cart to hasten our departure. But there seemed to be a few things on the cart already, hidden under the faded brick-red tarpaulin. Perhaps they were only baskets, into which our gear was to be unceremoniously heaped. There would be no point in our resisting them. We would only end up in a brawl. I felt a great weight settle on my back, as if my shoulder blades had turned to lead. I thought about the obstacles which had been thrown before us, and I did not know if these were a sign for Stanley and me to keep clambering over them and not to lose heart, or whether they were a sign that we should never have started on this voyage. At what point, I asked myself, does determination become foolishness? I wondered if that same question had passed through the mind of the guide Santorelli as he fell away into the blue-walled tomb of the glacier.

Now the man who had been walking behind the cart came forward. He wore a knee-length oilskin coat and gray-and-white-flecked trousers. On his head was a wool cap with a small brim of the kind I had seen newsboys wearing on the street corners of London. With a swipe of his hand, he removed his cap and bowed forward in greeting, revealing a polished bald head. "*Signori,*" he said.

"Good evening," we replied.

"I have brought you the dinner."

"I beg your pardon?" asked Stanley.

"The dinner," he repeated. "It is a gift."

"A gift from whom?" I asked.

He smiled, and for a moment his big eyes closed sleepily. In that moment, he looked like a big, contented cat. "This is from the manager of the Hotel Aosta. I am Paolo Ungaretti. I am the chef of this hotel."

Stunned by this announcement, I watched the two men who had been pulling the cart remove the old tarpaulin. Beneath lay a large wicker hamper. Beside it was a collapsible table and two chairs. The two men proceeded to set up the table, folding down its legs and carrying it past us to the clearing, where they made sure it stood on level ground. Then came the chairs, and the hamper, which, when opened, revealed plates and glasses, two bottles of wine, metal containers for food, and a white tablecloth. White. Here, in this world of mud and pine and shadows, it was as if they had clipped a piece of the distant glaciers and brought it down, neatly folded, to lay upon the table.

Ungaretti removed his coat, revealing a short chef's tunic. He tossed the coat up onto the cart and rubbed his hands together as he prepared to get down to work.

"But why is he doing this?" I asked.

Ungaretti pursed his lips and tilted one of his hands back and forth. "He says to me that he does not feel good about what happened between you and him when you arrive in Palladino. He says he hope you accept this for his apology."

"But why did he change his mind?" asked Stanley.

"Before you come here," said Ungaretti, "we did not like you. But when you come here, we see you are people like us. It is simple."

Stanley turned to me. "Do you think we should accept this?" he asked.

Ungaretti heard the question. He looked at the congealed stew in our mess tin and gestured at it with a flick of his fingers. The look on his face showed that even to gesture at it was more than he could bear. "This was your dinner?"

Stanley nodded.

Ungaretti reached down to one of the metal containers he had brought and removed the lid. "I have brought for you *zuppa friulana con l'orzo e basilico.*" A waft of steam rose from the container, bringing with it the smell of basil, onion, and garlic.

"I'll just sit down here," said Stanley, making his way to the table.

I did the same.

The two men, who must have been waiters in their pre–cart-pulling existence, laid the table, uncorked the wine, and even set between Stanley and me a small candle lantern.

Above us, the wind sluiced through the treetops. The flap of our tent rustled. A solitary raindrop dabbed the white cloth on the table.

Then, placed before us, was a soup so simple and so perfect that it almost made me cry.

But Stanley really did cry. He was blubbering great, shameless tears, which Ungaretti seemed to find entirely appropriate and the waiters politely ignored.

With the soup came a Tocai wine, heavy and mysterious, with layers of different flavors unfolding in our mouths.

While we ate the soup, Ungaretti stoked up the fire with some wood that he had brought. Crouched over the crackling

flames, he fried garlic in an iron pan, then added fresh rosemary leaves and arborio rice. For the next twenty minutes, he
stirred the rice with a wooden spoon, adding to it splashes of
beef stock from one bottle and white wine from another. He
never left the fire, squinting when the smoke blew in his face
and shifting on his haunches when his muscles cramped.

The waiters watched this as if in a trance.

Stanley and I did the same.

When the rice was done, Ungaretti stirred in butter and
shavings of Parmesan cheese. He scooped the mixture, which
was a glowing yellow flecked dark-green with the rosemary,
onto plates. *"Risotto,"* he said as he set it before us, *"col ros-
marino e vino blanco."*

There were more tears from Stanley, and toasts to the
waiters, who had at last begun to smile. And to Ungaretti, who
received our compliments with dignified solemnity.

The waiters broke out a bottle of grappa, and they and
Ungaretti toasted us from wooden cups.

We raised our cups to them and drank, feeling the grappa
burn along the branches of our veins.

For dessert, we ate little pastries made with honey, lemon,
and bitter orange.

Coffee was brewed on the fire, and by now we were not
divided between servers and patrons. We were comrades in
this odd and unforgettable occasion. The waiters inspected
the Rocket. Ungaretti, seated on the back of the cart with his
legs swinging gently back and forth, remembered his days as
an apprentice chef at the Polídor in Paris.

It was deep into the night when Stanley and I walked them
to the gate. We watched as they disappeared down the lane,
vanishing in the India-ink blackness, their course traceable
only by the rattle of the cart's wheels on the stones.

I knew I ought to head straight to bed. But I wasn't ready to settle down yet and decided to give the Italian tobacco a try. By the fading light of the fire, I rolled myself a smoke. No sooner had I got the thing lit, however, when Stanley banished me from the campsite, saying that if I insisted on insulting the fresh air with something so offensive I could do so someplace else. It occurred to me to mention that he still had a small supply of his own tobacco, which he could perhaps have shared. But I let it go and decided to take a walk instead, rather than listen to any more of his hacking.

Strolling along the edge of the wood, I looked down among the shadows of Palladino. Tiny cubes of light shone from the windows of those who could not find their way into the catacombs of sleep.

I reached the meadow where our parachutes had landed. Walking through the tall grass, soaking my boots and trouser legs with dew, I made my way to the hollow where we had hidden the silk shrouds and drop canisters by covering them with a layer of dead leaves and earth. The canisters were gone, of course; I had not expected to find them there. But it did me good to see these places again and to set them in a context other than the war.

Heading back into the darkness, I could barely find the path that ran down the middle of the woods. Cursing at myself for not bringing a torch and for not going back the same way I had come, I stumbled along, but it wasn't long before I realized I was lost. I was still on a path, but it was clearly not the right path. The one I had thought I was on ran straight through the forest, but this one twisted and turned, growing narrower and more rutted the farther I traveled.

I came to a clearing and stopped. The path seemed to have petered out altogether. The darkness was so complete that I felt myself growing dizzy. A breeze hissed faintly through the branches. At that moment, something brushed against me. At first, I thought it was a branch, but when I reached up to push it aside, my hand touched something soft.

I jumped back.

The thing, whatever it was, hung suspended in the air in front of me.

I backed up, and then bumped into something else, which swung away from me.

Spinning around, I lost my balance and tripped.

I fumbled in a pocket for my box of matches, then struck one and held it up.

Before the flame blew out, I looked up at a pair of eyes staring glassily down upon me.

It gave me such a shock that I cried out.

I lit another match, and this time, as the sulphur snapped and flared, I saw it was a deer, hanging by its antlers from a rope tied to a tree branch.

Another match, and now I saw more deer, their stomachs emptied and tongues lolling out, each one dangling just above the ground. They shifted slowly in the breeze, like abandoned marionettes.

A moment later, I heard Stanley's voice. Turning, I caught sight of a torch beam wobbling towards me through the trees. "Where are you?" he shouted. "Are you all right?" I called to him, and soon he was standing in front of me, out of breath, shining the torch beam around the carcasses.

There were a dozen of them at least. They formed a wall of bone and fur around us. Here and there, I saw pale marks on the bodies where the bullets had entered, tearing away patches of fur.

Beyond them, the blackness of the wood was complete, as

if the planet ended beyond those cold bodies, shearing away into space.

"I heard you shout," said Stanley. His hair was full of pine needles from thrashing through the trees.

"I got lost," I told him. "And then I stumbled into these things."

"What is all this?" he asked.

"It's a hunter's grove." I set my hand against one of the deer and gave it a gentle push. The rope creaked. It was the sound I had heard before. "They have to hang their kills to let the heat go out of the bodies. Then they can cut up the carcass. And since it isn't hunting season yet, they probably wanted these things kept as far out of the way as possible."

Stanley shined the torch around. Light reflected off the dried and open eyes.

It seemed like bad luck, running into this on the night before we left, but I tried to put the idea out of my head.

"Let's get out of here," said Stanley.

Rather than risk getting lost again, we followed the path out to the meadow, then went around the edge of the wood until we found our camp again.

Tucked back in my sleeping bag, I was just drifting off when Stanley nudged me.

"What's the matter?" I asked groggily.

"She tried to talk me out of it, you know."

"Who did?" I asked. "Out of what?"

"Helen. Out of coming on this trip with you."

I rubbed my hands against my cheeks, trying to wake myself. "She did? But why?"

Stanley paused.

I saw the silhouette of his face as he turned away from me.

"She said she didn't think you were lucky enough," he said.

I felt a constriction in my throat. "What kind of thing is that to say?" But even as I asked the question, I thought about those dead animals in the clearing and I knew exactly what kind of thing it was to say. He, too, had been thinking about luck. With all the preparation in the world, sometimes success or failure still boiled down to chance. It was the one thing you could not control, and because you could not control it, you tried to put it out of your mind as useless superstition. No matter how hard you tried, though, you couldn't help thinking about whether luck was working for you or against you.

"The thing is," continued Stanley, "she was wrong."

Through the mesh of fingers held against my face, I breathed in the smell of our canvas house. "Why?" I asked.

"Unlucky people don't have meals prepared for them by proper chefs in the middle of a forest."

"I hope you're right," I said.

III

ELEVEN

WE STOOD BEFORE THE ruins of the customs house. It was evening.

We had been marching all day.

My eyes stung with sweat. My shirt was soaked. I felt the slippery burn of blisters on my heels.

Stanley and I leaned against the coffin, gasping like fish until our hearts stopped hammering so hard against our chests. We passed a canteen back and forth, wiping the top on our sleeves.

"We'll make camp here," I said, screwing the metal cap back on the canteen.

"Thank God for that," grunted Stanley.

Wind off the glacier sliced into our faces, molding our clothes to our bodies and tugging at the straps which held our gear inside the cargo area on top of the coffin. The water of the Lago Dragone was dark and ruffled, glowing sapphire blue. Beyond it, the ice of the glacier hunched up to the sky and sank beneath the water, spouting little streams from cracks in its sheer wall.

Barbed-wire entanglements still blocked the road before the customs house. The rusted strands fell away as we stepped through them. The windows of the house were all smashed, the door gone. Wind moaned through the empty structure.

I had not known how it would feel to reach this place again. At first glance, however, the old building seemed to be nothing more than a collection of rotted wood and stone and broken glass. No nightmares clung to the shadows.

In any case, we were too tired to go on, the ground was too hard for pitching a tent, and the customs house provided the only available shelter from the wind. Not trusting its dilapidated floors, however, we unrolled our sleeping bags just outside the front door.

While Stanley unpacked the food, I went inside to scrounge up some wood for a fire. Stepping carefully over the creaky boards, I shined a torch over the mildewed walls. The impact marks of bullets were still clear to see, as well as places where the woodwork appeared to have caught fire. In a room at the back, I found two broken chairs piled in the corner. I dragged them outside and smashed them for kindling.

A short while later, with the fire crackling by our feet, Stanley and I sat on the coffin and watched the stars emerge from the periwinkle sky.

I kept waiting for this peaceful scene to come unraveled, for the past to bulldoze its way into the present. Of all the terrible things that had happened on that mission, the worst of them had happened here. But as the minutes passed, I began to relax. I felt like a prisoner who had escaped a punishment that had once seemed certain.

I glanced across and smiled at Stanley, who had gathered up a handful of old bullet cartridges. He set them in a row, clasped between his fingers and his thumb, and began to blow into them as if playing a panpipe. He gave a halting rendition of "Twinkle, Twinkle, Little Star" and then looked up, smiling.

I was relieved beyond words that those cartridges in his hand, some of which might have taken the lives of our friends or which I myself had used to kill, were only empty shells to me. I applauded and asked for an encore.

After dinner, we sat with arms folded, cigarettes dangling from our mouths, puffing away contentedly and looking at the night sky like spectators watching a movie.

It was not long before we saw a shooting star slice across the dark.

"Did you see that?" asked Stanley.

"I did," I replied. I stared at the place where the star had scratched across the sky.

"Now we get to make a wish," said Stanley.

But I was not thinking about that. The image of that falling star had jolted me out of my peace. It began slowly, but came on, gathering speed. I could not stop it. Riding the tail of that meteor, the demons flew hissing towards me.

❄

THE FLARE ARCED UP into the black and then burst, casting a bony light upon the ground as it drifted on its tiny parachute. Shadows stretched through the rain-sieved night, swaying with the motion of the flare. Rain pecked at my face. The spit and crackle of the flare filled my ears, and the smell of its smoke was bitter in my lungs.

I thought of the enemy, peering through the darkness, eyes dried out, searching for movement. I asked myself how they could have heard anything or seen anything on this miserable night. I wondered how many there were.

Finally the flare touched the ground in front of us and sputtered out. The world returned to black.

I began crawling forward again. The other men were already moving. Mud clung to my elbows and my knees. The gray paste found its way into the corners of my eyes, splashed between my teeth, and packed itself beneath my fingernails.

I had not gone more than a few feet when another flare went up. Jamming my face down in the mud, I tried not to breathe. After an eternity of drifting through the air, it hit the ground in front of us and lay crackling for a few more seconds before finally going out with a sigh.

We crawled forward again, moving in a ragged line. Whatever sound we made was drowned by the rain, which thrashed against a thousand shallow puddles.

Thirty yards from the wire, a third flare went up.

They must know we are here, I thought. But not one shot had been fired. Perhaps they were just a patrol, lost and nervous because of the storm and the gunfire earlier in the day, from which one of their men had not returned.

Ten yards farther on, the wire towered over us like the crest of a wave in the moment of its breaking.

Now I heard low voices coming from behind the wire. One sounded frightened. Then another voice cut him off.

I couldn't understand where they were. I knew they must be just behind the wire, but everything beyond the massive tangle was obscured by darkness.

The voices stopped.

The three of us reached the wire. Wind moaned through its coils. Raindrops gathered on each loop and curve, strangely beautiful in this ugly thicket. The plan had been to drag aside one of the individual frameworks and rush through the gap, but I now realized that the X-shaped frames were made of metal and not wood.

To my horror, I understood that we were completely stuck. We would not be able to climb over the wire. Nor would we be able to cut through in time.

I felt panic rising through my blood and filling the whites of my eyes, like the ancient monster of Loch Amon climbing through the black water, thrashing the darkness with its long tail, its mouth wide and claws outstretched. It took all the strength I had not to get up and run away.

At that moment, I saw Forbes pointing at the wire. He crawled across and whispered from so close that his lips brushed against my ear.

"There is a gap. There are two layers of wire. We can zigzag through it. The opening is ten feet to the right." Again he pointed.

We both looked across to where Sugden lay.

He nodded, to show he understood.

When I raised my head, the wire seemed to scratch into my eyes.

Choking down the fear, I rose slowly to my feet. My mud-clogged clothes hung heavily from my shivering body. My knees complained as they straightened. My grip tightened on the trench club.

I was standing. I could see nothing on the other side of the wire except the road, which trailed off into the darkness.

Where the hell were they?

I turned to look at Forbes and Sugden.

They were rising, as if the mud itself were taking shape.

No sound. Only the rain. Gray clouds tumbled by above.

That was when I saw the outline of a gun raised behind

the wire and felt as much as heard the bang of the flare going off. It blazed into the air and suddenly the white light was all around me, and there in that river of ink I saw two men behind the wire, buried up to their chests in the earth. Each one had a rifle with fixed bayonet raised to his shoulder. The rain was shining on their helmets.

A great weight fell away inside me then, as if my heart had become detached from whatever held it in place and was tumbling down the ladder of my ribs.

A voice called out from the trench, ordering us to halt.

None of us spoke.

There was the rotten-lung gasping of the flare above our heads.

In that bleached glare, I understood I was about to die.

Then there was an explosion in the trench, a cough of red fire and black smoke even darker than the night. The concussion blew past my face.

Sugden had thrown a grenade.

I heard people crying out.

Then came the flash of rifle fire. Blue sparks flicked through the blackness as bullets struck the wire. The tangled metal seemed to writhe and shift before my eyes.

I don't know how long I stood there, waiting for the bullets to shatter my bones. They snapped the air around me, like bullwhips cracking the sky.

But I was still on my feet.

I lunged for the gap in the wire, not stopping to hear if the others were following. The weight of my soaked clothes was almost too much to bear. I skidded in the mud. Rain thrashed against my face. I tumbled into the blackness of the trench. The ground rose up to meet me and I crashed against some wooden boards. A voice. Someone was moving towards me. I made out the hard-angled silhouette of a German helmet. I raised my arm, jammed the barrel of the gun against the thick wool of his tunic, and pulled the trigger.

Sparks flew out of the cylinder. The smell of gun smoke mixed with the burning wool of his clothes

He fell as if the ground had swallowed him up. He landed on his knees and his head slumped forward against me. I stepped aside and his face slammed down against the muddy boards.

Sugden and Forbes had made it through the wire. They crashed down into the trench open on either side of me, clods of dirt spraying from their boots. Water splashed up from the duckboards.

Gunfire was everywhere. I turned towards the customs house and my foot caught on one of the boards. As I sprawled, my hands tore on the splintery boards. Back on my feet again, I could barely move, my clothes felt so heavy. My heart felt like it was going to burst.

I stumbled forward.

Ahead of me, someone cried out, shrill and hideous. Then came a rapid, rhythmic pounding and the bestial roaring of Sugden beating a man to death.

Forbes moved past me. I saw his arm snap back and forward. We ducked down in the trench as the grenade he had thrown bounced against the wall of the customs house, then hit the ground behind the wall of sandbags.

The coughing roar of the explosion was followed by the sound of windows shattering. The door flew open. Smoke spilled out over the tops of the sandbags.

Now more explosions crashed about us. My ears were ringing.

Footsteps sounded on the wooden boards.

Forbes and I climbed out of the trench and took cover by the sandbags.

After putting the Webley back in its holster, I dropped the club and fished a grenade from my pocket. I pulled the pin, let the lever go, and threw it at the open doorway. Instead of landing deep inside the building, the grenade struck something just inside the doorway. Someone called out, and I realized it had hit a person standing in the dark. Red sparks filled the blackness, and a burning gasp of air washed over me. This time, I did not hear the sound of the explosion. My legs gave way in the concussion. Forbes and I lay there, stunned. My finger was still hooked around the grenade pin.

Taking up the club again, I clambered over the torn sandbags with Forbes following behind me. On the other side, a figure lay on his back. His chest was smoldering.

Now a man tumbled out of the customs house, rifle in hand, putting on his helmet. He almost crashed right into us. His face was ghostly white. I swung the club at him and felt a jolt in my wrist as the lead ball connected with his head. I swung my arm back, ready to hit him again, but he staggered back into a broken window frame, pitched into the shards of broken glass, and then lay still.

Taking out another grenade, my fingers fumbled for the ring. The other ring was still on my finger. I dropped the club as my mud-slippery hands tugged out the pin. Then I let the lever go and it sprang away. I pitched the grenade through one of the broken windows and threw myself down on the ground, my hands pressed to my ears.

With a stunning crash, the bomb went off. Glass and chips of wood showered down on top of me. Smoke retched out of the door and through the broken windowpanes.

I was lying there dazed when I heard the splintery wooden crack of a gun going off practically in my face.

A man was standing over me, holding out a long-barreled pistol. He had walked out of the smoke inside the customs house. Half of his left arm was missing. The sleeve of his tunic hung in shreds.

I could not see his face.

Am I hit? I thought. Oh Christ, am I hit?

But then I realized he was not pointing the gun at me.

He fired again. The spent cartridge fell and bounced off my chest.

I moved my hand slowly to my side and drew the Webley from its holster. Then, in one movement, I raised my arm and pulled the trigger.

Nothing happened. There wasn't even a click. The trigger seemed to have jammed.

The man looked down. He said something.

Bloody saliva splashed on my face.

He swung the gun down and pointed it at me.

I pulled the trigger again, and this time the Webley fired.

His head jolted back, but then he fell forward, collapsing on top of me.

I cried out and pushed him off. His body rolled away. I scrabbled back across the ground. Then I climbed shakily to my feet, my head still numb from the explosions. I looked around for Forbes, but he wasn't there, so I went into the building by myself.

At first, there was too much smoke to see. Then I made out scraps of paper burning on the floor. As my eyes grew accustomed to the gloom, I could discern a staircase leading up the right-hand wall of the room. At the bottom of these stairs lay a man. He was bald, with a thick roll of skin between the top of his neck and the base of his skull. He lay facedown against the bottom step. He wore no helmet or tunic, only a dirty gray shirt tucked into his trousers. A pair of braces stretched across his shoulders.

I pointed the gun at him, but he didn't move.

Outside, the gunfire had slackened.

Sugden was shouting, but I couldn't tell what he was saying.

Over the sound of his yelling, I heard a noise in the next room. Pressing my ear to the wall, I made out a muffled voice on the other side.

In a quiet, urgent tone, the man was repeating the same words over and over.

Standing back, I broke open the Webley, tipped out the empty cases, and reloaded the cylinder as best I could with my shaking fingers. Then I snapped the Webley shut, cocked the hammer, and fired into the wall at the place where I'd heard the voice. The darkness blinked with fire, and in the confines of the room, the noise was deafening. I kept firing until the cylinder clicked empty. Then I dashed through the doorway, down a short corridor, and into the room where I'd heard the voice. The door had been blown off its hinges by one of the earlier explosions. I couldn't see anything in there. Cordite smoke whirled around me.

Groping in my pocket, I took out my torch and turned it on.

Through the burning gray mist, I saw the heavy beams which supported the roof. In the middle stood a table, the legs of which were made of sawn-off branches with the bark still attached. On the table lay pieces of equipment—a gas-mask canister, canteens and a bread bag, binoculars.

As I played the beam around, hunting for the man whose

voice I'd heard, the light caught on bunks with chicken-wire netting instead of mattresses.

The smell of gunpowder clogged my lungs. I could taste it in my spit, like a coin in my mouth.

When the torch beam reached the corner of the room, I noticed a man sitting at a field desk, half hidden in the smoke as if behind a veil of dirty lace. Set up on a desk in front of him was a radio in a leather case. Wires snaked up from the radio, through the wall, and out of the customs house. Pale gouges, like splashes of paint, showed where my bullets had come through the wall.

The man was leaning forward, facing away from me. From the silver on his shoulder boards, I could tell he was an officer. He breathed heavily, still holding the black telephone receiver and whispering the same words over and over. He did not seem to notice the light of the torch.

I took one step forward and my feet crunched on broken glass.

He straightened up as he heard the noise, but still without turning around.

I aimed the gun at him but realized I had forgotten to reload it.

Slowly, he set down the receiver and turned to face me, squinting into the light.

At first it looked exactly as if he were wearing a red shirt beneath his unbuttoned tunic, but then I saw that he had been wounded in his chest.

In his hand, he clutched a small pistol.

"Drop that," I told him.

The man's pale eyes were shallow-set, his nose long and straight. He had a small, rounded chin. He spoke and his lips became flecked with blood.

I couldn't understand him. "Get up," I said, and jerked the barrel of the Webley away from the desk, hoping he could not see that my gun was empty.

The officer gently touched his hand to his neck and noticed the blood that came away on his fingers. He sighed and clicked his teeth together.

Outside the gunfire had stopped.

"For Christ's sake," I told him. "Get—" But I never finished the sentence.

The officer turned the pistol in his hand, his thumb inside the trigger guard, as if he meant to hand it to me. But instead of doing that, he set the barrel of the pistol against his forehead and pulled the trigger. His body jumped back in the chair, which fell against the wall but did not tip over. The man's feet dangled off the floor and his hands fell to his sides. His eyes were closed. The pistol dropped. Smoke slithered from the hole in his head. Behind him, blood ran down the wall.

I kept the Webley pointed at him for a long time, before finally lowering it.

My heart was beating too fast.

Sugden called my name.

I stumbled down the corridor and out into the night. The rain had stopped. Stars clustered in the sky.

Sugden called again.

"I'm here!" I croaked.

Wind moaned around the angles of the roof. The sound was like voices whispering all around me.

"Forbes is hurt!" shouted Sugden. "I can't find the medical kit!" His voice was shrill with panic.

I ran towards the sound of his voice, shining the torch in front of me.

Sugden was down in the trench, hunched over Forbes.

I jumped down beside them.

"I can't see enough to know where he is hit," Sugden shouted.

It was only now that I realized the trench was lined with concrete. It appeared to be some kind of drainage ditch for channeling runoff water from the lake past the customs house and down the steep slope on the other side.

"Let me take a look," I said.

When Sugden moved aside, the first thing I saw were Forbes's open eyes. The pupils were not dilated, but he continued to breathe in heavy and uneven gasps.

Moving the torch beam down the length of his body, I realized he has been shot in the stomach, as well as in the hip.

Past where he lay were two dead Germans, their bodies twisted against the side of the drainage ditch.

We cut open Forbes's clothing and discovered that both wounds had been caused by the same bullet, which had gone into his hip and exited out of his stomach.

Even with my limited medical training I knew he was not going to make it. I didn't say this to Sugden, but instead climbed out of the trench and ran back to find my pack, in which I'd stored the kit. Beyond the wire, I could make out the marks our crawling bodies had made when we'd come in.

When I got back, the medical kit clutched in my hand, I found Sugden slapping Forbes over and over on the cheek. "Wake up, wake up," he chanted under his breath.

Setting the green metal box on the ground, I opened it and looked at the neat little bundles of bandages, the white tape, and the sulfa powder. Then I set aside the angled scissors and the little morphine syrettes.

Looking at Forbes's wounds, I found myself already thinking past his death. The fact was that the mission had failed.

Sugden and I could not carry all the components for the beacon by ourselves. It would take two trips up the mountain, possibly three, and if that officer's radio was working, it would not be long before reinforcements arrived from down in the valley. We had to destroy the equipment and get out of here while we still could. The only question in my mind was whether to bring Forbes with us, on the slim chance that he might survive the journey, or to leave him here, hoping that the Germans might be able to save him, or to overdose him with morphine and put an end to his suffering as quickly as possible.

I was stunned by the coldness of my calculations. In the past, I'd been proud of my ability to think clearly, even in the most difficult situations we had faced together in the mountains. But this time, even though I knew it was more important than ever to think and act quickly, inside I felt as lifeless as the bodies of the dead men sprawled beside me in this trench.

Sugden sat back and put his face in his hands. "We should have turned back," he sobbed.

"You listen to me," I said, but my voice was so roughened by smoke that I barely recognized it. "If we had gone back down into the valley, the only thing we'd have run into would be half the bloody German army. Even if we'd given up trying to climb the mountain and pushed on to Switzerland, we'd still have had to come through here. That's why they chose this place to wait for us."

"But why were they here at all?" he moaned.

"I don't know. What we have to think about now is getting out of here, before another patrol comes up from the valley." I took Sugden by the arm and shook him. "Are you listening to me?"

I still didn't know if I was getting through to him.

"We'll take Forbes with us to Switzerland," I told him, making my decision. "That's the best we can do for him. Our job now is to get back alive."

Sugden lowered his hands to his knees. Dirt was smeared across his face. He nodded. My last words had brought him to his senses.

While Sugden did his best to dress the wound in Forbes's stomach, I went back into the customs house to find a stretcher. But there wasn't one. Instead, propped up against the side of the house, I found a wooden sled with a harness attached to it.

We gave Forbes a syrette of morphine, then loaded him onto the sled and wrapped him in gray blankets which we'd found on the beds in the customs house.

Behind the house we discovered a portable radio antenna, about six feet tall, standing on a collapsible tripod. The wires snaked back through a small hole drilled into the wall of the building. Only a few paces behind the customs house, the ground fell away steeply, patched with snow and boulders. A stone rolled off this place probably wouldn't have stopped until it reached the valley far below.

I unwrapped the pieces of the beacon and threw some of them as far out as I could into the lake. The rest I pitched off the steep slope. They clattered away down the mountain, shedding screws and wires and ringing against the rocks until they had vanished from sight

With two hours to go before dawn, we could hear the sound of trucks moving down in the valley. More soldiers had arrived, and we knew they would not wait for daylight before heading up the mountain.

As quickly as we could, Sugden and I headed out. Sugden carried a pack containing food and a tent, and I hauled the sled.

It was cold. Wind rumbled in the caverns of the glacier. Ice glowed blue in the light of the pale yellow moon.

❄

"ARE YOU ALL RIGHT?" It was Stanley. He stood in front of me, a cigarette smoldering in his fingers.

"What?" I asked.

"You were talking to yourself."

I shivered. I had no idea how much time had passed or what I had said. "This place," I muttered. I did not need to say more.

"I thought as much," he said, "with all these bullet cases lying around."

I got up from where I had been sitting on the coffin and walked out into the road.

"William," said Stanley.

I turned. "Yes?"

"I think it's time you told me everything, whether I want to hear it or not."

There was something in the way he spoke, a kind of absoluteness in his voice, which made clear that this chance would never come again. Stanley was the only one who could share this burden with me, and if I did not share it now, I would carry it alone and for the rest of my life. I had carried the weight of it already longer than I could stand, and I could not bear it anymore.

I told him all that I could remember, from the first days of training at Achnacarry, from the first gunshots, which had killed Armstrong and Whistler, to the memory of Sugden and me, after the customs house disaster, hauling the sled towards Switzerland.

I went on to tell him how Sugden did not speak on that long walk along the ruined road that led towards the border. It was noon of the following day before we realized that Forbes was dead. As I sat beside him, seeing the life gone out of his eyes, I could not summon any grief. That emotion, and others like it, had been swallowed in the darkness inside me. Instead, all I could think about was that despite all the time we had spent together, I had never really known him. We buried Forbes under a cairn of stones almost within sight of the Swiss frontier, too tired to speak or to feel anything more than exhaustion. Then Sugden and I sat on his grave and ate our emergency rations in silence. From there, we could just make out the summit of Carton's Rock, rising from the distant plain of ice.

Reaching the border at sunset, we found the Swiss customs house boarded up and empty. We were just beginning to wonder where our contacts might be when two men wearing civilian clothes appeared from a grove of birch trees, where they had been observing us. They turned out to be the SOE agents. They said they had not been certain who we were, since they had been told to expect five men.

They had brought civilian clothing, which we exchanged for our military gear. Our weapons were dismantled and the pieces buried. The rest of our stuff was hidden in a cave.

Three days later, bearing forged diplomatic passports, we were flown to Lisbon and from there, the following day, back to England.

We had been gone exactly one week.

Sugden and I were debriefed in a room at the Aldershot barracks. It was here that we learned why German soldiers had been in position at the customs house when the place was supposed to have been empty. It turned out that Zimanski, our parachute instructor at Achnacarry, had been passing information to the Germans with a short-wave radio he had hidden in a false-bottomed kit bag in his room. The debriefing officer told us that the only reason anyone from our group was still alive was because Zimanski had gotten the date wrong by one week. The Germans we ran into were an advance guard. If we had arrived a few days later, a whole company of mountain troops would have been in position and we would have been slaughtered.

"Where is Zimanski now?" Sugden asked.

The debriefing officer looked at us over the rim of his glasses, which were perched on the end of his nose. "He had an accident," replied the man.

By the time we parted company, things had gone completely to hell between me and Sugden.

I reported back to Achnacarry, and remained there until the end of the war.

Lindsay, the kilted officer in charge, filled me in on what had happened to Zimanski. "We only found out about him by accident. We went into his room after he had passed out from drinking his *spiritus*. We wanted to dismantle his brewing equipment rather than see him drink himself to death. We were trying to find all the various pieces when we turned up the hidden radio instead. After Zimanski was persuaded to tell us what he'd been up to, we took him up in the practice-jump plane. Got up to a few thousand feet and told him that when we landed we were going to hand him over to some of his old friends in the Free Polish Brigade. Zimanski asked us, rather emphatically, if there was any way he could avoid that. So we opened up the door and let him jump out. Without a parachute, of course. You know that thing he used to say about breaking every bone in your body? Apparently, it's absolutely true."

A replacement had not been found for Zimanski, since no recruits were coming through in those final months of the war. The mountaineering program had been shut down entirely. Piece by piece, the camp was dismantled. The staff members were reassigned to different corners of the earth. Barracks which had once held a hundred men were now only empty shells, home to nothing but mice and pigeons. The doors were blown open by the wind and remained that way. Windows broke and were not repaired. The twenty-foot-high assault-course jump fell down and was not rebuilt. In this forgotten place, Lindsay and I were also forgotten.

Lindsay could easily have moved his quarters to his manor house, located a mile up the road and equipped with luxuries it was difficult even to dream of in the ramshackle huts of the base. But I doubted if the thought of moving ever occurred to him. He had been given orders to man the barracks, and that was what he did. The lack of creature comforts did not trouble him in the least.

Even if I could not understand how his mind worked, I was grateful for his company. We spent a great deal of time sitting by the fire in his Quonset hut and reading old issues of *Yank* magazine left behind by the Americans who had trained here, while outside the never-ending Scottish rain came down. Sometimes, when even the rain became more appealing than another day of sitting inside, Lindsay and I would swathe ourselves in oilcloth jackets and stride out into the dreary countryside.

I was still at Achnacarry when news of the board of inquiry's recommendation came through. I hadn't even known there was going to be an inquiry, but later I learned that Sugden had demanded one. The medal, a Military Cross with its distinctive purple-and-white ribbon, followed quickly.

By then, Lindsay and I had lost all military bearing and were living more or less like hermits in the Scottish countryside.

In the end, Lindsay's Quonset hut was about the only thing left standing at Achnacarry. We had begun using pieces of wood from the old barracks to heat our fireplace, and the supply truck showed up rarely if at all.

When our demobilization orders at last came through, Lindsay returned to his estate and I went home to Painswick. But I was restless there and often woke from nightmares in the blackness of the English winter night.

"Was that when you decided to give up mountaineering for good?" asked Stanley, who until that moment had been listening without a sound.

I nodded. "Everything that climbing meant to me got turned upside down. All that I used to love about it, I hated from that moment on."

"But here we are again," said Stanley, gesturing across the lake towards the glacier we'd be climbing the next day. "And in spite of everything, there is no place I would rather be."

At first, I did not know what he meant. But then it dawned on me that there were things in both our lives, not only the climbing but people as well, whom we loved despite all reasoning. Stanley was right. At this moment in time, there was no place for us but here.

I felt the burden I had carried on my own begin to lift. It would never disappear completely, but I knew that I could bear it from now on.

"Thank you," I said.

"No, Auntie." Stanley shook his head. "I am the one who should be thanking you."

❄

I WOKE THE NEXT MORNING, back stiff from lying on the ground, and looked out into a mist was so thick I couldn't see the lake, even though it lay just across the road. My sleeping bag and the Kulmbacher mountain jacket I had rolled up as a pillow were beaded with the dew. The wind had died away and there was almost no sound, not even the lapping of water on the shore.

Over a breakfast of porridge and raisins, the scrape of metal spoons in our mess tins seemed unnaturally loud. Afterwards, we barely spoke as we washed our tins in the lake, flecks of oatmeal drifting down into the cold and glassy water. The fog, swirling all around, compelled us to be silent.

We set off, dragging the coffin around the edge of the lake.

By the time we reached the glacier, the mist had started to burn off. Even before we saw the sun, the ice began to glow a haunting greenish-blue. Its sides were not white but grayish brown, insanely ridged, and seemingly in motion, like a torrent of lava bearing down into the valleys.

After a thorough search, we at last found a slope that we could navigate. Then we strapped on our crampons and began to climb. With these daggers on our feet, our steps became slower but more certain, clinging to patches of ice like the claws of giant cats.

After an hour of hauling the coffin over sharp ridges, sliding down one side and climbing up another, I fetched the winch from its wine crate and carried it forward, leaving the coffin behind and paying out cable as I went.

When I reached the end of the cable's length, I wedged the winch behind a hump of ice and began to reel the coffin in like a huge fish, with Stanley pushing it from behind.

We kept this up for the rest of the day, stripped down to our bare backs in the sun.

I cranked the winch until my mind shut down, registering only degrees of pain. Now and then I would look up and see the coffin riding the ridges like a ship over an ocean turned to glass. Stanley would appear behind it, his pale skin reddened by the sun and his goggled eyes wide and emotionless. Then he and the coffin would tumble down behind the next ridge, only to reappear a moment later.

The ridges grew smaller but steeper as we neared the plateau of the glacier.

I had not spoken to Stanley in hours, except to yell directions or to let him know when my muscles had cramped and I needed to take a break.

He had responded only with waves or shouts whose words were lost among the crevices of ice.

At last, just when a part of my mind had become resolved to cranking this winch for the rest of my life, we emerged onto the smooth surface of the glacier's cap.

We collapsed on the ground, trying to catch our breath, eyes filled with the tea-brown light which filtered through the lenses of our goggles. Sitting up again, I looked down the side of the glacier to the lake. It seemed absurdly small, and the customs house nothing more than a speck at its edge. Even the road was reduced to a scribble of chalk, wandering dizzily around the mountainside. Of Palladino there was nothing. The town was hidden in the folds of the valley, which itself had vanished among other folds, blurring into the vastness of the ice-capped horizon.

We had climbed into the rafters of the world.

As I struggled to my feet, clumsy in my daggered boots, I remembered what Carton had said the first time I had gone to hear him speak. He had talked about how none of the things which allowed people to feel important—the money and the titles and the social connections and the ritzy tailored clothes—none of them counted for anything when you reached this place. And whereas down below your failures might be measured in scandal or gossip or lawsuits brought against you, up here your failures were measured in the crack of breaking bones, in cerebral edema, pleurisy, pneumonia, in pulmonary emboli, frostbite, and death. Words like these either drew you to them or sent you reeling in the opposite direction. Carton spoke as if this was a sorting of our species, each side looking uncomprehendingly at the other from the safety of the worlds which they called home.

The more I thought of Carton's last request, the less strange it seemed to me. Looking out across the blinding sea of white, with Carton's Rock still hidden out there somewhere in the blur of sun on snow, I understood that this place had been his home since the day he'd first set foot upon the glacier. Not the home of his body but the home of his soul, if such a thing existed. This was his sacred ground, and to be buried anywhere else, I realized, would only dishonor the body which had brought him here.

Stanley and I roped ourselves together and set off across the glacier, maintaining a twenty-foot distance between each other and the coffin. This way, if the ground opened up beneath us, we would be able to arrest our fall into anything except the largest hidden crevasse. We carried our ice axes at the ready, prepared to throw ourselves forward, digging the spike into the snow and bracing for the massive jolt which would accompany the other's fall.

The snow on top of the glacier was mostly frozen, so that our feet either did not sink in at all or only crunched down a few inches. In other places, all the snow had blown away, revealing the ice below. Here, the scraping of our bladed feet across the surface was like the slow and steady sharpening of knives. Where the ground leveled out, the snow was softer and deeper. Sometimes we had to stop and switch our crampons for snowshoes, which slowed us down considerably.

The Rocket at last began to move more smoothly, its runners no longer shrieking over the stones as if they were in agony. Instead, its passage made a steady whisper through the snow.

We marked our way across the glacier using the wands I had brought down with me from England. The orange paint stood out sharply against the snow and would, we hoped, guide us back across safe ground on our return. Every now and then, I looked back at the wands, which marked our wobbling path across the featureless white ground like a quiver full of arrows which had missed their mark.

We filled our canteens with snow and left them on the top of the Rocket so that the sun would warm the wool covers and melt what was inside. Whatever we drank came out as sweat.

In the hours which followed, my thoughts evaporated. I was aware of nothing but the angle of the land ahead and, in its slanting, the precise measure of the discomfort I would endure.

Sunset of that day found us in the middle of a white desert, where we pitched our tent like Bedouins among the frozen dunes. We ate without tasting the mush of beans, tinned peaches, and rubbery slabs of Danish ham which we shoveled into our mouths.

Afterwards, huddled in my sleeping bag, I was fading away into sleep when Stanley's voice exploded in my ears.

"Three things you cannot live without!" he shouted.

"What?" I groaned.

"Come on!" he said. "Name three things you cannot live without."

At the sound of that old game we used to play, I turned my head, slowly and painfully, until I could fix him with eyes made bloodshot by the smoke of our paraffin stove. "I am trying to sleep," I said, as slowly and menacingly as I could.

Stanley appeared to have recovered completely from his exhaustion, whereas I was still wallowing in mine. "Three things!" he said again, his voice annoyingly cheerful.

I groaned and dug my dirty fingers into the corners of my eyes. "You're not going to give up, are you?"

"No," he said.

I sighed. "All right." What seemed like an hour later, after much "constructive criticism" from Stanley, I had settled on three things. All of them were—not surprisingly, given our present condition—food. The first was Frank Cooper's Oxford Marmalade, the vintage kind, as well as Fortnum & Mason Christmas pudding and Camp Coffee. This last item was a kind of syrup made from coffee, sugar, and chicory. It had the consistency of dirty motor oil and was incredibly sweet. If you poured more than a couple of teaspoons into a glass of milk, it was undrinkable. But if you got the proportions exactly right, and if the milk was the correct temperature, it was very good. Stanley and I had practically lived off the stuff when we were studying for exams at school. Camp Coffee had been around forever. On the label of the bottle was a picture of a kilted Scottish soldier sitting on an large upended drum outside his campaign tent and drinking a cup of Camp Coffee. Flying from the tent was a red flag on which were the words "Ready Aye Ready." Standing next to the Scot was a turbaned Sikh in a blue uniform, the Scottish soldier's servant, who presumably had just made the coffee for his master, because his right arm was still raised as if he had only in that moment drawn back his hand.

I argued aggressively for Camp Coffee to be included and by now was wide awake. I had just finished pleading my case—very eloquently, I thought—when I realized that Stanley had fallen asleep.

✻

THE NEXT DAY, as we struggled on, I prayed for clouds to mask the sun, which blinded us even through our goggles. I was worried that I had not brought a second pair, since it would not have taken much to break the delicately curved lenses, which were held in place against the leather eye cushions only by tiny, rounded blades of metal. Without these goggles, I would have gone snow-blind in a matter of hours. I had experienced this once before, on a climb up Grossvenediger mountain in the Hohe Tauern Alps. I had not been badly blinded and recovered in a day or two, but even so I remembered the pain, as if someone had rubbed salt into my eyes.

The space we crossed showed on the map as a calm cream-colored emptiness no longer than my thumb, washed over with the calm pond ripples of contour lines. But standing here was like being on the anvil of the sun, on which it felt as if we would be hammered into particles of light.

I marched without any thought except of twilight, when the sound of our plodding footsteps could cease.

Stanley, on the other hand, proposed that we should discuss exactly what the kilted Scot on the Camp Coffee label was saying to his Indian servant. "Because I've always thought," said Stanley, "that his mouth was a little bit open and he does appear to be saying something."

"Perhaps he's saying, 'Thank you,'" I mumbled, hoping this might be enough to shut Stanley up.

No such luck.

"I think that Sikh looks bloody cheesed off," explained Stanley. "I think he must be saying—"

"The Sikh or the Scot?" I asked.

"The Sikh! I'm talking about the Sikh now."

"But you asked me what the Scot was saying."

"All right," he said exasperatedly, "you do the Scot and I'll do the Sikh."

"I'd rather do the Sikh myself," I told him.

"Fine!" he shouted.

"I think he's saying, 'How the hell did I end up working for a funny-looking little man like you? And why are you sitting on your drum? And I've put some special sauce in your coffee, by the way.'"

"Special sauce?" asked Stanley.

"Yes."

"Well, what's in it?"

"You figure it out."

"Well," said Stanley, "I would be saying, 'It's about bloody time. I've been sitting on this drum for over an hour. Where did you get to? What do you think I'm paying you for?'"

"But hold on a minute," I interrupted. "What if the Sikh didn't make him the coffee at all?"

"What are you talking about?"

"What if he's got his hand raised because he wants some coffee. He could just be saying, 'Can I try some of that?'"

"And the Scot would be saying, 'Bugger off and get your own coffee, laddie.'"

"He wouldn't say that," I protested.

"He would if I were him."

"It's talk like that which is losing us the Empire," I said.

This conversation lasted a disturbingly long time. Fortunately, there was no one else around to hear it.

I was grateful to Stanley for the stubbornness of his good humor, but that evening, even Stanley could not see the funny side of things as we unpacked the tent and other gear and realized we had lost the second of our two food containers. This had almost certainly happened during the scramble up onto the glacier two days before. I was positive that we had not left it behind at our last campsite. I had just assumed it was packed away with the other stuff we had not moved off the Rocket when we made camp.

My first reaction was to be furious with Stanley, since he was the one handling the coffin while I winched it forward over the ice. But I kept my mouth shut, both because it wouldn't have done any good to yell at him and because I hadn't noticed it myself at our last campsite, so I was at least partly to blame.

The food box we had been using until now was almost empty. As the truth of the matter sank in—that we had only two one-pint cans of olive oil and six cans of bean stew left, instead of twelve—my already empty stomach twisted inside me.

We decided not to go back for it. The thought of retracing our steps was too much to bear.

"We'll go on half rations," I said in a whisper.

Stanley nodded grimly.

"We'll find the box on our way back," I continued. "There's just about enough food to get us up the mountain." I held up one of the remaining bean cans, which had been dented slightly; the dent had already turned rusty. "I expect it's still all right," I said, tossing the can from one hand to the other and watching Stanley's face for some sign of agreement.

Two hours later, any visitor to our campsite would have

seen what looked like two large dogs insanely barking at the snow beneath their feet. Closer inspection would have revealed Stanley and me, noisily emptying our guts of rancid bean stew.

*

THE FOLLOWING DAY, as we dragged the Rocket mindlessly across a plateau of jade-green ice, a gust of wind grabbed my cap and skimmed it vertically into the blue.

We squinted up into the sun, waiting for it to come down again, but if it did we never saw it.

"I never did like your hat," said Stanley.

As a replacement, I unknotted my scarf and tied it around my head.

"Now you look like that Sikh in the Camp Coffee picture," remarked Stanley.

I glared at him.

Soon after this, Stanley began to complain that his special dozen-pocket climbing coat was too long and that the weight of it dragged on his thighs.

"Nothing you can do about it now," I told him.

"We'll see about that," replied Stanley.

After we had made camp at the end of that day, he used the folding scissors from his pocket knife to cut the jacket to a length just below his waist. He tried it on again and grinned with satisfaction. Loose strands of wool hung down around his legs as the twill cloth unraveled piece by piece. He reminded me of those sheep I used to see in the fields around Painswick, their dirty fur dragging in clumps along the ground.

Not satisfied with this, Stanley then tucked into his cap some of the material he had taken from the jacket. The shredded cloth now served as crude ear flaps, and made him look like a bloodhound.

For dinner that night, in order to conserve our food, we each drank half a can of olive oil and were too starved to care.

Stanley gulped it down and smacked his lips appreciatively. "I have," he said, "thanks to that breakfast you cooked me at your apartment the other day, experienced considerably worse." Then, as if to punish him for his rudeness, the left lens of his goggles fell out and dropped into the oil can, where it broke in half. Stanley looked down into the can. "Well, bugger," he said and busied himself cutting a piece from his scarf, which he then fitted into the empty eye socket of his goggles. He tried them on.

"You look like a pirate," I said.

"Give me your goggles, then," he replied.

I took the goggles from around my neck and tossed them in his lap.

"Thank you, Auntie," he said, and pressed the lenses against his eyes. He looked around the tent with short, birdlike movements of his head. Then Stanley gave a grunt of disapproval, took them off, and gave them back to me. "I'd rather look like a pirate."

Half an hour later, driven almost insane by Stanley's growly monologue about buried treasure, kissing the gunner's daughter, keelhauling, and the Black Spot, I felt sleep settle on me like a mist so thick that even Stanley's ranting could not penetrate it.

❄

THE NEXT DAY'S MARCH had us moving up a gradual incline. It was afternoon by the time we reached the crest of the rise. From here, the ground sloped away into a narrow valley, revealing lumps of rock and what looked like a cave at the bottom. The glacier above the cave had sagged down, revealing line after dirty line of ice, like the growth rings of a tree. Outside the cave there was no snow, only gray and muddy ground.

The wind flapped around the collar of my mountain jacket. The olive-brown color, which had hidden me so well in the San Rafaele woods, now stood out garishly against the white.

Beyond this valley, out across the countless rolling waves of snow, towered Carton's Rock. The rock stood by itself, and the first impression was of a ship with black sails, moving slowly through an ocean made of clouds. It was like a mirage, shimmering in the heat haze which rose off the ice. The dirt and silt of its lower elevations gave way to cleaner snow, which the sun had polished to a mirror shine. How far away it was, I could not tell.

The valley extended too far in either direction for us to consider going around it. In order to stay on course for the rock, we had no choice but to head down into the valley, climb back up the other side, and then keep going.

Stanley stood behind me, leaning against the coffin with a smoldering cigarette pinched in ratty fingerless granny gloves, while I fished the compass from my pack to take a bearing before we started down into the valley. The compass was a heavy brass thing with a disk inside made from mother-of-pearl, on which all the degrees were marked, and a flip-up sight which allowed me to aim the compass like a gun. I looked through the sight, feeling the powder of dried salt in the corners of my eyes crumble as the muscles of my face tensed. I was waiting for the little disk to stop spinning so I could get a proper reading when I heard a swishing sound, and turned to see that Stanley was no longer leaning against the coffin. Instead, he had climbed up onto it as if he were riding a strange metallic horse. Now he and the coffin were sliding very slowly down the hill. Soon the Rocket had come level with me and I found myself walking down the slope beside it, since we were all still tied together with the climbing rope.

"What exactly do you think you are doing?" I asked, stashing the compass and coiling up the rope as it grew slack.

"You'd better get on," he replied. "I think the Rocket is taking off."

He was moving faster now. With the gathering speed, the runners seemed to be rising from the snow as they moved forward. I had to run to keep up. Then I was galloping down the slope. Soon, I knew, I would be left behind. Without giving it another thought, I jumped aboard. I only managed to slump over the coffin, legs sticking out one way, my stomach on the coffin's lid, and my head only a few inches from the ground, before the coffin began to move with a speed that drew involuntary shouts from Stan and me.

I had a view of snow sliding beneath us and a sudden glimpse of a narrow crevasse, hacked as if with the blade of a huge ax, falling away beneath us. The coffin sliced over it as if on an invisible bridge.

By now, I was pushed back against the fins of the Rocket, where the remainder of our gear was stored. Stanley was holding on to a rope, heels digging into the sides of the coffin as if spurring on the great metal horse, and was making cowboy noises as we careened down the slope.

With a crash we reached the valley floor and shot out across the flat ground, heading for the mouth of the cave. It looked as if we might shoot straight into it, but we were already losing speed, and the runners began to sink back down into the snow.

We came to a whispering stop, just where the dirty snow gave way to pasty gray earth at the mouth of the cave.

I slid forward off the coffin, careful not to impale myself on my own crampons.

Stanley was still straddling the coffin, holding the rope as if a sharp tug and a click of the tongue would send us racing on across the snow. "That was brilliant!" he shouted.

"You could have killed us," I gasped, and was about to list the half dozen ways in which he could have accomplished this when Stanley flapped his hand in the air and made a dry spitting sound through his teeth.

"Quiet, you old fusspot!" he commanded.

Muttering under my breath, I untied myself from the mad cowboy and his tin pony.

The huge cliff of sagging ice, rising at least a hundred feet above us, looked as if it might come crashing down at any moment. The buckled lines of dirt embedded in the snow were like a warning, proof that this glacier was in motion, and that its usual imperceptibly slow course was never to be trusted.

Despite the danger, Stanley and I could not help walking into the cave, drawn into it as if by some strange music which played deep in the catacombs inside.

The air was damp and there were puddles on the ground. There had to be a spring of some kind here, melting the ice from below. The arching walls and ceiling of the cave were vivid blue and dimpled like the sides of a beer glass.

We stood there for a while, listening to the steady drip of water from the walls.

I was just about to say that we should turn around when I caught sight of something hanging from the ceiling of the cave. At first it looked like a branch, but as I stepped forward,

I realized it was the wing of a bird. It was a large wing, as long as my arm and still with the feathers attached, hanging down vertically as if reaching for the floor. The feathers were brown, almost black, shimmering purple and green like the feathers of a starling. The ceiling was high enough here that I could stand directly beneath the wing. Above the place where it protruded from the ice I could see the rest of the bird, or part of it, anyway. The bird was far larger than any of the crows or ravens I had seen in these mountains. I could just make out, blurred inside the ice, the large hooked beak of the bird, whose neck had been twisted around, and a band of white stretching from its eyes to the beginning of its beak. The chest appeared to be a dirty, reddish white.

Stanley stood beside me. He reached up to touch the feathers, and as soon as his fingers reached them, a handful of them fluttered down onto the ground. "What do you think it is?" he asked.

At first, I could not remember the name I wanted to say, but now it appeared, rising through the dark inside my head. "A lammergeier."

"There aren't any lammergeiers here," said Stanley.

"Not anymore," I replied. "But it is a lammergeier." I was sure of it now, recalling pictures of its white body and black wings and the masklike streak across its eyes. I did not know how long the great vulture had been gone from the Alps, but I had heard of its reputation for carrying off lambs and dogs and even babies, flying them thousands of feet into the air and then dropping them to their deaths. Birds like these had wingspans of nine feet and still existed in some parts of the Middle East, Spain, and the Himalayas. But not here. Not anymore.

It was as if, in reaching this place, we had stepped backwards through time, to a place where the years were not counted in seasons but in centuries, in the slow creep of the glaciers, almost unmeasurable on the scale of human lives.

We left the cave, our clothes dampened by the dripping air, and after roping up began to drag the coffin through a rock-strewn gully which ran in from the side of the valley.

Halfway up, the gully widened out into knee-deep snow. We were just stopping to put on our snowshoes when the avalanche hit.

First I heard a deep, soft thumping, like the sound of a giant wing beating the air above me. Then the ground began to move beneath my feet. There was no time to be afraid. Next, I had the sensation almost of swimming. For the first few seconds, I thrashed my arms and legs to keep my head above the level of the sliding snow.

But the more I tumbled, the more disoriented I became. Then I was just falling. Whiteness thundered all around me. It tumbled and hissed out of darkness into light. The air was slapped from my lungs and with a glimpse of daylight slapped back in again. I experienced the strange calm of waiting to die. Helpless. Blind. No way to fight the falling. My body shuddered as it struck something hard. But there was no pain, only the knowledge that damage had been done. I grew numb. My limbs became strangers, twisted and contorted as I tumbled down. I clung to the silence deep inside myself, surrounded by the roaring which was all around me and through me and then was gone. The rope wrenched at my waist, putting pressure on my ribs. I felt sure I would be ripped in half. Then, with one last mighty sigh, everything suddenly came to a stop. I could not breathe or move. I opened my eyes and saw only the gray haze of light above. My chest was on fire. Frantically, my arms punched upwards. Sun poured down on me like molten brass. I spat the fire from my lungs and gasped in the cold air. I began to dig my way out, pawing the glassy grit until at last I saw my boots again. Each crossed thread of my clothing was tamped with snow. My socks and the knots of my bootlaces were knotted with ice. Still I could not get up. It was the rope, wound too tight around me. From the pocket of my coat I pulled my old Opinel knife, prized it open, and cut myself loose like a just-born creature slicing its own umbilical cord.

I stood waist-deep in the blinding snow, and it was only when I had untangled my goggles from around my neck and set them once more against my eyes that I could see. In light the color of weak tea, I stared at the debris of the avalanche, which lay in the shape of a fan, dirty and clumped, all the way down to the floor of the valley. The cave had been swallowed up. It was hard even to see where the opening had been.

Looking back up the valley, I saw the rope rise from the snow fifty feet away and the coffin wedged against the gray blade of a rock jutting from the ice below.

Stanley's face jumped into my head. I glanced around but saw no sign of him.

I began to wade across the slope, calling his name. But he was nowhere. All I could see was the smooth sheet of the avalanche. I reached the rope and tugged at it. The thick brown sinew jumped above the surface of the snow. As fast as I could, I traced it down to where I knew he must be. Then I started digging like a dog. Snow flew everywhere.

I saw his hair first, and then his face, which was turning blue. I raked away the snow around his chest and pulled him up, and when I dropped him down again upon the surface of the slope, he spat a gob of bloody snow into the air and gasped and sat upright. I hammered on his back and he spat up more snow, which melted in bloody slime across his chest. I cut the rope with my Opinel knife and tried to get him to stand. He wobbled on his feet, coughing and retching. I brushed the snow from his hair. His pockets were filled with it.

We were like scarecrows stuffed with ice, which had found its way down our shirts, up our noses, into our ears and which melted now in painful chips like broken glass inside our bellies.

Across the slope, a gust of wind stirred up phantoms of snow. The glittering dust twirled and took on human shapes. I saw faces, shifting as if glimpsed through a curtain of water. I could make out their hands and the rags of clothes and I heard the whisper of voices.

They were like the ancient ghosts of those buried so deep that even their spirits became trapped. Uncovered now by this same avalanche that had almost buried us, they left the frozen wreckage of their bones. They swirled away across the fields of blinding white, brushing past us in a sighing crystal cloud. We seemed to have strayed beyond the boundaries of our world, into a place where neither the living nor the dead were meant to be.

✳

"I THINK I BROKE A TOOTH," said Stanley. He stuck his fingers in his mouth, bloody saliva trickling out across his hand. "Thought so," he said, turning the tooth this way and that, to examine it from different angles. He spat again. The speckles of red sank away into the white.

"Are you in a lot of pain?" I asked.

He shrugged. "I don't know. My head feels like it's filled with bees." Carefully he put the tooth in the pocket of his mountain coat and replaced his goggles, which had been forced down around his neck but at least had not been lost. He tried to smile. "I'm fine," he told me. "Really, I'm fine."

Despite what he said, I could tell he had been badly shaken.

He must have been in a lot of pain, too, but he was not the type to show it. He could complain easily enough about his badly thought-out mountain jacket, but pain he would not show. Only in the crooked line of his windburned lips could the strain be read.

We made our way back to the coffin and dug it loose from the rock. The top had received a large dent, and some things were missing from the compartment. We had lost our stove and a bag of spare clothing, but the tent, the sleeping bags, and the rest of the food were still roped in.

Compared to others I had seen, this was a small avalanche, barely a shrug of the vast snowfields which lay ahead of us. In the past, I had watched whole hillsides give way. The force of them was almost unimaginable, and I remembered a story I'd once heard of a forestry worker in Glarus, Switzerland. In 1910, he had been thrown two thousand feet into the sky by the force of the air preceding an avalanche. He was carried half a mile and dumped, alive, into a snowbank. The six men he had been working with were all killed. You hear a story like that and you think it cannot possibly be true, but then you see an avalanche, and hear the terrible roar of the falling snow, and suddenly you know that it could happen after all.

Stanley and I had been thrown down some two hundred feet. If the coffin had not become stuck, the slide could have carried us ten times that distance, and would certainly have buried us beyond all possibility of digging ourselves out. If we had been buried, the chances were that no one would ever have known what happened and we would have ended up suspended in time like that lammergeier.

Strapping on our snowshoes, but leaving our crampons attached so that we could keep our grip on the slope, we made our way out of the valley.

By the time we emerged, clouds had come in from the north and the temperature had slid below zero, with the wind-chill taking it even lower. In the dimming light, I pulled my goggles down around my neck and felt the freezing gusts against my eyes.

We checked our ropes and began to drag the coffin on towards Carton's Rock, but after two hours the mountain suddenly disappeared behind a wall of boiling white. Only then did we realize we were walking into a storm. We stopped. Now, without the sound of the Rocket sliding over the glacier, we could hear the howling of the storm's approach.

Stanley's face was drawn and pale. He had taken off his goggles but the welts around his eyes remained. "Should we turn back?" he asked, raising his voice above the wind.

I went to my pack, which was strapped into the Rocket's cargo area, and took out a pair of binoculars. Searching the ground ahead of us, I saw a lump of stone jutting from the snow about four hundred meters off. I pointed it out to Stanley. "We could pitch the tent behind that," I said. "Ride out the storm that way. Stan, the only place behind us is the valley, and the storm will overtake us long before we reach it."

"I didn't mean just to the valley," he said.

His words caught me by surprise. I thought about his brave-face talk of how he would get this done even if it was the last thing he ever did, and it made me angry to hear this from him now. Replacing my goggles, I turned away from him and straightened the harness on my shoulders. Then I began to drag the Rocket forward into the wind. As Stanley's section of the rope grew taut, I came to a stop. Leaning forward in the traces, I waited for Stanley to make up his mind, to join me or to untie himself and give up.

I heard, even over the sound of the approaching storm, a

kind of groaning swear from Stanley. Then the pressure on my harness was released and we were moving forward once again.

We marched as quickly as we could, hoping to reach the rock before the storm rode over us. If we did not get there in time, we might lose our way and never find the rock. And even if we did, without the time to pitch the tent, there would not be enough shelter.

Hard pellets of snow rattled across the ground towards us, bouncing up into our faces and tearing at our windburned cheeks. Ice crystals rattled against the lenses of my goggles.

The wind grew stronger. We were leaning into it, far beyond the point of normal balance, teeth bared. The noise of the storm was a constant rolling thunder on our ears. As hard as we pulled the Rocket, it seemed to be pulling just as hard in the opposite direction, as if we were locked in a tug-of-war with the ghost of Carton himself.

The white wall was closer now, towering above us and seeming to devour the earth over which it passed.

Stanley's words began to repeat in my head, like a grim echo of Sugden's demand that we turn back from our mission during the war. I had dismissed Stanley's wanting to turn back as simple cowardice, but now, with this storm about to break over us, I wondered if he was the one being reasonable, and not me. I had been thinking of all of this in terms of how we would be judged when we returned. There, in the back of my mind, sat a jury made up of people like Sugden, Pringle, my father, and even Mrs. Reave. And there were the dead as well: Carton himself, and the faces of Whistler, Armstrong, and Forbes, already fading into impressionistic blurs as my memory slowly washed away their features, like the stone angels in the Palladino cemetery.

But out here, I had to force myself to understand, the only

decisions that mattered were the ones that kept us alive, no matter how they would be seen when we returned. Only we could know what we were living through. Only we could make a balance of the danger and the drive to succeed. If I allowed myself to forget that, the chances were that we would not be coming back.

The wind was all around us in an awful banshee squall which vibrated through my body as if it meant to shake apart my bones by the force of sound alone.

Plumes of snow were rising from behind the rock, corkscrewing like devil horns into the air.

I turned to look at Stanley. I could not see his face, only his stooped form and the mechanical rising and falling of his legs, almost lost in the seething snow.

I realized now that we would have no time to pitch our tent, nor would it have done us any good to try to find shelter inside it. This storm was too strong. It would blow the canvas to shreds. We should have gone back down into the valley. At least there, the wind might have left us alone.

My eyes were playing tricks on me. The streaks of snow on the rock seemed to be changing shape, forming letters and numbers, then disappearing again into meaningless blurs of white. Then the letters reappeared again. It was maddening. I could even read them now, a huge letter J and under it the numbers 231135.

I turned my head just in time to see Stanley raise his arm and point towards the stone. His mouth moved but his words were lost in the wind.

Looking back at the rock, I realized suddenly that it was not a stone at all but the tail fin of a plane. The ridge of snow that trailed off to its left must be the rest of the plane.

We were close now. There was no doubt about the letters.

Windblown snow poured like an inverted waterfall from behind the tail fin. The ground shook underneath us. The sky had disappeared.

We reached the fin, which was much larger than I had thought. Wind shrieked around the weather-beaten metal.

Stanley and I tore off our harnesses and undid our ropes. Then we began kicking and clawing at the ridge, moving away the snow until we reached the side of the aircraft. My gloved hand passed over the olive-painted metal, feeling the bumps of rivets, but no way in.

Then Stanley cried out. He was farther down the ridge and had found a hole in the side of the plane. It looked like some kind of doorway. He bent down and scrabbled inside. I saw his feet kicking like a swimmer's, and then he was gone. A second later, his head reappeared and then an arm, beckoning me in. I left the Rocket and dove at the hole, flailing my way into the dark and then falling onto some kind of step. From there, I rolled onto a narrow, bumpy floor.

Outside, the storm had overtaken us. Only the dimmest yellowish light showed through the hole in the snow.

I covered my face with my hands, feeling the torn wool of my gloves clogged with ice. I was sure this wind would rip the plane apart. I imagined Carton's coffin being swept away back in the direction we had come.

Stanley crawled over to me and we lay there, listening to the storm. The wind changed pitch, growing even stronger, and the sloping metal walls groaned around us.

After a minute, I pulled my hands from my eyes and looked around. There was almost no light now. The hole through which we'd crawled had already been covered by snow, dampening the noise of the storm, which we could feel more than we could see, in the shuddering of the ribbed fuselage. I fished in my pocket for my torch and switched it on. The air glittered with tiny drifting crystals of snow. The torch beam passed over tangles of wire hanging from the ceiling. Lifting myself up, I saw that the narrow floor space on which I lay was made of plywood, and the bumps were in fact empty bullet cases, each one the length of my palm and as thick as my thumb.

Stanley raised his head up off the floor. Immediately in front of him was a low, curved dome of metal, looking strangely like an eyeball in the half-light.

Attached to a metal post directly behind me was a large machine gun, pointing at the ceiling. A snake of ammunition wound out of the breech, the copper-headed bullets sheathed with ice. There was another large post on the side through which I had crawled into the plane, but only a shred of torn metal where a second gun must once have been fixed.

It looked like an American machine gun, probably a .50-caliber, in which case I guessed this machine was one of those B-24 Liberators I had once seen flying overhead.

Towards the front of the plane lay a tangle of boxes, a large yellow object rounded at both ends like a giant vitamin pill, and, at the bottom of this heap, a pair of legs in heavy, rubber-soled boots.

I did not register any sense of horror at seeing the dead man. Perhaps this was because, to judge from the ferocity of the storm outside, I had narrowly escaped becoming one myself. Maybe it was also because he must have been dead for a long time. Instead of sadness or revulsion or pity, I found myself preoccupied with little details, like the way the rubber soles had been worn down at the heels, the way his legs were wrapped in some kind of sheepskin trousers with a shiny lacquer finish on the outside of the leather.

The dead man, and everything else which jammed the passageway, must have been thrown forward by the impact of the plane hitting the glacier. I knew that somewhere up ahead of it must be the cockpit, unless the whole front of the plane had been sheared off in the crash.

Stanley got up and hobbled over to a seat built into the wall just to the left of the jammed corridor. Above the seat was a small table, on which rested a radio receiver. Next to it was a Morse code tapper. The plate and the receiver were completely covered in a thin layer of frost. Stanley wiped away some of the crystals, revealing a metal plate on which the Morse code alphabet had been printed. Then he cleaned off the receiver and read aloud the white letters printed on its black surface: "Signal Corps. U.S. Army Air Forces. BC-348-C."

"I thought this was an American plane," I said, my breath fogging the still air. I remembered what Carton and Lindsay had told me at Achnacarry, about planes crashing into the mountains. I wondered if the men who flew this plane would have made it home safely if we had managed to put the beacon on Carton's Rock.

"Are you all right?" asked Stanley.

I told him what I was thinking about.

"It may be true that they would have reached home, but if they had, you and I would now be dead out there in the snow." Stanley pressed absentmindedly at the Morse code tapper. "You didn't bring any food in, did you?"

I shook my head.

Stanley peered around at the metal sides of the plane. "I think I know how my uncle feels right about now," he said.

"I wonder how long the storm will last," I said.

Then we were both silent, as if some answer from the storm itself might reach us on the moaning wind outside. The arched walls shuddered all around, planting in my rattled brain the thought that we had somehow stumbled into a real rocket ship and the noise of the storm was the sound of our engine as we climbed up through the airless stratosphere.

TWELVE

Two days later, the storm still screamed around the carcass of the plane, which groaned as if it were a living and tormented thing.

Inside the creaking hull, we lived in dead men's clothes and passed the time by smoking dead men's cigarettes. After my torch batteries gave out, the only light came from a candle lamp which Stanley had been carrying in his pocket. He had forgotten to store it away the last time we made camp and had been too lazy to unpack the bag where it belonged. We rationed ourselves to a few hours a day, crowding around the greasy flame like two pale and gloomy moths.

Three times we had gone out into the storm to find the Rocket, in the hopes of unpacking our sleeping bags and retrieving some of our food, as well as the miner-type headlamps we had brought. The first time, I could not find the

Rocket and staggered around in the whirling clouds of white, afraid not only that the coffin had been blown away but also that I would not be able to find my way back to the shelter of the plane.

Something happened to me out there which filled me both with terror and with awe. As I wandered about in the snow, twisted this way and that by the wind, I had the sudden feeling that I was not alone. Everyone has had this sensation, sitting in a room, perhaps, and realizing that someone else has entered. You turn and see that other person. You make yourself believe you must have heard something, because otherwise how could you have known? It was that same feeling, and I immediately assumed that Stanley had come out to join me in the search. I spun around, trying to see where he was, simultaneously annoyed that he would have left the shelter of the cave, because now we could both be lost, but also glad to have his company. I kept turning, the storm ripping at my clothes and snow spraying across the ground and peppering my legs like ivory shotgun pellets. There was no one else. I even reached out into the gray haze, not trusting my eyes, afraid that there might be someone right in front of me whom I could not see and at the same time worried that my eyes were right and nobody was there. But the more my empty hands reached out into the screeching wind, the more certain I became that my first instincts had been correct. It was as if, in leaving behind the world we knew, Stanley and I had stumbled into a place where not only the boundaries of space had changed but also the boundaries of perception. My mind, once contained within the white walls of my skull, now seemed to flood out through its shield of bone.

And now I knew, or thought I knew, that this presence in

the air around me was Carton himself. Not the doctored remnants of the man inside his coffin but all of him, here and alive and aware, only hidden from the flimsy powers of my sight.

But in that instant I forgot about the cold, and the wind, and about everything else except standing there, my arms outstretched, too amazed to let the fear take over.

After some time, I didn't know how long, I stumbled back to the plane and crawled inside.

Stanley had torn up a piece of plywood from the floor. We used that as a primitive door to seal up the snow hole.

I shook my head when Stanley's wordless question showed across his face, the right side of which was swollen from his broken tooth.

He sat back beside the candle and folded his arms and sighed.

I wanted to tell him what had happened out there, but as I tried to put it into words, I realized it couldn't be done. And now that the event had passed, I could no longer be sure, as I had been before, that it had actually taken place.

The second time, after staggering around in the swirling white for half an hour, Stanley found the Rocket buried under a mound of snow about a hundred feet back from where we had left it when the storm hit. By then, Stanley was too cold to be able to dig away the snow and was forced to retreat to the plane.

Although our hovel in the fuselage was sheltered from the wind, it was still below freezing inside. At first, it didn't cross our minds to take the clothing from the dead man. Then, as we sat shivering side by side, Stanley and I found ourselves staring, by the candle's feeble light, at the sheepskin trousers and the clunky fur-lined boots. There was no need to discuss what we were thinking. We had extra clothing, and sleeping bags, too, but all of that was buried in the Rocket. If we could get to that, we might be able to avoid the unpleasantness of stripping the corpse. But one way or another, we had to find a way to stay warm, or we would freeze to death in here. After twenty-four hours trapped inside the plane with the storm still raging outside, the threat of this was no longer a possibility but a certainty.

We decided to make another attempt to retrieve our gear from the Rocket. On the first two trips out, we had gone only one at a time, in order to be able to keep the hole open and make sure the one outside could find his way back. This time, we decided we would both have to go. We armed ourselves with pieces of plywood prized up off the floor, removed the door, and stuck our heads outside.

"Straight ahead," Stanley shouted in my ear over the screeching of the wind. His mittened hand chopped in the direction of the Rocket, now completely buried under snow.

I slapped him twice on the back and we crawled out.

The wind was so strong that we could barely stand. We lumbered forward, hunched like animals unused to walking on two legs, constantly glancing back at the entrance to our cave. Afraid of losing track of each other, we held hands. By the time we reached the bank of snow under which the Rocket had been buried, our mittens had fused together in a frozen handshake.

Already I was imagining myself tucked into my sleeping bag, eating bean stew from a can, a dozen candles burning around me. We worked fast, grunting with the effort.

Even though he was standing right next to me, all I could see of Stanley was a bowed gray form with a misshapen head, as if he were not solid but only a bizarre compression of the air.

Almost as soon as we began work, our plywood shovels struck a layer of ice, like a blanket of glass over the coffin, against which the wood splintered and broke. When we tried to use the smaller pieces, they broke and splintered once again. We could see the perforated sides of the cargo container and the outlines of the bags lashed neatly in place. Beneath the ice, only a few inches away, lay all that we needed to survive.

As Stanley's shovel cracked into yet another piece, he gave a strange, whining growl and threw away the scraps of wood. Then he tore off his mittens and began scratching madly at the ice. This did no good at all, leaving only faint chalky trails on the surface.

I threw away my own shovel and patted him on the arm, to tell him it was no use.

But he swatted my hand away and began to pound against the coffin, the strange, bestial cries continuing.

I hooked my hands around his chest and began to drag him back towards the plane.

At first he resisted, but then he went slack in my arms, as if he had fainted. He hung there, dead weight, while I shuffled backwards towards the plane.

I fell into the entrance and the two of us floundered into the fuselage.

For a while, we both just lay there, half on top of each other, huddled in the darkness. Then I reached across and fumbled for the candle lamp. Once I had it in my hand, I lit a match.

The first thing I saw, when the flame hissed into life, was Stanley's face.

The sight of him shocked me. It was his eyes. They were exactly like the eyes of my father's mastiff when I'd brought it to the vet's to be put down. The old dog, grown tired of its silly name and helpless owner, had become so weak that it could not stand up. My father had been too upset to come along, so I'd had to carry it in from the car by myself, no easy task since the mastiff weighed over a hundred pounds. From the look in its eyes, I could tell that it knew what was about to happen. I set the dog down on the floor of the vet's office.

The vet, a red-faced man named Plunkett, with white hair and a white mustache gone yellow at the ends, was already filling a syringe. Dr. Plunkett turned to me and nodded. "It will be all right," he said.

I took one last look at Trouble.

He was watching me, his jowls draped on the floor and his black nose twitching as he drew in shallow breaths. I looked for some forgiveness in those eyes, but there was only the blindness of fear.

Now those eyes were Stanley's.

I was also beginning to break. I seemed to be falling away inside myself, growing fainter, melting away.

I don't know how long I had been lying there when suddenly a jolt passed through me, like the shudders of an earthquake against the insides of my ribs. I scrambled to my feet.

Stanley remained on the ground, eyes closed, lips turning blue.

"You'll die if you lie there any longer!" I shouted at him. When he did not move, I kicked him.

His eyes opened.

"Come on!" I yelled. "Get the clothes off that corpse before you turn into one."

I stamped over to the pile of wreckage and began tearing away at it. I was expecting it to be incredibly heavy but, to my surprise, some of the boxes were only made of cardboard instead of metal. Even more surprising, most of them were filled with long strips of tin foil, which spilled out over the floor like confetti. The only heavy objects were the large yellow cylinders, which turned out to be for oxygen, although these were cracked and empty now.

The dead man lay at the bottom of this heap, arms at his sides, hands inside brown fur-lined gloves. His head was swathed in a leather flying helmet and face covered by a rubber oxygen mask with only a shred of the hose remaining. The rest appeared to have been violently torn away. He wore large goggles with a single lens over both eyes, unlike the goggles Stanley and I wore, which had separate lenses for each eyepiece. Mercifully, we could not see his eyes, as the lens had been shattered and the inside was coated with ice.

He was completely frozen, and even though we managed to undo the zipper on his sheepskin jacket, we would have had to break his arms to remove it. So instead, we lifted him carefully off the floor and cut the jacket down the middle of his back. We were then able to peel it away.

Stanley immediately put this on and fastened it around him with his trouser belt, while I removed the sheepskin trousers, which, thankfully, had zips from the top to the bottom of both legs and so did not have to be cut.

Beneath the sheepskin outer layer, the dead man appeared to have several more layers of clothing, all buried beneath an olive gabardine flying suit. In one of the leg pockets attached to the front of each shin, I found an unopened emergency-ration tin.

After five minutes of flapping his arms, Stanley pronounced himself warm. "For the first time in bloody ages," he added. He then went and tugged the gloves off the dead man's hands.

This was our first real look at the corpse. Until now, he had remained anonymous beneath his clothing. But now the alabaster-white fingers, the nails flat gray and blackened at the tips, pointed at us as if casting a spell. The shape of them reminded me of Carton's hands, and the way that he aimed them in greeting.

Stanley's own hands were held in front of him in the same rigid shape by the still-frozen gloves. Slowly, as the minutes passed, the fingers of the gloves began to wiggle as the warmth of Stanley's body loosened the leather. He bent down, picked up some of the tin foil, and sprinkled it over the dead man, covering him up as if with a matting of flowers.

Meanwhile, I struggled into the trousers, and soon my kneecaps stopped feeling like chips of ice beneath the goose-bumped skin.

Beyond where the boxes of foil had piled up was a door. I turned the handle, set my shoulder to it, and fell into an empty space where, I realized from numbers printed up and down the metal supports, the bombs must have been stored. Beyond this point was the cockpit. I could see the backs of the seats belonging to the pilot and copilot, and between these the engine throttle handles. The front of the plane had caved in, and it looked as if the controls had been smashed into the seats. Moving forward, I saw that both seats were empty. The rest of the crew must have bailed out, leaving the dead man behind. I wondered how far the plane might have flown without anyone at the controls. Miles perhaps. Maybe hundreds of miles.

I returned to the foil-strewn cave to find that Stanley had discovered a parachute, which had been hanging on a rack on the wall. He had opened it and now stood draped like a monstrous bride in the folds of the white shroud. He had opened the emergency-ration tin and was nibbling at the rock-hard chocolate.

I stared at him.

He gave me a haughty look. "Not exactly Friday afternoon at the Montague, but at least things have improved enough that I feel confident in saying that they could be worse."

I took the piece of chocolate he held out and gnawed at it until a lump broke free. It was not like regular chocolate, even when it wasn't frozen. The stuff contained a gritty mixture of coffee, cocoa, and, I think, some kind of milk powder. It was better than nothing but not by much.

Further rifling of the man's pockets revealed a half-full pack of Lucky Strikes, with the logo "It's Toasted" on the green-and-red packaging.

From then on, Stanley and I were more or less comfortable on our bed of tin foil, both of us wrapped in pieces of silk parachute to keep warm, letting clumps of chocolate dissolve inside our mouths and smoking our carefully rationed supply of cigarettes.

The candle ran out, but it no longer mattered. I drifted off to sleep, dreaming that the storm had quit and we were on our way again.

Sliding back into consciousness again, I realized that something was different. I blinked, but my eyes were useless. I sniffed but smelled nothing other than my own stale breath. Suddenly I knew what it was. It was quiet.

The storm had finished.

I nudged Stanley awake.

We dug our way out yet again and crawled into a world lit almost bright as day by the full, white face of the moon.

Standing, we looked around us. As far as we could see, the rolling surface of the glacier was covered with glittering snow. It was as if the stars themselves had fallen from the sky and come to rest among us.

In the distance stood Carton's Rock. The black stone seemed to merge with the night sky, leaving the streaks of ice and snow suspended like flames in the night.

Stanley's breath plumed about his head. The sheepskin jacket, which had begun to come apart, hung in shreds from his arms and his back.

We swept off as much of the snow as we could from the Rocket, then sat down with our backs against the ice. For a long time, we looked at Carton's Rock drifting in the strange sapphire light.

The next morning, after a few hours' rest inside the plane, we woke to find light streaming in through the sides of the hole we had walled up with plywood. After removing the plywood, I poked my head out through the opening and watched the rising sun spread like an egg yolk across the snow.

Leaving the plane, we had to put our goggles on. It was too bright for the naked eye to see. And it was hot. We soon shed the remains of our extra clothing. The Rocket, too, gave up its crust of ice, and we gorged on beans and ham before shouldering our traces and heading out again across the glacier.

The willow wands we had planted to mark our path had all been blown away. I wondered how far they had gone. With the force of the storm, there was no telling. I imagined them spun into the sky and falling to earth in some Italian's garden like toothpicks from the gods.

❊

WE MARCHED UNDER THE fierce and cloudless sky.

The silhouette of Carton's Rock stretched across the empty whiteness.

We stopped to stare at a leaf which had been carried in by the wind. Its edges were trimmed with the rusty browns and reds of autumn colors. Where the leaf lay on the ice, the sun had warmed it, melting a perfect indentation.

Then we moved on.

Our skin burned into painful maps of red, with tiny blisters pebbling our noses, ears, and cheeks. Only the space around our eyes, protected by the goggles, retained its original paleness. Our lips became horribly chapped, and whenever I relaxed my hands, they curled into clawing fists around the memory of the rope.

Sometime around noon, Stan and I dropped in our tracks. We lay like overridden horses, wheezing with exhaustion.

"Get up," I told him.

"You get up," he replied.

The coffin loomed between us. Sometimes it clicked in the sun, like a car with its engine just switched off.

"You get up and then I'll get up," I mumbled into the snow.

"First you get up."

I rose to my knees, head hanging down, my mittened hands like the paws of a half-invented beast, then staggered to my feet. "On your feet," I told the figure sprawled on the other side of the coffin.

Slowly, Stanley turned his head. The one glass eye blinked back the sun. Then, with a curse, he stood.

Occasionally, we would crawl into the shade of a tarpaulin and pull the goggles from our faces. No expression showed on Stanley's face, which looked to me as if it had been chipped from pink granite.

It was early evening when we reached that hard gray line of shadow cast down by Carton's Rock. As soon as we crossed into it, the cold closed around us like a trap made out of light.

We had gone only a few feet when I heard a groaning

sound from the snow beneath my feet. Stanley was walking away to my left, so that we pulled the Rocket behind us in the V formation we had found to be most effective.

Slowly we both came to a stop.

The earth grumbled again.

Stanley and I looked at each other.

And then suddenly he was gone.

The coffin jerked across the snow towards him, and I watched in amazement as the rope which connected me to the coffin snapped tight like a whip, tore me off my feet, and pulled me forward, facedown in the snow. And then I was being dragged, my guts jammed up under my ribs and the wind jolted from my lungs.

I raised my ice ax, jammed it into the snow, and leaned on it with all the strength I had left. Chips of snow and ice sprayed up around the ax blade, spitting into my face. As suddenly as it had started, everything came to a stop. For a moment, I just lay there, the pressure of the rope still painful across my middle, drawing the air carefully into my chest. As soon as I had my breath back, I called out to Stan.

There was no reply.

I called again.

This time, I heard his voice.

I turned my head slowly, afraid that my grip on the ice ax would slip.

The rope which attached him to the coffin disappeared into a small hole in the ground.

"Get me out!" he called, his words muffled underground.

I could hear his ice ax clacking against the ice walls of a crevasse as he tried to find a grip so he could begin climbing up. Judging from the length of the rope before it trailed into

314 | PAUL WATKINS

the hole, I knew that he could not be more than ten feet down. I looked around for a place to anchor the rope, but there was none. "Prusik knot!" I yelled. "Tie a Prusik knot!"

We both carried extra lengths of rope for tying these knots, which would allow us to climb up the main rope without the risk of sliding down again. The knot could be slid up the main rope and then pulled taut by the weight of the climber. In this way, Stanley could, at least in theory, haul himself out of the hole.

The coffin shifted, with a dry, grating sound.

I kicked my feet deeper into the snow, to find a better grip. The side of my face rested against the edge of the ax head, the other end being buried into the snow. My hands were cramping. The bulge of the leather envelope containing Carton's poems jabbed into my chest from its pocket in my coat. As the minutes went by, I could feel the growing strain in my elbow joints and in the muscles under my arms. I just lay there and tried not to think. The cold worked its way up through my trousers. My toes went numb. The rope never slackened. Sometimes, I felt it jolt as Stanley moved around inside the crevasse.

Then I heard a gasp and saw Stanley's hand fly up out of the hole. The next thing I saw was his leg, and then the other leg, and finally the rest of him. For a moment, he lay at the side of the hole, then he scrabbled forward, until he was lying by the coffin.

He had lost his goggles, and his clothes were soaked from butting up against the wall of the crevasse. Other than that, he seemed unhurt.

As soon as I knew he was clear of the hole, I pulled up the ice ax and stepped over to the coffin. I dragged it away, keeping

an eye out for sunken areas in the snow, in case another crevasse might be lying just beneath the surface, or the same
crevasse might spread wider underground than it appeared.

While I was doing this, I saw Stanley struggling to untie
the rope around his middle. His half-frozen hands clawed at
the knot until it came loose. He breathed in shallow gasps, a
strand of spit dangling from his lips. He pulled the rope away
and let it drop at his feet. Then he turned and began running
back in the direction we had come from.

"Stan?" I said, but my voice was faint. I did not have the
strength to stop him, but only watched as he clomped away,
chunks of snow kicking up from his boot heels. I wondered
how far he would get.

He passed through the arc of shadow and out into the sun.
The colors seemed to jump back into his clothes—his red neck
scarf, the pale blue of his canteen—as he left this cage of black
and white. Without his goggles, he must have been blinded
immediately. His arms began to flail, the weight of his damp
clothes and his climbing boots dragging him down. He carried
on another few paces and then dropped. He seemed to fall in
slow motion, landing on his knees and then pitching facedown
into the snow. Condensation rose from his clothes as if he had
become a pile of smoldering rags.

I began to walk towards him. I got as far as the rope
allowed before the weight of the coffin brought me to a stop,
making me feel like a chained dog. I did not have the energy
to undo myself from the rope. I just stood there.

At last, Stanley rose to his feet. He slapped the clumps of
snow from his trousers, then turned and began walking back
towards me.

It was not until he slipped again into the grayness of the

shadows that I could see he had been crying. Now that the colors had gone from him again, and with condensation still rising from his body, he resembled nothing more than the burnt-out stick of a match.

Still leashed to the coffin, I held out my arms to him.

He stopped a few paces out of reach.

Slowly, I let my arms fall to my sides. "It will be all right," I said, realizing as the words left my mouth that this was the same thing Dr. Plunkett had told me when I'd brought my father's dog to be put down.

"My goggles," said Stanley, fingertips dabbing at his tears. "I think they might be on a ledge down there."

Five minutes later, with Stanley anchoring me, I crawled forward over the uneven snow, feeling sick as the ground shifted beneath my chest. I reached the edge of the hole and looked down.

The crevasse spread wide beneath the hole, like the inside of an egg on whose thin crust I was now lying. The central part of the cavern disappeared into darkness. It seemed to reach into the belly of the earth. The air was stale. No sound came from below. Even the rivulets of water that dribbled down its walls were silent. I could make out the brittle teeth of icicles hanging down from the roof of the cavern. The snow along the sides was frothed into huge mushrooms. The wall Stanley had climbed to the surface was scarred where he had kicked away the icicles and trampled the delicate coral of frost. And there were his one-eyed goggles, just as he had said, resting on a lip of ice by the surface. I reached down with my ice ax, hooked the goggles by the strap, and, lifting the ax, slid the goggles down until they stopped against my hand.

I slithered back, hearing icicles snap away from the ceiling just beneath me and fall, crashing like glass, down the black throat of the crevasse.

*

By NIGHTFALL, we had reached the first outcrops of boulders that lay around the base of Carton's Rock. At one of these, we stopped to gather water from an overhang, where urgent Morse code droplets fell into the canteens gripped by our shaking hands. Looking down at my feet, I noticed that where my boots had left their imprints in the snow the space was red as blood. I looked at the heels of my boots, to see if I had somehow injured myself without feeling it. But there were no wounds, and now Stanley had noticed the same gory slush in his own bootprints. As we moved on from the place where we had stopped, the red marks faded away. When they had gone completely, and the marks of our boots had returned to their usual ghost-white shells, we looked back at the boulder, almost as if expecting to see the stone rear up like a gashed and crippled animal and fall back dead into the snow.

We made camp in a small clearing which was protected from the wind by two arms of rock. They reached down like an embrace around our little tent. In this place, tall pillars of ice had grown from steady streams of water dripping down during the day and then freezing again at night until they resembled the ruins of a second Parthenon.

Our dinner was a handful of broken biscuit crumbs which I gathered from the bottom of my pockets.

High above us, the wind whistled as if through a giant organ pipe, sometimes playing single long notes and then changing pitch and screeching crazily until it died down again.

I felt like a castaway who had found an island after days of drifting in the ocean. At first, I was overwhelmed by a sense of relief at having reached something solid, where I could shelter from the wind and hide away among the overhanging stones. Hiding from what, I didn't know. Maybe just from the openness of the white tundra. To lean against the cold solidity of rock helped chase from my head the demons which had found their way into my skull these past few days. I wanted to stay here. I could not stand the thought of going back out onto the glacier. But this relief was replaced almost immediately by the knowledge that we could not remain long. There was no food. No way to make a fire and keep warm. And what shelter this place offered was little more than a place just to curl up and die.

Stanley was nearly frozen. We hung his wet clothes inside the tent, where they steamed and smelled as our bodies heated up the space. Shuddering inside our sleeping bags, we shared a cigarette, forehead to forehead in the confines of the tent. The harsh smoke burned in our empty stomachs.

Once I had warmed up a little, I went outside to check that our cargo was battened down for the night. When this was done, I stood staring up at the rock. Automatically, my eyes began to trace the paths of routes that we might take. The rock itself was a mass of intersecting gullies, some choked with snow and others whittled clean by the wind. The high point was rounded, like the ball of a shoulder, on the western edge of the rock. A summit ridge ran evenly across the top of the rock, but if it was wide enough to cross or whether it was mined with overhanging cornices of snow, I could not tell from where I stood.

I crawled back inside the tent. The last sound I heard before I fell into the chasm of sleep was the wind, piping its strange music as if from the land of my dreams, not from the frozen world in which my body lay.

THIRTEEN

B Y THE END OF the following day, despite having removed all the gear from the Rocket to lighten the load, Stanley and I had moved only a third of the way up the Rock. We had followed what I thought was the best route, a gully mostly stripped of snow which zigzagged like a lightning bolt up the southern face. The gully was too narrow for both of us to pull side by side, so one pushed from behind while the other pulled from the front. Above the gully stood a wall of snow and ice and finally, beyond that, more gently sloping ground that led to a large snub-nosed rock at the summit.

We were more exhausted now than we had ever been in our lives. At sunset, we left the coffin wedged between two rocks at the top of the gully and retreated to our tent. The way down took only a few minutes, as we slid from one shifting plate of stone to the next.

I was miserable at how little ground we had gained. Once

more I felt the urge to give in, just to leave the coffin and head back. If anyone ever came out here again and found the coffin, we could say the wind had blown it down from the top. The temptation to do this had grown so overwhelming that it had almost transformed into a need. I knew that if I so much as framed my thoughts with words, it would all be over. The only thing that stopped me was the knowledge that I would have that lie inside me for the rest of my life. It would eat its way out of me like a cancer. In the end, I knew, the pain I would inflict upon myself later would be worse than anything I felt now.

What was going through Stanley's head I did not know and did not ask. Nor did he question me. It was as if our thoughts had become dangerous, and speaking them would only conjure demons from the crystal air we breathed.

That night, I woke with a start. I went to check my watch but found that it had stopped. Suddenly remembering what it was that had woken me, I crawled out of the tent.

This freezing night had stilled the dripping icicles. The snow along the summit ridge was glittering like broken glass. In the steel-blue light thrown down by the moon, I tossed aside objects from our neatly stacked pile of gear until I came to the box that contained the winch. I tore off the lid and pitched it away. Then I lifted the winch and tried to fit it into my rucksack. But it would not go. I sat down in the snow, chewing my thumbnail, lost in thought and staring at the forked path of the Milky Way, which stretched from the horizon and disappeared into the rocks above my head.

By morning, I had fashioned a set of straps around the winch. I'd used some climbing rope to make a sort of net around the box, then attached the straps from my rucksack.

When Stanley crawled out of the tent, he found me staggering around with the wooden box attached to my back.

Seeing that the lower edge was digging into my back, he retreated into the tent once more and then reappeared with the cutoff piece of his climbing jacket, which he had been using as earflaps on his hat.

He wound this material around the rope which ran along the bottom edge of the box, transforming it into padding.

When I lifted it onto my back and no longer felt the sharp edge of the wood grating against my spine, I knew that this might work after all. It had to work. The only way to haul the Rocket up the rock face was to lift it with the winch.

After a few mouthfuls of cold bean stew, we set off up the gully. Stanley carried our two coils of climbing rope, as well as rock pitons, crampons, and a rock hammer. I climbed with the winch on my back, using our two ice axes like walking sticks as I crept from rock to rock.

We reached the coffin two hours later. A light snow was falling. Flakes dusted the coffin's top, gradually covering it, like tiny pieces of a puzzle being fitted into place.

Leaving the winch behind, I strapped the crampons onto my boots, roped up, and began to climb the slope. After so many days of hauling the Rocket and the last few hours of the box's uneven weight on my back, the climb felt easy as I advanced, stabbing my stilettoed boots into the snow and swinging the axes, one after the other, as I moved.

The slope was covered with a thin layer of snow, which became compact a few inches below the surface. I could feel the axes sinking into the snow and sometimes ringing against ice or rock.

Every twenty feet I hammered a piton, which looked like a thick nail with a ring at the end, into the ice. I threaded the rope through the ring, then rested for a minute before carrying on again.

During these rests, I looked down at Stanley, my eyes trailing along the umbilical cord of climbing rope which connected me to him.

Stanley sat on the winch box, the end of the rope held loosely in his hand, looking up at me. His face was a cat's tongue of pink, blurred with the snow that crossed the air between us.

The ice wall leveled out on a sloping shelf of ground made up of crushed gray rock. From there, perhaps a hundred yards away over a jumbled mass of larger stones, stood the blunted gray pinnacle that marked the summit. Snow blew in my face and gathered in the cracks among the stones. White sky merged with snow, reducing the world around me to the grainy bleakness of a black-and-white photo. Looking out over the precipice, I could see nothing of the glacier, and not even our tent at the foot of the rock.

I hammered a piton into a slab of rock, but the stone was rotten and flaked apart with every blow from my hammer. On my second try, I found a more solid rock. The piton rang as it spiked, unlike the dull thump it had made when piercing the bad rock.

I anchored my second rope and lowered it down to Stanley. While he tied up the winch, I lay on my back on the uneven ground and closed my eyes.

The next thing I knew, Stanley was tugging at the rope to show that the winch was secure. I began to haul it up, hand over hand, and was soon drenched in sweat. When the box at last appeared over the lip of the ice wall, I dragged it all the way to me before releasing my grip on the rope. Then I set my blistered palms in a patch of snow and hoped that the pain would subside.

I fixed the box to the clip at the end of the winch cable and lowered it back down to Stanley. While he attached the cable to one of the holding bars at the front of the coffin, I roped the winch to a large boulder and then sat behind it, sore hands gripping each of the winding handles, waiting for the signal.

I waited a long time, and was just beginning to wonder what had happened when Stanley appeared over the edge of the ice wall, having climbed the same rope I had used. He lay panting on his back for a moment. Then he gasped, "It's all set."

I began to wind the winch, and it soon became clear to me that I would not have been able to complete the task alone. Stanley and I took turns cranking the handles, while the teeth of the winch clicked slowly and the cable sawed into the ice. Unfamiliar rhythms pounded in my head, and were answered by the tom-tom drumming of my heart. Fragments of songs tramped tunelessly across my mind. Sweat poured out of me. My arms began to shake convulsively.

At last, after over an hour, the snout of the coffin appeared at the top of the wall.

We then had to fix more ropes to it and drag the coffin onto the ground where we stood.

When this was done, I lay on my side, shoveling snow into my mouth with bloody hands and choking it down along with all the grit that it contained.

Then it was time to drag the coffin once again.

In that final stretch to the summit, the coffin screeched over the sharp, upended stones, pitching forward and clattering down. The runners were torn from their mounts, but we no longer cared. The fins of the cargo space were smashed first one way and then another and then they, too, ripped from their welded seams. The coffin's sides were gouged with streaks of stone and lichen. We shoved it forward, torn hands leaving red smears across the metal. The body thumped about inside, and a half-mad part of me was glad to think of that as I slammed my boot into the coffin and noticed the dent of my heel in the once-sleek structure. I noticed the same wild look on Stanley's face that I knew must be on mine. With gritted teeth, he shoulder-barged the coffin, falling as his balance slid away and cursing as he tumbled down among the stones. At last, we reached the base of the pinnacle and could go no farther. We collapsed against the wreckage of the coffin, our panting breaths fogging the air.

The snow had stopped. The clouds had blown away. I had not noticed it until now.

Bronzy light fell warm upon our faces, polishing the stones on which we lay.

Clambering to my feet, I looked out over the glacier. The ice was like a sea of molten lava, and even when I put the goggles back against my eyes, the light was too strong to see anything other than the blazing reflection of the sun.

For a moment, surrounded by this fierce glare, I thought back to the miraculous light of the alpenglow which had appeared around us all those years ago and the nameless fear its memory had brought me ever since the day I fainted on the hill behind my father's house. But this sun sparked no nightmare in my head. It was as if the bad dreams were being burned away and the space they left behind made clean and new again.

A faint breeze brushed against the tatters of my clothes, cooling the sweat of the climb.

Below me, in the gullies which spread like fingers down the slope of Carton's Rock, crumbled snow and shingle debris showed where avalanches had come to rest. On the other side of the rock, the slope sheared away, dropping almost vertically onto the dirt-rimmed glacier.

I was surprised to feel no sense of achievement. Nor did I feel any lack of achievement. The only thing I felt was exhaustion.

Stanley stood beside me. "I suppose we'd better read the poems," he said.

I had completely forgotten about them. I reached inside my coat. The leather envelope was still there. With the blade of my Opinel knife, still sharp despite being peppered with rust from lying in the damp wool of my jacket, I cut the stitches from the leather. The hide was dark with moisture, its once-neat rectangular shape now warped and crushed. Working the tip of the knife along the white threads, I popped them loose and emptied out the contents of the envelope.

Along with a bundle of paper, I was surprised to see two small cigars drop into the snow. Quickly, I picked them up. "I hope you've got some matches," I said.

Stanley's eyes were fixed on the cigars. "How thoughtful," he said, with such sincerity that he seemed ready to take back every rotten thing he'd ever said about his uncle. Stanley rummaged in his pocket and his hand emerged with a bashed-up yellow box of Swan Vestas. Hesitantly, he shook the box, and we were both relieved to hear the rustle of matches inside. He tossed them to me and I handed him the poems, on which the handwritten ink had blurred like the colored paper of a litmus test.

"I think you should be the one to read them," I said.

Stanley shrugged. "I'll do my best."

I lowered myself onto the coffin, ready as an audience of one.

While Stanley glanced through the poems, I cut the ends

of the cigars with my knife and then, with my jacket pulled up over my head and both cigars clenched between my teeth, carefully scraped the red heads of the matches against the ragged striking paper on the side of the box. The first two blew out before they even reached the cigar, so I struck three of them at once, and soon a blue haze of tobacco smoke was wafting out from under my soggy woolen tent.

I shrugged my jacket back over my shoulders and held one of the cigars out to Stanley. "Which poems did he choose?" I asked. "Or did he write them himself?"

Stanley seemed to be frozen, just staring at the paper.

From far away across the glacier came the rumbling thunder of another avalanche.

"Stan," I said quietly, still holding out the cigar.

"He never climbed it."

"Climbed what?" The smoke pinched at my eyes.

"This!" He jammed his heel into the snow. "This rock!" Then he plucked the cigar from between my fingers, and in the moment when he set it between his teeth, I was startled by how much he looked like his uncle.

I, in turn, snatched the paper from his hand and began to read.

"My Dear Boys," the letter began. "By now, if all has gone well, you will be on the top of Carton's Rock. And so, I hope, will I. I am glad to have made it at last, in body if not in spirit. I could not have done it without you. I mean this literally, as I must now confess to you that your first ascent of my mountain is mine as well."

I raised my head from the letter. The sun poured into my eyes, the full shield of its blaze against my face. The shadows of ridges, invisible before, now cast themselves across the chalk-white fields below.

Stanley lay on his back, eyes closed, laughing quietly.

"What's so bloody funny?" I shouted.

He just shook his head and laughed again.

When my eyes returned to the pages, shards of sunlight remained branded on my sight.

The letter went on to explain how Carton and his guide, Santorelli, had come within sight of the rock on their third day of trekking across the glacier. Shortly afterwards, a blizzard had come down upon them. As they pressed on, hoping to find some shelter from the storm, the ground gave way beneath Santorelli and he fell into a crevasse. The rope held, and Carton had the presence of mind to fall upon his ice ax, which prevented him from being dragged down into the crevasse as well.

"But this," wrote Carton, "was where our luck ran out."

Earlier in the day, Carton had removed his rope in order to adjust his clothing. He had retied the knot himself, and it was this knot which now gave way. The rope slipped from his waist and Santorelli tumbled into the abyss that lay beneath.

"It was then that a nightmare began for me which has never truly ended," wrote Carton. "I have never spoken about it, or written it down until now."

According to the letter, Carton had wandered for what he later calculated to be twelve days, although at the time he had lost track of how long he had been gone. He had only a small amount of food and the bedroll that was tied over one shoulder with which to keep warm. He survived by digging holes and hiding inside them, out of the wind. He discovered that laying his dark red handkerchief out on the ground would melt the snow beneath, and he could squeeze the water from the handkerchief into his mouth. Eventually, he stumbled back into the village of Palladino. At first, he was too exhausted to make clear what had happened. It was only hours after, as

328 | Paul Watkins

he lay in the warmth of a bed, that he conceived of the lie he
told to the people of Palladino and later the world.

"I had to make something of it," he explained, "for
Santorelli's sake as well as for my own. To justify his death and
my own suffering. As soon as I could speak, I told them we had
been to the top and that the accident took place on the way
down. By the time I was strong enough to return to England,
the story had already spread. From then on it was done and
could never be undone. The legend took on a life of its own,
and I found I could no longer live without it. In the years
ahead, of all the lies I told to keep the legend and myself alive,
the one that troubled me the most was saying I had glimpsed
the view that you have now before you. I hope it is as beautiful as I have let the world believe. You are the first to know the
truth, and what you do now with that truth I leave entirely in
your hands. With great affection, your friend, Henry Carton."

My first instinct as to what would happen now was that
Stanley and I should pitch the coffin off the ridge and send it
falling thousands of feet into the rubble of avalanche debris
below. In fact, I wondered why Stanley had not already done
this.

But Stanley was still lying there, still laughing, as if the
spirit of Carton had leapt inside his head and it was Carton,
not Stanley, whose mocking croak I heard from underneath
the plume of cigar smoke.

"Well?" I asked.

The laughter wheezed into silence. Stanley returned to a
sitting position. "Well what?"

"Are you going to tell me what you're finding so hilarious?"
Stanley held out his hands, palms up. "We're here!"

"So what? I'm damned if I'll let him get away with this."

"He already has gotten away with it." He reached across and slapped the side of the coffin, which resounded with a hollow boom. "Isn't that right, Uncle?"

"As soon as we get back to Palladino, I'm going to tell them the truth about your uncle."

"Suit yourself," said Stanley. "He is past caring now."

"But don't you care?" I asked.

Stanley raised himself to a sitting position and removed the well-chewed cigar from his mouth. "Don't you see? We made it. That's all that matters now!" He reached across, took the letter from my hand, then slowly crumpled the pages and threw them off the precipice.

For a long time, we did not speak.

We went back to puffing our cigars, the soft incense of the tobacco smoke rising into the clear sky.

It was Stanley who broke the silence. "You do with the knowledge what you want," he said. "As far as I'm concerned, the matter is closed."

It was not closed for me, but there was nothing more to say.

Our journey down the mountain and back across the glacier survives in my memory as a semiconscious march through night and day and on again into the night. Sleep and waking merged. The last of our rations were finished off by the end of the first day of the descent. From then on, we were permanently hungry.

Now and then, I turned to look back at Carton's Rock, which vanished into the glacier like a ship sinking into a calm ocean. Then it was gone, as if it had never existed. I turned again and plodded on.

We barely spoke, Stanley and I. Partly it was because we were too tired. Partly it was because we had nothing to say.

330 | Paul Watkins

And what little we could have said would have ended in an argument. I was still bitter about Carton's deceit, and Stanley's ability to take it as a joke only served to make me angry at him, too. In my exhausted mind, the two became conspirators. I wanted to accuse him of this treachery. I wanted to blame someone who could still be blamed and give a damn about it.

That anger was the only thing which kept me going.

As our strength began to fail, we cast away pieces of our gear, leaving the glacier strewn with mess kits, tent pegs, binoculars, and shreds of filthy clothing.

To keep ourselves moving, we advanced across the glacier in short stages, choosing some feature of the land in front of us—an outcrop of rock, a dip in the ice where a shadow had collected, or even some imagined wrinkle in the distant snow, appearing like a mirage to Stanley or to me but not to both. Then one would follow the other, like a blind man following his dog. Sometimes these stages lasted only minutes, sometimes hours. They allowed us to trick our minds away from the total distance we knew we had to cross. Gladly we duped each other and ourselves as the eye-cutting brightness of day gave way to the gunmetal blue of night.

We sang to keep a rhythm in our march, coughing out old hymns we never knew our minds had stored away. In the frost-tinseled air, our chapped lips split and bled and the words of those hymns formed on the salty metal of our blood.

I drifted in and out of dreams so vivid that while I sat beside my father in his garden, drinking tea, or gorged on bread and strawberry jam in some nameless empty space inside my head or ran my finger down the trench of Darcey Kidder's spine out in the middle of St. Vernon's moonlit playing fields, all the pain in my twisted knees would go. Nor did I feel the shriek of sunburn on my cheeks and nose, or the dull thump of frostbite in the blackened skin of my fingertips and ears. Then the daydreams would vanish, like birds flushed from tall grass, leaving me again inside the stubborn, plodding carcass of my body.

Other times, my crumbling brain delivered to the light behind my eyes half-finished arguments from years before, or conversations I might have had but didn't. And these I battled through, fists clenched with indignation at the arrogance of words which had never been spoken.

Hunger twisted in us, tying knots in our intestines and untying them again. Menus appeared before us and we read them out, slobbering words lost in bubbles of spit and gnawing on the emptiness of air.

One evening, in a hollow in the snow, we found the bones of some small animal, brought there perhaps by some hunting bird to eat in peace. We sucked the rotten marrow from the yellowed sticks of bone, turned back to back to hide from each other the things we had become.

When we finally staggered down off the glacier, I was so lost inside my head with thoughts of what I would tell the world about the liar Henry Carton, I barely grasped that we were safe again. The return journey had taken us five days, although I could not have reckoned it at the time. It seemed to me I had spent my whole existence out there on the ice, and the flowers in the meadow of the San Rafaele woods all seemed to belong to the memories of someone else's life.

We arrived in Palladino just as a group of local mountaineers, headed by Salvatore Santorelli, were in their final stage of preparation before heading out to try to recover our bodies.

Helen was there. News had reached her in London that Stanley and I were long overdue, and she had flown down to help in the rescue.

My thoughts were so sluggish that I walked right past her without recognizing who she was. Even when I did realize, my mind was so jumbled that seeing her in Palladino, which should have taken me by surprise, only merged into the haze of shock that I was also here, and that the journey was over at last.

She, along with the entire population of the village and one lone photojournalist from a small newspaper based down the road in Domodossola, welcomed us with the stunned happiness accorded those who have been given up for dead.

We stood by the fountain. People were whirling around us. Faces loomed into view, smiling and chattering in Italian and broken English. Music blared out of the café. Children shrieked and dodged among the grown-ups. A bottle of wine was put in my hand. Then the bottle of wine was taken away and I found myself holding a fist-sized piece of cheese. A woman with pale green eyes kissed me on one filthy cheek, and then I was empty-handed again. I turned to say something to Stanley, but he was not there.

Then I saw him sitting with Helen on a bench across the road. They hugged and she began crying. She brushed the back of her hand down the side of his face, as if to wipe away the scorched red of his sunburned skin. He took her hands in his and kissed them.

The photographer from Domodossola appeared in front of me and held up his camera, asking if he could take my picture.

I nodded and made a halfhearted attempt to stand up straight.

When he had moved on, I turned and washed my face in the clear water of the fountain. The cold brought me back to my senses. I stood and felt droplets trickling down my back. I realized then that I was standing just where Carton had stood when he had had his own picture taken after coming down from the glacier. I also realized, because I felt it myself, how lonely he must have been. It was not only at this place, surrounded by all these people, but on the ice. The terrible, bone-hollowing fear of dying out there alone. Until this moment, I had not grasped the weight of that solitude, and the burden that he must have carried for the rest of his life after that.

Seeing Stanley and Helen together, locked in whispers and embracing, I understood suddenly why Carton had taken his own life. As much as Stanley had needed Carton, all the while pretending to loathe him, Carton had needed his nephew. Carton had tried to shield his devotion behind a screen of bluster and family obligation, but the truth had been easy to see. Upon the arrival of Helen Paradise, and the realization that she was not like the other women who had drifted through Stanley's life, Carton had known that the bond between him and his nephew was about to break. With that, and all the suffering his daily life entailed, Carton's reason for living had expired like the magazine subscriptions in his club.

Despite the popularity, or lack of it, which had dominated his life, Carton had been a lonely man. The loneliness had followed him everywhere, like a black dog skulking in his shadow.

He must have known that no one would understand such loneliness, not in the million-faced whirlwind of the city or even here, in this tiny Italian village. On the glacier's ice, there were no lights of cozy fires, no sound of church bells in the distance. There was only the angry sun or the blind eye of the moon, enough to make a person feel as if he'd been marooned on an empty planet, that all the people he had ever met were only dreams, and that he was alone and had always been alone.

Only now did I know how he had felt. Standing now where Carton had once stood, I realized that I could not tell the secret he had shared with us. Nor, in my mind, was he diminished by the truth he had revealed in his letter. For me, he had simply changed into a different kind of hero.

✳

AFTER SEVERAL DAYS SPENT recovering in a hospital in Domodossola, we returned to London.

By the time we arrived, Stanley and Helen were engaged.

Descending from the train at Victoria Station, Stanley and I were surprised to see a newspaper headline announcing that the Rocket Men had perished.

"A slight exaggeration," said Stanley.

"But only slight," I added.

Exaggeration though it was, we soon discovered that the news of our deaths had spread more quickly than the news of our having survived. Some of the papers had already printed our obituaries, and a number of bookmakers had already paid off those who'd bet on our not returning home.

The first thing I did after saying good-bye to Helen and Stanley was jump in a cab and head straight for St. Vernon's. I didn't stop at the school, however. Instead, I had the cabbie drop me off at Darcey Kidder's house.

After rapping my knuckles on the door, I stood back. It was only then that I gave any thought to how disheveled I must look. I just had time to claw my hair roughly into shape before the door opened and I found myself looking not at Darcey Kidder but at a man about my own age, with a bottle of beer in his hand.

He was wearing a collarless shirt whose untucked ends trailed down around his knees. He was also barefoot, smart wool trouser cuffs draped across his toes. "Can I help you with something?" he asked.

"I was looking for Darcey Kidder," I stammered. "Perhaps I've got the wrong house."

"Oh." He nodded. "She's gone, I'm afraid."

"Gone?"

"Yes. Moved out. I'm the new tenant."

"Did she leave a forwarding address?" I stammered.

He shrugged. "Not with me, she didn't."

Walking back across the fields, I thought about the looks on the faces of Higgins and Houseman when I told them about this. I wondered what my own face looked like, too. The feeling of such a missed opportunity is like no other feeling in the world. All other regrets seem trivial beside it, and you find yourself wondering if you might have another life someday, and you swear that if you do, you'll never make the same mistake again.

The next day, after discovering from the St. Vernon's registrar that Darcey had "left no instructions to have her address forwarded to members of the staff," there was nothing for me to do but try to set aside my disappointment and lose myself in the many interviews that lay ahead. Most of these took place in the cramped space of the Montague Banquet Room, where I experienced the same uneasiness at being surrounded by so many people as I had felt when I'd returned from my first trip to the Alps.

The first chance I got, I caught a train down to Stroud and then walked home along tree-shaded lanes.

My father was waiting for me. That first evening home, in front of the wheezing coal fire, I told him everything I could. When I had finished talking, he went up to the mantelpiece and took down the medal in its box.

"You have earned this more than once," he said. Then he closed the box and handed it to me, and he said nothing when

I threw it in the fire, as if he had known all along what should be done.

Sipping our tin mugs of tea, we watched in silence as the box smoked and then burned, and a while later we saw a trickle of molten metal dripping through the grate onto the stone floor of the fireplace.

One week later, the school year began. I found myself once more in the opening faculty meetings, while the headmaster and various department heads droned on about changes to the school regulations, the dining hall dress code, and compulsory chapel attendance. I breathed in that particular smell of the school, the way it always rested strange and unfamiliar in my lungs those first days back, before I grew used to it again.

On my way out of the meetings, I was accosted by a delegation of groundskeepers, wanting to know if they could have their winch back. I told them that their winch was on the side of a mountain in the Alps. That same day, I went out and bought them a new one, and the sphinx-faced men were satisfied.

Then the students began to arrive and I was soon caught up again in the mad rush of boarding-school life, with no time for uneasiness, or even to reflect on the weeks since I'd set out on the journey.

The time for that reflection came in bits and pieces during the months ahead, along with the realization that I still liked teaching. The comfort and sense of purpose I found in this chaotic existence was not something to feel guilty about, as I had once worried. Rather, I took it as a sign that I was built for this work, even if it was not always easy and not always enjoyable, either. This was what I had been put on earth to do, I decided, so I thought I'd stay around awhile, instead of moving on.

But things were not the same since Darcey Kidder had moved on. Higgins, Houseman, and I mourned her loss in a way that was both stoic and sincere. We told ourselves that it was meant to be, and reminded ourselves that we had predicted this from the first day she walked into our lives. There was something rather poetic about the way she had always been unreachable. Without ever having known it, she had laid claim to a piece of our hearts, which we gladly gave away and saved for her alone.

It was always amazing to me how, even after decades of working at the school, faculty members who left or retired faded so quickly from our thoughts. It was one of the necessary brutalities of life at a school like this, that the memory of the school was only ever four years long. After that amount of time, the entire student body would have rotated through, and we among the faculty, caught up in the daily rush of things, also tended to forget.

Darcey was different. Maybe she didn't deserve to be, but Higgins and Houseman and I didn't spend too much time trying to figure it out. We just agreed that it was a fact. If we could have said exactly why she'd had such an effect on us, the effect probably wouldn't have happened at all.

On those nights when we played blackjack up in Higgins's loft, the Busch-Rathenow binoculars, with which we had watched her lights switch off behind the curtains of her house, remained untouched. When yet another nameless lodger moved in to her old house, those lights came on again. Then it was our own curtains that we drew, rather than be reminded of the brief and hopelessly one-sided love affair we'd had with Darcey Kidder.

Later that year, I was the best man at Stanley's wedding.

Watching the two of them go down the aisle, I was forced, for the first time, to take seriously the idea that a bachelor's life awaited me.

But the gods were not finished with me yet.

It was just before the Christmas holidays began, when St. Vernon's hosted its annual dance with the girls of Islington Ladies College. This was usually a miserable experience for Higgins and Houseman and me. Our job was to make sure that everything ran smoothly, that the ladies were not interfered with, that the band, made up of old men who never seemed to get any older, did not get drunk and fall over. Out of a grim sense of duty we danced with the ancient school nurse and the laundry lady and the headmaster's never-smiling and all-judging wife.

I was propping up the wall over by the drinks stand, wondering when Higgins would return from having left to "check on something" over an hour ago.

Houseman, in his traditional role as punch server, was, for the benefit of the adults, expertly spiking the otherwise nonalcoholic punch served out to the students. For this, he employed such deftness that no one but those receiving their rum-inspired drinks ever caught on.

The headmaster appeared, a blue silk cummerbund shimmering around his waist. "Gentlemen," he said. "Another year goes by."

We nodded and made halfhearted mumbles of agreement.

"I've got an early Christmas present for you," he continued.

I wondered what this might be, and hoped it was not one of the overstocked domed glass paperweights with the school logo, which were bought in bulk and given out at every opportunity. I already had about six of them, and they lay like crystal blisters on my desk.

My huffy thoughts were interrupted by the headmaster,

who announced that another teacher had just been hired for our department.

On numerous occasions, we had petitioned the board of trustees for another faculty member to help with the workload. Each time, our request had been "deferred." This meant, according to Higgins, that they didn't have the guts to tell us no outright, but that we had no chance in hell of actually gaining a new colleague.

"God, that really is good news," said Houseman, unable to hide his astonishment. "I thought it was another bloody paperweight!"

The headmaster did not smile at this, of course.

"That's fantastic, sir," I said, hoping to defuse the situation.

"Yes," drawled the headmaster, uncertain whether to comment on Houseman's lack of school spirit or whatever category of cheekiness his remark fell under. After a moment's hesitation, he breathed in sharply and said, "Well!" to show that he had let the matter pass.

Houseman stirred the sudsy punch and, almost imperceptibly, sighed with relief.

"There she is now," said the headmaster. He jerked his chin towards the entrance of the hall.

And there stood Darcey Kidder, as if she'd never gone away. She was looking around nervously, but she smiled when she saw Houseman and me. She walked straight over, weaving past the dancing couples who plodded woodenly across the floor.

"I heard you were dead," she told me with a smile.

"I get that a lot," I replied.

Houseman held out a glass of punch. "*Tamam*," he muttered when she took it from his hand.

"Darcey," I said, "please don't go away again."

"You're one to talk," she answered.

I leaned across and kissed her on the cheek.

It was at this moment that we realized the music had stopped. In fact, everything had stopped. The entire hall, including the old men in the band, were standing completely still and staring at us.

The first person who spoke was the headmaster's wife. "Well, it's about time!" she announced.

The band took this as their cue and struck up another song.

We danced, Darcey Kidder and I.

And so began a lifelong revelation that loving someone at a distance is fine for poetry and novels, but loving a person close-up is a far more satisfying occupation.

The following year, we were married.

For a wedding present, Higgins gave me his Busch-Rathenow binoculars.

Houseman's present was his declaration that he would allow me to go on living, despite the fact that I had broken his heart.

Darcey and I stayed at St. Vernon's. We had two children, a girl and a boy. Eventually, the boy became a student at St. Vernon's. Our daughter went on to Islington Ladies College, where she was mortified to have to dance with me each year at the St. Vernon's Christmas dance.

Twice a year, I led groups of students on hiking trips to Scotland, Wales, and the Lake District. Sometimes even Stanley came along, and it was thanks to him that the students were soon calling me Auntie, a name that stuck with me for the rest of my teaching career.

When not in the mountains, Stanley and I continued to spend our Friday evenings at the Montague. In time, however, our wine ration of a bottle each was reduced to one between two and, eventually, to a single glass of port. This we raised in silent tribute to the ghost of Mr. Barber, whose portrait now hung on the wall.

When my father passed away, I inherited the house in Painswick. I meant to sell the place, but when Darcey and I went back to settle the estate, and stood among the roses in his garden, we decided that we couldn't let it go. From then on, that was where we spent our summers, and as our children grew they alternately loathed and loved the time they spent in that quiet Cotswold town.

At the end of every summer, on the evening before I was due to return to school, I walked up to the beacon hill and said good-bye to the place before returning to the city. The sun would have gone by the time I reached the top. I would smell autumn in the air. The valleys below would be blanketed in mist, which always settled on the landscape at this time of year. Here and there, in places where the mist was thin, the lights of houses would glow in the dark. The white sheen of the fog would remind me of the way the glacier had looked from the summit of Carton's Rock. At times like this, I'd remember how thoroughly the gods had dismantled the life I'd once thought was perfection. And then I'd say a silent prayer of thanks for the new life they'd given me instead.

Now the only climbing that I do is on the staircase in my house, being too frail for anything else. It used to be that people asked me what I loved about those distant summits I'd once reached, but now they just ask what I miss.

The answer is that I miss nothing.

The mountains I have seen are deep inside me now.

They touch the sky on the horizons of my mind.

They burn in the miracle light.